Josephine Herbst

The Executioner Waits

WARNER BOOKS

A Warner Communications Company

Warner Books, Inc.
75 Rockefeller Plaza
New York, N.Y. 10019

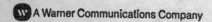 A Warner Communications Company

Printed in the United States of America

First Warner Books Printing: August, 1985

10 9 8 7 6 5 4 3 2 1

"Miss Herbst is in the process of painting a fresco of our times. . .I believe that the publication of this second volume in her trilogy establishes her right to be considered one of few major novelists in America today."

—Horace Gregory, 1934

THE EXECUTIONER WAITS

The Great War is over. The boys are back from France and the young couples eagerly look forward to the promised prosperity and a new era of opportunity. Anne Trexler Wendel had done the best she could for her children but money was scarce and times were hard. Now her daughters Rosamond and Victoria must make their own way in a time of turbulent and complicated change—and join a very different generation of Americans.

"A rich and tender and terrible book, violent in its pity for those who, like Rosamond and Jerry, are frustrated by the inevitable forces of our society; and in it Miss Herbst comes into her full powers."

—New Republic, 1934

"A historic document of great value; what men and women from every walk of life said and thought between 1918 and 1929 is accurately recorded."

—Saturday Review of Literature, 1934

"Because of the height of its purpose, the artistry of its execution, because it is the second successful volume in a trilogy, and because the spirit of the times and not a member of the protagonist Trexler family is the real hero of the story, this is one of the outstanding novels of the year. With this volume Miss Herbst has fortified the position in the front rank of women novelists which she won with the first installment of the trilogy, *Pity Is Not Enough*."

—Atlanta Journal, 1934

Novels by
Josephine Herbst

The Executioner Waits
Pity is not Enough
Rope of Gold*

Published by
WARNER BOOKS   *forthcoming

CONTENTS

INTRODUCTION

THE EXECUTIONER WAITS is the pivotal novel in a trilogy that begins, with *Pity Is Not Enough,* in the period after the Civil War, and ends, with *Rope of Gold,* on the eve of World War II. Continuing the saga of the family introduced in the first volume, the second is about the later lives of "Poor Joe" Trexler's brothers and sisters, particularly David and Anne, and of Anne's daughters, particularly Victoria and Rosamond. The time is the 1920s. Based, like its predecessor, on the real history of Josephine Herbst's real family, *The Executioner Waits* is a novel of many parts, many people, and many themes. It is also, to a considerable extent, her own story.

Of the many things that distinguish the "Trexler trilogy" from comparable trilogies of the Depression era such as James Farrell's *Studs Lonigan* or John Dos Passos' *USA,* perhaps the most important is the centrality of women. From the grandmother of the first volume, to the mother of the second, to the daughters of the second and third, it is the female line whose experience provides the link between the generations. In addition to the portraits of the nineteenth-century women, "Mem" and Anne, the portraits of Victoria and Rosamond are among the earliest representations of modern women in American fiction. The modernity of Victoria and Rosamond consists, above all, in their desire for independence. "Don't be stupid and shut your eyes and imagine that the only things in life worth while come from men and what people call romance," cautions Anne in one of the foreshadowing interchapters of the first volume, and the girls do not. They seek not only love, but work. In passages which clearly capture a frustration not unknown today, they see all their efforts to get an education end only in business school and the chance to "sit solemnly at some business man's feet while he cleared his throat and began "Yours of the 19th received and contents noted." Nor do they find love any easier. Rosamond, though she is married, dies as a result of an accidental, unaffordable pregnancy—something that actually happened to the youngest, favorite sister of Josephine Herbst—and Victoria's bohemian affair with Jonathan Chance is very uncertain. The women are bold, but they are vulnerable. The protections of their mother's era are gone. This is not the image of the 1920s as it has come down to us in works largely written by men: it is women from their own point of view, in which one of the implications of freedom is the possibility of ending up alone.

But *The Executioner Waits* is not only a novel of women. Like *Pity Is Not Enough* it is also an historical novel: specifically a novel of the early twentieth-century radical movement. In the sense that *Pity Is Not Enough* is "about" capitalism, *The Executioner Waits* is "about" the rise of opposition to capitalism during the 1920s. From the singing Wobblies to the striking meat packers, from San Francisco to New York, the novel is full of vignettes of the emerging "movement"; and its exploration of the continuing hardships of Anne and Amos Wendel, the difficulties of Rosamond Wendel and Jerry Stauffer, and the inauspicious beginnings of Victoria Wendel and Jonathan Chance provide its justification. Interchapters, which in *Pity Is Not Enough,* foretell the characters' personal histories, here, with their mood of resistance, foretell the political. The solidarity of the farmers in the first interchapter, at the beginning, is echoed by the solidarity of workers in the main text at the end. The time is the 1920s—but the direction is toward the 1930s. The inchoate dissatisfactions felt by individuals such as Rosamond and Victoria all across the country will soon coalesce into a political force: that is the "idea" of the novel. It is very much a novel of becoming.

The chief incarnation of capitalism in *The Executioner Waits* is the successful but selfish banker David Trexler, who has so much but gives so little to his family. The youngest brother of "Poor" (but generous) Joe, and poor (but generous) Anne, he is very much their moral opposite. His self-satisfied but self-deluded character is perhaps best captured in the scene in which he imagines his neighbors remarking to one another on his all-too-modest good works: "There goes Mr. Trexler, the philanthropist, he does so many nice things, and all so quietly." Another representative of capitalism is the philistine father of Jonathan Chance who would rather write his son moralistic, self-serving letters than trouble to understand him. ("It was. . .a horrible example of the way people were warped all out of shape to find out that a father could have it in his power to help his son and not help him," thinks Victoria, to which "People get different when they begin to get money. You were lucky to have parents who didn't have much," is Jonathan's response.) What is interesting about these portraits, as in so much of the writing of Josephine Herbst, is how close to the real-life originals they came. Relatives of Herbst's uncle Daniel Fry found her representation of the Oregon banker perfectly apt. The letter denouncing Jonathan Chance's life of "vice and vagabondism" and stopping a check previously proffered to help buy a house is a letter the real father of Herbst's real husband John Herrmann actually wrote. The story of Victoria and Jonathan's "shotgun wedding"—including the reasons for it—is one of the autobiographical highlights of the book. So harsh they may at times read like stereotypes, Herbst's capitalists were nonetheless not invented. She was interested in the relationships between money and social control both in and out of the family and she found plenty of evidence for her perceptions. If the portraits seem exaggerated, remember: it was not a very subtle era.

The Executioner Waits appeared at a time of immense social upheaval, 1934, and several of its interchapters are dated the same year. A book which depicts the forces of capital and the forces of labor in growing combat, it leaves us with the representative of capital—David—observing the determination of the representatives of labor—workers at the funeral of a fallen striker—without prescribing which side will win. The same audacity which characterized Josephine Herbst's use of current political materials in her historical trilogy also characterized her use of materials from her marriage, which was in fact dissolving just as the novel celebrating its beginnings was being released. Both in terms of political developments and in terms of her life, she was tossing things into her novel almost as soon as they happened, and she did not know how it would end.

—Elinor Langer

ABOUT THE AUTHOR

Josephine Herbst was born in Sioux City, Iowa, in 1892 and died in New York City in 1969. A writer of considerable reputation—her work was often compared to that of her friends and contemporaries John Dos Passos and Ernest Hemingway—in addition to her 1930s trilogy *Pity Is Not Enough* (1933), *The Executioner Waits* (1934) and *Rope of Gold* (1939), she published four other novels, two in the 1920s and two in the 1940s, and one nonfiction book, a biography, in the 1950s. She was also noted for her journalism—dramatic eyewitness accounts of the midwestern farm strikes, the radical movement in Cuba, and the resistance to Hitler in Germany, which appeared in major newspapers and periodicals during the 1930s—and, later, for her criticism, essays and memoirs. She received many prizes and awards, including a Guggenheim Fellowship for fiction in 1936, a grant from the Rockefeller Foundation in 1965, and an award from the National Institute of Arts and Letters in 1966. A complete biography, *Josephine Herbst: The Story She Could Never Tell,* by Elinor Langer, is also available from Warner Books.

I. FOURTH INHERITANCE

A BANKRUPT man is a jump ahead of a bankrupt town. Until the day when Amos Wendel failed in business, Anne Wendel hoped for capital and looked back frantically on the chances lost forever.

"Only think," she'd say to her four girls, "your uncle had the pick of all the Deadwood mines. He was in the Black Hills from the start. Why didn't he get in on Homestake instead of Escondido? Who knows what might have happened?"

"Would you have married father?" Rosamond said.

"Who knows?" said Anne Wendel. "I probably wouldn't have met him."

"Then we'd have had another man for father. Perhaps that Mr. Gason that gave you the gold opera glasses," said Nancy.

"Don't be silly," said Anne Wendel. "But if Joe had picked Homestake, generous as he was, I'd have had all the advantages, you can mark my words."

Sometimes she would remember a still greater lost chance. "Why my father might have bought lots in Chicago when it was just a swamp. He was there in 1845 and wrote in his diary, *someday this will be a great city.* Think what it would mean today if he had staked out one lot for himself. Papa wouldn't wear himself to a bone, we'd have all we wanted to eat and wear, books and travel."

"Travel, that's what I want," said Vicky.

"It would be a different life, I can tell you," said their mother. "He was on his way to Wisconsin then, to pick out land for some Swiss immigrants coming up from St. Louis. He thought of a dozen things for other people, how to get the boats off the flats when they got stuck, and when they came to Mineral Point he knew where spring water was. He has it all down in black and white, a careful man like that, mint julep, 10 cents, letter to wife, 25 cents, coat mended, 35 cents, and wouldn't you think a man with his mind about him would have thought of staking out a nice property in Chicago for his posterity?"

"We wouldn't have Papa for a father then either, would we?" said Rosamond.

Amos Wendel had bought a little implement business, crippled from the start by want of capital. The Cuban War of 1898 had patched things somewhat. Amos had laid that to McKinley enterprise, and although Anne Wendel was a democrat to the marrow like her brothers, she put a mourning picture for the martyred president in their window and draped Mem's widow veil around it. It was the biggest picture in the block and had the biggest drape around it.

But 1903 was bad for crops. A heavy frost came too soon. Amos looked out early one morning in September and groaned. Corn needed two weeks more weather. Wheat was a failure in that section. Thousands of acres in Iowa grew nothing that bad year but wild sunflower. And 1907 was bad, they had lost several hundred dollars in a bank that failed. In 1911 it was a bad, bad year. They had just bought the house the year before to cheat the landlord of his eternal rent, and it looked as if they would lose it. And in 1914 Amos Wendel went on the rocks just when the wave of war was beginning to do the farmer a little good. He had failed, out and out, with no more hope of a business to worry over.

"It's enough to wear away a stone," Anne Wendel said a little wildly, because all the wills had been willed that she could think of. Aunty Blank had willed every stitch of handloomed linen and every pewter plate and all those handsome rubbed walnut pieces to Lizzie, her adopted daughter, back in 1899, when Lizzie hadn't had the grace even to write that poor Aunty was on her deathbed. Aunty had parceled out four hundred dollars apiece to her nieces, Anne Wendel and Hortense Ripley, but look what happened. Sunk in Papa's business and drained off like so much rain on rocky soil.

Then Mem had willed to the two sisters, her son Aaron's promise to pay his debt to her with town lots for her daughters. Do things alles freundlich, she had said when dying. She had fallen on the floor in her lavender dress, with coffee on the stove and sweetpeas coming into blossom. David, the pampered youngest, was gadding around in Europe taking in the Passion Play and the Paris Exposition. The prosperous boy had never realized what it meant to an old woman, eighty-two, to live alone with nothing but rags to tear into strips for rugs and bits of painting to do over and over of Mt. Hood and Hood River at Sunset and Lone Rock in Storm. For a woman who had spent a lifetime working hand and foot for others and never idle, it was hard even in such old age to slow to little nothings.

She had taken advantage of her son's absence to die and to be laid on the white spread while Hortense was sent for. "Alles freundlich," she had said, puzzled that since her fall the world and its creatures seemed upside down and her daughter appeared to listen with tears on an upside down face, feet sticking in the air and clock half way on the floor and the ceiling for a carpet. Annoyed she had been, rising and frowning, brushing it aside.

"Stand right," she had snapped, glaring at her daughter. "Don't try to be funny," and poor Hortense had hovered over her. But it was all wrong, she had to leave this life with everything leering in a crazy way and no sure belief that they would send the right pillows to Anne or divide the silver tea set fairly, or worst of all, get Aaron to settle up his just debts.

But all the living children, Anne Wendel, David and Aaron Trexler, and Hortense Ripley, fell in with Mem's last command, Alles freundlich. Anne complained a little that the pillows seemed like feather bed pillows but David, who had returned from Paris sporting a red tie only sixty days after his mother was in the ground, wrote Anne that he was shocked she should imagine there might be better pillows. "Alles freundlich," he said, asserting that he and Hortense had sorted everything to the best of their ability. Then, wise boy, he knew how to touch the right chord and wrote plaintively of his return to religion.

"Ella and I are going to join the church. I got back to home influences through Mem. Like the sailor we may wander but hope to reach port someday. Moral and spiritual education are good for those who have children to rear. We need to educate them for a safe landing and this is to the educated mariner as natural as the beating of a pulse."

Anne Wendel melted and forgot her complaints of the feathers and ceased to cry over the pathetic black bonnets that they had crushed thoughtlessly into the china from her mother's home. "Nothing that is truly good and beautiful can vanish from the earth," she told her children as they stood around her awed at the contents of the barrel from Oregon that seemed to yield pieces of Grandma's person almost as living as her head and arms. Her little black cape, the squirrel piece, stockings with a darning ball and needle still in place.

When the old piano came, that their mother had played O Listen to the Mocking Bird on in her youth, they clasped its heavy handsome legs and played doll house beneath it but Mem's will was the last they were to benefit from for a long time. It had been toward the end of 1902 and for years no other member of the Trexler family thought of dying.

The Wendels made the best of things in Oxtail, Iowa, where they seemed to have been stranded on an island with wealthier relatives to the west and east. Sometimes the situation they were in burst out all of a sudden. Anne Wendel might be fitting a dress for one of the girls.

"Stand still now, do you want it longer or is this right?"

"The style's longer, isn't it? It sags on the side."

"All right. I know that, I'll take that up, stand still now." Then from her mouth, crooked with pins, she let pins fall, words popping suddenly. "I know full well *in the right place* Papa's abilities would in these years have made us independent." Her oval face tightened as she spoke, the arched dark brows tragic and solemn. "Full well," she repeated in a somber voice.

But to all that, there was as yet no answer.

She was so pressed for cash, so worried that her two youngest would get caught in life without an advantage to their names that when the letter about Uncle Aaron came, her mind leaped to its conclusion. "Sick, and with that Sally like a hawk over him. Why he might die without a will if no one of his own people come to help him."

MISERS DIE TOO

When Aaron Trexler smashed his thumb on a surveying job on the road to Millville, New Jersey, he remembered one of Mem's wise sayings: "No good comes from Millville." She had been against the town, no one knew why but time was proving her right. The thing bled and he had to quit the job.

"Better get that boy of yours on the job to help you," said Mr. Wrenn.

"He's getting educated, not that it will do much good if the war keeps up in Europe."

"I bet you his education won't get him any better business than you've got right here," Wrenn said, as the two of them got into Aaron's Ford. The thumb throbbed and no doubt it was a mistake to wrap it in a dirty handkerchief.

"A man can't stay in a business like mine this long and not get known and do business," said Aaron Trexler. "Better take the wheel Wrenn this darned thing is bleeding."

It had looked for awhile as if they would have to slice off the thumb. Aaron went around with a bandage as big as a hornet's nest. The curious thing was that as the thumb began to heal, Aaron began to sicken. His color turned yellowish and his gray-green eyes had the look of a sick cat's. He was penned in with his wife Sally spying on all he did and clamping down like a bite on his liberties. As he grew weaker he stayed at his office to all hours, crawling home, afraid to go to bed for fear he'd not get up again. One morning he couldn't budge. When Sally stood over him, scornful and silent, he managed to sit up.

"I'll be home today," he said.

"Oh you'll be home today, will you Mister High and Mighty, thank you for the compliment," said Sally. He got up from his bed in his scant nightshirt and wrapped his old bathrobe around him.

"Watch out woman," said Aaron, staring at her feet in the red kid slippers. "I'm not too sick to cut you off yet."

"Oh you'll not cut me off," said Sally. "What doesn't come one way will come another. You'll not cut your Son off, I think." She was right; what else had it been about all these years but the boy. He'd put up with fire and brimstone only to have her turn him against his own father.

"You've done enough devil's work, get me some breakfast," said Aaron. She set the food on a cleared edge of a cluttered table. It was cooked nicely and hot.

"Now then," he said after breakfast. "Get me paper and pencil and I'll send a note to Wrenn." She let him write it, fold it in a cocked hat and hand it to her.

"What's this for?"

"Send it," said Aaron. "Get a boy." She turned it over, looking at him with the same ironical twist to her mouth that had fascinated him back in 1890 when he was already old enough to know better. Then, at fifty, he had admired her good sense, her trim figure, her red hair, like his sister's. No man had turned her into such a fury, no, it had been another woman, that Madeleine McNarry and her tattling mouth, who had sown more trouble in her day than an army.

"Please soon," said Aaron. Still holding the note gingerly, Sally withdrew and Aaron sat hunched for an hour, why didn't Wrenn come? He did not show up that day nor the next when Aaron was too weak to leave his bed. Sally sent for the doctor then but never budged from his side. Aaron's eyes probed the doctor's, longing for a chance for a private word. If he would only send her from the room for hot water, for a glass. No, nothing.

The next day and the next he lay trapped. He saw himself gradually sinking, heard one day the hypercritical voice of his wife assuring Wrenn's voice that her husband couldn't see anyone. "Oh Wrenn," he called and was surprised that his voice was such a whisper. That night he took himself in hand and asked for whiskey.

In the morning he got up, staggered downstairs, one step at a time. "Lord have mercy," said Sally.

"Now Sally," said Aaron firmly. "Use your wits. Wrenn wants to buy two Sea Isle lots and promised me cash for them. I've been trying to get him to come to close the deal. You've blocked me, I give you credit. Come to your senses, you know you always get a nice little divvy out of all the deeds you condescend to sign, don't you?" She nodded. "Well, get dressed and send for Wrenn."

When Wrenn came she was all sugar. "How do you think he looks, Mr. Wrenn?" she said.

"Bad," said Wrenn. "Very bad. You ought to be in bed."

"Never mind that," said Aaron. "Now Wrenn I want to go to my lawyer's to sign this, understand." He lifted one eyebrow.

"Of course," said Wrenn, answering by a lift of his eyebrow. "It's the only way to do business, especially with this piece where seems to me there was flaw of title." They got into Wrenn's car, Sally alone on the back seat, and drove slowly along the street that Aaron had laid out for Flemmer when he was a young man. Flemmer had been full of projects then about making a little Italy out of Grapeville. Grapes would multiply and make everybody rich and wine would flow and the town would grow like a mushroom. Now Flemmer was cold in the grave, his three boys quarreled over the will and his old maid sister couldn't bear the sight of a decanter.

"Here we are," said Wrenn, not gallantly to Mrs. Trexler, who had got herself up in a brown suit and gloves that were too long in the fingers. When they got to Roundtree's office, the old lawyer did not at first recognize his friend.

"Trexler, I'll be damned." He got up, came around, an old man assisting one younger but feebler than himself. "What's been ailing you?"

"Don't know," said Aaron. "Let's get to business." He pulled out the papers and, peering at them, stiffly signed.

"Now Aaron, set your mind at rest," said Roundtree as Wrenn briskly signed his check and, blowing on it, handed it over.

"I'm going to," said Aaron, beads of sweat on his forehead. "I'm not going back home and I want you gentlemen as witnesses." The two men stared and Sally fired up.

"What?" said Roundtree.

"I'm not going home. I'm going out to Tonis's house, they know how to care for the sick. Roundtree, you've had me here a dozen times in my life, talking of leaving my wife and every time you've persuaded me to go back to her. Why, I don't know. But now I've made up my mind. I'm not going."

"He's not right in the head," said Sally heatedly. "None of his family are, why one of them went plain looney and they are all cracked, everyone. I've had a battle all my life to protect our child and now he humiliates me before others. But I can stand it, I've put up with so much I can stand this. I've worn my feet off waiting on him."

"Never mind, Mrs. Trexler," said Roundtree smoothly. "You need rest yourself. I think it's all for the best that your husband has a little change. Mr. Tonis's house is very quiet, nicely managed, I heard she was a first rate cook and had been a nurse once. And you should rest," he soothed, nodding and winking toward her, as if she alone were in his confidence.

They got rid of her with one device and another and they packed up his bones again and rattled him off to the Tonis's. Mr. Wrenn waited a few days, then got off a letter to David Trexler, the wealthy brother, in Roseland, Oregon.

Grapeville, New Jersey, Feb. 5, 1918

Dear Sir:

This is Monday afternoon. Mr. Trexler went to board with Mr. and Mrs. Tonis on Grove Ave. He used his wits to get away. Mr. Trexler sold me a piece of land for $500 and insisted that I take himself and wife to the lawyer's office to transact the business. After they got there, Mr. Trexler refused to go back home and told Mr. Roundtree to take him to Tonis's which he did. Mrs. Trexler of course protested. I was on the spot and Mrs. Trexler expressed herself but to no avail. I visited Mr. Trexler last evening and this afternoon. He looks greatly emaciated but is comfortable and seems so relieved to get away from his prison home. He told me he has been trying to reach me for a week but could not and her kind treatment had long ceased to be. The Tonis's are used to caring for people and I think will look after him well. I believe where he is is better than a hospital. I hope he stays and does not go home.

Enoch Wrenn

David Trexler received this letter in his office at the drug store. He sat tapping reflectively with a pencil. Let's see, Aaron was born in 1840, that would make him seventy-eight, poor fellow, he would no doubt not get up again. Aaron was almost old enough to be his father, 19 years older, he himself had been born in fifty-nine, just a month before their father died. After all these years, his eyes moistened at the thought of himself as the little fatherless child who had made such a battle in life and, of all the Trexlers, had won such conspicuous success. Poor Joe, wrecked, the girls married to good men who lacked acute business sense, and Aaron who might die with say twenty, maybe thirty thousand, not more considering the way his she-devil of a wife had tied his hands with her refusals to sign deeds. Like Joe's wife, a regular spitfire, while he had been fortunate not only in a business way but in having such a wife as Ella.

He got his sister Mrs. Ripley on the phone. "Hortense," he said briskly. He loved to think of her at the other end of the line, answering sweetly in hopes of a big grocery order, her start of disappointment at the crack of his voice. Considering all the business he had thrown her way, to say nothing of the free bayrum and liniment, a little gratitude now and then wouldn't be amiss; but no she was stingy even of that. "Hortense, had a letter from

Wrenn and poor Aaron is down and out. Couldn't you take a trip back there and straighten things out?" He could hear her clear answer; no, Milton was not well and Eloise had a bad abscessed tooth. But he pretended deafness to irritate, roaring "What? What's that?" until she had repeated the tedious answers three times. Drawing in his mouth, making faces and eyes of enjoyment, he went on talking to his sister. They agreed that Anne was the proper one to make the trip. Her girls were either married or scattered and Amos's business was gone. If the brother and sister in Oregon put up the cash, Anne could make the trip and of course they could get back the money from Aaron's estate.

David Trexler immediately wrote his sister in Oxtail, Iowa. "And keep your eye on Sally. She's capable of poisoning you. In my opinion she's crazy and should be committed. If he doesn't divorce her, she will chew up everything and not leave him enough for a decent burial. Get him to make a will. He should take care of you and Hortense and leave that woman with a pittance."

The news was actually a godsend in his home that evening. Since both his boys had been shipped overseas his big house was gloomy as a tomb. He was glad to be staggering under a heavy load of work at the office. It gave him an excuse to stay away from the long faces of his wife and daughter Sue. Not that Sue was so crazy about her brothers; her grievance went deeper to some hidden personal sore of her own. Her hidden woe would join her father's rancor in a stream of violence against the war, against the way Bryan, David's idol, had been unceremoniously shoved out of the picture, and in a lower key, with heads together, against the trouble makers in the town, those meddlers and humiliators who had dared to nose their way into Trexler's affairs and to bring down his pride.

In the midst of pressing work, the flash would explode in his mind, the negative exposed, the same old picture tiresomely photographed. It was always the same scene, repeating itself endlessly, the parlor in his home, the delegation of men he had known all his life in Roseland facing him with impertinent, triumphant hostility.

"Dave," Trimble, President of Chamber of Commerce had said. "We are all thinking of your interests and of the interests of our country. It pains us to come here. But duty cannot be shirked in times like this." Even in memory, David Trexler wanted to snicker at the pretentious speech, the faces set up solemnly like a flock of cards. "Your place of business flies no flag, your house has none. Your boys miraculously escaped the draft with you on the draft board. Before we entered the war, you were out and out pro-German. Now suspicion has fastened on you and it is time for a showdown."

"Our people never believed in war, on principle," he began.

"Slacker," hissed from the back. Yes, Jack Larson who had missed out on the paving bid when Dave was on City Council.

"I say they were Mennonites, they did not believe in it."

"Be a man, Dave, you're a Congregationalist," said Snyder, Head of the church committee who had voted on his membership and then went around saying they couldn't afford to lose out on such a moneybags.

"Quibbling won't get you any place Dave. We aren't buyers bidding for your cascara bark and peppermint." Archie Erskine. Furniture and coffins. David had a terrible urge to laugh. He could feel laughter bubbling like gas in his belly, he was afraid it would spout suddenly from his mouth and finish him. They stood there solemnly and he had to warn himself that this was indeed an all too solemn moment. They were jailing suspects. Only the other day he had heard that Doc Trainor who had been in the same class with him in Philadelphia had been mauled by a crowd, then jailed.

"Get it over, now Dave, we're your friends, and we might as well tell you we've come for proof of your loyalty. Are you willing to kiss the flag and repeat the oath?"

David Trexler had not answered. He was wondering how he could get even. The best way would be to make money hand over fist, buy bank stock, control it, get in the banking game, then squeeze.

"Brother Trexler," said the soothing voice of Rev. Aldrich. David glared in his direction; he wasn't his pastor and didn't care for that cheap Methodist familiarity. But he could feel the ring tightening. Archie Erskine had had a glass of beer, maybe whiskey.

Look at the criminal shave on Tusk Coy's mug. He heard the side door click and light steps going upstairs.

"Quick boys, my wife," and he ushered them deftly into the long billiard room opening from the living room. He had had this room fitted up with one of the handsomest tables money could buy; not that it was used often but it gave tone to his establishment.

"Now gentlemen," he said briskly.

"Don't take it that way, Dave," said Tusky Coy, getting chummy as he saw Dave meant to toe the line. "We're only thinking of your own good."

"Hurry, my wife has come home. What do you want?"

"Just swear allegiance, Dave," said Trimble. "Say after me. I swear allegiance to my flag."

"I swear allegiance to my flag."

"And to the country for which it stands. . . ."

"And to the country. . . ." The words spoken by Trimble seemed ugly and he felt crawling and mean. If only they would forget the kissing business. But Snyder remembered. A corner of the flag was held out to him relentlessly. He took it gingerly, looking out miserably at the group of "friends." He put it to his lips.

"Atta boy," said Tusky Coy hilariously, clapping his shoulder. "Nothing so difficult, was it? Now boys, let's forget all about this and keep it under our hats. Tell no one, not even the little woman. We know Dave is with us, and let's show him we know it by respecting what's gone on in this room just as sacredly as if we had sworn oaths." Everybody agreed; now they were laughing nervously and someone was joking about the blarney stone that had to be kissed standing on your head, it was said. Anyhow the flag was easier than that. Now they were shuffling out of the room, eyes down a little, eager to get home to their wives and begin retailing the sacred news, all under promise of not to tell, of course.

When they were gone, David Trexler walked upstairs. He went to the bathroom and carefully brushed his teeth. The paste tasted sweet, not like the soap Mem had used that time she had washed his mouth for lying about playing marbles on Sunday. He rubbed the brush along the soap as it lay in the dish and scrubbed again.

David Trexler often went to the washroom of his store and, while washing his hands, found himself drawing a soapy finger along his teeth. He could not wash out the resistance he felt toward the war. He liked to howl about his principles against war but he knew in his heart that they had nothing to do with it. In the beginning he had feared the war, afraid that it would interfere with his drug business. He had instinctively sympathized with the German cause. Way back in 1914, he was already saying that we would get into it. He liked to think that he sensed events before their time and knew the meaning of history. Actually he kept a strict eye on the market. Watch Morgan. When the twelve billion loan went out to England, David Trexler stiffened his resistance but he watched his stocks and bonds and bought heavily in U.S. Steel and industrials. He got in on a lumber combine. David Trexler made money before the day the European nations went to war, but after that date, his money bred money, the stuff was fertile as a grain field in good growing weather.

Yet David Trexler could not look back upon the beginning of his great rise without pain. It was on that very day that he had felt betrayal in his private life. His wife's younger sister, Millie, on whom he had lavished a father's love, had eloped. She had opened a chapter that he thought closed forever. Years before, when she came home from the Pharmaceutical College in Philadelphia he had had it out with her about that man who had dared write her love letters. He had ripped open the letter, read the shameless words, confronted the girl with the proof of her infamy. How could she carry on behind his back when he had put so much money into her education expecting to make a useful clerk of her for his own store? She had promised never to write, never to see that man again, had quietly taken up her life. Who could say she did not have a comfortable home with trips and presents, just like one of the family. Wasn't that enough?

During that June of 1914, David Trexler had made gratifying progress in the control of his affairs. His son David had just graduated from the same college that had graduated himself and Millie. Millie had gone east to the national convention of druggists and D. O. considered that such a move would help smooth over the slight break in affairs due to young Dave coming into the business.

As the son, Dave naturally stood in line over Millie, who on account of her long service might feel some slight. No such intention was in Trexler's mind. But Millie was, after all, a woman. Millie had gone off cheerfully, more affectionately than usual, crying a little at the station. He and Mamma had started off on a swing through the mountains to Crater Lake.

The fact is that they had been very lonesome on their little trip. Business was slack and he was following his usual course of buying heavily when prices were down. He bought chittum bark that trip at astonishing lows. For what else had he built a warehouse, if not to take advantage of such little tricks of the trade. He profited out of the Crater Lake venture and came back toward the end of July expecting to find a nice little family running along smoothly.

Millie would be back and they would all have some good laughs at news of the convention and at the number of poor forlorn druggists who had begged to exchange photographs with her. They would lay the photos on the table and he would analyze each one and have the whole family in stitches.

It was evening when the car swung into the rose-lined drive and edged slowly toward the house. They could see a white dress on the veranda and, to hide his pleasure, D. O. complained as they passed one of the spraying hoses on the vast lawn, "Darn thing too close to the drive." A strong fragrance of heliotrope and rose-bloom was in the air. The grass was newly mown. The little lights of the town were coming out in the houses below as Trexler came out of the garage to join his wife who stood quietly on the lawn.

"Where's everybody?" David said, huffed at not being instantly met with open arms. As they neared the porch, Sue came down the steps and kissed them both. Dave, Jr. was at the store, little Pussy-dee was in bed, Daniel was at the Sampson's.

"Millie? Where's Millie," said David, his head up and his bright blue eyes suspicious and angry. Funny thing she wouldn't be around when she might know they would be coming home.

"Millie's not coming home," said Sue. "Papa, I guess there's some news in there you won't like. I didn't open the letter until Maud Danish came over. She'd had one too. She should be ashamed to show her face here and I told her so too."

"What are you talking about," said David. He put the bag he was carrying down and stood firmly as he did when about to close a deal with a man who was not exactly ready to sell at that price. "What's the meaning of all this?"

"Oh, David," said Ella. He looked at her angrily but she had turned very pale. "Let's go in," said Ella. They all went up the steps.

"Now just explain please," said David.

"Oh that letter will explain," said Sue, her face strangely like her father's. "Of all the ungrateful things and the treacherous things, all these years behind our backs."

"What, what?" shouted David. "Can't you make sense?"

"She's married," said Sue. "Married to that man, after all these years. Here's the letter." She put the letter in his hand. He glared at Sue and jerked it out of the envelope. Ella was very pale and sat down on the sofa. She spoke up now, "Now Dave."

David Trexler read the letter, muttering words aloud. Then he turned toward Ella. "Never speak to me of that woman again. To shame me before everybody, to brazenly elope. Yes, madam," he said addressing his wife. "She's married. In the holy bonds with that lecherous hound who never in all these years kept his nose off the scent. Why he's been smelling around all this time, think of that, and writing her on the sly, I've no doubt."

"Oh of course, that's what I tried to tell you," broke in Sue. "Maud Danish, she's been the go-between all these years. Eighteen years of deceit, pretending to be our friend and receiving letters from that man for Millie who has had the disloyalty to accept them. After her sacred promise to you."

Ella opened her mouth to speak but thought better of it. There was misery enough without reminding Sue that she too had promised her father never to see a certain young man again and had seen him; not that it did much good considering he afterwards drowned in the Columbia.

"To think Maud knew it," said David.

"Knew it? She aided and abetted Millie. If you have any spunk, Papa, you'll never let that woman set foot in this house again."

Between the two raging Trexlers poor Ella Trexler sat very pale, her hands in her lap. "Did you know of this, Mamma?" said David, whirling on her.

"No, Dave, of course not. Not a word. What does she say?"

"What does she say?" His hands shook so he could hardly smooth out the pages. "Here it is, the most brazen letter I ever hope to read.

" 'I am married to John Shane because we have loved each other all our lives.'

"*All our lives*," aped David.

" 'I obeyed you as long as I felt I was needed in the store and until Dave finished school but he can take my place now and perhaps you will not mind if I have a little happiness too. I shall never forget your kindness to me and pray you will forgive me for marrying this way but I felt my husband had a right to this secrecy and it was his wish. We were married this morning and I hope you will remember all the happy times we had together as I shall all my life long. I hope you will understand and see that I felt I should give John some of my life after all these years.'

"There's a young lady for you," he shouted. "Eloping at her age. You'd think age would give one sense; no, it seems to soften the brain. A woman who had excellent offers waits until she is an old maid to fall into the arms of a fortune hunter. Of course all he wants is her money that she's saved all these years due to our generosity."

"She hasn't much," said Ella timidly but, as David turned purple and looked ready to strike her, she quietly left the room.

The big house turned all lights off early that night but David Trexler did not go to bed for a long time. He went furiously to his office and made changes in his will and tore up papers and wrote orders and cut everybody's salary, his son's included, and he laid, in short, the foundations for a sudden strong spurt of financial success. Then he wrote a curt note to his sister to say there was no fool like an old fool and that Millie, that 180 pound darling, that chubby little morsel, had decided to elope in her second childhood and had allied herself to a low type who was only a fortune hunter but who had kept his nose to the scent for a long time, give him credit. It only proved what a base fellow he was and how ruled by his lusts and David had burned into his brain as with a hot iron the lustful letter that man had written Millie years before and he had thought he had scotched the snake, but no, the snake always bites the hand that feeds it and so it had been with Millie on whom God knows he had lavished all the affection of a kind and loving father.

And as he wrote this, he broke down in his little office and, to his deep anger and shame, felt the hot tears on his hot face. He crawled home when the sky was beginning to be light and sat on the porch in a chair looking at the sun coming up over the roofs of the town and little houses. On the porch of his big house he sat all collapsed, and when the newsboy flung the morning paper it hit his knee and he reached down languidly, unrolled it, and stared uncomprehendingly for several minutes at the great black headlines:

AUSTRIA DECLARES WAR

Rushes Vast Army Into Serbia

RUSSIA MASSES ON BORDER

He unrolled the paper firmly, sitting erect. By God. War. Was it possible? Nobody could say he hadn't bought that chittum bark in the nick of time. Prices would soar now. He got up, walked briskly into the house, up the stairs, and into the bathroom. The upstairs had that sleepy hushed look. In the bathroom he plunged his face and head into the washbowl, rubbed himself dry briskly, looked in the glass at his shiny bald head, the pink cheeks, the blue eyes, and the neat clipped moustache. He took a long drink of cold water and bustled into the bedroom. In the bed his wife made a vast mountain that did not stir but opened its eyes. "Oh Dave, why don't you come to bed?" she said.

"Nonsense," said Dave. "Where are my clean shirts? Do you know what's happening while we fume about our miserable little ungrateful affairs? Well, war, that's what's the matter. Europe is at war." He actually looked cheerful and Ella got up and began to dress.

Thank God something had turned up to distract him.

With Wrenn's letter in his hand, David Trexler toiled up the hill toward his house. He took pride in using his legs and felt that the continual use of cars showed decadence in the race. He had three cars in his garage and a light truck at his house on the coast, and the possession of these articles was enough. The big flag that had swung from its massive pole in front of the house ever since the vigilantes had called, banged away in a stiff breeze that had a smell of the ocean in it. There wasn't a more expensive flag in Roseland.

Since the boys had left, the remaining family had crowded closer together at the dinner table and leaves had been taken out to make it shorter. He was nearer to Ella than he had been in all the years of their marriage. He thought to himself it was true in more ways than one. With the table stretched out, they had had room for company and not only their growing children but Millie had found a place at their board. As he thought of Millie, he slashed at his meat and Ella looked up surprised.

"Mercy, Dave, is it that tough?"

"No, Mamma," said David. "I keep thinking of Aaron. Now if Anne can't go, what would your idea be?"

Sue looked up and said, "You can't go, you're doing the work of three men now with the boys gone and every clerk rushing off to war."

"I know that," said David. "I wouldn't be surprised Mamma if this was the poor fellow's last sickness."

"He's old," said Ella, "it's to be expected and with young boys dying all the time in Europe, I can't get worked up about him."

Sue gave a little snort and little Pussy-dee went on helping herself to more mashed potatoes. "Why don't you stop that child, Mother?" Sue said. "Can't you see she is swelling up and getting so stout she'll burst open? Who will love you if you keep on like that?"

Pussy-dee leaned over her plate and stopped scooping potatoes into her pretty mouth. Her curls dangled into her eyes that now slowly filled with tears.

"Sue don't make her cry. Papa will always love you, don't cry. Fat never stopped anyone from loving," said David. He opened his mouth and let it hang looking at his wife with a funny light in his eyes. "Why, bless you, Ella was a rail when I married her but she put on the flesh by the ton and did that ever stop me?" He had it on his tongue to add that Millie, running off at 39 to make a mad marriage with a railroad clerk, had been no featherweight. His mouth stayed open a little and his eyes showed all too plainly his thoughts.

"I know what's going on in your mind, Papa," said Sue. "All I can say is that some marriages are worse than none."

"Glad to hear you've so much sense," said David, annoyed to be reminded that Sue always read him like a book. He could have reminded her of a few follies of her own, like getting herself engaged to that boy who had the misfortune, not that it wasn't providential for her, to get drowned in the Columbia. Why, she cut up so about that episode that he had never dared cross her since. He was certain that the way she kept to herself, getting sour and shy of men, was just to spite him because he had not let her have her head in that instance.

"Let's try to be peaceable, there's none in the world and we might as well try to have a little in the home," said David, but he had not really felt at home since the vigilantes had invaded the premises. He pushed his chair back from the table, fished around in his pocket for a cigar, and went out to the big veranda to walk up and down.

Some boys and girls in one of the houses below were playing ukuleles and their dancing figures, hugged together, bobbed past the lighted window. Perhaps his taste wasn't of the best but music like that got under his skin. He couldn't for the life of him remember an opera score but to this day he felt a shiver remembering the weird wild voices of the cowboys and girls lurching on their horses that night at Shantico.

They had been driving all day through sagebrush that flowed over the flattened country in eastern Oregon like waves. At sunset they could see Jefferson, Mt. Hood, and Adams. That's how clear the air was. When they stopped the car the silence was so intense it hurt the ear. Rabbits hopped in front of the car. Shantico had burned down, there was only the wreck of the old red hotel, but the bar was intact, standing there like a set on a stage. Cowboys and girls, half drunk, half silly, lounged about while his party made up beds in the open on big piles of straw. The night was so white you could have read print. The cowboys and girls rode off singing, you could hear that singing long after they were gone. In the night he sat up and saw the three snow-capped peaks and the white faces of the sleepers. Millie lay like a child with an arm flung backward.

Millie, always coming back to Millie. Damn and be damned. He walked faster and faster, and only when Sue stuck her head out the door calling, "Heaven's sake, father, think of someone else, you're driving us crazy," did he stop and look out toward the sky where the big silk flag flapped to show the town that he was loyal.

Anne Wendel no sooner received the letter from her brother than she mounted the steep steps to the attic and dragged the old trunk from its corner. Maybe it was a sin to be so elated about a trip that might end in Aaron's death, but how could she help it when in all these years she had never stirred from the town but twice, once on a trip to Oregon financed by David the year he made the deal on hops and again with David when he took her to the Democratic Convention at Denver and they had stopped in Lincoln, Nebraska, to see Bryan who gave her a pebble he had picked up by the sea of Galilee.

At that she was better off than Mrs. Belisle who had lived in the red house on the alley and bought a pint of milk a day. Sometimes she would come while Amos was still milking and stand in her black dress, that sagged at the waist, holding her big lumpy pale baby on her arm. That was the hardest baby to find something cute to say about; he looked like a grandpa with his long face and pointed bluish nose. When Mrs. Belisle said she wouldn't need milk anymore, she was going to wean the baby, it was the first time Anne had ever heard of a bottle baby being weaned from the bottle so young. She came right out and told the mother it was wrong to take milk from a child that young. What a shy thing she had been and how reluctantly she'd finally admitted she couldn't afford the pint. Amos had poured a quart out for her from the big pail and told her to come every night and never say a word about the price anymore. There was a woman who had never traveled, had only been to Riverside Park once in her life, and yet she lived just a few doors away from the Wendels.

How many times since that night, years ago, had Anne Wendel not thought of Mrs. Belisle and sometimes, when she sat up late sewing on some dress for the girls or setting the bread for the next day or just sitting wondering where the money would come from, it almost seemed as if a magnet was trying to draw them out of their house to Mrs. Belisle's house, that finally stood vacant, infested with rats, by the alley. If she got frantic sometimes and had appealed to her brothers, it was because that threat seemed more and more imminent as the years went on. It wasn't only that sickness seemed to cluster around her family and she'd nursed her children through some of the hardest cases the doctor had ever seen, but a kind of threat seemed always hanging above them, waiting to swoop down upon them and to gobble up the little advantages she and Amos had scraped together.

She couldn't remember the time when she hadn't nourished some plan that would save her little family and bring to her children the advantages she herself had lacked. They were always ready for anything that would turn an honest penny or save one; not that they had ever been able to accomplish much. When they got sweet potatoes from Jersey to resell to the Oxtail merchants, that was certain to be the year when the price dropped and the profit was nothing.

And when she read the article that the soil of Iowa was said to be like that near the Rhine, how they had talked and spent an excited evening planting acres of grapes on that high bluff over the Missouri. The crop was harvested, sold, and the profits pocketed and spent, the children packed to college, the house refurnished, a new mattress for the children's room, a new rug for the bedroom and *a house all their own*. Around the lamp of an evening, all that cycle was lived through and enjoyed and, when the children had gone to bed and the excitement died, she and Amos had looked at one another and laughed a little.

If now and then she was puzzled at her two youngest girls, and the way they talked about life as if it were soda pop and could be had in a bottle, she tried to fall in with all their plans, practical or impractical. She thanked her stars that she had been mad enough to dream of some kind of a grand future for her children. If only money did not play such a part. But it always seemed as if everything hung upon the need to get together a few pennies. Many was the time when she saw the chance to make something in real estate slip for lack of a small sum that would make them independent and prosperous. That small sum, how it hung like a ripe pear out of reach.

No wonder she had sometimes swallowed her pride and had appealed to one or the other of her two brothers. Not that it had brought her good, for at the moment of need, some pressing venture seemed always to be engaging all the resources the brothers had. Even in 1916, the year that Mrs. Belisle had stopped the pint of milk, and one of David's children had boasted of the 800 per cent dividends Papa's United States Steel was bringing him, David himself had muttered about his business absorbing all his profits. Her timid suggestion, that he help her girls to college, fell like a stone from a high building. David had bolted from fretting and anxious relatives to Alaska with all his family. Vicky had gone on with her job of cutting stencils and sent Rosamond money all that year for a taste of college at Wisconsin.

It almost seemed as if their uncle's indifference stiffened her girls' stubbornness and made them more determined than ever to get what they were after. Not that she approved of the bitter way they spoke of their uncle; compared to many a brother he was good as gold. Some rich brothers wouldn't have bothered to take her to Denver or to remember her at Christmas with little checks.

But she would never forget the look on Vicky's face, the year she taught school in the country and came home for weekends, changing from the train to the streetcar in the suburbs instead of at the downtown depot in order to save a nickel, coming home one Saturday, sitting at the table with her thin wrists and circles under her eyes, reading one of her uncle's letters with the snapshots of the

Cadillac and the family party tricked out in their best as they were about to start off for Death Valley.

It was all very well to say that a year or two didn't matter in a young person's life. She had put in so many years in her own girlhood, toiling away like a mole underground at the Grapeville place, that she knew only too well a few years made all the difference in the world. And if she sometimes liked to quietly open the drawer where Vicky kept her papers, after the girl had gone to bed, to read some jotting in her notebook that she had copied from somewhere, like *To suffer or to win, to be a hammer or an anvil. Goethe*, it was to comfort herself. Everything would come out right, it would have to; with her two hands she would push back trouble and wrestle with death itself.

But it was easier to hold off death than to hold off torn tablecloths and worn bedclothes and curtains that had hung in the same place year in and year out. A battered coffee pot is sometimes harder to contend with morning after morning than sickness in the house. Yet what a triumph when the girls finally walked off. Papa had hardly recognized his own daughter when Vicky showed up at the train in her new suit, actually on her way to California. It wasn't every girl would go so far, but she was like her uncle, like poor Joe, who was always setting his hopes on some far off place. And Rosamond coming home from Wisconsin, pretty as a picture with her trunk full of snapshots and her head full of new and dangerous ideas.

Few women had as much variety in their children as she did. When they were little, people used to shake their heads and say that they never saw a family who resembled one another less. Nancy was thin and dark and Clara smooth and fair and Vicky was middling fair and thin and Rosamond was lovely. Sickness was nothing to the other troubles she'd nursed those girls through.

Take the two oldest. What a wrangle they had made about the size of their waists, holding to the tape measure and squeezing and breathing in, tears running down their faces, each one claiming to be smaller than the other. "Now there's no difference," she would say, stopping everything to measure them while they held their breaths, just girls of 12 and 13, but in those days waists were important matters. By the time the two younger came along with a gap of almost ten years between, corsets were out of fashion.

She and Amos had to bear lectures from their two eldest that would astonish one. Religion with them had been as bad as small-pox. A handsome revivalist had upset the Wendel home for years, dragging the older girls to meetings morning and night, weekday and Sunday. They had the temerity to lecture their mother and to accuse her of not being a "christian." When she wanted to see them pretty and learning to dance, they were praying and testifying at prayer meetings.

It was unnatural and she worried about it more than she did about Vicky and Rosamond when they announced they did not believe in immortality and doubted what was meant by the soul. She had gone through phases of that nature herself but had never come out so boldly. She was a little frightened at the calm way in which they appeared to put marriage on the shelf. Experience, she told them, was a great teacher and marriage was the experience of the ages.

All the same it was a triumph and an excitement in her life to have bright girls who could read a newspaper and get worked up about affairs of the world and yet wanted to dance when they heard music and talked about riding in airplanes and all the new inventions with so much familiarity and ease. It made all the sacrifice of helping them to college seem a blessing, and if she skimped and saved with never a drop in the bucket and all their efforts only keeping them fed and clothed just enough to cover nakedness, it helped to imagine that her children were going to find life bright and ready for living.

She contented herself with writing little homilies to them like "I am always thinking of the influence on your character of college," and "Don't let your fresh youth be worn away by brainless idiots at dances," and "Don't think the rich girls will be those you will like the best or want to know most," all the time hoping that they would take care of their health as that was the most important thing in the world.

And if certain phases her girls passed through gave her sleepless nights, she tried to remember that gradually they outlived their little spasms. Take Vicky who had bullied them during her high-school days with her snobbish ways and the notion she was better than the rest. Her triumphs in highschool had gone to her head and she had bossed her older sisters, complained of their grammar, and primly said "That is not I" in a way to make one's face crack. No one ever made more of a virtue of reading and she read the house down, scolding poor Clara and Nancy for their tastes in books and lording it over them all, dictating table manners and snubbing members of the family, if she met them in public, in a most obnoxious way. Only Papa's failure had put humbleness in the girl.

As for Rosamond, she was at that very minute a source of great concern. After two years of country school-teaching she had had, with Vicky's help, one year at the university at Madison. The year had not reconciled her to ordinary ways of earning a living. She was pestered by letters from "men" she had met at college. One of the boys had shown up as a reporter on the local paper and, when the worry he caused subsided by his departure, Rosamond gave more trouble by having a married man's attentions center on her. All Corny Stebbins's talk about Pancho Villa and the war in Mexico where he had been a correspondent didn't pull the wool over Anne Wendel's eyes and hide the fact that he was a man not to be trusted.

She had been only too glad to have Jerry Stauffer come along, a nice fresh boy from the country, with brains and ideals. The girls could make light of such qualities if it pleased them; in the end they would find no husband would wear long without them.

Rosamond had really cast off some of the gloom of her disappointment in having to work at routine office jobs, after she knew young Stauffer. His father ran a dairy farm and the two young people were just beginning to enjoy themselves, rattling around the hills near Oxtail on moonlight nights in the milk truck, when the war took him off. Rosamond had quit her job in Oxtail, had moved discontentedly to San Francisco to be with Vicky and now, after all that moving around, had finally made up her mind to marry Jerry, who was stationed at Manhattan, Kansas.

It would puzzle anyone, even a mother, to explain why her girl needed to make so many moves before she finally decided to make

the right one. Anne Wendel had never been one to push her girls
into marriage but there was no doubt in her mind that marriage
would steady Rosamond. The two eldest had taken to it without
question; they had never ventured from home like the two youngest, had waited on the door step for a good man to come along.
Times changed a great deal in a few short years.

She sat on the floor of the attic, unpacking the old trunk, lifting
out the children's baby clothes and her own wedding gown that had
been worn only that one day and then wrapped in blue cloths to
keep it from yellowing. Her whole household was in a state of
movement and it was hard to focus on her brother Aaron, sick and
abandoned, when the very business of taking a train provided
bustle and stir in the world.

Amos Wendel accepted his wife's new move to Grapeville. Since
he had failed in business, he had not a word to say about his
daughters' lives and he considered Anne had better judgment
about what she wanted to do than he did. He did not understand
why his two youngest girls wanted to chase all over the country and
for Vicky to work so hard for a little education was a puzzle that he
was proud of. He went to the train when the different moves were
made, his mouth trembling a little under the big moustache, tears
in his eyes.

"Well, daughter," he would say, "I don't know what it is you're
after but I wish you luck." The resignation with which he said this
made Vicky cry resentful tears for miles after the train had started
across Nebraska. No one meant to leave him out of their plans, but
they did. Before the day he brought the clock home four years
before, he might have put in his oar, but after that he let things go.

THE CLOCK GOES BACK

Amos Wendel came home with a present on the very day that the accountants from Omaha were figuring to put his little business on the rocks. The present was a little gold clock and the alarm was like a tune from a music box. On the way home on the streetcar he began to have cold feet about his present. He could hardly explain to himself how he had come to step up in the auctioneer's room and buy it. Someone had bid a dollar. Then it had been raised to $1.25. At two dollars the auctioneer had set the alarm and it had gone off, a clear little tune. It was like a music box Anne was always talking about that had belonged to her brother Joe.

"Now gentlemen, listen to that tune. Where will you find a genuine singing clock like this for ten dollars. What am I bid for this little Swiss masterpiece? Just think of waking up in the morning to sweet music." He waited, wound her again and let her go. It was a lovely tune. "Only imagine, gents, what this tune is called. A regular import, gents, called appropriately, *I love you*." He paused, holding out the clock. Wendel had cleared his throat and to his own surprise, said, "$2.25."

He had stepped into the auction room because it was warm and filled with men who were out of work as he himself would soon be. He wanted to be with the crowd and to feel that he wasn't the only man in the world who was getting it in the neck. The day before a bunch of outofworks had stormed the City Hall and the hose had been turned on them. When he looked around him, the men in the auction room depressed him—some weren't shaved, their necks looked thin, their coats shabby. When the auctioneer began his speech, Amos spotted Ricketts and a few other business men who showed up in this crowd not so much by their clothes as by their easy way of lounging, laughing and looking on.

He hoped they wouldn't realize what was going on at his place. The accountants would be busy for a week; he wanted that time to

27

move around with his head up. When a fat man in a corner raised his bid on the clock, Amos spoke up and raised him. It was a game and he took pleasure in thinking he was pulling the wool over the eyes of fellows like Ricketts. A man who could buy a clock wasn't dead on his feet.

Between bids he looked down and the soaked shoes of the man next him stood spongily in the midst of little pools of melted snow. When Amos made a bid, the man seemed to raise himself on his toes and more water sloshed out of the shoes. Amos's own shoes needed soling and he knew that if he got the clock he could not get new soles, but he kept on raising and at $3.75 the clock was his.

When he got out on the street, his pocket sagging with the little clock, he felt uncomfortable remembering that fellow's shoes. He bought a cigar and swore at himself for his extravagance. Something seemed to be pushing him into the wrong places. He should be down with the outofworks looking at the employment boards and he was haunting auction rooms, buying cigars. But, by god, didn't he have a right to buy a present for his wife after all these years? Was he to be shoved off the map with never a chance to bring home something that wasn't strictly useful? He had been in business twenty-five years and had put every cent back, hoping to get ahead. The future was dark but he felt he had a right to a little present.

"Here's a little present for you, Anne," he said shyly when he got home. "A present?" she said. "This is a great time for presents. Did someone give it to you?" He had to shake his head. When she saw it was a clock, she looked amazed. "A clock. We don't need a clock."

"Wait" said Amos, "let me." He wound the alarm delicately, set it down. "Wait," he said smiling, but something inside felt very heavy. When the tune began, Anne smiled, but she kept right after him, "You didn't pay real money for it, did you?"

"Only $3.75," he admitted. "At an auction."

"At a time like this, when the children need so much. I never heard of such a thing. You take it right back. They were just taking advantage of you, that's all. Take it right back, I don't want to look at it again." She had wrapped it up and had even tied the string. There it lay on the mantelpiece shaming him.

After supper she had written letters furiously at the dining table, her pen scratching away. He knew very well she was probably writing to that big bloater on the coast, David Trexler, who was too busy looking out for number one to listen to his sister. She would have to find out by trying, he told himself, getting a chuckle out of the disappointment bound to follow such an appeal. Only a few months later, when David was crowing about his chittum bark deals and how 1914 was making a turning point in the affairs of the world, Amos remembered that night, and his wife's frantic appeal for help that went unanswered. It was a consolation to him to know that he was right about some things even if he failed in business and was foolish enough to buy clocks.

When morning came, he did not know what to do about the clock. He took it to the store and while he waited for the accountants, he and Jake the drayman stared at the dirty snow. "Don't know of anyone who would want a clock, do you?" said Amos.

"Don't know as I do," said Jake, staring at the clock while Amos wound the alarm. "That's quite a little trick," said Jake as the tune played. "Let's see." He stared out the window again, his eyes on the second floor above Perry's Seed Store. "By gum, I got it. Just wait. I got you a customer."

Amos followed Jake's eye. "Well," he said slowly, "do you think that would do?"

"Do?" said Jake. "You want your money, don't you? Mabel's a good scout." Amos knew it was foolish to feel like that about a clock. And Mabel Moore had been a little girl once, innocent as any child. She was a fine figure of a woman now, moving as softly along the street as if she weighed one hundred instead of well over two hundred. But even when Jake came back grinning, later in the day, stuffing the money into Amos's hand with "Here you are, she took it like candy, I told you she was a good scout," he felt funny about the whole business. He felt bad about it and looked across the street at the windows where occasionally heads, brighter than they should be, showed themselves. His clock was in a funny kind of home, that's one sure thing. He wondered what Anne would say. He made up his mind he wouldn't think of it anymore.

FIRST BIG TRIP

"And I hope it isn't bad news," said Mrs. Beeger hopefully, emerging from the kitchen just a trifle, with a hot water bottle for Gramma Beeger tremblingly held aloft in one hand, as if for an offering.

Rosamond Wendel read the telegram again to put off answering that too sweet and self-sacrificing woman, who lived so exclusively for others. Then she swallowed hard, looked up, and said in a dry voice, "It's not very good news." She saw no reason to take Mrs. Beeger into her confidence and even the sorrowful face, put on with such genuine belief in the grief that lay in wait throughout the world, couldn't make her confide. She was still shaky when she opened the bedroom door. "What was it?" said Vicky.

"I guess that's the end of our little plans," said Rosamond, pushing the telegram under Vicky's nose. Vicky read it and said, "Why? You aren't going to let troops moving stop you, are you? He says maybe a week, maybe ten days. That's something." She picked up the hair brush again, brushing vigorously. Ten days—why, for ten hours it would be worth it. What else was life except to be snatched on the run in the midst of bombs bursting and the future as uncertain as shifting sand? "You aren't going to let that stop you, I hope," she said.

Rosamond was already not letting it stop her and was getting into her street clothes, buttoning the skirt of her new smart blue suit that had looked so lovely the day she left Oxtail and Corny Stebbins had stood outside on the train platform looking up at her, with her family perfectly conscious of him and trying to ignore him in a little disapproving huddle ten feet away. He had touched his fingers to his lips as the train began to move, his brown eyes trying to say all the things that he had whispered into her ear in the public places that were all Oxtail allowed for the attentions of a married man. If she had had these pretty clothes perhaps Norman would not have gone off so lightheartedly months before. He had jumped at the chance to go with an ambulance unit and she had been the one to stand on the platform and watch him go, with his funny ugly and bright face smiling entirely too cheerfully at her. No one she had ever known made such a game of everything, he had even liked Oxtail and thought she was queer and spoiled not to make friends in the town and get into its life.

No one but Jerry understood her. If she got there in time, she would tell him how hard it had been to live so far away from him. He would even understand why she had to go away from him, to really see him. Up close to him, she hadn't been sure, but she was sure out here away from everyone who had admired her, and only the letters of Stebbins coming monotonously with hints that he would get a divorce if she gave him hope. She loved him. She wanted to run to him as she had never wanted to run to anyone. He wouldn't disapprove of her as she felt that her family did; even Vicky's arguments to go east and marry Jerry had a sniff of doubt in them.

"I'm going to wire him I'm coming," she said, powdering her face lightly, rubbing a slight bit of rouge on her cheeks that were so like the Blessed Damozel of Dante Rossetti. The one thing she had liked about that fellow Bruce at Wisconsin was his way of linking her to other things. "You look like the Blessed Damozel," he said, "leaning out of heaven," and, yes, her face with heavy lidded eyes and the mass of electric hair and the long strong throat, yes, they were like. . . . But how tinny all those words had seemed at last. She had come to feel tinny herself, tinking around, catching the rays of smiles and approval and being distracted. But what could distract her from typing, when that was what she had to do eight hours, nine hours, every day for the Drummond Lighterage Company. A few months before she came to California, with hopes of no one knows what exciting future, a lighterage company had been nothing in her life. If she thought of jobs, it was "interesting" work, maybe newspaper work, because after all not many girls had been as good in English as she had in the University of Wisconsin.

She could remember perfectly like a bell that she must ring over and over to remind her that there was sound in the world and not just a vacuum, the words of Prof. Leonard, spoken seriously, not lightly or as a compliment the way men talked to her when they wanted to arouse her interest in *them*, "for years I haven't had so promising a student." The words hadn't kept her from going to business school so she could sit solemnly at some business man's feet while he cleared his throat and began "Yours of the 19th received and contents noted." She said it to herself when she was too tired to read and wondered if her brains might not just petrify and harden, so that afterwhile she would battle for the right to work overtime for her boss, glad to receive his praise "and I wouldn't know what to do without Miss Wendel. She's my right hand."

But, chilly as the grave, was the need to be necessary to the Drummond Lighterage Company. Norman was in France, writing witty things to her and passages that read as if he had been reading H. G. Wells. Perhaps he did read Wells, in between emptying chamber pots and dressing wounds and hearing hollow groans that made him retch. He had confessed it, like a little boy, and she had answered so warm, so full of feeling for his woe and the woe of all the world, that he had shrugged back quickly into his witty Jewish shell, leaving her outside, even following up his quick retreat with a long scolding letter to her on being self-sufficient and strong, and on the necessity to scorn marriage and its ties and keep free. The words Keep Free—how often they were hurled at her and how often she had hurled them at others. Keep Free, Keep Free.

Jerry was the only man she'd ever known who had not cared if he kept free. No, he had wanted to marry her, with a real heavy old-fashioned gold ring, and he had listened to everything; there was not one in the world she had told so much. It had been an acid test to tell him all she thought and felt and how she had struggled against Stebbins, who had fascinated her with his superior experience and his way of talking so strong about life. She had shown him Norman's letters full of hatred for Stebbins and warning her against Stebbins and his loose ways with women, and then she had laughed herself sick at Stebbins's warnings of Norman, that "dirty little opportunist" who had been nice to her "only because he wanted to amuse himself while stuck in Oxtail."

If only Vicky didn't sit there mending the run in her stocking with such a determined look as if *she* were the one who was making up her mind, and for desperate things, to hang on the gallows, to live or to die. "I'll phone about trains for you," she was saying now, as they went ahead with their toilets, taking turns at the mirror. And then Vicky's voice a little sharp could be heard rising in Mrs. Beeger's hall demanding to know what time trains left for Kansas City.

"One goes at two this afternoon," she said, coming again into the room as Rosamond was fitting the little purple toque on her head. Not many girls could take a cheap hat, give it a twist, add a feather ornament and the lining with the words, "Charmant, Paris," printed on white silk that served all her cheap hats so that if pulled from the head carelessly, it lay there proving that style was hers. She pulled the hat down now, a little on one side—the blue suit pulled down, the little jacket making her very slim—took the slip from her sister's hand as if it were an order, and read it. They looked at one another.

"Do you think I should really go, Vicky," she said, not because her mind wasn't determined but because it suddenly seemed heartless to leave her sister. Such an elaborate scheme of excuses had been raised to bring her out to the coast. When Vicky had the bad luck to break her arm, how she had leaped upon that reason for going to her sister. "Why, someone must go," she had argued. "It's not right to leave her all alone out there." Not that Vicky hadn't managed very ably. She had even saved money ahead so that the accident was almost a vacation. But none of the good times had happened. Vicky's friends were older people, much older than Vicky. It didn't mean much to Rosamond that they worked on newspapers. They looked snuffy and were not the brilliant exciting people she at that time longed to meet. At that time she was continually hoping to solve her life by meeting brilliant and exciting people who would be able to find her "interesting" work and with whom life might seem to be beginning.

"Why, of course," said Vicky. "I don't see why you doubt it at

all. Of course, I'd like it if you stayed here. I thought we'd go
around together, see things."

"What things?" said Rosamond. "We wouldn't have money. We
haven't even gone to Cliff House. Think of being out here and not
even seeing the ocean. It's awful. But that's the way it has been. I
know you've been busy and your arm . . . ."

"You haven't any patience," said Vicky. "No holding power at
all. When I came here, did I know anyone? No. I enjoyed it
anyhow. I was so glad to be out of Oxtail, I didn't care if nothing
else happened. You know as well as I do that I had to finish my
exams before we had much pleasure. I made up my mind to see the
year through, though why I don't just know except that I began
and I ought to stick it out. Now it's nearly over and you go away.
That's the way with everything."

Rosamond could hardly bear it. There was something tragic
about the way Vicky said it, with an all too conclusive feeling in the
words. What had gone wrong with her now? As if bones broken
wasn't enough. She would soon be finished with the exams and
then she would have to get a job too. Did a few years of college
keep you from the Drummond Lighterage Company? One year
hadn't saved her, perhaps two might save Vicky.

Vicky was walking around the room, picking things up, making
excuses not to look her sister in the face. It was early in the day.
There was no use going to the Drummond Lighterage any more. "I
think we ought to go out to Cliff House so you could see the
ocean," Vicky said. "It's a sin and shame to go back to hot Kansas
without seeing the ocean. You never saw it since we all came out,
when you were a baby—not more than three and I was five.
Remember how we used to pour sand down our necks from a bottle
and then watch our bloomers swell up like rubber balloons?

"And how Mother tied a rope around me when we went in
bathing because I went so far out?

"And the pancakes we ate?"

They couldn't even begin remembering without a dialogue that
might have seemed rehearsed. So many times in Oxtail's blistering
summers the Wendels had recalled that one blissful summer, the
cool mountain streams, the little brook trout. Year after year, in

hot rooms, with curtains and windows sealed tight and hot air blowing in as from an oven through any opened door, they had talked over their One Good Time. The train ride, the mother with her four little girls, the big Oregon strawberries, the yard where the pear trees grew, Grandma's cool house with the bed and little steps. They could drug many a hot day with clam-digging that was in the past and gone, with lush ferns that grew as high as little Rosamond had been, with daisies and foxgloves and forget-me-nots that grew without any hand to plant them. The whole summer had spread out over many summers. It was a sin and shame to go back on the ocean.

"We could go out on the streetcar and get back in time," said Vicky. "It's awful not to see it. What would mother say?"

"What about me? I'd feel terrible not to see it." But the streetcar was a seasick and lurching affair, and the view high up of the blue blue water was not like Oregon. Even the sea lions did not interest Rosamond. The ocean was not nice out here in the midst of hot dog stands and people who pushed toy balloons in your face. She felt timid and a little frightened, as if everything in the world was bound to be disappointing and never again would the ocean appear fresh and sparkling, seen between two huge firs from the seat of Uncle David's carryall.

"Look there, there she is, roll on thou deep and dark blue ocean, roll," Uncle David had chanted, holding on to his niece's tiny skirts and pointing, sniffing greedily too and yelling, "Smell that, Anne, oh you people from the plains, what do you ever get to compare with it?"

Anne had sniffed, defending for a moment the Iowa fall days and the smell of burning leaves and the haze and golden light, but the ocean was like the ocean of her own youth, it brought back the Cape May days, and "Smell it," she told her children as they looked and smelled, stuffing themselves with the sight and smell to last them for years in the dry midlands.

The sun was too hot and the dazzle on the water made her dizzy. More than ever, Rosamond longed for train time. Suppose the troops would leave suddenly without her? She could almost feel it plunge up and down but there was no use cultivating idle fears. She was even glad she had seen the ocean. It was not so good as an ocean. It was not like the ocean she remembered. It was just another thing she did not mind leaving behind. There would be new things, not old ones. No matter how badly everything went in Camp Funston, she wouldn't let herself feel disappointed. She was tired of feeling always let down, always hopeful for something that never happened.

Vicky sitting beside her tried to look at the ocean from the car window. She felt that Rosamond was unappreciative and was always running from one thing to another. It took stamina, she thought proudly, to bear things. But the next moment she was almost weeping inside of herself with rage. What good had it done? What good? It was not bearing up uselessly all the time that mattered.

There was Rosamond now, looking fresh and lovely, and as she climbed up the steps of the train she looked down at her sister. How much she looked like her baby picture that had been enlarged and hung on the dining room wall for years, almost a part of every meal. The same big eyes—only the tiny rather corkscrew curls, that never would fluff out big and round like Vicky's own, were missing. The two sisters looked at each other; tears began to come. They stood looking as the train moved slowly. Rosamond was so like that picture, like her baby days when she used to sing at the door between her bedroom and the dining room where Papa and Mamma and the bigger children sat at breakfast.

> Open the door for the chillens,
> Gather them into the folden,
> Teach them the gospel of Jesus
> Tell them the tory he told.

sang the baby, confidently, brightly, knowing nothing of doorknobs or handles, thinking her song, that she had heard the older ones sing after coming home from revival meeting, opened doors. And then all of them had stopped eating, Papa had tiptoed over and opened the door for baby who stepped out in her nightgown and wide eyes into the arms of her family, the sisters getting up from their chairs to hug her, mother pushing her high chair back and baby herself with bare toes, triumphant and happy, *loved*.

"Don't be a dog in the manger, Barney, introduce me to the girl friend," said the young man with the scar, pushing in past two stout ladies to the back of the café table where Barney Blum sat with Victoria trying to cheer her up because she felt so alone now her sister was gone.

"Sure, Victoria Wendel, Chris Caseman." Caseman shook hands seriously looking at her intently. "Haven't we met somewhere?" he said, continuing to hold her hand.

"Now don't pull that, Chris," said Barney. "That's too old."

OVER THERE   OVER THERE

"Damn that noise, isn't there anywhere you can go without that racket, why don't they keep quiet," said Caseman nervously, still holding hands.

"Maybe we did meet," said Vicky slowly, letting her hand relax in his warm hand.

"Oh we did, I'm certain of it, I remember your eyes." He looked intently into her eyes and a party at the next table now joined in with the orchestra

OVER THERE   OVER THERE

"I wish to god they'd go over there, they wouldn't toot so loud if they got a few dirty shells in their mouths."

"Not so loud, Caseman," said Barney.

"I mean it," said Caseman. "Dirty sonsofbitches, singing for the fun of it while the other guys, the poor buggers with nothing to lose but their tails are in the mud."

"Now I remember," said Vicky. "We *did* meet. You're the fellow in Doc Baumann's class at the University of Iowa who got in the fight about the Colorado coal fields."

"The Ludlow massacre, you mean," said Caseman looking at her. "Holy Jesus, were you there? Remember that hightoned fellow with the curly hair who made the argument about this being a free country and people had the right to work if they wanted to."

"Yes, and you said that was baby talk and if they had the right to work they had to strike."

"She remembers that," said Caseman. "What a jewel. I don't remember but it sounds like me."

"He's still spouting that stuff," said Barney, beginning to look at the holding hands with uneasiness.

"I'm glad to hear that," said Vicky.

"Yes sir, I'm still saying the same thing and will till the final conflict," he smiled at Vicky. Barney frowned, embarrassed as if someone had started to undress. He looked around uneasily. "Say, Caseman, you ought to pipe down in public places, that is, if you value your own skin."

"My skin? Christ almighty, they're all the same. What do you tag around with this man for, kid? His own skin, my own skin, your own skin. It's all they think of."

"You're not fair," said Vicky, "he isn't really like that. He's only cautious."

"It's all the same. Where were we?" He looked sharply and triumphantly at Barney who slunk back in his seat, his head aching, wishing he were ten years younger and had gone to France. His kid brother was seeing life. Barney read over and over the gory passages of his brother's letters, written with restraint to show how hardboiled his gang were even when one of them lost his eyesight, had to be sent back from the lines, forever blind. He ached to belong to some battalion like that, he was a lone fighter for the cause. Let such loose-mouthed fools as Caseman talk. Socialism wasn't made in a day. And even on the Bulletin, he worked stuff in. It counted to get even a line across, he argued, picking up the evening paper as it lay on the restaurant table, the headlines roaring at him. His own small lost line with the double meaning was hidden somewhere. He turned pages.

"And what I remember best about that Colorado mess—where were we? What was the command? *Shoot everything that moves.*

There you are. The perfect slogan of the system. If it moves, shoot it. And let me tell you, they shot. I was out there and they trained their rifles on the ruined tents and waited for even a dog to crawl. The perfect slogan."

"You ought to pipe down," said Barney. "There's a dick been looking at you."

"I hope I do his eyes good," said Caseman, but he shifted and looked at the chubby man with the neatly polished black shoes, staring at them over a glass of beer.

"Lily is expecting us back for that birthday cake, Vicky, don't you think we'd better run along?"

"Oh to hell with the birthday cake," said Caseman.

"We promised," said Vicky smiling from Caseman to Barney. "Perhaps I'll see you again."

"You have to," said Caseman, solemnly. Barney tried to run down Caseman as they drove toward Oakland and the birthday cake. "He's a good guy but talks too much. That doesn't help anything. He's narrow and all he'll do is to get himself locked up. What good does it do if you are in jail?" He grinned sideways at Victoria who sat huddled on her side. She felt a thousand miles away from him. Caseman wasn't cautious like Barney. He wasn't surrounded with a battery of sisters. She couldn't forget overnight how guilty the sisters had tried to make her feel. They couldn't help themselves, it was the way they were made, but when they had pounced on her demanding, "Are you sure, Victoria, that you care for all of us equally"—when Barney had proposed that she board at their house—she had stormed out of the Blum house.

"I wouldn't come to live here now if it were the last place on earth," she had said. "Of course I don't like you all equally. I like Barney best, why not?" She could see at this minute, at any minute, the two shocked faces of the intense sincere sisters bending over the railing of the second-floor stairs, looking down at her as she raced out the door. They thought of her as strong-willed and selfish and she couldn't answer that kind of logic. Didn't they have feelings? Didn't they ever want to make love or run crazy on the hills? Not that Barney was very good at it. He had even cleared his throat, huskily, separating himself from her, saying painfully, "I

don't think this is very good for us, do you? I don't seem to sleep
very well when I go home. I . . ." What could she say? If he didn't
have sense to understand how silly it seemed, just standing like two
horses in a field, rubbing noses under a tree, being "friends,"
whatever that is, then she couldn't do anything about it.

But Barney was moving gracefully, happily now, around the
living room of the Blum home and Victoria sat on the couch beside
the Old Patriarch, Mr. Blum, with his fine white head and his
bright dark eyes, and his warm way of touching her that she only
wished he had passed on to his son. They were all talking now,
about the war and the horrors of war and free speech, and the
curious superior way they talked seemed old-fashioned. Victoria
looked around wondering if she could just slip out and go home.
But no, she was a Family Friend, and so sat while the cake was cut.
KEEP OUT KEEP OFF THE GRASS PRIVATE PROP-
ERTY   KEEP OFF   SHOOT EVERY LIVING THING   and
with her arm around Lily's waist she sang with the rest of them,
"There's a long long trail awinding into the land of my dreams,"
hoping that she would see Caseman again.

He hadn't changed much since that day in the spring of 1914,
just before Papa's business had failed, and he had gotten into a
scrap in Doc Baumann's course. He had quit the class with his
pocket bulging with newspapers, looking mad and excitable, and
all the girls had huddled out in a bunch, embarrassed as if a bar-
room brawl had barely been averted. The silly sheeplike way they
had acted still stuck to her and she had hated being in skirts at the
time while all the men bulged out the door after Caseman, excited
and argumentative. She had made resolutions to read up on all
those questions and then Papa's business had failed. She had gone
back to Oxtail, lugging her suitcase up the path one night around
ten. Papa was singing to Clara's newest baby:

> And I would give all my greenbacks
> For those bright days of yore
> When little Nelly Lane and I
> Slid down the cellar door.

She had gone into the house and stripped off her finery and it seemed a million years ago since she was that girl, looking out the window of the Tower Room at the moonlight on the Missouri. She thought of herself as very old now, and in fact her sister Clara was married at her age, twenty-one. Rosamond was younger still, and on this very night as they cut cake was racing across the continent. BRIDE RACES WITH WAR FOR BRIDEGROOM read Barney's paper, running a little story in a box that would certainly please Anne Wendel and Nancy even more. Nancy would clip it out and put it in her Memory Book, that was so full of happenings that seemed to come to everyone but herself. Only her lone wedding announcement and the little occasions when she entertained the Ouija Girls played much of a part.

"And what are you going to do my dear now the college year is over?" sweet old Mr. Blum was saying.

"I guess I'll have to get a job," said Vicky, wishing the whole line of job hunts forever behind her instead of beginning again. But she knew how to write good letters. They all fell for that line about being more keen for the opportunity to work up than for any money involved, as if wages meant nothing to her. The funny thing was that in the beginning she had believed it.

Anne Wendel had the pleasure of getting out wedding announcements for her daughter Rosamond's marriage to Corporal Jeremiah Walton Stauffer at Manhattan, Kansas, and, if she could only afford printed ones instead of engraved, it was less painful now that it was wartime and even a virtue. She pinned up a little service flag with a star in it in the front window and Jerry Stauffer's mother forgave her and was sorry for the woman who had sons only by marriage. When Rosamond's letter came with the brief details of the marriage, she gloated over the line that no matter what happened, she would never forget these days, like an oasis in a desert.

When Rosamond's train arrived in Manhattan, Jerry could not even meet it and she had gone to a hotel until five o'clock. Then they tried to buy flowers but there wasn't a petal in the whole dusty

town. They finally hunted up a minister and found a Congregationalist and he married them after hastily clamping on a clean collar
while his wife put the kids to bed and came out smiling with a new
gaudy scarf draped over her wrenlike person. They had been
married with an old-fashioned gold ring, not one of those tinny
newfangled ones, and afterwards walked around the streets in a
daze, holding hands and giggling and standing solemnly before
windows of bedroom furniture and kitchen displays.

"I don't know why we look at such things," said Rosamond.

"There's nothing else in this town to look at," said Jerry, and
both kept away from the idea that perhaps they might never have a
home at all. They even drifted into the library and looked around
for books that might enlighten them on married life. Suddenly they
felt terribly young and ignorant and a little scared, but there was
nothing in sight but *What every Mother should know* and *What to
tell your child*. They walked the streets hand in hand, looking in
windows and marveling at electric contrivances. Between windows
they would look at each other, afraid to talk about the future.

"What'll we do when you come back?" said Rosamond, determined to face it. Already she had terrible fears that he might not
come back, or even worse, come back like that Canadian soldier, in
a basket with his legs shot off. Terrible events happened that
changed everything. She had tried to talk to Victoria of these fears.
"What could happen that could change everything?" she had said.
"Nothing," Vicky had answered in her provoking, stubborn way.
"Nothing, except death." "I know of things, I can think of things,"
she had said, feeling scared as she use to when little and someone
began telling ghost stories.

"Lord knows what we'll do," said Jerry. "I may be an old man.
The war may go on and on, a Hundred Years' War."

"It couldn't do that, everyone would be killed off."

"That could happen," said Jerry, but he would rather look in
windows some more and imagine both of them with fishing tackle
going up into the mountains for a good vacation. Solitary soldiers
brushed past them. In a doorway, a kid sat scrawling, "Dear Sid,
Dear Ma, Dear Clem," on cards, writing over and over, "Getting

out of this dump soon, look for word from across the pond, don't do anything I wouldn't do. Bill."

Jerry bought a box covered with sea shells glued in rhythmical pattern around a painted lighthouse with *Greetings from Atlantic City* in bright green, and Rosamond bought a tiny picture frame of braided grass and *Good Luck* studded in gold nails, and they exchanged their presents in their own room with the brown shades and the spotted wall paper and a lithograph of *The Storm,* showing two young lovers without a curl out of place, just like the movies, prancing in a false panic along a woodsy road before a huge stagey cloud.

Rosamond was proud of Jerry's clumsiness. She had had enough of smart adept fingers that always seemed to know it all. Little they knew. It was feeling that counted. And Jerry's eyes looking up at her, as he bit his lip and wrestled with the tight button on her slipper, made her want to cry. She was glad when the button came off and rolled under the dresser so that they both had to hunt it, getting all dusty and pretending to be shocked at the big rolls of dust underneath the heavy chest. The button was clear at the back, and they sat on the floor looking at it in Jerry's hand, laughing, and holding to one another, getting suddenly terribly weak and scared and happy. They forgot all about sending telegrams to the relatives until the next morning. Only Rosamond's sister Clara cried at the news, while her four children stood around pleased and awed at the violence of mamma's sudden tears. Nancy in Seattle insisted on going to a movie to celebrate, and she and her husband, Clifford Radford, held hands during the entire performance and afterwards had chocolate fudge sundaes.

CHEAT THE CHEATER

As soon as Anne Wendel reached Grapeville, she wrote Amos:

"Aaron looks far worse than I expected. I wouldn't have known the poor fellow. I don't think he will ever get well again. He has to pay $15 every week to that Sally. The day I came he had paid what he owed and asked his son to bring his books and some papers to the office. The son never showed up and Aaron finally sent a man with a note. Would you believe it, that demon of a woman wouldn't let the man in the yard. She flew at him in a rage and when Aaron heard of it he just groaned and said, 'I'm so discouraged, I wish I were dead.' Take your medicine and leave your shirts for the woman by the alley to do."

Sally had no terrors for Anne Wendel. She wished she could see her sister-in-law face to face, and took walks past the house on Elmer Street. The front lawn was ragged, an unkempt cat sat superiorly on the porch, and in an upstairs window a woman's pale face glared for a moment in a rim of wiry gray hair. "That's Sally," Anne said but she did not tell her brother of her little trip. Aaron was too ill to be bothered and it was trouble enough to wrench money from him for the little expenses of each day. He took advantage of his sickness to be very weak when Anne needed money, even pretending deafness to put off the fatal moment.

But the daily tussle for funds did not spoil her pleasure in being in the town where she had spent her girlhood. She took strolls almost every day past the old homestead that still stood in the midst of its original acres. It was no longer spick and span, the neat rows of currant and berry bushes had disappeared. The big pine near the house had had its head lopped off by lightning. The front door, from which Joe had bolted to the Black Hills, had two shotgun holes in it where idle boys had fired for fun when the house was empty.

Tenants who came and went had left little monuments of ashes and tin cans behind them. Where was all that order that Mem had worked so hard for in the old days! How she had struggled with weeds and flowers so that El Dorado might continue to be the show place of Grapeville that it had been when Mrs. Ferrol first bought it and in a picture hat planted flowers, working with a little trowel for hours among their roots. The place needed a scythe, paint, and constant attention. There was nothing so grasping as a house and land. They demanded eternal vigilance and, when denied, took mean revenges. Each day she kept a sharp eye out for the first cherry blossom and to see if that wistaria vine would actually bloom as it had of old.

When she was obliged to draw on her own resources for cash, she consoled herself with Aaron's promise, made the first day, that she was not to worry, he "would take care of her." She planned dozens of uses for whatever sum he might leave her, paid off the debt on the Oxtail home and the judgments against them, sent pretty dresses to each of her four girls and repainted the porch. Sums much larger than any she dare dream of controlling, flowed through her hands constantly in these visions. Her cheerful letters home put a spur on them all. Amos took pleasure in saving the bulk of his wages to surprise his wife when she should come home. The entire family seemed to have made a fresh start in the world. Even Rosamond, back in Oxtail, after Jerry had moved to France with the troops, did not waste her time aimlessly grieving. She pulled herself together and packed a trunk and started off for Seattle where Nancy and Clifford were holding down jobs. On the train all the women angled for a handsome French officer in his beautiful blue uniform and, after they had reached Montana, he began hunting out Rosamond from the observation car crowd, pretending to be delighted at her college French.

David Trexler gave only a small fraction of his attention to his sister Anne's letters about their brother. "Look here," he grumbled, "Aaron has got himself tied up in knots again. Anne can't get at any cash because he's so involved in real estate he hasn't any. I'm not going to advance a cent unless I know that woman is to be kept from benefiting by his will. It would just be rewarding her for being a dirty dog all her life. If he wants to get a divorce, I'll help him." Letters between Anne and himself went back and forth and Anne was often in dire straits for lack of cash. She had moved her brother from the Tonis house and had installed him in one of the rooms of his office. It made a lot of work for her but it cost much less and Aaron actually seemed to pick up, surrounded by his papers and big office safe and old books.

"I don't want a penny myself but see to it he divorces that woman if he wants me to advance cash without security. I am sending a hundred if he secures it by a note on the Elmer St. property." Groaning as if his bones were being twisted, Aaron had signed the note; but there were repairs for different houses, daily expenses, and the fifteen a week for Sally that soon put them in the hole again and made it necessary to negotiate advances from the bank on property.

David was annoyed by these interruptions. He longed for peace and fretted for the time when his children would be married and establishing homes on the pieces of land at the base of his own property. Of course, he would expect his children to pay for this property, just to keep alive their self-respect, but he liked to stand on the porch as if it were the prow of a battleship and look into the valley where he hoped to see the cottages of his children, like so many little tug boats, lying at ease some day.

Ella fell in with his ambition. She spent her idle hours making elaborate quilts pieced together by hand like the ones her own grandmother had made. She planned one apiece for each of her probable grandchildren and liked to consult David as to the number they might expect. "Don't count your chickens before they are hatched, Mamma," he said, frowning. Sue was certainly at the marriageable age, but she insisted on being unsociable and never saw a soul except the girl in the library who was engaged to a young engineer who had just graduated from college. It made David furious to hear Sue worry about the future of this pair who could not marry because engineers were a drug on the market and he could not find a job. She should be starting a family of her own, worry about her babies and their diapers, not moon around.

Every now and then he would scold Ella for the way she had brought up that girl in such a stiffnecked way that she was unmanageable, and Ella took it all quietly, piecing away on her quilts, sure that if she kept still David would soon exhaust himself.

If nothing else presented itself, he could always find a reason to blow up in the grievance he felt in not owning as many old relics of his family as Anne, who had no boys to pass on the name. But he was not a grabber for relics yet. He had his hands full with his different enterprises and spent night after night at the office, straining his eyes and nerves for children that he irritably sized up as unworthy of all he was doing for them.

When Sue came back from a chatty afternoon with the young librarian, she couldn't bear the stiff way the chairs stood, and the sight of the two huge red and blue glass emblems of the drug trade that David Trexler kept for sentiment in his front hall, one on each side of the hat rack, set her teeth on edge. She growled at Pussydee for not folding her hair ribbons and swished through the house like an evil wind. "She's a regular bear tonight," complained Ella.

"A bear?" said David, raising his eyebrows and darting one of his cutting looks at his daughter. "Well, don't growl around me. What you need is responsibility, young lady. Why, my mother had half a dozen children at your age and no time for empty headed discontent. If you've nothing else to do, why not write your poor brothers?"

But Sue had no real feeling for her brothers who were already wrapped up in their own concerns. Young Dave was so much in love he wrote only to his girl Charlotte and his mother. His letters to his mother were always about a sore tooth or the way he felt like sleeping every minute of the day or how awful it was not even to hear the sound of guns, just pitched down in a lot of mud waiting like flies on dead horsemeat.

In her talks with her friend, Sue envied her Aunt Anne's daughters, who were getting married or moving round or holding interesting jobs. Even David Trexler occasionally gave his daughter a prod for letting Anne's daughters get ahead of her. "Do you want to be an old maid," he bawled one night after a particularly aggravating letter from Anne all about the romance of her youngest.

When Aaron Trexler was better, the brother and sister made a little trip to Sea Isle. Anne Wendel pushed her brother in a wheel chair up and down the board walk. He had wasted to almost nothing and was no weight to push. In a way, his mind was more active than ever. It continually fretted about his son. "Have we any letters today?" he would ask a dozen times.

"Nothing today," Anne always answered.

"Why doesn't Timothy write? I asked him to attend to the Clark rents and he pays no attention to me."

It was a pity that a man could never face the truth about his own child. The boy was the mother's tool and wrote only to hound the father for her weekly allowance. He even had the nerve to make threats. "The money had better get here if you want to avoid complications," wrote Timothy. Aaron read the scrap, shriveling down in his chair, feeling the humiliation of years. She had the upper hand, that woman, but how had she branded the boy so against him? He had been generous to his son, sent him to the University of Pennsylvania, spared no expense. The boy had even elected to follow his father and was studying civil engineering. He would take over his office, his very tools. The sextant that Aaron's own grandfather had used in his early surveys in Lehigh County, would pass to the boy.

It was no use for Anne to tell Aaron not to pay any more attention to such a son. The father had built up a little security for no one else. It began to get under Anne's skin that she should be worried every day about money for their keep, while the son was kept in idleness and his future guaranteed by the father's niggardliness to his sister.

In the mornings when she had him washed, sitting in his clean bathrobe, eating slowly with his thin old hand, she'd try to begin working money out of him for the expenses of the day. "We'll need some groceries today, Aaron, we're all out of coffee." He would pretend not to hear, eating slowly, his eyes vacant. He had only allowed two days at Sea Isle because of the expense. It was cheaper in Grapeville in his office.

"Do you want to live like a pauper?" Anne had finally to yell at him. Then he turned his mild blues eyes slowly on her. Yes, he was willing to shell out a little money. Anything for peace. She had to remember how he had always been the compromiser so far back as she could remember. In every family squabble it was Aaron who had stood uncomfortably, looking from one to the other. "Let's have peace," he said. He thought of himself now, in his armchair and old bathrobe, as a man who had wanted nothing all his life but peace.

When he wheeled out to his main office, where his desk and the safe and all his documents piled high on the shelves barricaded him from the door, he could touch with his hand a dozen files with clippings of the quarrels of families and property fights that had separated father and son. He liked to console himself with such evidence and feel that it was human fate that caused him in his old age to stand alone.

Anne Wendel felt a deep real sympathy for her brother during the first weeks of her visit. She was bitter against his wife Sally and the boy. She was so willing to relieve him of care, and felt important collecting rents and keeping track of insurance due. It was only after she saw how hard it was to get money from him that she began to sour. It began to dawn on her that her two brothers, Aaron and David, were using her to save themselves good money. David could afford to help his brother and Aaron could afford to help himself. They could between them hire a woman to keep the place clean, they could hire a boy to run errands. At night, dead tired, she sat alone in the dark office, hurt that her brothers did not try to save her steps. When rents came in, the money was sucked up in a dozen ways. Everything seemed more important to Aaron Trexler than his sister.

When Timothy came to see his father, he barely spoke to his aunt. He passed at once through the outer office into the inner room, where two voices could often be heard rising argumenta- tively. The visit was certain to end in a trip to the safe. The son would wheel his father out to the big safe and stand behind the wheel chair as the dials clicked. Often he would not even thank his father for the bills handed out so gingerly.

Anne began to wonder what sin could make Aaron bear his lot so humbly. She looked sharply at her brother who sometimes even now liked to ramble on about the old days in Grapeville that seemed so pleasant. She had worked for her brothers then, handing over every cent that the hens and fruit made to the boys. They were always getting into scrapes, always on the border of disgrace or trouble. How inconsiderately they had run their lives, and yet even now she was thrilled to think of the high-handed way they had dared to be. Why, Aaron himself had had the nerve to install Mrs.

Ferrol, his mistress, in the very house that he afterwards bought for his mother. He had visited her under the very noses of the town gossips; she had borne him two children. She remembered the day she found Mrs. Ferrol's shoes in the bottom drawer of Aaron's desk, several years after the lonely woman had died. It was only then that she knew the truth. That's how mysterious he had been.

Sitting in the darkening office with the big elms outside casting such a sheltered light, she pitied poor Mrs. Ferrol who had died giving birth to Aaron's child. She had died, all alone, in a Philadelphia hospital and Aaron had not even set up a stone. He had let her mother take the other children, take the body, carry off every scrap that was Mrs. Ferrol. Only in the memories of his sisters, Hortense and Anne, had Mrs. Ferrol survived. She survived now. It was astonishing how real she seemed. Why, he had treated her cruelly. He no doubt treated Sally cruelly. What about Madeleine McNarry! There was a black spot.

Rummaging in the drawer that had once held the shoes, she found the clippings about Madeleine, yellow, but the haunting selfish face, with the headlines of her suicide still intact, looked out at Anne. He had wronged Sally, his young wife, with his mad infatuation for her half-sister Madeleine and then he had no doubt wronged the girl herself. Why, he had been in league against them all, against her. Peacemaker indeed. She felt actually indignant for all of the injured ones.

Sometimes she wondered what had happened to Mrs. Ferrol's shoes that at first he had saved. Had he burned them down to their very buttons? It looked like it. In the back of the big safe he kept the oldest relics of the Trexler family, a little wooden toy like a jack in the box, carved by hand, a heavy old watch that struck chimes. She liked to peer in at these things and calculate how she might divert them to her own children. Certainly Timothy did not deserve them. He was no Trexler. He was his mother's child and she had so warped her boy that he would never look at another woman. He would have no heirs, and sometimes she wondered, as she watched the father feverishly rummage in his safe for some present for his son, if he realized that the line would die with him.

One day when they came back from a little airing, the safe had been tampered with. "Just look Anne, you look, I can't see but someone has been tampering with this safe." He trembled as his sister leaned past him, reaching in with her hands into the dark cavern of the safe, feeling around. The relics were gone.

"They're gone," she said. "Stolen."

"He's been here. He got that combination watching me. Pretty smart."

"It's not smart to steal," said Anne coldly. But she could not bear to rub it into the father that his son was a thief. He had taken them only to hurt the old man. What could he care for relics? When he came brazenly to the office the next day, she went out on the landing and confronted him with his crime.

"Yes," he admitted. "I took them. To hide them from you. They belong to me. Everything my father has belongs to me and my mother." He had sailed past her and she had listened in vain for some word of reproach from Aaron's room. The foolish man was actually condoning the son's misdeeds.

Now Aaron did seem really in league against her. Why, he would die without a will, without making the faintest provision for her. The money she had paid out, the money he owed her from long ago, the lots he had promised Hortense and herself as a payment of the debt he owed their mother, where were these sums? Was she going to die and not leave her a penny? It looked like it. Gladly would she have taken care of him, free and with pleasure, if he had not treated her like this, making her worry and fret for the benefit of his child.

You'd think his was the only child on earth.

When she wrote to David complaining of the situation, she got cold comfort. All he could tell her was to see that Aaron got a divorce. As if a man on his last legs had interest in a thing like that. It made her feel very alone in the old town where their family life had once flourished. It was practically a judgment on Aaron when his hand suddenly became too feeble to sign his own checks. He was frightened at his helplessness.

"Don't let the boy know," he said, looking at his hand, helpless as a piece of wood. "If they find out I can't write, they'll get everything from me. What'll we do, Anne?"

"I can write like you, Aaron," said Anne. "The other day I was thinking when I cashed one of your checks how your writing seemed a little different from one day to the next. If it looks funny, they won't notice, they're so used to it now." She took the pen and made a bold start. "How's that?"

"Fine," said Aaron. "Fine." He looked at her doubtfully, but she was plumping up his pillows, trying to hide her tears at his sudden final helplessness. When he was settled for the night, the problem of the will began to haunt her all over again. It wasn't right for him to worry her so. When morning came she tried to bring the subject around to a will but it was hard to remind him of his condition. She fussed all morning with papers and sorted out bills and now and then came to the door of his room with some little remark like "Remember what trouble poor Mem had because father never made a will." Then, when he did not answer, she brought the whole subject quickly around to his lunch. "Would you like a nice omelet today, do you think?" she said, "one with jelly rolled up in it." And she'd go on describing it to distract him from the will that she now regretted mentioning.

All the same Mr. Roundtree the lawyer stopped her on the street to warn her he should make a will. Nothing seemed important about poor Aaron anymore except his will.

He brought it up himself one night after a long hard day. By hints and proddings, Anne actually got him started dictating what he desired. When he began, "The old Trexler Homestead, to David Trexler, Anne Wendel and Hortense Ripley, share and share alike," she could not help pausing and saying, "But Aaron, will David expect it? After all, he has enough." The old man did not even answer, shut his eyes tight for a second, and then went on with the items. His wife to be cut off with the least the law allowed—to his son, everything.

When she finally saw that all she'd get was a sliver of the homestead, she spoke up and said, "Aaron, don't you think it would be nice to remember your nieces and nephews with a little something? You never did a thing for them all your life and now's your chance." She thought how handy a hundred would be for Victoria and Rosamond. The girls had never had spending money;

what a pleasure to give them a chance to buy some new clothes, even a whole outfit, such as they often talked about.

Aaron didn't answer. His body seemed to shrink down in the bed as if to hide from her. Outside boys were playing in the street, calling to one another in the game Duck on the Rock. The angry voices of two boys quarreling, yelled, "I'll throw a dornick at you." When Aaron would not speak, Anne got up quickly and went into the other room. To think that her brother had spent a lifetime in this town, in this very office, and for no one really but himself. It was not right to spoil him and give him his way up to the very end. He wouldn't miss a hundred dollars. Not when he was dead. For all the nieces and nephews, and she'd want all, even David's children to share equally, it would cost only a little.

She could hear him tapping on the table. He could tap for things he wanted, but how much of an ear had he ever given to the vain taps of others? She went into his little bedroom and stood looking at him. He could feel her enmity at a glance and was scared in all his freezing bones that she might abandon him. It would cost a terrible sum to go to a sanitarium. Or back to a nursing home.

"How much do you think the girls should have?" he said, slyly, raising his head.

"A hundred's little enough, the boys too."

"No, I can't do anything for the boys, they can help themselves. And I think fifty is plenty. I haven't money to fling around, Anne."

"You aren't flinging it around when you give it to your nieces. Don't you want them to have a nice thought of you?"

He didn't answer but as she began making notes for the will again, he said feebly, "Make it fifty." And as he saw her scribbling away, he added, "Did you make it fifty? I want the girls to have something," he went on as if the idea had been his own.

"I fixed it all right," said Anne. She had written a hundred and a hundred it remained, even in Roundtree's final draft that had to be signed by Anne because Aaron's hand was too weak and wavering. She wasn't at all sorry for her deception. He would never know it and the children deserved it.

Making the will pulled the man together, and if through the summer he seemed to hang by a hair, it was a very strong hair.

What life there was in him lived in his eyes that kept a sharp lookout as Anne signed the checks under his nose. In the evenings when he dropped to sleep, Anne went for walks alone. The town had not grown much since the early days, but the trees had grown. She wished she had a garden to dig in, to rid her hands of the smell of the sick room. If only Amos remembered to water the window box and put stakes around the woodbine near the alley. When she got control of the homestead she'd take up slips from the wistaria and from the trumpet vine to transplant in Iowa. The children could laugh at the White Elephant as they were always calling the Oxtail house, but it sheltered them all. It would prove a good investment, once she fixed it up. Fixing it up was such fun that she put in new plumbing and hardwood floors, all the way to the cemetery and back, and was installing a new furnace as she went in to take a last look at her brother. He was lying as she had left him, his head thrown back. Now that his son had stolen the relics, he did not pester his father anymore.

The brother and sister were left alone with occasionally a few calls on the phone from old friends. Letters from her children brought the only fresh air to the sick room. Nancy and her husband were getting along in Seattle, but the big money people talked about in shipyard work was just another bursted bubble. Clifford had a job in the shipyard but at no fancy pay and if Nancy had not found a filing job with the Northern Pacific, they would have had a hard time of it. Now the government was running the railroad, wages were up, and Nancy was proud of her salary that came up to Clifford's.

When Rosamond arrived, the three of them went around together and made trips up the Sound on Sundays. Nancy wrote that Rosamond was very untactful and said things in the boarding house that just got the boarders riled up for no good whatsoever. She had gotten into a scrap, when someone was complaining at the big wages the shipyard people got and how workers were making money hand over fist and spending it for cheap jewelry and clothes. "Why not?" she had insisted. "What could be sillier than the way rich people spend their money, on dogs and drinking and jewels and gambling?" Nancy had pressed her foot under the table but the girl had gone right on. "Of course, Mother," wrote Nancy, "I know it's just because Jerry is gone and she feels it more than she lets on but all the same it's embarrassing and Cliff doesn't help any. He even made things worse by saying that he hadn't seen anything of the high wages in the shipyards, only a few men got them. It just makes the whole boarding house down on us and I wish you'd say a few words to Rosamond when you write her."

But there seemed no way for Anne Wendel to control her children. She had to trust to luck and their early training. She wrote Rosamond that she hoped she would always be considerate of others and try to remember that different opinions could live in the world side by side. She wished the war would end, so her two youngest could settle down and have children. Life was useless unless lived for others. She was beginning to feel the pinch of old age that, without children, would seem insupportable.

Her daughter Clara was too busy with her four children to write often but sometimes late at night, very tired, she managed to scrawl off a few lines to say that Papa seemed well and was over to dinner and she wished she was as good at dosing the children for their little illnesses the way her mother had been with her aconite and belladonna that had always worked like a charm.

When Vicky wrote from San Francisco that she had had an offer of $150 a month to go to a mining camp in Chile for a three-year contract, Anne's heart stood still for a second, but the girl had no idea of taking up the proposition. "The money's nothing," she wrote. "I worked so long to save for this year in college and now I don't want to save anymore. I don't want to bury myself in a little town. Right now I want to hear music and see plays and know people. Life, that's what I want." But if she had turned down one job, she landed on her feet with another.

"What do you think, Aaron, Vicky's in a law office, she gets $25 a week and sits at a desk with nothing on it but a vase with a flower."

"She ought to save some of that," said Aaron.

"Oh, she will," said Anne. "She says she's going to buy me a wrist watch."

"Better tell her not to begin that business. We had one member of our family run on the rocks making presents." He squinted at his sister in a triumphant way and Anne shot back at him. "At least, Joe made a lot of people happy with his generosity. None of us should ever say a word against poor Joe."

"It doesn't hurt to learn a lesson from him, does it?" said Aaron, looking around him, but Anne hoped she might die before she learned the kind of lesson Aaron had learned. Joe, mad and dead, was better off than Aaron holding on to life that was no good to him or anybody else. The brother was frightened at her coldness. He was always afraid that she might desert him and leave him to the mercy of strangers. He fumbled with the cover on his bed, tried to think of some old memory that would reunite them.

"How about reading me a little?" he said. "I think I could sleep if I was read to a little. I don't know any better reading than our father's diaries. You see if you can't pick me a piece from them." Yes, he had touched the right chord. Her face had softened, she was fumbling among the old books and drawing out the one bound in calfskin.

She opened to the account of the finding of the settlement for the Swiss immigrants back in 1845 in Wisconsin. As she began, Aaron relaxed in his bed. His voice that so often was so weak, spoke up to comment in a strong firm way.

"Our road led us through regions that would rejoice the eye of the most despondent, (*he leadeth me beside the still waters*) many miles of the Prairies on which countless herds of cattle could have bathed in the thick rich grass. Then again through pleasant woods, good water everywhere and pure air, here and there a settler; at times we stopped and asked for and received buttermilk. (*Thy rod and thy staff shall comfort me*) We strode forward stoutly, not certain that we were following the right course and at 2 p.m. came to a farmhouse where we drank buttermilk again and had a good meal with coffee and salad. (*He anointeth my head with oil*) The people here are said to work only one fourth of the year, half of which they plant and hoe and the other half they harvest and gather their crops; the remainder of the time is spent in hunting or other favorite enjoyment or they lay on their backs and smoke cigars. (*Surely goodness and mercy shall follow me all the days of my life*) The cattle cause no care. They come towards the evening to the dwellings and if milk is needed so much is milked as they need, and then they are again driven off to the woods or prairies. Sheep are kept mostly for wool, as the flesh of these animals has little value. (*I shall dwell in the house of the Lord forever*)"

As Anne finished the passage, she looked sideways at her brother. She was terribly disturbed to hear him quote scripture. She had lived apart from him for many years but she had seen nothing in his letters to show that he had gone back on his old atheistic beliefs. It was a shock to hear him now, worse than if a believer had begun swearing on his death bed that there was no god. What could it mean? She said, "My throat hurts a little, I'll wait before I read anymore." He nodded from bed, lost in a kind of trance. When she was reading, he was a boy again at Nazareth Hall listening to his father. He could remember the clover field and the firm way his father had pointed out the spot where the new railroad was to come through. "Right through the gap," his father had said. "It will come that way and change everything."

In the other room, Anne wished for someone to talk to, some well person. She was sure it would soon be over but to have Aaron speak religion was a living decay. Still it might be just the sound of the words he loved. She couldn't believe the way he used to think was done with. Only that afternoon, rummaging among old papers, she had come across clippings that he had saved about the anarchists who had been executed back in the Eighties. He had got very excited at the time because they, too, were atheists. She remembered very clearly the letters he had written about them. She pulled out the old envelope and, in the little stuffy room, tried to keep her mind on the yellow print. But these men had stuck it out, to the death. They had believed in something beside the almighty dollar. As she read the speeches, tears rolled down her face. She despised her brother for his weakness and hoped he would not ask her to read to him again. He had taken up religion, it was clear as day, because he had long ago given up the world. His son was the world, a selfish ruined boy, whose life Aaron himself had had a hand in blighting forever. He had laid his hand on his wife, and on everyone, wilfully, to do what he liked, and when he had finished, he had taken up God.

She was angry and furious, as if she had been drawn into his schemes without full knowledge. So, he could put her off with a share no bigger than David got, or Hortense got, and they in their cool homes taking it easy. She would help herself if he wouldn't help her. She would see to it that her children weren't stunted by his selfishness. She had signed papers and deeds, checks and accounts. If her hand was good for one thing, it was good for another. Those lots he had promised her, what about them? Deeds to them were in the bottom drawer. She got them out, looked them over. Everything was set in another drawer, where papers with Notary Seals were prepared in expectation of the secret sales he carried on under other names to circumvent Sally. She pulled out three blanks, filled them in, and went to bed with a steady heart.

In the morning she could see at a glance he was worse. He did not even see her when she came in with his breakfast and, on her way across the square to the doctor's, she stepped into the courthouse to file the deeds made out to Anne Trexler Wendel for one dollar and other valuable considerations.

When she came back with the doctor, he was dead. She did not feel guilty. The guilty one was dead.

Amos Wendel consented to come to Grapeville for the funeral, as he was full of ideas about that Sally and afraid the woman might choose to throw acid in Anne's face at the very grave. She did not even show up at the funeral and Amos planned an almost immediate return to Oxtail.

"But aren't you going up country to see your relatives?" said Anne. "Why, it's been more than twenty-five years since you've been to Lewisburg. You ought to take time off for that." To back up her ideas she brought out David's letter urging Amos to stick around Grapeville until the estate was in a more settled condition. That finished any doubt in Amos's mind.

"It's all right for David to talk. He's his own boss. I'm not. I'm not going to risk losing the job I have for any estate. Besides, I don't see that I'm needed. You can handle it as well as anyone."

Amos had brought her a bunch of violets in a purple box tied with a silver ribbon, and their little visit together in Grapeville was almost like a second honeymoon. They hired a horse and buggy and drove around the roads outside of Grapeville. When Amos was gone, Anne began assorting Aaron's old papers and came across a bundle of Amos's letters to her and hers to him that had been left there at the time their first baby was born in the old homestead. Amos had been on the road then with grand ideas about the future. "I keep thinking all week of our walk in the woods and how happy you were. How I wish your life could be one of unbroken happiness," he wrote.

"What I long for is your happiness," she had written him, and he wrote, "There is nothing I desire so much as your happiness." No one could say they had not tried to bring happiness to one another. But poverty is a bitter weed. The little daily pinching, the anxiety. The letters freed her of any doubts she might have had about the lots that she had signed over to herself. They weren't worth much anyhow, not more than five hundred dollars, but they would mean a little capital. She could sell the homestead, she and Hortense, and realize a little something more. It would be hard to know how to invest that money. Just so they had a little security at the end of their days and the girls got help when they needed it most. When David wrote giving up his share of the homestead, glad to be rid of a responsibility that might prove to cost more than it brought, she wrote Hortense that she was certain they could cut up the land in parcels, sell it for town lots and double the money.

She actually took more pleasure in meeting townspeople on the street and held her head a little higher. She owned something, she owned property. An awful lot of money had been spent on railroad fares lately, it was a good thing that the family owned something at last.

WHITE HEADED BOY

Jonathan Chance did not have a distinct remembrance of the year the world war broke out. All the summers were nice in Northern Michigan. He remembered they were at Torch Lake that year. Afterwards they went further North and the cottages at Torch began to run down.

The Chance family never lived in a run-down place. Everything had to be spick and span, just like Mr. Chance kept his clothes, with a box for each of his several hats and drawers full of neat piles of beautiful ties and the finest underwear and crisp shirts and dozens of pure linen handkerchiefs, and the linen closet was the same, piles of sheets that felt like silk and bathtowels big as sheets and rose-colored plush bathmats and embroidered bureau scarfs by the score and table linen, with cutouts and fine drawn work, that Jonathan hated the sight of when he finally broke from his home.

But coming back the time his mother died, he got hold of some letters. They had been cached in a drawer of her dresser, along with a bottle of fine whiskey that had been the mystery of the house for years. The mother had allowed Jonathan's father to think her son had stolen the bottle and had consumed it in secret. She had kept up this fiction year in and year out, and it had been a great aid to her in casting blame on her favorite boy for other matters, once he became involved with a woman.

She was dead when he found all his letters and the bottle, and, as it was the afternoon of the funeral, it only seemed pathetic to think of the little game she had played. He took his letters, and his sister hid the whiskey, and among those letters there was one 1914 item that refreshed his memory about that time.

It was written to his mother at Torch Lake from their home in Benton.

Sept. 4, 1914

Dear Mother:

I arrived safely this morning. It was a hard ride. As soon as I got here Papa made me start working in the store and he wouldn't offer me any money and kept giving me the devil for not holding my broom right and I am so near dead tired now that I can hardly hold my head up. Gee I wish I was back on torchlake. Papa won't let me work for Bert, he says I've got to work here. He'll wish he hadn't made me though. How's Ed getting along. The dog's getting along fine. I haven't seen Uncle Jake. He is driving the car. With Love.

Jonathan.

That fall he had a tussle with his father about going to work again for Bert at the bicycle repair shop. His father didn't like the idea of his boy working out. People around town talked that it looked funny for Mr. Chance to let his boy work when school was enough for a kid his age. At noon he always cycled to Bert's and kept his eyes open, maybe tinkered with a cleaning job, while Bert got his lunch. Then he had to bike home and gobble his own lunch and, if he was late at school, he always got off by telling teacher he worked. As Mr. Chance was one of the best fixed men in Benton, some people thought it was a mistake for the boy to be allowed to work in a dirty bike shop but Mr. Chance, and his wife too, were secretly delighted at what looked like a sign of ambition. He was the first grandchild of old Jonathan Chance and, among the wide circle of family connections, was looked upon from the start as the White Headed Boy.

What really turned Mr. Chance from Bert's bike shop for his son, was the way the boy insisted on spending Sundays with his employer. That fall of 1914, Mr. Chance had resolved to keep Jonathan employed at his own store, but his strict notions of discipline prevented him from giving the boy more than a dime a week.

The upshot was that Jonathan made such sloppy work of the little jobs around the place and was always so late, always playing hooky from school with the northend gang when he could, that Mr. Chance gave in and let him go back to Bert's.

The first victory Jonathan Chance won from his father was in that year. He went back to Bert's and spent every Sunday, same as ever having dinner with Bert Johnson and his wife. In the mornings he was choir boy in the Episcopal Church where his father was warden, but in the afternoons he was treated like a grownup, smoked one of Bert's pipes, and cracked jokes with Mrs. Johnson and some of her cronies. Sometimes they would have a little beer or wine and play a game of cards.

"There's nothing in the bike business anymore," Bert said, tilting his chair back. He was a great hand to have the women fuss around, handing him his beer and making a lot of him. Later when he got a divorce from his wife, it was a surprise to Jonathan. He was a man then, and Mrs. Johnson told him tearfully that her husband was all brag and no go and she couldn't put up with it any longer. She was a corset fitter and had reached the time of life when, if ease is all she could get out of life, she might as well take it alone.

When his mother came down from Torch, she had ragged at him for his dirty hands and for going to Bert's, but he said, "Aw mother, I've got to learn something. I learn a lot at Bert's. How'm I going to learn about machines if I don't begin now?"

"Never you mind about machines, just you keep your hands clean when you come to supper. It'll be time enough for machines later." But afterwards when she told her husband, the two chuckled about it. They were careful not to let the boy see how much they approved of him. From the very start they expected him to carry on the tradition of old Jonathan Chance and they were always looking for signs to confirm their hopes. The trouble was that they saw only the money-making streak in old Jonathan Chance. They miscalculated on the variety in the old man, who in spite of his enormous capacity to cop all the best real estate in town, maintain a business, get a wedge into the banking game, still had liked to play the accordion, smoke many pipes, keep diaries, and write long newsy letters about political matters to the papers and long descriptive ones when he chanced to travel. He had died, also, with a number of little mysteries that the thoroughly sedate sons preferred to leave unraveled. They had inherited only their father's regularity and it was not their fault. The father had trained his boys in that way, had kept them apprentices to his fine saddle and leather manufacturing business at low wages for years while the business grew and became finally solid.

He had drilled his sons in such steady saving ways that his death came too late to release a spending instinct in any of them. Abel Chance never saw a good reason why his boy Jonathan should have pocket money. When he caught the boy lying to get something to jingle around in his pocket like other kids, he thrashed him soundly. On Sunday, he always passed the plate and sat very proud when his boy, the tallest in the choir, came down the aisle behind all the others, his handsome head held high.

The parents fondly shut their eyes to the boy's preferences, that very early in the game might have indicated that a split in the money-making urge was going to cause trouble somewhere. Jonathan never took to the "nice boys" his parents preferred he play with. He was always followed by a horde of rowdy northend kids and, as he had a big yard on the bank of the river, a wonderful cave, a tree house and a father with a cellar of beer from which he could occasionally snitch a bottle, he was seldom alone. If the parents found fault with this tendency, they had to give credit to the kid for taking a paper route, when only a tyke of nine, that got him out of bed with an alarm at five every day. He was ingenious as the devil, too, picking up little jobs that no one ever heard of, and at that time, hadn't a lazy bone in his body.

Of course, it was disgusting the way he would loaf with the men at the mill out at his uncle Graham's place. They liked to get a boy smoking and chewing and he was ready for anything. When he was practically a baby of seven, he'd leave a houseful of his aunt's guests and tear out back of the mill to sit with those big loafers, guffawing over dear knows what. His mother washed his mouth out after a go at tobacco once, right before the men, but the minute she let him loose, he took the boat and rowed to the other side under the piles and got out a chaw that he'd hid in his pants and took a big bite and spit a long vicious spit way out into the river.

That winter at Bert's they talked more about this man Ford and his little new bus than they did about the war in Europe. People said Ford was going to revolutionize industry, and one Sunday Bert read a piece out loud from the papers about Ford and how all he was doing was practising the golden rule. "The golden rule pays in business," the headline ran. The women always listened attentively, even respectfully.

Mrs. Goodman, a dressmaker from rooms upstairs, came down after dinner and sat around with them, her white plump arms in sleeves of elbow length propped on the table. "I don't know the time when five a day coming in steady wouldn't look good to me," she said airily, shaking her head, with its switch of lighter hair wound around on top in a little mound. "How about you, Belle?"

Belle quit looking at the heel of her shoe that she had stretched her leg the better to see. "Well, look at that shoe. I don't know what ails shoes these days. I always run down my left shoe and my right stays fit as a fiddle. When have I seen five dollars a day, I'd like to know? But I bet they have to work for it. I never see anything people get for nothing."

"It's a new idea in business, mother," said Bert. "Who does the spending? The people who work, don't they? Who makes up the bulk of this country? You'd think to read the Supplements there," pointing his long finger at a pile, "that it was the high-fliers who are always taking champagne baths and buying strings of pearls for chorus ladies and divorcing each other, worse than if they were dogs running around after every new bitch. But don't you believe it. It's people like you and me makes up this country. And if we don't buy, they don't sell. Take this car," went on Bert, turning to look full at Jonathan who was backed to the wall with his chair tilted in an adult fashion, pipe in mouth, comfortable family spitoon near by. "Take this little car. Why does he make a car like that? He'll clean up, is already. The people can't buy expensive cars. Why, the blasted snobs all wanted to make swanky cars. Take Rhingold. He's got a good car. I heard from one of the men there that Rhingold wanted to make a cheap car but he couldn't get the idea over. His cronies wanted to make a swell model that they could feel puffed up about when it passed on the street. There goes one of our models. There goes your Aunt Fannie's fanny, if you ask me. Fools, they're fools in comparison to this man Ford."

"The Rhino's piled up dough, though. You ought to hear my mother, she's always telling how much we would have made if we'd gone into it at the start instead of steam wagons," said Jonathan. The women looked at him respectfully while he talked. Mrs. Johnson got up, her corset creaking slightly under her stiff Sunday taffeta, and went to the cupboard, opened a tin box and brought out some homemade cookies. Lifting her eyebrows and smiling and pointing to the cookies, she set them down before the man and the boy so as not to disturb the talk. Then she settled down again, listening and nodding, every now and then distracted by a further contemplation of her heel. At such a moment the two women caught each other's eye and nodded commiseratingly.

"Sure, Rhingold makes money. Of course. The market's wide open and not yet choked up. He'll make money for quite awhile, how long I don't know. So far as that goes, the same goes with Ford. So many manufacturers are trying to get on the bandwagon that they can't all make a fortune and they'll all begin aping Ford soon. Watch out. All the same, what I say goes, it's people like us who keep the stores open. Those Sunday Supplement squirts, like as not, are too tony to shop in America anyhow. Nothing but an import is good enough for them, I'd bet my shirt." He was looking hot as he said it, and Mrs. Goodman tactfully brought the subject around to the nice choir the lodge had and such fine voices. That Mr. Rumsey in the meatmarket had the clearest tenor and you'd never know it seeing him cut steaks and chops. It just shows all the lights hidden behind bushels, if we only knew.

Bert listened moodily. He hated to be sidetracked like that. The women couldn't stand it if you showed a little heat. All they wanted was everything nice, nice pleasant talk and a lot of grins. He looked at Jonathan who was paying no attention to Mrs. Goodman's talk. "I look to see the day," he said, "when everybody who wants to—wants to mind you, because you always got old maids like Miss Brody who prefer a horse—when everybody who wants a car will have one."

"Ain't he the prophet though," said Mrs. Johnson admiringly.

"Bert, if you could only do as well at seeing your own business as you do others. I tell him and tell him that bikes are going out so fast, there's nothing in repairing. He learned back when bikes were the rage, he was a kid then, and he's stuck through all the changes to motorcycles and I expect if they got anything else on two wheels, Bert would travel along. But the traveling's no good on that road— I tell you, Bert, if you don't switch into something else, you'll be up the creek without a paddle. At your time of life, it's not so easy."

Bert flushed and his neck under the neat gray shirt thickened and he couldn't think of a word for a minute, just knocked out his pipe and got up and glared. "My time of life, talk sense, there's a woman for you, wants to make me out in second childhood so she can run things. Beware of women, Johnny, they'll weaken you in one way or the other."

"I didn't mean anything Papa," said Mrs. Johnson. Mrs. Goodman said she wished they could have a little beer, and she'd a mind to run upstairs and bring down those two bottles that Mike McGraw brought her last night for sitting up to twelve to finish his wife's black silk for the funeral. Bert said, "We got beer, keep it," and Belle said, "Why, the idea May, don't think of it. Papa's got beer." They brought out four small bottles and let Jonathan open them. He poured carefully to keep the foam down and after a few swigs Bert began tuning up on "There was a jolly sailor, O."

When Jonathan Chance left the Johnson house it was always so cozy and by that time more cronies had come in and they were sitting around free and easy talking about the races down south or how Bert had seen Dan Patch when he was a colt. The parlor at home looked pretty gloomy, nice but nothing exciting. And he was always careful to run upstairs first to wash his hands and brush the tobacco odor out of his mouth.

In 1914 it was hard to know where to invest money and sometimes Mr. and Mrs. Chance would have quite an argument. As she had tipped off her husband on a good thing once and he had used his own judgment to his sorrow, she usually had the last word. Jonathan would stand yawning in the doorway, and at last make an excuse to go to bed. If he put a towel at the crack, his mother couldn't see how long he kept the light on reading.

In spite of not proving a demon investor, Mr. Chance kept tight hold of his purse strings and, what with the inheritance from his father, it was a fat purse. But his hold was snug enough to shoot Jonathan out on jobs in the summer when he might have lolled around in northern Michigan with his kid sisters and brother. In 1916 Bert let the bike business go and trailed toward Ohio with the idea of going into one of the new trucking factories. Jonathan got a job as lifesaver on a lake beach and, when his mother came after him as if he was a baby and humiliated him by telling everyone his real age, he struck off for himself selling garden seeds all over West Virginia and Ohio. He'd rather wear his ass raw bouncing on the saddle over the West Virginia mountains than be bossed around at the lake anymore. His parents thought fatuously that you couldn't hold a born moneymaker down.

No one can say if it were not just the idea of leaving home that made Jonathan so patriotic in 1918 and so anxious to get into the War. He could hardly wait until he was old enough to enroll in the R.O.T.C., but he was eighteen that November and then the armistice had to come along and spoil all his chances. He was in his last year at highschool and he and Terry Blount had made some peppy Liberty Loan speeches. People were saying he ought to go into politics or "Mr. Chance, you ought to make a lawyer out of that boy." He had stacked up pretty hot on the highschool debates too, but the school paper that he really wanted to get on wouldn't have him because of the teachers. He never had any respect for them and kept ragging them and so they got even and paid him off. At the dances, where some of the teachers chaperoned, he was polite as you please, because he was cutting such a swath with the girls that he could afford to spread himself even with enemies.

But at public dance halls where he really longed to shine, he got the cold shoulder from little toughies. He would stand, almost the tallest boy present, his dark eyes blazing and resentful, his mouth still half smiling, one shoulder hunched a little higher than the other, looking after some common little brat who had snippily told him to go chase himself.

He and his Liberty Loan side-kick Terry Blount got an idea to become revivalists and go down the Mississippi on the river boats stopping at all the towns and maybe sell patent medicines too. They cooked up a fine gag but it never got any further. For one thing, Jonathan realized he was being groomed for a topnotch success and at that time he was not actively against it. He was a whizz on the road, selling, and could sell anything from an old toothbrush to imitation pearls. "I could sell a wooden leg or a wooden egg," he would boast, laughing his funny silent laugh, his mouth stretched wide and crooked and no sound coming out— only, if he were seated, a slap on the knee, delivered slowly and resoundingly as if to clinch the matter. "By the time I'm thirty I can have a million if I want," he told Terry Blount. But the way he said "if I want," with his eyes looking somewhere else, did not look so good for his parents' fond hopes.

He was no longer a choir boy and, although he went to church, read Schopenhauer afterwards and felt mature and cynical, especially about women. His cynicism didn't prevent him from getting several violent crushes and he fell for beautiful vain girls who could not resist having as many boys around as possible. When he got hold of Walt Whitman, he read every night and never had any respect for the minister of their church again when, after calling on him and bringing the subject to literature, he mentioned *Leaves of Grass* and the clergyman had taken a brand new copy down from his own shelves to finger in a patronizing way. "But what's this," he said, angry. "This is the way I treat it," and he had torn out the Children of Adam poems, ripped them across again and flung them into a basket. "Filth," he said, his face contorting to suggest all the backhouse words. "That's the way to treat it. Dangerous. And in my opinion a mind capable of conceiving those poems is incapable of conceiving anything of a really noble nature."

The minister must have told Jonathan's folks about his query because his mother searched his room pretty thoroughly after that and, in a deceptively sweet way, asked him about his reading. He wasn't fooled though and kept mum. His parents realized he was difficult to direct, full of the old Nick really, but consoled themselves by thinking such traits usually indicated superior powers.

When the armistice came there was an undercurrent of disappointment in more breasts than Jonathan's. Some of the business men were afraid profits would drop but others said that reconstruction in Europe would take care of any surplus. The uneasiness penetrated to the wage earners and talk of strikes in other cities spurred on even the employees of Jonathan Chance & Sons to ask for higher wages. The employees of the Chance store were in an awkward position for a strike. Many of them had been in the business thirty years. They had been brought over from Germany and you couldn't duplicate their kind anywhere in the country. The Chances, father and sons, had always treated their help in a nice fatherly way. They gave them fair wages, provided good working conditions, and at Christmas sent turkeys to the families if the season was a good one.

Benton was an open shop town. It had been kept open shop at the cost of some broken heads and a couple of bullet wounds years back. The town bragged about its open shop character. It was really Rhingold's town. When his lecherous old eye spotted a man's wife he wanted, he got her. She became his, more or less openly, and was even proud of it. "I see Mrs. Bascomb is going to Florida on the Rhingold's yacht," one woman would say to another, with a lift of the eyebrows and a certain envy. Rhingold knew his business. He provided what is known as fair wages, a clean factory, and a handsome club room with movies, pool tables and an occasional lecturer who spoke of the poor living conditions for the working classes of Europe and of the highest standards in the world enjoyed by the working classes of this country where the lowliest may hope to rise to walk among the mighty if he has the ability.

In spite of these visible and invisible cords around the working people of Benton, an unrest was spreading and causing uneasiness. Some of the sounder people of the town laid it to the Wilson propaganda talk about self-determination for little nations and to the democratic slogans that had put the idea into the heads of the workers that they should be allowed more of a say-so in their own affairs.

"Wilson has all the flaws of the professor," they said. "It sounds grand on paper, but will it work?" The men who were employing others didn't think anything would work except the firm guiding hand of the intelligent employer on the dumb employed. With the war over, a good deal of energy that had gone into Liberty Loan drives and Red Cross work broke out in suspicion about Red propaganda. Pro-Germans became Bolsheviks, and even young Jonathan came home with a cock-and-bull story about his teacher in Ec being a Red.

Abel Chance had kept his head more than most during the war and had not been much taken in with atrocity stories. His memory of his German mother prevented that. And now he said, "Don't shoot your mouth off without thinking. In the first place, find out what that revolution was about in Russia. They've got a right to do what they want, same as we have. I don't like to hear you talk like a parrot."

"Well, but everybody says how they had a reign of terror," said Jonathan.

"Everybody says—there you go again—don't be so hasty."

His father's words really impressed Jonathan. What Mr. Chance had in mind was a nice Christian forbearance. He took some things of his church literally, such as a tolerant attitude toward beliefs of others and the poor ye have with you always.

He could see no reason for discontent among the Chance workmen. What astonished the two brothers in the firm was their demand for a union. A union in an open shop town. "There's no reason for a union," said Abel Chance to Kemmerer, the oldest workman. "You know you have only to come to us and we'll talk it over. Higher wages, this is no time for them, man. Business is tightening, not expanding."

"Living conditions are up, Mr. Chance," said Kemmerer. "They have gone up 17 percent this last year and our wages have stood still."

"Well," said Mr. Chance. "Living conditions for my brother and me went up, too. We are all in the same boat." He wasn't going to stand and argue. But he did not know that his son was every night in the home of one or the other of the workmen listening to argument.

When he was a little shaver, Jonathan had come in the back door and sneaked up the stairs to the workroom for a talk with Gottlieb or Krause. Krause had a wonderful bitch that he took duck hunting every fall. He always asked for a little vacation in the fall and he and his wife took the dog and went off into the wilds. He had snapshots in his pocket of the dog and himself holding a brace of ducks and grinning. He also made his own beer in a big clean cellar.

From the time he was fifteen, Jonathan went over to this man's house where they also treated him like a grownup, as Bert and his wife did.

Sometimes the man and boy would go down into the basement and light up, the man a heavy pipe and the boy a lighter one that Krause loaned him. His father wouldn't let him own pipes yet, and it was not like the gun that had also been refused him so that he had to buy one for his father for Christmas in order to get one in the family.

When Jonathan heard of the disturbance in the store he was right out at Krause's. Some of the men from the store were down in the basement and, with the exception of two or three, didn't know just how to take Jonathan. Krause set them right with a few words in German. They were talking union. One of them, a little man with sharp eyes said that it was shameful to be such slaves as not to have a union. "Be men," he said. "Now's your time. The spring rush will be coming, they got to have you. There ain't better workmen in the country than you fellows. Fifth Avenue would be nuts to get you old fellows. But where are you now? Prices shoot up but does the wages? No. You know what business was done and in whose pocket it went."

They sat around drinking beer and smoking and Krause took Jonathan aside and said what did he think his old man would do about it? Jonathan didn't have an idea but he said that his old man would have to meet their terms, and, he said, if he doesn't you fight him, he'll give in. Everybody was pleased at the kid's talk. Jonathan meant it. A curious inner fire kept him edging to the front of his chair. He wanted to make a speech too but had nothing to say. He had read in history though, only that winter, that in the middle ages there were fighting men in the old guilds, some of them had been revolutionaries of their day. His throat felt dry and he gulped down his beer quickly. Krause was talking his quiet slow way. "No one of us says Mr. Chance isn't a good employer or considerate. He is. It's not that. It's something else, it's like this fellow here says, it's we must have a union and be grown up not just little fellows that can be spanked and put to bed if we ain't good."

"You stick up for your rights, make him come across," said Jonathan. "You should have a union if you want one."

"The boy's right," said Krause, his eyes melting at the fervor of young Jonathan. Every man was heartened by Jonathan's speech. Now it was over, he slipped back in his chair, a tall very slim boy, a little embarrassed and leaning down to rumple the ears of the bitch hunter who was lying as close to his feet as she could. "Good girl," Jonathan said, huskily. He was so moved he was afraid to look up at the men. It was wonderful here, such warm friendly feeling. He jumped up when Krause went for more beer and filled the glasses at the keg. Mrs. Krause came tiptoeing down the stairs with a tray full of pretzels. He took them from her and passed them to everyone, sometimes in his zeal he passed twice but the men noticing it, pretended it was all right and smiled indulgently.

When they went out of the basement that night, it was set to go and the faces of the men looked serene in the light of a full moon. Jonathan felt like a conspirator and, when he fell over the hall mat coming into his house and his father called from his bedroom, "Who's that?" he answered, "It's only me," meekly and the words seemed inadequate and foolish after the fine evening.

Bunker Hill, U. S. Route 20. 1932

The old man stirring the ground with a stick was the first to lift his head. "There she comes," he said.

Six of the big fellows got up slowly from the earth and taking hold of their sticks moved toward the road. The one man left behind put another chunk on the fire and shivering held out his hands. It was cold in the cut the way it gets sometimes at the full of the moon with one of those clean blue skies that are as blue at night as in the day. The tall corn growing almost up to the road made a good windbreak for the fire. The flames were steady. The big guys stood ready by the road swinging their sticks gently as the whine of a motor coming up grade hummed through the cut.

"That ain't no truck," said the man by the fire. It sounded to him smaller than a truck, a car maybe, but coming up it had an ominous get-ready noise like during the war when a shell was about to crash. He couldn't get out of the habit of cowering inside at that kind of a noise. "It ain't a truck, I tell you." A big car nosed through the cut, slid gently down hill toward the boys. The old farmer backed up and was first to sit down again by the fire.

The car slid down past them, passed and stopped. The men by the fire squatted and paid no attention. As someone came toward them, the old fellow turned, said softly, "Oh it's *Him*."

He came toward them humbly, with the crawling timidity of a yellow bitch dog who knows the feel of a stone.

"Hello boys," He said, making his voice loud and jovial.

"Hello," said two of the boys.

"How're things going, boys," says He.

"First rate," says the old man, scowling.

"Now listen boys," He says, edging toward them and beginning to talk fast. "You can take me out in them fields and beat me up with a rock, by jesus, if you can't, if you think I had anything to do with the other night. Listen boys, I'm regular, not special. Those

73

deputies that was out here slugging around didn't know you boys. Why I'm with you, heart's blood. You know that, don't you, boys?"

"Why don't you throw that badge you got hid under your lapel in the fire if you're with us," says the old man.

"Now boys, you know me, listen I'm here tonight with my old man. He's back there in the car, I had to bring him he's so lonesome. You know what tonight is? Why I lost my mother just a year ago, this very night, and I've got my old father, he's seventy-six year old, back there in the car. You'll lose your fight boys, but I'm with you, heart's blood."

"How'd you know we'll lose," said one of the boys getting up to his six feet and looking down at the little whiffet. The deputy backed a little uneasily and said, "Of course you'll lose, you know that. You got everything against you. You can't go shutting off food from the babies like you're doing. The whole outfit in town's against you, you're choking off trade too. Why they're not routing cars to the Black Hills anymore through Oxtail, all on account of you fellows. You can't win, boys, but I'm with you and I don't want no hard feelings, I just want to explain. That's why I came out here." He leaned down peering into the faces of the sitters with his own foolish flushed conciliatory face.

"If you weren't with them the other night, why didn't you tip us off instead of letting them slide in here by surprise?"

"Now boys, I didn't know a word about it, honest to god I didn't. You can ask my old father, he'll tell you. I was eating supper with him that night and afterwards him and me took in a movie. That's because he's so lonesome, he can tell you. We lost my mother just a year ago tonight. You boys got this thing by the wrong leg. Keep the farmers off the road, then you'll not have any trouble."

"No," said the old man. "I expect not. The packing house will get our nice hogs that costs us money to haul in to them, the Rogers Brothers will get our good milk to distribute and fatten up on, sure we get you."

"Boys, they'll hook you for every hook in the road if you talk like that, I'm warning you, I'm your friend."

"Say, they've hooked us already. And we've got too many friends like you," said the shivery man. "The woods is so full we can't see the trees. Get me, we're helping ourselves. Would we be here if our backs weren't to the wall? You belong with the Chamber of Commerce outfit, go back and tell them to mind their business and not go sneaking to the governor asking for gunmen and we'll mind ours."

"Boys," He said in a weepy voice. "There's plenty sons of bitches trying to do you dirt, I'll say that, but I ain't one. I'm with you and I had nothing to do with that dirty raid the other night. I swear to god, I'm with you. Well, I got to take my poor old man home, but I'll see you soon, maybe bring you a dish of oatmeal in the morning." He laughed nervously, plucking at a string of hair that dangled little boy fashion over his nose. "I'll help any way I can boys, don't forget I warned you. So long," He got in his car, started her and turned, the car went up the hill, whimpered through the cut.

"He's tanked up," said the old man, "and guilty as hell. He pushed the whole bunch of deputies on us, I know by the green look he's got, can't look you in the eyes. Say, he's scared we'll beat him up. And let me tell you, we can do it. They ain't the only ones who can get guns either. That corn ain't growing tall for nothing. If we can hide there, we can shoot there, I say. It's been done before."

At the word shoot, the shivery guy held out his hands to the fire. A log fell and sparks spit out and the men drew closer around it. They sat there talking quietly, wondering if the other roads to town were being guarded too or had they doublecrossed the boys by telling them it was all up, picketing was over.

The town of Oxtail, Iowa, lay on the other side of the cut, hid by the yellow hills. A glare in even that white moonlit sky showed where it was, drawing the roads to it, sucking the country in.

"The damn old spider," said the old man, his eyes on the glare. "We fed it long enough."

"I heard big news tonight, forgot to tell you," said one of the boys. "One of the Meyer Brothers shot himself, I think it was Henry. He shot himself because that business is cracking up so fast that if they don't get some insurance it's all over. The other four brothers will get the insurance for the business. That's what they say."

"Is that right? Are they going downhill that fast?"

"Sure, they're on the toboggan, they are all on the slide and they want us to plug it up with hog meat, that's the way I see it."

They stirred their sticks softly in the soft dust, and now and then town noises sounded far off and faint. The town had swelled during the up-and-up years. It had swallowed little farms, turned country into swanky additions and golf courses for the town boys. Now it was strangling on its own cud, it lay there like a sick cow, choked with what it had eaten, its life drained to the eastern seaboard, its substance sold out and its citizens, frantic, passing the buck to the farmers. "Look at you, what you're doing, bringing us more bad times, keeping away our trade."

Oxtail lay, as always, between the Big Sioux and the Missouri. Ruin had fallen upon it. The white lights on the downtown streets had given way to the cheaper red neon. A rocking chair contest went on in a Pierce Street café. Rock, rock, rocking in your rocking chair. The Meyer Brothers, now four, solemnly stood by the bier of their brother in the funeral parlor. His insurance was large enough to stop a gap but not enough to dam a river.

They remembered the pushcart days and how Henry had been the boldest of them all. Now they were floorwalkers in their own mongrel store, the shoes sold out to Minno of New York, the women's wear to Baumfeld. The mortician hovered anxiously near the brothers. He felt he had done a fine job and he was upset not to be congratulated on his work of art. The corpse lay in a natural way with hands crossed upon its breast and a faint red color painted on the stiff gray cheeks.

This was no time for the Meyer boys to be so snotty. They ought to give credit where credit is due, especially considering a bullet always makes a nasty job for any man, even a skillful mortician like himself.

II. YOU CAN LIVE FOREVER

IF SHE had been like her sister Clara who had been so good at enduring things, tight corsets and tight shoes, Victoria wouldn't mind it so much to be trailing along to the Big Ball of the year in a Family Party with the Blums, instead of as Barney's special guest. But, of course, Lulu Blum would probably have a fit if such a thing occurred.

"Oh it is lovely for all of us to go together," she lied as she squeezed in past old Mr. Blum's knees and sat safely between Lulu and Barney, with Lulu resting her long arm caressingly along the back of the seat where it could reassure itself against Barney's coat. "And you look a perfect picture," to Lulu who, dressed as Old Lady Hubbard, lacked nothing except the dog and his bone.

"What about yourself, my dear?" said Papa Blum, who had wound a sheet around himself and hoped he looked like Socrates although he was far too handsome. Barney's sister Nelly hugged her corner, a modest Lady Macbeth, while her husband as Diogenes was wondering if anyone would recognize him without his tub.

"Seems to me we've got too much Greek influence here," joked

Barney. "Father, you and Reynolds must have been stewing up in your room together to come out like that."

"Oh, but there's no connection, an entirely different era," said old Mr. Blum. He was still eyeing Victoria. "I can't just make out what you are," he said.

"I shouldn't tell, should I?" said Victoria looking at Barney. "It was Barney's idea. I wasn't going but Barney came around and said he thought I should. My uncle, you know. I just got the telegram from my mother and thought I wouldn't go."

"I know, my child, but there's no use sitting home and missing such a nice party. Your uncle wouldn't want you to and certainly not your mother. We can't bring back the dead and life belongs to youth." He beamed with pleasure and Victoria felt the uneasy arm of Lulu reaching across her neck for Barney. "I suppose you're right," said Victoria, but she had never seen Uncle Aaron in all her life and it did seem useless to cry about a perfect stranger. But hearing that he was dead had nothing to do with Uncle Aaron. Uncle Joe, who had died just before she was born, was more real than Uncle Aaron and somehow Uncle Aaron's dying reminded her of the tragic way she had come into the world, just on the heels of her mad uncle's death. "Name the boy for me," he had said. And then it had turned out only another girl.

"But you didn't say what you were?" said Mr. Blum.

"Let him guess," said Barney.

"No one could guess what *you* are with that crazy dirty old sweat shirt on and he's sewed the letter *I* on the back, Father, heaven only knows why, he won't tell *me*," said Lulu enviously craning around Vicky to look at Barney accusingly.

"Let 'em guess," said Barney again, flippantly and happily, drumming on the glass and feeling good because that very afternoon he had put over something pretty on the desk. Got in a few sharp words against the way they were rounding up everyone on that bastard Syndicalist law that shut the free mouths of people as if they'd been born under a Kaiser.

"Oh tell us," said Nelly, "we're nearly there."

But the taxicab stopped and the whole party faced the flight of steps. Diogenes, lost without his tub, stepped out self-consciously on the pavement. Socrates, more at home, followed. Victoria, suddenly afraid her skirts were too short, hung behind but Barney gave her a nudge and they got out. Lulu bounced out, looking the most presentable of the outfit.

"Now if we get separated, let's all meet by the cloak room exactly on the hour," said Barney.

"Why should we separate?" said Lulu, alarmed and holding grimly to Barney's arm.

"We might," said Barney, "and if we do, at the hour, every hour, cloak room. Come on girls," and taking hold of Vicky on one side, with Lulu taking hold of him on the other, he charged up the flight of steps. The others tried to move easily after him and Diogenes stumbled near the top and got out his pipe to steady himself.

"Well, professor," challenged a voice, and hearty Mr. McKee held out his hand in a grim shake. "Say, I hear there's trouble brewing out your way. Anything in it?"

"What do you mean?"

"Oh I hear you're a nest of Bolsheviks over there at that University and the whole gang is liable to get the bum's rush."

"Well," said Diogenes, stuffing his pipe deliberately, "you know more than I do. I'm in it so perhaps I don't see so much." He hoped he had put that carelessly enough. Yes, old McKee was swallowing it down, breathing heavily and privately convinced that the whole staff were sly dogs linked up with gold from Kaiser Bill or somewhere. "What you doing here?"

"I?" said McKee. "Tut-tut. Can't a man sell insurance and still try to get rid of his libido?"

"See that girl over there, with my brother? You ought to get acquainted with her. She's here as Suppressed Desire."

"Why, Reynolds," said Nelly. "You promised not to tell."

"Oh she won't mind, she can handle him," said Diogenes with too much admiration in his voice. Lady Macbeth drew herself up and said drily, "I think her skirt is too short, Reynolds, but I suppose that's what men like."

"She's got pretty legs," said Reynolds, watching the legs through the door.

"I thought you were above such crude ideas," said Lady Macbeth, laughing in a desperate and unhappy way that made Diogenes take his pipe out of his mouth and look at her soberly. Heavens couldn't a man see another woman without his wife always leaping to conclusions. The whole business was a biological trap, why make such a pretense about freedom when there wasn't any? He stood aside while Lady Macbeth checked her coat and, still holding the pipe, moved moodily with her into the big ballroom.

It was the only affair that had been held in a long time and even now, if it were not to raise money for the political prisoners and their families, many people, the Colonel Goods, for instance, would not have come. His handsome white beard above a Chinese Mandarin's robe was moving graciously aside for the eternal Columbine with her tiny black mask.

"Now for a long evening pretending to have fun," sighed Diogenes, looking at Barney enviously as he galloped absurdly past with his letter I ripping toward the top slightly. The big black letter was causing a lot of comment and Diogenes moved softly from group to group, happy that his dollar was paying for some political prisoner's kid or wife while he was free to give lectures on English literature, especially on that old fool Wordsworth with his "I'd rather be a pagan with a creed outworn so might I standing on this pleasant lee have glimpses that would make me less forlorn have sight of Proteus rising from the sea or see old Triton blow his wreathed horn."

"Penny for your thoughts, Mr. Reynolds Blake," said Miss Twining of the Domestic Science department as she bounced by on McKee's arm. Reynolds waved his pipe jovially, even his gesture had a hopeless bitter quality to it, as if to deny the whole business and to admit that he hadn't had the guts to stand up to his convictions, go to the stake, go to jail, like all the brave for whom these fools were dancing in such sweet charity.

"Penny for your thoughts, Mr. Blake," said Emory Duncan passing pompously with Mrs. Duncan, dressed as the Queen of Sheba in a cardboard crown with long false curls and paste jewels bought in the ten cent store, displaying the plump tops of two pale bosoms a little the worse for wear.

"Ha, ha," laughed Blake, waving his hand, now empty of the

pipe, and trying to imply, with an eyebrow raised at the pulchritudinous Mrs. Duncan, that no thought other than of herself could survive that lovely lovely presence. Waving a fan sweetly, graciously, lovely Mrs. Duncan wafted down the room on the arm of her cavalier King David. So much marshmallow sweetness everywhere. No wonder that his own Nelly, with her hard and brittle body and sour bitter ways, bitten and dreary through no fault of her own—no wonder she was full of tang for him, thought Diogenes, peering around and looking gratefully out the window to the sound of tugboats that booed softly and dashed around with an almost extra noise, as if someone had perhaps escaped from Alcazar, some poor soul, desperate for freedom. "And they say that they get perfectly terrible treatment, tied to the bars and hoses turned on, beaten too."

"Don't believe everything you hear, Miss Walden," and from the right, "But I had a friend who was told absolutely direct that they were being treated like the middle ages," and what was shocking was the shocking conversational tones of the speakers that rubbed on the nerves of Diogenes with his guilt of forsaken martyrdom. Oh, if he had followed his own way, had come right out, said, "No, I do not believe in war." He had hid behind Nelly's skirts, so glad to hide. Mixed and muddled, he looked out over the assorted gaieties of the ballroom and Barney came bouncing by again with that little Vicky. What a cool straight glance she could give one. She'd dished blundering McKee with one sweep. "Hey, I bet I know what you are," he'd roared. "My Suppressed Desire."

"Guess you'll have to keep on suppressing it," said Vicky, turning flatly away from him and taking up with a boy who was not in costume. She was dancing with him again now. Barney was looking around uneasily and got to the door too late, as it flipped open and closed again too late on her short gauzy skirt.

"Seen anything of my suppressed desire," he said grinning, as he came up to Diogenes.

"No more than you saw, she went through that door," said Diogenes.

"Say Rey, you having a good time?"

"Of course not," said Diogenes.

"You think too much, Rey, take it easy, like me. You're only young once," he grinned happily and stalked off just as Old Lady Hubbard decided that she had been sitting out dances quite long enough. "Now Barney," she said, "you ought to be ashamed to leave me alone all evening, I've waited and waited by the cloak room."

Diogenes looked out the window again. The night outside was fine and clear and he could see the boy not in costume and Vicky— he could tell by her short ballet skirts—move quickly across the little plaza and over by the wall. He was pressing her backward against the wall now, tilting her head back and her arms were around his neck; they were so tight together you'd never get them apart. That's what she wanted. That's what they wanted. He felt small and helpless and tears came into his eyes. He moved hastily away from the window. They were playing that damned There's a Long Long Trail a Winding, and Barney was standing by the piano with a group, pretending to lead them with a rung of a chair that someone had crazily broken for that sole purpose. Old Mr. Blum, in his mild pose of the hemlock-poisoned Socrates, started across the slippery floor and, walking past the row of windows, Diogenes had to look again, he had to look, and looked out the window into the plaza, yes they were still there, they were there, shameless and positive as daylight, still in each other's arms.

He hurried away from the window as Barney, spotting him, waved and beckoned. No, he didn't belong in the plaza, but beside the piano with the rest of the weak-kneed of the world who didn't have the guts, who couldn't make the grade.

"Mister Reynolds Blake," said a positive firm voice and, yes, it was old lady Blackstone with her rhinestone buckles still buckled above her ancient heart, fastening for some mysterious reason the same type of uniform garment that had held her erect for some seventy odd years. "I'm terribly glad to see you," he said shaking her hands, holding to her as if he were drowning, "come over here, let's talk." Yes, come over here, my good honest, sane woman, let me sit down and look at you. You at least were honest. "I intend to support those I.W.W.'s to the last ditch," she had said, separating herself the last night their little group of earnest thinkers had met to discuss what to do next. "They are honest men and they have the courage of their convictions." He could see her now, as she sat down almost meekly, so pleased at his kind attention, as she was that night, standing up very boldly in her absurd buckles and the stiff hair that no one could ever be sure was not a wig. "I shall stand by those boys," she had trumpeted, so that every soul there had crumbled more or less at her tones, "to my last gasp. They are honest, and there is damned little honesty in this world, you can take my word for it." Yes, she had blared forth like a brass trumpet and they had all filed out, muttering that they would have to sleep on it, and no use to come to a decision now and the result had been that the Little Group of Earnest Thinkers had quit thinking. They had bought War Loans and Red Cross stamps instead.

"You're a sight for sore eyes," said Diogenes, breathlessly, holding tight to her.

"I told you you'd be sorry," she said sagely, shaking her too wise head kindly. He nodded looking around uneasily. "My boy," she went on, "in this life there's very little fun if you've lost your own self-respect. You did wrong. You should have come out." She thumped her steely chest that was buttressed to the left with the rhinestone. "Like me," she added with another thump.

"I know," he said, gratefully, holding her hand and looking desperately at her. "I realize all that and even now I'm thinking...."

"Think?" She laughed. "My boy, that's all you will ever do. Think. The world's going too fast. Think. Well, I don't mean to be cruel but sometimes cruelty is welcome after all this goo-goo stuff." She wrinkled her nose at the too-sweet shepherdess who was prancing past. "I can't stomach it, and I've got an iron digestion."

"Oh I guess it's fun for them" said Diogenes, but he longed for a sudden spurt of courage. He fancied himself springing lightly to one of the gold-legged seats in the ballroom. "Ladies and gentlemen, let us stop our merrymaking to remember that at this hour in the jails of the land those who had more courage than we joymakers are lying on their stony pillows." He could see himself with his face blazing with indignation. He had never had a chance to play a decent rôle. But he had longed to write plays with decent rôles for others. His wife could not understand the crazy impulse that had sent him to New York, long before he met her, to hang around the theater, taking a prompter's job, just to find out how it was done. The wooden things he'd tried to write were still locked up in the attic. They never came to life and he himself had never really come to life. His job at the university was just a mouthing compared to what he felt inside of himself. He was a man locked within a man. What could ever set him free? He looked around at the dancers hopping past him in genial oblivion. The Iron Woman was sipping a little punch beside him, enjoying herself, her capacity for hatred endowing her with great powers for pleasure, sipping away, nodding to the better looking of the young men. "As I told you, my boy, I never have and never shall go back on you-know-who," she said, as Barney lumbered up, looking worried. "Say Diogenes, old kid, have you seen Vic?"

Diogenes jerked his finger cruelly toward the window. "She's out there," he said, proud of himself for once in his life speaking up and not sidestepping. "She's in the plaza."

"And what might you be, young man?" said Mrs. Blackstone, craning to see all around the sweat shirt to Barney's rear. "Guess," said Barney.

"Oh I'm not good at that sort of thing, I can't imagine."

"He's an Inferiority Complex," said Diogenes.

"Goodness, as if there weren't too many already. What's come over the young men? Take my advice, and forget that kind of morbidity. Inferiority Complex. Why, you're much too nice to be afflicted that way, young man. Forget it. Take my advice, forget it." She shook her head at Barney and as he moved away, laughing a little weakly, she whirled on Diogenes. "This party depresses me. I never saw such people to take the starch out of living. Give me a nice old home for cripples, they've got more zest. They really have. Think over what I said, my dear. Be like me." She thumped her chest again and getting to her feet, made a direct charge toward the door before Diogenes could stop her.

The trip home was not very lively. Old Lady Hubbard sulked because she had been ignored all evening and Barney was paying too much attention to Vicky who thought to herself that the only reason he was exerting himself was because he had seen her with that other boy. Diogenes was silent beside the even more silent Lady Macbeth and only Socrates commented in his kindly voice about the evening.

"Did they make any money?" said Diogenes, rousing himself.

"Not much," said Barney. "The darn hall cost so much, then advertising, the music and so on. I don't think they made more than twenty dollars."

"My God," said Diogenes. He squirmed uncomfortably. "Why it would have been better to take up a collection," he said.

"Oh no, Rey, you got to figure on the publicity value."

"Yes, but if you don't get any returns, I don't see what good it is."

"You're in too much of a hurry, that's all," said Barney comfortably.

"You got to remember people don't live forever," said Rey, "especially if they haven't any money to live on." He slouched down in his corner, feeling thoroughly disagreeable and the pleasing voice of Socrates counseling patience, grated like chalk on a blackboard.

"You're not talking much," he said to Vic, just to be saying something. "About as much as Nelly," said Vic smiling at Lady Macbeth. Socrates kept up a steady kindly chatter until the taxicab stopped at Vicky's place and she insisted on hopping out alone.

In a few minutes she was in bed and in a few hours she would be up again and off to the office with a darn fresh rose for the vase. The party was already a thing of the past, its memory sagging like a broken arm. They hadn't even made money. Talk, talk, talk, that's all they did. No matter what the party was, she was always back in this room, as tight as a box. Riding in the cab with the Blums, she had longed to shout some bad word. They were all so nice. Barney was such a gentleman. No wonder she occasionally liked a rough neck like Rand Natches. He knew what a moon is for, that's one thing you could say for him. If the girls back in

Oxtail could see her now, they wouldn't think that the only thing she was, was "smart." Victoria Wendel is such a bright girl, but Rosamond is just lovely. No wonder she never wanted to see Oxtail again. Now she was feeling the same way about San Francisco and the whole Bay region. What a silly she had been to think that college could mean very much. Maybe if you were straight from a nice home, it would mean more. But she had been working for three years, teaching in a country school, making fires with the thermometer below zero, *Oh teacher, a tramp has been here again and broke another window getting in.* Then Hides and Furs: *I'll pay you thirteen cents for that muskrat, not a cent more* (you're a good buyer kid, go to it). Then dictation (Oxtail Credit Ass'n.): If we do not receive payment we will begin suit at once. But Mr. Berry, he's written, *Dear sirs, they have taken the shop away from me, the balloon has went up.* The whole squeeze-a-penny-and-you-make-a-dime didn't develop respect, and what if the professor of Political Science was a brother-in-law of President Wilson. His calm gentlemanly exposition of The State and Duty toward the State, what did it really mean? Who was his State? Well might she ask and herself feeling as lost as a drop of water in an ocean. The year she had worked for so long, was over. *The balloon has went up.* She was back in harness again, taking dictation, saving money. Always saving, as if there was nothing else in the world to do. Barney had seen her in the plaza with Rand but it didn't mean anything; he had ridden off with his whole family. Caseman had gone away. She had run into him that very afternoon and he had walked along with her, his hat in his hand, making fun of the party. "Why, bless you, they won't make a red cent, at least not much, they never do, it's run for them, not for the political prisoners, this washes them clean, a kind of catharsis." He had been right, the thing was a flop. Everywhere talk and pity, pity, pity, until it made her feel as hard as nails. Nancy and Clara had always complained how hard she and Rosamond were. They hadn't cried at the movies, they laughed at Clara's long courting telephone conversations with Donald. When Clara had spent hours every night for months burning a leather toilet set for Donald, only to ruin it, she and Rosamond had sympathized but in the end they had laughed, they had to, she looked funny with her poor little red nose all cried up. Nancy had scolded them for hardboiled brats. Caseman was on the train at this minute; he wasn't like Barney, he was different, yet she probably would never see him again.

Tomorrow she would go to the office with another fresh rose. "Goodmorning Mr. Rinklemeyer, Goodmorning Mr. Trumbal, Goodmorning Mr. Drayton." No wonder she had taken a course in beekeeping at the university. At least you used your hands. It was something to be able to lift comb honey and brood out of a hive, to let bees crawl an inch thick over wrists and not wink an eyelash. She wouldn't mind having a hundred hives to watch, break out worker cells to make a queen, lay in the royal jelly, close it up with tweezers and a bit of wax. If she had a cow to milk or some ducks to feed. She was so lonesome for something real. No wonder people huddled in families and spent their lives feeding and caring for one another. It was no fun alone at Mrs. Beeger's, going every day with a fresh rose, doing little nonsensical tasks and reading scraps of law books that were all about property or crime. A lot of windy empty words that made even a simple transfer of a house a long deadly process. No wonder the Wobblies were always yelling for direct action. But Caseman said you can't work it that way. He was heading north, so he said, "into trouble." Trouble would be a godsend. Trouble would be fine. Anything would be good except sitting around day after day waiting for a dinner invitation to the Blums' and hearing the same old talk, talk, talk. Trouble, she loved trouble. Why, when she was a baby in arms, the neighbors used to call her Little Pugilist. She was always trying to batter away at someone. Anything but sitting with a fresh rose.

If she was in Seattle now, she could save more money. Rosamond and Nancy were there, they could take a place together. Here she was talking of saving money again, after she was sick to death of it those three years she'd been saving to go back to college. Oh, but it was good to be saving for something. To have something to live for, outside yourself. Like Caseman. If she could talk to him again. Going north, he said, into trouble.

There was something healthy about trouble. Why, all the troubles that their family had headed into had not dragged them down so much as just sticking a rose in a vase dragged her down, day after day. How many would it be in a year now? Enough to make a fine funeral blanket to throw over a casket.

"How about tomorrow night," Rand Natches had said. "We could go somewhere, dance, do something." If she hadn't suddenly felt finished with the whole Bay region, it would be fun. But fun didn't prevent you from putting roses on the desk every day. Rand was just a nice boy. When she was a kid hearing the train whistles she had more good sense. The trains talked straight. Get going. Move along. And in Seattle she could save some money, think about what to do next. Plan. The word plan fused up in her mind like a little firecracker, it burst and spattered like the kind that went off damply and surprised you while you still held on to them. Plan, what plan? Her mother was full of plans, she had ideas of making money by selling the White Elephant, of sending them each a hundred dollars from Uncle Aaron's estate, of all of them riding around and around in a little car. She could see herself sitting with the others, still feeling out of the picture. Oh for something *real*. For love, like she could feel in her bones existed somewhere, for something that took you along like a great river.

Well, at least, she had thirty-five dollars in the bank, twenty-two seventy-three in her pocketbook and that was enough. She did not even bother to call at the office the next day, let the old rose wither; she hauled out her money, had the pleasure of hearing Barney's voice start over the phone as she said crisply and with, she hoped, mystery, "I'm off, to Seattle!" "How long will you be gone?" "Always, I'm not coming back." "Hy Vic, what's the matter?" "Goodbye, and good luck," she had said, giggling suddenly, hanging up the receiver and heading for the train. As the train crossed the border she wired Mr. Trumbal, CALLED SUDDENLY SEATTLE SORRY LETTER FOLLOWS.

The letter never followed. It was worth two days' wages left behind, just to be free of the rose.

THE SIDE LINES

Anne Wendel was very pleased to hear that all the exiles were at last together in one spot. If the younger ones got sick, Nancy would be at hand and it was always safest to have a man around. She looked forward to the time when the family could be together again in Oxtail, not that she ever hoped to keep the two youngest there for good. Sally was causing trouble and she was waiting to see what that woman intended to do about her dower rights in the old homestead. It all depended on Sally's age. If she was under 47 she should get 20 per cent, if over, 15 per cent. Sally was being ridiculous and pretending to be 47. Anne would have to do some sleuth work and dig up her brother's marriage license in Philadelphia.

She went out to look over the three lots in South Vineland, taking as much pleasure in the excursion as if it had been a picnic. The sun was so pleasant and the blackberry bushes on her land were full and ripe with berries. Italian children were busy picking, watching her with sharp black eyes. She sat down on a boulder, took out a little pie she had brought along and slowly ate, enjoying every crumb. No one would know what fun it was to sit on her very own land and to look at the bushes and grass and wonder if they would become part of a house when the property was sold. She would sell it, of course; she could not afford to own it. The money would help fix up the White Elephant and she could sell that and make them all happy. Such a warm happy feeling filled her at the very idea that all her calculations stopped with the mere selling. To sell was enough, to have some money in her hands so she could do a few of the things she had always longed to do, maybe go to the Black Hills where Joe had lived or to that town of New Glarus in Wisconsin that her father had located so many years before.

The good that was sure to flow out of the money seemed to flow

out of the earth as she sat on the boulder eating her little pie. She
thought that now she could help her children get the right start and
guide their lives into useful rich channels. Crumbs from the pie
dropped to her lap; she brushed them off and they fell to the
ground where a little bird pecked at them with his bright beak.

Their mother's plans and optimism were an old story to the
Wendel girls. Long ago they had laughed and agreed that Mamma
would never sell the White Elephant. They had said it bitterly,
when they were forced to contribute for its upkeep during the years
when the two youngest wanted to save for college. The White
Elephant had never been a cheap monster, it had housed them but
it was always demanding paint and repairs. Plumbing went wrong,
the furnace didn't work. It was a constant worry and care. Long
ago Vicky and Rosamond had shelved the White Elephant as a
possible gold mine. If it made Mamma happy, that was all that
could be expected. But wages were so high in Seattle that winter,
until after the soldiers began coming back and gutting the market
with cheap labor, that the girls saved month by month. Even
Nancy and Clifford saved, and Clifford began talking vaguely of
getting a little business of his own, maybe buying into an automo-
bile agency.

The armistice had let everyone down and, in the boarding house
out near the university where the sisters and Clifford had breakfast
and dinner, a suspicious nagging crept into the conversation that
had been open and gay before the bells rang all night and crowds
heaved in the downtown streets yelling and happy. A few business
couples eating at the place talked sourly of leaving before the ship
yards quit and business began flattening out. Students in the
R.O.T.C. felt cheated that they had not got into the excitement.
The boarding house lady Mrs. Caspar was worried because now
she could not keep on indefinitely telling the story that Mr. Caspar
was east on "war work." Sooner or later he would have to return or
the boarders would continually wonder why. She would rather
drop dead than admit that he had just run off with a stenographer.
She would protect her children, if she had to send her husband to
Austria, and get him shot, to do it.

Sometimes after a hard day with all her muscles aching she

would sit rocking upstairs, seeing herself a widow, in decent black, peered at from behind the neighbor's sympathetic window curtains. "Poor Papa," she would say, showing that handsome scamp's photo that stood in a frame that cost three dollars on the parlor table. If she died for it, she'd keep up her pride and the boarding house was good; business people paid better than students and it was only because she could see the time when they would be leaving that she got so provoked at those two Wendel girls, the single one and that married one, Mrs. Stauffer, for always starting arguments at the table. Still, the men liked it, they fired up and got excited the way you'd think only a leg show would affect them. It was a lesson to her and she felt sometimes as if immorality was going on right at the table when those two girls would start at it, bold as brass, criticizing the world. And the worst was the way they came out defending those Bolsheviks in Russia. Oh what a high-handed way to do things. You'd think they'd show some discretion. The way the war made girls carry on was a caution. If it wasn't running outright with men, it was flaunting opinions that did credit to no decent woman, right in the faces of a whole table of the young and innocent. Why they had the nerve, those girls, to laugh at what everyone knows is true; everyone knows that the revolution was just to nationalize women, so as to give them license. Liberty was one thing, license was another, and she certainly approved of the way the government was rounding up loose talkers and suspicious characters. Cigarette smoking was one thing she did not approve of in a lady and she had seen, with her two eyes, those two girls on the front porch with two of the best boys, one of them a young lieutenant, smoking. All she could say was that, try as she might, she couldn't help making her spine a little stiffer when she served them their pie after that. A girl with her husband at the front—and the other one, who knows how far she carried her high talk?

It was all right as long as people were still singing songs and feeling all bound together in a great common purpose like the war; she could tolerate a little of that then perhaps, a little talk and so on but now that she felt so terribly let down, with Papa a constant worry and the fear that any day people might begin to insist, "But when is Mr. Caspar coming home from his war work, Mrs. Caspar," her nerves were on edge and she was in no condition to handle a big strike. No indeed. The flu had been bad enough, with one fatality right in the house and several days going by with not more than two boarders showing up at that long table. No one could say she had shirked, she'd been on her feet early and late. Feeding people was no joke, but add to that nursing the sick and you had a bill of requirements that would shake an ox. And she was no ox, thank you, in spite of her heavy build. She could see, bit by bit, her boarding table split up, first arguments, then high wrangling tones about the Fourteen Points. What a mistake that was, as if we shouldn't punish those Huns, punish them so they couldn't rise again. Why, there was one evening when she had waited in the kitchen absolutely trembling with the pudding in her hand ready to throw it at that Victoria Wendel when she had gone on about the kind of peace that would only make another future war. Prison was too good for a girl like that. What did she know about anything? Wait until her husband walked out right under her nose with a frippery stenographer, and what did she have that his own wife didn't have, what, I ask you? She'd been a good wife, never one to say no to anything, no matter how tired. And what a reward. She clattered the dishes now, glancing over her shoulder at the cook. The roast beef was too rare, the salad lacked that dab of mayonnaise. She was as tired of that dab as of her old hat but what else was there? She watched the plates go into the babbling room and waited.

"What they talking about tonight?" she said, when Clarence came out in his white coat.

"The strike."

"Is there going to be one?" said Mrs. Caspar.

"You bet your life," said Clarence, stacking up the soup plates and arming himself with the roast beef.

"What's that? Clarence Upstone," said Mrs. Caspar. "What ails you? Why, those men have no right to strike, just selfish, that's all. What right have they? Do I strike? No, I have to go on, day after day, slaving away. Of course," she amended quickly so that he wouldn't get suspicious, "I'm glad to do it, it keeps me busy while my husband is at his war work. I'm glad to contribute to my country." He had gone into the dining room and the voices had subsided with the appearance of food.

When he came out again, she rinsed her plump arms and began arranging the desert. "What is that they're saying? Is there going to be a strike? Oh, we are in for it. Me, in a business like this, with a general strike." She looked at him scared and furious. "What do they say in there?"

"They don't know anything," said Clarence. "Nobody does but the strikers. The papers say it's pretty bad, food will be scarce, lights will go off. . . . "

"Ooh," said Mrs. Caspar. "Lights. Oh, we'll have robbers and thugs running around breaking in, nothing will be safe, nothing." She clutched her breasts, whirling around to the cupboard. "Coffee, beans, sugar, prunes, flour, eggs, why it will take every cent I've got and can scrape together to lay in food. And lights. Oooh. What can we do?"

"Kerosene," said Clarence cheerfully, hoping they would strike with a vengeance, strike hard, strike Mrs. Caspar and all her kind who were thick-headed and hard of heart. Why, she had bickered with him about his meals and always gave him the leftovers and even tried to slip leftover food from the boarders' plates onto his if he didn't keep an eye open. No wonder her old man had dished her. War work. Pretty good. You had to call it something. He snickered.

"What's that?" said Mrs. Caspar, whirling at him. "I hope I didn't hear a laugh. I surely hope not in a time like this."

"I was only trying to keep from sneezing, I think I'm catching a cold, Mrs. Caspar," said Clarence.

"Take those drops I gave you, I can't afford colds around here not after that siege of flu. If I had to live through that again, I'd say, bury me. But this strike, Clarence, are you *sure*. What right have they? Suppose I struck, what would happen? Can I give myself such a luxury, no, I have to work." She clattered the plates and Clarence began arming himself ready to charge into the dining room. "Give that to those Wendel girls," said Mrs. Caspar indicating two plates with slightly smaller puddings and less sauce. "I miscalculated and it didn't quite hold out." Clarence shouldering his burden pushed into the dining room and plunked the two stingy portions down in front of Mr. and Mrs. Granger. Mrs. Granger eyed her portion critically and sniffed slightly, whispering to Mr. Granger. The Granger portions were placed carefully before Victoria and Rosamond.

"Begin eating," whispered Clarence to Victoria, "before the old lady sticks her nose in the door." Victoria and Rosamond took big bites and when Mrs. Caspar breezed in with, "Everything all right, folks?" Rosamond spoke up with the rest, "Just fine, thank you, Mrs. Caspar."

After dinner Mrs. Caspar asked advice from everyone as to the strike and the boarders were practically agreed that it was plain greed and selfishness that led to strike talk. The Wendel girls and Nancy and Clifford put their wraps on and left without a word. Outside Nancy said, "Can't you two girls be a little more tactful? About this strike particularly. Everyone is worried and worked up, why do you rub it in? I don't think you girls ought to take out your personal grievances on the boarding house like that."

"I don't even know what you mean," said Victoria.

"Yes, you do," said Nancy. "You're just sore because things didn't turn out the way you liked in San Francisco, I know all about it, that Barney and his family acting so slow, and Rosamond is upset about Jerry. But you girls ought to learn tact. Neither of you used to be this way except that you always were provoking, both of you. Why, when Clara and I used to come home with fellows you darned kids would be at the window flattening your noses."

"I suppose the ship yards men are mad at their sweeties and that's why they are striking," said Rosamond. "I suppose that's it, isn't it, Clifford?"

"That's another thing altogether," said Nancy virtuously, galloping a little ahead of the rest as they came to a corner. "Quite another thing. You girls aren't ship yards workers. Why do you have to stick on their side for? With a whole city against them. I can't understand it." She felt grieved as if they had insulted her personally and spoiled her chances for fun.

"Why don't you read the Seattle *Union Record* instead of the P-I then and maybe you'd find out," said Vicky.

"*That* paper," said Clifford, laughing.

"Oh laugh," said Rosamond hooking her arm into Vicky's. The street lights paled and the street ahead under the dark trees was very black and shiny.

"Look, the lights are going out, see them blink," said Nancy, taking an extra skip. Something was going to happen at last. "What if the whole place goes dark?"

"We bought candles this afternoon," said Vicky. But the lights were already coming back strong. Then they flickered. Somewhere in the power house someone was about to turn off the lights.

Nancy and Clifford went one way, Rosamond and Vicky another. At their rooming house, their landlady Mrs. Parks had a row of candles waiting on the hall table. "Did you see those lights flicker? I don't know what we're coming to," she said cheerfully. "Oh we're certain to see trouble."

Trouble. Everyone talking of trouble. Caseman had headed north into "trouble." Like as not he was in this city and knew all about the strike. It was more than the two girls knew. Some said it was a protest against sending munitions to Siberia, some said it was against a wage cut, some said it was just plain cussedness on the part of labor. The two girls could only climb the stairs and sit down in their rooms, read a book, darn a few stockings. Outside a rain began gently on the heavy expensive window pane. The Parks had built a very good house. They had put all of Mrs. Parks's little inheritance into their home. The roomers slept on the best beds and paid good prices too. The only thing was that the radiators rarely were as hot as they should be. Mrs. Parks saved on the heat. The house took a great deal of fuel and was, all in all, a Great Expense. Still, it was worth it. What else did they have? "Our little home is all we have," Mrs. Parks often explained. That very afternoon she had laid in a store of food, plenty of candles. Thousands of housewives and hotel keepers and restaurant keepers did the same. Little stores did a sudden business in oldtime kerosene lamps. Every now and then the lights flickered but did not go out.

The rain changed to snow and a soft persistent snow fell for twenty hours. It fell along the street car tracks and piled in little ridges, then it smoothed over into soft drifts. Mrs. Caspar's boarders struggled out into the snow, grieved and sore at the weather. It was another sign from heaven that everything was against them. At a time like this, with returned soldiers beginning to straggle in for jobs, it wasn't safe to stay home. If you got a cut, you took it. What a nerve those ship yards guys had to strike against a cut. Everyone else was getting it in the neck, why not them? The little bevy from Mrs. Caspar's straggled out, grumbling and comparing notes. In the midst of falling snow, scab trucks and jitneys slid alongside charging fifty cents for the ride.

Nancy Radford had been so embarrassed at her sisters the evening before that she went without her breakfast rather than face the boarding house crew. Rosamond and Vicky ate in a stony silence. By evening Nancy decided to face the boarding house again but she asked the girls as a personal favor please not to make themselves conspicuous. The entire table was grimly waiting for terrible events. Someone said chopped glass would be put into food. Poison would be poured in the city water supply.

"I've spiked that," said Mrs. Caspar. "We won't drink a living death in this house. I've filled every bathtub and every utensil in sight. Hardly had a thing left to cook with tonight."

"No baths then," said Mr. Draper.

"No baths, Mr. Draper, if you want water to drink."

Clarence in his white coat, the two Wendel girls, and a young man with a suspicion of baldness looked at one another, Victoria snickered, the young man winked. Clarence dodged into the kitchen.

"In my day when a young girl talked as free as those girls, we knew where to place her. Nice girls didn't talk like that, in my day," said Mrs. Caspar. "Mr. Caspar wouldn't like to hear such talk in this house, not with him away on patriotic war work. I shudder to think of what he would do if he were here." She shrugged her shoulders, a little more certain of herself. That very afternoon she had read a long piece about war work in Austria and how workers were being sent over to Hungary and Armenia to take charge of relief. When she had digested the article she could begin

her new story about Papa. Would it be better to send him to
Armenia or Vienna? Probably Armenia, it sounded very remote
and anything might happen.

Clarence dropped a pan. Mrs. Caspar jumped and looked angry.
"My nerves, goodness no wonder, with revolution in our midst." A
loud report from the street brought a little scream from highstrung
Mrs. Galveston. "It's only a blowout," said Mr. Draper sarcastically. "Don't worry, we've got plenty of water to drink."

The lights were going strong. The street cars hadn't been running for hours. The power plant was said to be in the hands of the
enemy.

"What enemy?" said Rosamond.

"Why the strikers, of course," said Mr. Draper. "Strikers and
strikes should be outlawed."

"Enemy to *you*, Mr. Draper," said Rosamond sweetly.

"The newspapers print lies. It's all lies about the ground glass,
they just say that to get people worked up."

"I suppose you have Inside Information," said Mrs. Galveston in
an angry voice.

"I know it isn't true," said Vicky, "and I know something about
newspapers, I knew some newspaper people," she bragged trying to
make what she said sound important and impressive, "in San
Francisco and they told me that news isn't always the truth by any
means." She looked from one angry doubting face to another.
"What are you so sore about? The men on strike never hurt you,
why do you act so mad at them?" Mr. Granger winked at Mr.
Draper. In his opinion modern girls put themselves forward
entirely too much.

"Well, Miss Wendel," said Mr. Draper, "we've got water in this
house anyhow. We are loaded up with enough water to fill an
elephant, so why worry?"

"Talking of worry," spoke up Grandma Elkins, "I was worried
sick this afternoon when I thought little Freddie had swallowed a
button. One minute he was playing with my workbasket and the
next the button was in his mouth. I thought sure he'd swallowed it,
but it turned up later."

Talk drifted away from the strike and the Wendel girls, who

were marooned, took themselves off for a walk in the rain. "Do you think Jerry will ever come home again?" said Rosamond. "I feel awful. The boarding house hates us and the strikers don't even know we exist. We might as well be on an island."

"I know I'm sick of the rain," said Victoria. "We might as well be wax flowers under glass. Why weren't we old enough to get sent overseas to see things? Seems to me we're always stuck in the wrong place. How much money you got saved?"

"About ninety dollars," said Rosamond. "Why?"

"Oh nothing," said Vicky. "I was just thinking."

THE SCISSORBILLS

Amos Wendel belonged to that large class of individuals designated in the daily newspaper cartoons as Mr. Average Citizen, Mr. Voter, or sometimes as Mr. Consumer, and always pictured as small, inept, with a scared face, skinny body and a hat too big for the head. Mr. Wendel did not have a scared face. Although he had failed in business, he had a calm clear skin and mild clear blue eyes. An old-fashioned moustache hid a mouth, that, in his boyhood pictures taken in Pennsylvania when his father was still owner of a very prosperous farm, was sensitive and lacked the fighting quality that his brother-in-law Joe Trexler had, in a boyhood picture taken at about the same time.

Amos Wendel had never had the fire of ambition that had driven Joe Trexler to the South and the Black Hills. He had instead a kind of stubborn resistance to ill-fortune. When he lost his business in 1914 he was only a jump ahead of countless others. Fifteen years later, when he was almost at the end of his life, he had plenty of company. He was even better off than the new recruits, for he had by that time adjusted himself pretty well and he had been earning money steadily as a worker for fifteen years.

He had had to make no great change in his way of life when he started working for Bryant Brothers instead of himself. As a business man, seller of farm machinery, he had never been enough of a success to put on many airs. He had never achieved a stiff white collar and black suit at work like Mr. Carlton, who set up an implement store in the same block, cleaned up on real estate, and shot himself when the whistle finally blew.

With Amos Wendel, it was easy sailing in a way. He had worked pretty hard, had been always on the run, working on machinery and repairing it; he was a first-rate mechanic. He kept his hands in shape with a good grease soap but his table manners had long ago taken on the easy edge of the farm trade. When the boys came to town they always had lunch with Amos at Sommer's Saloon, the cleanest place in town, or at Ma Baumgarten's joint where the apfelmuss and the hasenpfeffer were the best ever. If Amos forgot and occasionally used a knife for a fork in his home, it wasn't out of disrespect for his wife and girls but because the longer he lived the more like his associates he became. He had begun life on a farm and, when his feet touched farm soil, he forgot that he was the man who should get a note for the new plow or foreclose on the harrow. The fields looked wonderful, the corn was prime, or the frost had ruined crops that needed two weeks more weather. He would stand, feet apart, skinny strong legs in baggy pants, lips pursed on an old pipe, fairly eating up the look of the land. If it hadn't been for his wife always craving town advantages for the girls, he would have taken a flier years before at farming again and would have fared about like the rest of them.

In 1919, a good many of Amos's old customers were cheerful for the first time in their lives, although no one had much more jack. Old Man Bronson was buying another hundred acres, the Ericson boys were tying up with a good 300, the Pattersons, father and son, were building a new silo and investing in tractors to take care of their swollen acres. A lot of the boys were talking of buying farms, and quitting renting, and some of the old timers who had been squatting on good land that was bought for a song in the old days, were selling out at the fancy prices and beating it for sunny California.

"Well Amos, how about you and me beatin' it for sunny California?" said Gus, the helper at the Bryant Warehouse, as he and Amos loaded the trucks for the Brackwood outfit.

"Wouldn't be bad, would it?" said Amos a little sharply. He didn't like to talk on the job, it took wind, and besides, with the war over, there wasn't a day but a young fellow in a soldier suit came nosing around asking for work. An old fellow had to keep spry or he'd get the can. He'd got a cut as it was.

"Oranges," said Gus, "sunshine, palm trees, ocean waves, flower in winter, oranges. . . ." He stopped, recognizing that he had said that once, drew a hand across his forehead, removed his hat and carefully wiped the sweaty band. "Oranges," he repeated as if they griped him worst of all. "Know what we pay for them, sixty cents a dozen. My wife has to have them, the doctor says, but sixty cents, holy smoke. The good ones."

"I saw some little fellows for forty," said Amos, resting a moment.

"No juice in those buggers. We tried them out. They're a sell. No sir, know what my brother told me? Oranges rotting all over the damn state out there, laying there like pebbles, rotting. He saw that in California, saw apples rot in Washington, saw peaches rot in Michigan, saw them dump watermelon in the Mississippi. What do you think of it? And he's smart too, he'll be here if the Legion lets them come. Why not, Wobblies are Americans ain't they?"

Amos looked warily across the big warehouse floor toward the office, but Gus wasn't a loud talker and he was speaking quietly now. The newspapers had kept fireworks going for weeks about the I.W.W. Amos read the two town papers regularly every night, and, while they differed on some situations, on the I.W.W. they were alike as two peas.

Only last night he had read how action was going to be taken to save Oxtail from becoming a harbor for I.W.W. Several labor leaders said it was the city council's duty to censure the mayor, who was going to let them meet if he had his way, and another labor leader had said the mayor was not the only culprit, several Oxtail employers had given work to I.W.W.

Amos was chewing this editorial in his mind, as Gus talked. "He's a real guy, Ed is, he's a fighter," said Gus. "I got tied up with my family or I'd be right with him. First it was my older brother's family, it was Frank's wife that tied me up. When he got killed, she had to have help until she married again. Then I put my own neck in the noose, not that it ain't nice, nine times out of ten, but wait till you see Ed, you'll think you've missed living. He doesn't live the life of Riley, either, get me, he knocks around, fights, works, knows everything. Why say, I've heard that kid talking how they beat their way from Portland to Chicago ten years ago, saved $800 railroad fare and sold songs and took up collections, passing the hat. When they got there they had $175.13. Think of that. They went like a wind over this damned country; to hear him talk was like hearing a conductor calling out railroad stations. It made you feel you were a fool not to get on the train. He'd tell about Little Falls, Lawrence, Wheatland, the Masaba Range. Last time he was here he just got out of jail." Gus lowered his voice and looked around carefully, took out a chaw of tobacco and bit a hunk, rewrapped the hunk in a handkerchief, put it slowly in his hip pocket, went on. "He was in all right for not getting in the war and they'd had fights all up and down the coast, Fresno, San Diego, Seattle, and Everett." As he said the names, Gus singsonged in a conductor's voice, his head lifted chanting. "He sat in our kitchen, I can see him with his big legs crossed and sucking away at one of my corncobs and singing out those names, jesus, it made me so mad to think I'd sunk my life. There comes a time when it sours, it's no good, Maud and me quarreled more when he was there than in our whole lives before or since. Seemed as if I couldn't stand it, feeling tied to apron strings. Fresno, San Diego, Little Falls, Butte. Yes, at Butte something pretty terrible happened, they strung up a lame man and ripped out his balls the goddamned lice, I can see Ed turn purple talking of it, and he could tell stories about more parts of this country and more people, say, you and me is dead men compared to him."

"We can't all be like that, where'd the population be, how'd the work get done?" said Amos, but he was stirred up in spite of himself. It was lucky his two youngest girls weren't boys; they did enough hell raising as it was, god knows what they'd have done if they'd been boys. He felt that Gus was exaggerating, too. Those guys lived a hard life, lice, bugs, no good food. "They get rotten meals, Gus."

"No rottener than most of us, I bet you, and say about work, don't let them fool you. They're the workers of the world, those boys, those stiffs from Washington and Oregon, guess you never seen those boys, why they could throw five of you and me," said Gus, " and as for work, I know Ed, he's a demon for work. He worked old man Silver's farm, you know that old cuss, mean as you make them, but even he gives the palm to Ed, says he's the best hired man he ever fed. Said so the other day when he was in here gassin' and puttin' on airs because he's so chummy with banker Hollis, say, he thinks he's so smart because his credit's good. Take another five hundred Mr. Silver this Hollis says, why, you need a new roof to your barn, your farm needs more modern equipment, a thousand's as easy to get as five hundred. Are they so lousy with dough they have to beg you to take it, I asks him. Oh no, he smirks, it's only to us farmers who are a good investment. Good investment. What farm land ain't good at this minute, but how long will it last? I've seen good times come and go again. I says to Silver, time'll tell if it's a good investment, but he was the worst patronizing old halfass I ever see, he says, now Gus, he says, you ain't so smart. You'd have started up a little business for yourself long ago, says he, and be your own boss. I was so mad I could have knocked his nose off, but I didn't, just swallowed my cud, that's all, I was so mad at him and his superior airs at getting so chummy with Hollis. I bet you Ed would have been able to pay him out, like that," he stretched his arm out and flicked a finger at an imaginary fly.

Amos said, "We'd better get going here, Bryant will be coming around soon. Get busy, you got the gift of the gab Gus even if you never got a little business started and considering I lost my business, seems to me you weren't so dumb. We're in the same boat, only you got there without so much trouble, that's all."

When Amos Wendel picked up his paper from his front porch that evening the headlines were still about the menace of the

Industrial Workers of the World. Mayor Handy was putting up a stiff fight.

Not that Amos thought any too highly of the mayor. There was something doubtful about a fellow who had been preacher in a regular church, then in a labor church, then mayor. He still talked the language of the pews and it was Amos's experience that the majority didn't think anymore about religion than he did. It bothered him to hear the mayor mix labor and the soul. The fellow was well meaning and sincere according to his lights but he wasn't going to get over what he meant, that was certain. No one quite knew what he was driving at. He wasn't a church man anymore and he wasn't a laboring man. He just hung there, holding out his hopes and they didn't seem to fit in.

This convention business sure got the newspaper's goat. To read, you'd think barbarian hordes were on their way. Amos had never got very close to any of the movements that stirred the town. They were generated higher up than he stood. The big fellows, the Meyers, the Brackwoods, the Troys and Mellers, those were the boys, with their hands in their pockets on a lookout against strikes, that hated the Wobblies. Why, he knew dozens of Wobblies. Off and on they were sure to bob up on any farm. They were pretty certain to be good help once they learned the ropes. Like as not they'd got themselves on some black list in town and took to the farm as a last resort. They'd work hard, catch on quick, but not stand the long hours as patiently as your fellow with hopes of a family and owning a place of his own. Don't know as you could blame them. Nowadays there weren't many farm hands graduated to farms and, when they did, it was harder picking than in the old days.

Amos's evenings at home were mostly the same, a quiet lonely supper, maybe he would eat at his daughter's for a change but her four kids were rambunctious and got on his nerves. After supper, the dishes, then the paper and a letter to his wife or one of the girls. He was certainly taken off his feet a couple nights after Gus's tirade, when he heard steps on the porch and someone call, "Hello Papa," and if there weren't Rosamond and Vic. A man can take a lot of pride in two handsome full-grown girls, and he felt pretty set-up at their stylish clothes and ways.

"What you two doing here?" he said, blushing and smiling.

"Papa, you look better than when we were here, I believe you like it better alone," Vic said, coming in and taking in the neat rooms with an eye. There were his socks all washed out by hand and hung over a chair back. The dishes put away. "When is mother coming home, she's gadding enough to last a lifetime."

"Pshaw," said Amos, "your mother's got more ideas than a cranberry merchant. I don't know what she's up to, some trouble now in getting Sally to release her dower right to the homestead and then you know Mamma. She'll find things to do where no one else could, and she's got some notion she can make money buying tax property and then we can all ride around like Rockefeller."

It was certainly nice to have the girls home. They were all over the place airing out the rooms and he couldn't keep track of their plans. Seemed that Rosamond was on her way to Detroit hoping that Jerry would soon turn up from overseas. As for Vic, she'd her mind set on going to New York, he couldn't figure out why.

"Say, my girls have got your brother Ed beat a mile. They track all over the country like pigeons," he boasted to Gus.

"Yeah," said Gus. "Say, they ought to meet up. Ed's coming all right, got a card from him from Sheridan, Wyoming, he'll be here any day now. Do you think they'll make trouble for the boys here?"

He looked worried. He wasn't only worried for Ed but his wife had been nagging him since she read the papers that a movement was on foot to drive the I.W.W. out of Oxtail.

"Public Safety demands this action. A crime wave always follows an I.W.W. convention. They are a band of criminals preaching anarchy and overthrow. The only way to insure safety of our women and children is to nip the movement in the bud. Run them clean out of town. They are the riffraff of humanity, refuse to work and are leeches and parasites."

His wife had read the whole bloody paragraph out loud to him. "What about it?" she said. "Now it's bad enough to give the kids a black eye with your coming home drunk last week. What will the neighbors think of us now if your brother Ed comes with his loud ways and his singing? Why, the last time he came and brought his hoodlums up here they were bursting their lungs until four in the morning, keeping respectable neighbors awake. And let me tell you," she went on, shaking the cup in her hand which she was about to refill with coffee, "let me tell you, I've my hands full without anymore of that. You'll be getting fired, if they hear of it at Bryant's, and then what?"

"Oh shoosh with it, a lot of hot air, don't you know better than to always be reading them papers? Full of lies."

"Full of lies? Listen to him," she wailed holding out her arm oratorically and appealing to the baby in his highchair. "Listen to your father, as if he were the fount of truth."

"I'll stand for a lot," said Gus, rising suddenly and approaching threateningly, "but about Ed, shut up. We're lice compared to Ed. Lice. The papers are filth. If you are stubborn and so set you can't know the reason the papers are riding them, when you know those fellows've gone through hell while I've been sitting here every night taking it easy smoking my pipe. Oh you make me want to wring your neck," he stopped, astonished at his vehemence as was his wife. She calmly began wiping the cup she had intended to refill with coffee, and placed it on the shelf.

"Don't get upset now, I didn't mean anything only for your good," she said, placatingly. "And do try to keep things a little quiet here when Ed comes. There's no use advertising everything to the neighbors."

"To hell with the neighbors," he said slamming out of the house. But it worried him.

"What do you think, Amos?" he said.

"The mayor's a sensible man but he hasn't got much power, that is, the legion and chamber of commerce and it looks as if the labor union leaders are all against him, but you don't hear people as a whole holding anything against the I.W.W. coming here. It's only in the papers, seems to me. Say, did you see that writeup calling them the 'I Want Whiskeys'?"

"No, I didn't," said Gus, "but I bet my wife did. She's an eagle's eye for that kind of thing. You know, Amos, Ed's had a couple of tough breaks since I seen him last. I'm real anxious to see him this time. He'll talk your arm off. You ought to come up to the house and bring the girls. Say, would you now? You know the wife would take it all right about Ed if your girls showed up, she'd think the thing was all o.k. That's the kind she is," he said bitterly, looking at Amos hopefully.

Amos stuffed his pipe with tobacco slowly, puffing judiciously and looking at Gus as if he were considering the proposition. Inside he was terribly pleased that Gus considered it such an honor to have the girls. If only the girls would go. Should he take a chance and make a promise like that. "Why Gus, the girls aren't going to be here long you know, but I'm sure they'd like to come up, we'll all come, whenever you say, Gus."

Gus said that he'd ask the old woman and that they'd sure have a grand time. "Ed's a card. He's better than vodville. He's an evening all to himself," said Gus.

The two men were very excited and yet they went through all the chores of the day with outer calm. At lunch time, they were not hungry and talked dreamily of little things. Amos said the way his girls got around was a caution. "And they always get good jobs, too, but then they've got education."

"That's the ticket," said Gus.

"Vic always was smart," said Amos. "When she was little, I remember one time I was unloading a pile of wood in our yard and she spoke up and said, Why don't you drive up to the cellar door and throw it right down and then you won't have to carry it twice. I said then, see what education does, just in fun you know, she was only in the grades then, but it's a fact, all the same."

"Ed never had anything to speak of, but he's read a lot, always can tell you more about politics and what's going to happen in the world."

That night when they were all at dinner at daughter Clara's house, he broached the subject of going to Gus's place. He could hardly eat all during the nice meal Clara had cooked, for thinking about it and hoping the girls would not refuse. Clara had put the two younger children to bed and the oldest boy and the older girl were all dressed up like a circus. He always felt a little awkward and shy at Clara's house, she put on so much style, and her husband Donald Monroe had a kind of patronizing way with him that didn't set any too well.

"Why do you go to so much trouble, Clara?" Victoria said, as the dinner plates were carefully removed and the coffee and dessert came on, the pudding piled into little glass dishes and topped with whipped cream, the coffee with little spoons beside the cups on small saucers.

"It's no trouble," said Clara, in a hurt voice. She felt that she had failed to put the affair on in the proper manner if the stress of preparation showed. "Why, once I get the children out of the way, it's no bother at all." Her husband looked up complacently and said, "What else would she do with her time, hey?" winking and making a joke out of it.

"I can think of lots I'd rather do," said Rosamond.

"Wait till Jerry comes back and you get settled down," said Don, "then'll you'll sing another tune, or he'll sing it for you."

"We aren't going to keep house," said Rosamond. "I'm going to keep on working, if I can find a job." She flushed a little as she said it, because she knew that when she went to Detroit she was counting on Corny Stebbins to help her find something interesting to do. She didn't want anyone in the family but Vic to know that Stebbins, who had them all so upset by his attentions before she married Jerry, was in Detroit.

"I think that's nice for a time," said Clara, who liked harmony. "That is, for a while. A job will get monotonous but you can always quit."

"I don't see how we could live otherwise," said Rosamond a little irritated. She hated these family parties and she was upset at herself for disliking them so much. It was awful to feel so ill at ease with your own people. The Monroes with their worship of nice china, and always some new improvement on the installment plan, got on her nerves. "Jerry won't have a job, and heavens knows what he will do. He hasn't any training, he doesn't like the farm. I don't know what will happen to us." She tried to keep a peevish quality from her voice but she was tired and anxious. It had been a terrible year, so anxious and so lonely. Even now, it was all darkness and mystery. No one knew when the government would condescend to let Jerry come home.

"Oh, you'll get along," said Donald heartily. "Your old man will get a job. They're preferring the soldier boys, wouldn't be surprised any day to go down and find one in uniform sitting at my desk." He smiled and offered the unsmiling Mr. Wendel a cigar.

"Thanks," said Mr. Wendel, "don't care if I do. These things are fancier than my brand. Try one," and he handed one of his two for five to Donald.

"No thanks," said Donald politely, "you keep it, I've got my tastes pretty well set in the cigar line. The boss set me right on cigars. He smokes those boys, the kind I gave you, and sticks to the one brand. He says it's like mixing drinks. Only gives you a bad taste and I believe he's right."

"I couldn't say as to that," said Mr. Wendel. Vicky smiled at her father whose stiff unbending way of speech with his son-in-law always remained the same. Amos seeing her smile, smiled back warmly and tenderly, his whole face melting. He took the cigar from under his large old-fashioned moustache and said, "Say Vic, what would you say to going up to Gus's place some night next week? He was telling me his brother's coming and he thought maybe it would be kind of fun, his wife's upset about the brother and she'd take it nicer if you and Rosamond were there. What would you say?"

"Sure," said Vic. "Did you hear Rosamond? Papa wants us to go to Gus's place. Sure we'll go Papa."

"Gus will be pleased all right," said Mr. Wendel. In his pleasure he flicked off the ash jauntily and forgot himself so far as to say to Don, "Pretty good cigar."

"Yeah," said Donald. "It's about as good as you'll get at the price. The time I was in New York to the main office, they had a box of Corona Coronas on the desk, one of those will do me a lifetime. They're a fine cigar but not for me. This little number will do me."

"What's the wife upset about Gus's brother for," said Vic.

"Oh, nothing much," said Amos. "He's one of these I.W.W., it seems."

"Huh," said Donald, bristling. "Don't wonder she's upset. Say, take a tip from me. If you want to be a good friend to Gus, take him a tip from me. Keep it under your hat where it came from, but they aren't going to let those bums meet here, they're going to run them out of town."

"They, they," said Rosamond. "Who do you mean by they?"

"I mean the responsible men in this town. A committee met with the boss only yesterday. I heard all about it. Brason, you know him, Dad," he said familiarly turning toward Amos, "Brason, the lawyer."

"Yes," said Vicky, "I know him all right. What about him?"

"He said this town was facing a crisis in its history. We'd be run over by I.W.W., if the solid business men didn't take a stand. Why, you know yourself, with strikes breaking out all over and this damn Bolshevist stuff in the air, how dangerous it is to let those bums in."

"I'd like to hear who the rest of the solid citizens are. I can guess all right, the Troys, the Brackwoods, the Mellers."

"Sure," said Don. "They're the guys whose interests need protecting most, naturally, what would this town be without them?"

"A damn good place," said Vicky.

"Vicky," said Clara in a low voice, "the children." The two brats had perked up at the sound of the swear word and the boy grinned.

"Aaw mother, that's nothing new," he said. "Say, you should hear Bud Allison, he can tear off more bad words. Say Vic, you ought to hear him, he gets them off by the carload."

"That'll do," said Clara. "I guess you kids had better get ready for bed, now."

"Oh shucks," said the boy, "just when things begin to get hot, we have to go to bed. I ain't going."

"You'll do as your mother tells you," said Donald in a threatening father voice.

"Aaw shucks," said the kid, "I never have any fun."

"Come along now," said Clara in a too sweet mother voice. "You have to go to school tomorrow, you know," she went on persuasively, trying pathetically to carry off her dinner in the nice pleasant way that she had dreamed it should go. "Come now," she added more firmly.

"Aw shucks," said the boy, "damn it," he said daringly slanting a swift glance of triumph at Vic. "Good night, Vicky."

"You cut out such language, young man," said Donald, red in the face. "Goodnight," called Vic, laughing.

"Nighty-night," echoed the little girl tagging after her brother.

"Well, now that they're off, I'd like you to tell me what those friends of yours propose to do," said Vic.

"I've known a lot of I.W.W., they're all right," said Amos Wendel. "A little wild, but nothing to get the whole town in a stew about."

"It's that crack-brained mayor," said Don. "He's anxious to get himself made chief billy goat of something or other, mark my words."

"Well, he must think he's got someone behind him or he wouldn't dare insist the convention meet here. Did you ever think of that, Don? I guess a lot of people can't be so against it."

"Then they are as unsettled as the I.W.W. Why, the times are too dangerous to allow such a thing, but I'm surprised that you don't show more sense, Vicky, with all your education."

"Education, hell," said Vic.

"Well you are in a swell mood, I must say," said Don, smiling and genial now that the kids and his wife were out of range of such a bad influence. "What's eating you? You're young, good looking, why the world's your oyster if you want it." He tapped his cigar in a fancy way on the tray and leaned back. "I should think you'd see which side your bread's buttered on Vic. The bums aren't going to get you any place, not by a tin hat, they aren't. Unless in jail. And take my tip, that brother of Gus's will be roosting there if he doesn't watch his step."

"On what charge," said Rosamond, in a carefully controlled voice. She had made up her mind not to get into a squabble with Don. Dinners at Clara's almost always ended in some kind of a fuss and she wasn't going to let herself get drawn into the combat. It wasn't worth it. She pretended now to be indifferent, playing with her spoon, and looking past Donald's left ear, but it was a puzzle to her why the very tone of his voice and his manner of sitting with arrogant head in the air, made her want to fight more than eat.

"Charge?" said Donald. "How do I know. They'll be plenty of charges. Why, I read only last night in the papers that a crime wave follows the I.W.W. conventions as inevitably as night the day."

Vicky and Rosamond turned and smiled at one another. Amos Wendel smiled at the girls. He felt very happy. They had promised to go to Gus's and they were having a tiff with Donald. It made the three close together, the way they were in the old days when the girls were little and he and mamma and the two little ones took long walks out to Smith's Villa on Sunday. They all walked along four abreast, sometimes, holding hands.

Vic scraped her chair back and getting up yawned. "Well, what do you say to going home, Papa?" she said.

"I'll get the car," said Donald.

"Don't bother," said Rosamond, "let's walk, it isn't far, shall we?"

"Sure," said Amos, very happy, "let's have a little walk after our fine supper. Thank you, Clara, for the fine supper," he said as Clara came into the room.

When the three were out on the walk, the two girls put their father between them and hooking their arms in his, began slowly walking home. "Donald is a fool," said Vicky.

"Who ever thought differently?" said Rosamond. Amos chuckled.

"You girls won't forget about going to Gus's," he said.

"Just let us know what night, and we'll be there, Papa," said Rosamond.

"Do you think there's anything in what Donald said?" said Vic.

Mr. Wendel thought there was a good deal to it, but he wasn't going to give that windbag credit. "Pshaw, no," he said. "He's talking. They're all talking. I don't think anything will happen."

"A lot happened out on the west coast," said Vic, "they didn't stop at killing either."

"Oxtail's different," said Amos, none too sure. He hoped that poor old Gus wouldn't have his hands full with his hell-raising brother. When they got home, he got out the little notebook where he kept notations of the interest paid, his insurance up to date, and holding it out like a little boy's school book, said timidly, "What do you think of that? I guess Mamma will be surprised when she sees how much I've paid off this winter, won't she?"

Vic took the book and, with Rosamond looking over her shoulder, read it. It was all down in tiny careful figures, and both girls praised their father. He was very pleased and went off to bed at peace with the world.

The two girls sat under the old-fashioned gas mantle, their faces pale and hair of almost identically the same fair color brushed back from their foreheads. They sat that way for minutes. The kitchen clock ticked, an early spring rain began slowly plopping against the window, a soft timid splash. "I wish Papa hadn't gone to bed," said Rosamond. "I'd like to play the old piano tonight. I found a stack of mother's old music today. Ben Hur Chariot Race, O Listen to the Mocking Bird, and Floyd's Retreat. Remember?"

"Yes, and what happened to the hanging lamp with the roses that used to dangle over the piano and once belonged to Uncle Joe?"

"I don't know, but they've still got the old china," said Rosamond looking at the glassed-in corner cupboard where Mamma kept the old family relics. The Adams plate, the slipware pie plates, the blue bowl that Vicky used to eat bread and milk from when she was a good girl, and even the Easter egg with the date 1830 on its shiny garnet-colored sides in Greatuncle Jacob's sugar bowl.

"I found another piece today, *Wenn er nicht wieder kommt*," said Rosamond. "I bet mother used to play it when she was hoping Mr. Gason would come back. Funny he never did, isn't it?" Suppose Jerry never came back, just got trapped and blown to bits by an old shell or got flu. She didn't want to be one of the lost ones of the family, consoling herself with old songs. Not that their mother had let herself be lost; once she and Vicky had found her girlhood diary in the attic and the words "Farewell, sad days, I go to my new life and may I make *him* happy, is my fervent wish." The old-fashioned, highflown language hadn't hidden Anne Wendel's real longing to make her husband happy. She envied her mother's singleness of purpose; nowadays there were so many things to wish for. She had to do more than hope for happiness, Jerry would have to find something to do, they'd have to live. It seemed harder and harder and you'd think with all the improvements in ways of living, it would be easier.

"I guess we'll never know the truth about Mr. Gason," said Vicky. Mr. Gason was a young man in a photograph album who had given wonderful presents that still survived. The gold opera glasses were as solid as Uncle Joe's silver tea set. The solid presents of the romantic males who had run away stood up well with years. No one ever heard a word against Mr. Gason or Uncle Joe, the most generous brother. For that matter, no one heard a word against Amos Wendel either. Anne Wendel was always praising Papa, and when the children used to quarrel would often say, "Now I'd run away, I declare I would, if it weren't for your father."

The little notebook with all the items was not so romantic as the opera glasses or the silver tea set. Amos Wendel had lost his business. Even before he had lost it, he had been for a long time in hot water. It wasn't very exciting in a town like Oxtail; no wonder their mother had furbished up the heroes of her past. Why, Vicky herself was always putting her best foot forward, hinting at deep affairs that were no more than a ripple, and who could help feeling something more like the lovely Mrs. Ferrol, victim of love, than Vic Wendel, a working girl. There was a kind of terrible satisfaction in that kind of unhappiness that no one could explain. Like the time she had learned the poem, "Lie still my hear, my aching heart, my silent heart, lie still and break, life and the world and mine own self have changed for his dear sake," and yet there hadn't been a sign of a soul to break her heart about. How could there be, seeing she had been eleven years old at the time, with so much heart-break in the attic, stored in old letters, gotten out on rainy days, relished

because in Oxtail there wasn't even a theater that amounted to
much. The Peavy Grand had presented Uncle Tom's Cabin years
ago, but nothing much since then. Once Joe Jefferson had come
and Mamma had hauled them up to the gallery to see him. Of
course there were the movies, but it wasn't a real substitute for life.

Nothing was. And sitting in the White Elephant was just as bad
as crawling into a spider's web. Both of the girls could feel a kind
of pleasant melancholy and, if they didn't take the train soon, they
would be back in the same old rut.

The little notebook was a terrible warning. And what reward
had their father gotten for all his goodness? Vicky made up her
mind to say something the very next morning about Uncle David,
that selfish Monument, and how he was nothing in comparison to a
man like her father, who was the salt of the earth.

But when morning came it was not so easy to say anything.
After all, Amos Wendel did not expect it. He was so bewildered
with words. He only hoped to get the girls down to the warehouse
and see how he was fixed. And in broad daylight the murky
feelings of the night before were a little dim. It was nonsense to be
afraid they would get stuck in this town again. Nothing could keep
them. The excitement of the I.W.W. about to meet was much more
real than John Gason's opera glasses. Rosamond dashed off the
Ben Hur Chariot Race while Vicky washed the dishes. Then they
ransacked the house for Rosamond's belongings. She meant to take
the little she possessed to Detroit. The stacks of rather useless
things beside her trunk toppled to the floor.

"Don't take so much," said Vicky. "All that junk."

"I never want to come back here again," said Rosamond,
"except of course to visit mother and Papa." If only she could find
that cornbread recipe that mother used to have. Would it be all
right to take the old sugar box? Some girls might like to take
something out of the parlor, but there was nothing there but the old
piano and the pictures Vicky had influenced her mother to get
when she was in highschool, Sir Galahad, Corot's Dance of Spring,
Hope. Now no one, except Anne Wendel, had any use for the
pictures. But the sugar box or the bread board ought to bring good
luck. Not that she expected to cook much. She wouldn't have a

chance in the tiny apartment she and Jerry would be bound to have. Maybe they'd have only a room. Letters were so unsatisfactory. They seemed to draw thin all the feeling between the two and make the future full of doubts. Jerry never wrote of their plans anymore. Only about how much he longed to see her. She longed to see him but she was anxious about their life. They ought to get more education, they'd have to be very smart if they weren't going to let themselves be dragged down to some routine jobs somewhere. He would think it funny, if she came along carrying a sugar box and a bread board. When she was little and everything was simple, she used to watch her mother roll out the pie dough and sprinkle sugar on the cinnamon buns and wipe the round brown loaves of bread warm from the oven with a little rag dipped in butter. Every corner of the house smelled good in those days, not like a stuffy room, where she hung her clothes always living in a trunk. She was tired of a trunk and sometimes felt guilty imagining herself on a farm with peach orchards in blossom and chickens running about and a blue sky full of white racing clouds like a picture on a calendar.

"Don't carry off things you won't need," said Vicky. She had packed up Aunty Blank's old bone-handled knife and fork for herself, just for luck.

In the middle of the morning, Amos Wendel called up to say that Ed had come and that Mayor Handy was going to make his speech at the opening of the convention as per schedule.

"What about not letting them meet? Is there going to be trouble?" said Vicky.

"I don't know about that, you might go along downtown and see if anything turns up. But don't get mixed up in anything." Lower Fourth Street had nothing spectacular to offer. Opposite the I.W.W. hall a few idlers stood watching three policemen swing clubs at the foot of the stairs leading up. At upstairs windows, backs pressed against the glass and roars of applause leaked to the ordinary street below. The Wendel girls felt out of place and hurried on to Papa's warehouse. He had no time for them but Gus grinned and waved to them, and Papa ran over to say that they

would go to Gus's that night as it wasn't certain how long they'd let
the boys stick around town.

BENIGN DOUBLE CROSS

As the Wendel girls walked past the I.W.W. hall, Mayor Handy
was making his welcome speech to the delegates. After all the pow-
wow from the Chamber of Commerce and the Legion, it was
disappointing to find only 54 delegates, 12 deputy sheriffs, federal
officers, and one auburn haired woman. The Sheriff had pushed his
way past the door guard, yelling, "The hell I can't come in here.
I'm the sheriff." As the Mayor talked, he faced a number of
posters on the dirty brown walls. The jagged big letters bawled at
him from the sides and even from the back between the windows.
Smoke from a corncob pipe got in his eyes.

ONE BIG UNION
AN INJURY TO ONE IS AN INJURY TO ALL
ARISE YE PRISONERS OF STARVATION
NO GOD, NO MASTER

Everywhere his eye fell, Mayor Handy saw writings that went
against his deepest grain. He must keep tight rein of himself and
try to show these rash men a little light. He was conscious, as he
spoke, of the town beyond the window and of a dozen offices where
at that minute the biggest guns of the town were in secret excited
conclave. It was a man's fight to buck that crowd, but he could do
it. He felt all his nerves strong for the battle of the right that had
been carried on, first in God's church and then in the arena of
politics. It took courage to see that Christianity was fruitless kept
in airtight churches. The politicians poisoned the roots of life, he
would go out after them, he would become one of them. He would
purify and lift. Standing before the 54 men and the one woman, he
felt very much like a school teacher before a group of rather unruly

boys. He had taught school and had worked on his father's farm and the farms of neighbors as a hand, knew the long hours and the short pay. The years since that time had drained this memory somewhat and he had, with the aid of an older brother, worked himself through college and was even a product of a course at Harvard. He tried now as he balanced on the platform to make a synthesis of all this rich experience to offer to these roughnecks who were not among the highly advantaged of the earth and deserved therefore the help of those who were more enlightened, like himself.

Not until he came to the words, "The preamble to your constitution begins with these words, *The working class and the employing class have nothing in common*," did the hall become so still you could have heard a pin drop. The smoke bothered Handy who never smoke or drank, but he went on in a level voice, now and then turning his head stiffly to take in a little group sitting on the edge of the platform. "I would call your attention to another statement heard today: The interest of the worker and the employer are one."

As he said this, he paused as if to clinch the argument. No one moved. A chair squeaked as it scraped backward.

"These two statements appear to be absolutely and hopelessly contradictory," he went on, encouraged by the deep silence. "Yet I can see how a man may find plausible arguments for either of them. I believe the latter contains the higher truth.

"The people of France during the last four years, when the nation was struggling for its life, have risen to the point where interests of capitalist and laborer, of officer and private soldier, were one and the same. The world is moving toward that point of view—moving more rapidly in the last few years probably than ever before in history. It is the higher point of view. Therefore it is the point of view that is going to prevail ultimately."

A kind of heavy dull patience sat on the shoulders of the men in the audience and on the shoulders of Gus's brother, Ed Bates, third row toward the aisle. He wondered how long the preacher would keep it up. Christ, what palaver, as if a man could forget the hot tar poured on open wounds at Tulsa. Sure, the boys had come out for a few decent conditions and look what they got. Listen to him

talk as if the big bosses and working stiffs could have a nice picnic
and talk things over. Please pass the potato chips. How about a
little ham? The picnic in Tulsa had been a ride in the dark—black
snake whips. Easy now, easy Ed, said Ed to himself, go slow,
remember this guy did us a good turn. The Legion would like to
give him a ride for this. He may even get the recall. Easy.

Easy went the Mayor's voice sliding into its admonitions for the
wayward boys. His speech was slow and sometimes sounded the
language of a hymn. He had a desire as he stood there to tell them
about his mother who had come on a river boat to this state down
the Ohio and up the Missouri. Of the tall grass his father had to
turn under to get the beginnings of a farm. He melted in that hall
at all those listening faces, he was their guardian, he had protected
them, had given them shelter, they were his lambs.

"The worst enemies of progress are they who hope to reap a
sudden reward, or a reward for which they have given no
equivalent of honest toil. This is true no matter in what social rank
a man may be classed." He stopped, felt almost as if an "amen"
must be breathed out of his watchful congregation. A tall fellow in
one corner spit into a nearby spittoon, slowly and with interest,
measuring the exact right distance. Mr. Handy turned his face
away, went on to his lesson.

"There are men who would tempt you to believe that the day is
coming when men will go and take by violence what they want. I
wish to say with all earnestness that such an idea has absolutely
not a shadow of a chance of success in America. It will not be
tolerated a moment."

Ed Bates smiled down into his hands that were held loosely over
his face, as he propped his head on his knees. It couldn't last much
longer; then they could get down to business. It would end, like all
things, like the fellow worker singing, "Hold the Fort" that day on
the deck of the Verona at Everett with the picnic baskets around
and the kids and wives standing there and the drunken skunks, out
to save America, had fired anyhow. They got him and the song
stopped. "Hold the Fort," the fellow worker sang, holding to the
rail and sinking to his knees, pouring blood he was and singing,
"Hold the Fort." That was a fine song.

"I just want you to know that I know a little of what you meet sometimes," went on Handy's precise voice, "and that to keep one's soul right, and to be an honest man who is giving value received as he goes through life and to stand first of all for order and constitutional methods in human society, is the only way. There is absolutely no chance for anything else in America. There are too many people just like myself who have got a little plot of ground a little bigger than this room that is the product of their whole life's savings and who will fight for it even if they have to fight alone. Now I want every man of you to rid yourself of the idea you can take the world by violence. For you can never do it. It is just a matter of plain common sense to cut that out, because it won't go."

The teacher voice slid to the preacher voice, thanked them for their attention in tones of a benediction and it was over. The men applauded politely, the sheriff growled as Mayor Handy brushed by, "How's teacher's pet?" Outside near the entrance a big car was drawn up and former Mayor Henderson and a couple of bigwigs sat looking up at the windows of the hall curiously. "Mayor, you made a mistake there. I wouldn't have done it." He shook his head a little playfully, what was one man's poison was another man's meat and he could cash in on this prank of the Mayor's in fine shape. The Mayor crossed the street alone and getting into his Ford drove toward City Hall.

He went into his office and went over his speech in memory. he felt good and brave. "I will fight the good fight," he said squaring his jaws with a little contraction of the muscles. He knew without the shadow of doubt that Henderson and his gang would start recall proceedings. He would show them. The daily papers would be against him but he would win. The people were behind him. As he said the word *people* to himself, he thought of them as a group in a kind of mist, like a congregation waiting to hear the final prayer. He had clean skirts, his speech this morning had cleared up any doubts anyone might have. No one could say *he* was for violence. He was for law and order. When it came to labor he was with Gompers, who like himself, had begun to labor as a child. With the wolf at his own door, Gompers had gone out to toil for the betterment of the masses, yet Capital had found him a fair and helpful friend.

Mayor Handy took out his crisp handkerchief and carefully polished his glasses. He was beginning to part his hair with a little comb when a knock on the door made him hastily jam it in his pocket.

His secretary stepped inside, said in a low voice, "It's a delegation. From the Chamber of Commerce."

"Show them in," said Handy, straightening his tie, and getting to his feet with his hands squared on the desk before him.

"Well, gentlemen," said the mayor as the miscellaneous group shoved into the room.

"We're here to talk turkey," said the spokesman, getting up close to the desk. "All right to go ahead?"

"Fire away," said the Mayor.

"All right, here goes. Henderson is going to start a recall. That may not be news to you, but what about this? We've been angling for eastern capital for a dozen different enterprises. They'll back out if we don't clean up this town. Get rid of the I.W.W. and take a firm stand. Capital won't come to a town with a stink like this."

"It's no stink," said Mayor Handy. He reached to the corner of his desk. "I assure you gentlemen that papers all over the country, particularly in the east, the more intelligent weeklies, *The New Republic* and the *Nation* . . . "

"Never heard of them, Mayor. But I can tell you what the organ of the Chambers of Commerce says. I can tell you what business says. And that's what counts. What a lot of highbrows think can't build factories for us or get loans for some of the boys who are feeling a little shaky. Now then, this gang is going to back Henderson unless you give us a little leeway. We'll clean you out if you don't talk our language, that's all."

"What's your idea?" said Handy. A compromise would be better than to lose all. He would stall for time but go back on his principles of free speech, never.

"Well, you've had your little party," said the spokesman. "You said your little speech this morning. Now how about making a little news tonight that the papers can print; don't need to be rough, but say let a meeting be broken up. You can even wait until after it is over."

"Absolutely not, gentlemen."

"Wait a minute. Take it easy. We know you can't turn about face. But how about letting the Legion take things over. Keep the bluecoats out if you want. Just let us tip them off to stay clear for awhile. That will show the world where good old Oxtail stands on this question."

"I'm dead against it," said the Mayor but in not a very strong voice.

"Listen, they've got criminals here with this outfit. Bill Haywood, been in Leavenworth a year, what do you think of that? I tell you Mayor, why don't you be an ostrich, for the good of the town, we'll take all the responsibility. And if this goes on, well, I told you, it's hands down."

Mayor Handy didn't answer. He looked out the window and the delegation looked at him. The spokesman stared hard for several minutes, then smiled slowly. "O.K., Mayor. I get you. Mum's the word. And it will be all over in a second and the recall will be knocked in a cocked hat, too. All we care about is to get that eastern capital moving." He grinned, the other boys grinned, and the delegation backed off, leaving Mayor Handy looking uncertainly out the window.

"I can still stop them," he said, but it would take a little time to think over. There were many sides to the question. He had been fair to labor that morning, perhaps he was being unfair to capital if he refused the boys. His brow cleared and he made up his mind to keep up the good fight and stand for reelection under recall. "I'll win," he said. But he was uneasy. Suppose things did not go off well that evening.

"Now boys, take it easy. We don't need guns but guts."

"Got plenty of them, Charley."

"We meet tomorrow at six at Jake's place. Detour in a body to Oberholzer's farm and stand by. The bank or the insurance company will have a bidder but if you bring along a rope, Sam, and sort of dangle it inconspicuous, maybe he'll take the hint. No bids over a dollar. We don't want to lay out cash. It only goes back to the bank boys, and they chewed us up long enough. They're laughin' up their sleeves at us, we're such nice easy marks."

"They got Mellon and Mellon is president. You thought you voted last time for Hoover, but no boys, it was Andy Mellon. He sees that his pal Charley Dawes doesn't get into trouble. Hands out eightymillion for poor downtrodden Charley. But we can't get two cents for hogs. Corn ain't worth taking in. I says, I says I'll feed the corn to the hogs and see how big a hog can grow. Got one nearly 700 pound now but what for should I take it to the packing house? To feed them packing house kings? No, sir. I'll feed my stock and eat my own victuals. Let the rats eat the corn. I got my electricity turned off, no phone.

"But boys, this is the breadbasket of the world. We're living right in it. Folks can get along without neckties, they can do without hats. It's not so hard to let your hair grow if you need a cover. But by god, you can't do without food. We're feeding them bankers and politicians and what are they doing to us? They got us lined up against the wall. They got the wooden shoes all laid out ready for our feet. Boys, they don't care if we lose our homes or if our kids can't go to school. If things don't go right with them, they take a bank holiday and we pay for it. They let our savings be gobbled up and we ain't got no kick. It's the law. The law's all for them, boys. We get the promises. For twelve years they ain't kept one promise they made us. I'll eat a bale of hay for every promise they kept.

"The mayor of Oxtail is a double crosser. Take a delegation there and he'll smile and rub his hands and say ain't it a pity but they're doing all they can. But what goes on behind our backs? What?" He paused and glowered at the mob of farmers who stood solid as if they had been planted and grown there. Nobody spoke.

"He skedaddles off to the governor, him and the big guns, and they ask for outside militia. He knows he can't get our local boys to shoot you down boys. They won't do it. They know what it is we're up against. Then he gets a promise and he comes back and scares your leaders off. 'Boys, you don't want no bloodshed, do you boys.' He tries to make out as if the pickets was paid. PAID. Ain't that good boys, paid. Why if we had a nickel we'd pay ourselves. We don't need no agitators he's talking about. We're all agitators ourselves. We're agitating for our rights and our freedom boys, and tomorrow is a showdown. We ain't got the *Daily News* back of us no more, the mayor scared off that fellow too, said he wouldn't get no more advertising. But boys, we got our own two hands. They ain't licked us. We'll show them it's tough to swallow an elephant. Now boys tomorrow when some slicker wearing good clothes while you and me can't buy overalls steps up pretty as you please to say his piece, stand together. Shake the rope, Sam. And now for the vote, just to be regular." He grinned turning his big head slowly, his legs stiff in the old overalls, his lean hand rubbing his unshaved cheek. His eye roams around, back of the mob of overalled men to the barns, the full corn crib, the dilapidated machinery, the rich fertile fields that have pitched him into poverty; he counts the hands, raised high up at the end of stiff blue jacketed arms, all hard working hands whose industry has brought them only trouble.

"That's right, boys," he says, in a quiet voice. "I make it unanimous."

MARTYRS TO A CAUSE

When her brother's property added up to around thirty thousand dollars and all but a smidge went to his son, Anne Wendel began to feel grieved at the way Aaron had treated her. It wouldn't have hurt him to have given her a little money, for the first time in his life. She had given up months of her life for him, nursing him and leaving her family to shift for itself. He might have made it easier for her when he was alive. He could have given her some cash outright in his will. The lots she had salvaged for herself were hard to sell. It would be months before she could find a buyer.

In letters to David Trexler she spoke of her discontent. He was up in arms for his sister against his brother. It was very easy to be indignant about Aaron's shortcomings, and David himself was getting to the time of life when he longed for approbation from his relatives. He had been made executor of the will, along with the lawyer Roundtree. "Just put in a claim for services rendered to the estate," he wrote his sister. "I'll guarantee I won't sign another check for the benefit of that son Timothy unless your claim is paid. Make it proper but don't cheat yourself."

Roundtree agreed with Trexler and thought that the least she should charge was eight hundred dollars. She had been with her brother more than a year. She had certainly earned it. What had Aaron ever done for his sisters or his own mother? Timothy was a young man with a good education, who, if he cared to utilize it, could make considerable out of the business his father had left him. He'd never miss the eight hundred. As for Sally, hadn't she ordered their own mother out of the house? Wrote the nastiest letters and treated Mem like a dog. It was practically a virtue to divert eight hundred dollars from her. She forgot that only a short time before she had actually felt sorry for Sally, and when Roundtree seemed to think the claim would be settled without trouble, she went back to a sympathetic attitude toward the widow. Not

124

that she wanted to be friends. That was impossible, still Aaron had wronged his wife. When a young woman adores her husband and then suddenly turns to bitter unending hatred, there must be a reason. Madeleine McNarry was reason enough. Aaron had taken on all the vices and airs of Mr. Flemmer, the millionaire for whom he had been an agent in all his real estate deals. He had no doubt learned many a thing from such a man. People said that Flemmer had brought Italian laborers over on false pretenses to start a vineyard and that it was only an excuse to sell them real estate. He had got cheap labor for the knitting factory and he had sold his land. Aaron had got a divvy on everything sold.

Alone in the old offices that had been Aaron's Anne Wendel went over and over in her mind the life her brother had had. The more she went into it, the more she felt justified in having signed over to herself the deeds to the three lots on the day Aaron died. She did not regret, she wished she had picked better specimens. But the more she considered the past, the more it seemed only right that she take the old diaries and letters of their father that she found in the office. She gradually found good reasons for adding to the little innocent store of possessions that piled up in her trunk.

She had learned a few tricks from her brother about buying up property for taxes and, now that she had leisure, she poked around in nearby country following leads on property fairly desirable. She saw herself as negotiating quite a little nest egg as day after day went by.

Hortense Ripley was prodding her to clear up the matter of Sally's age so they could sell the homestead. She goaded her on to filch as much as she could from Aaron's estate on account of her claim. At a distance, Hortense's remarks looked like an intense interest in her welfare and Anne was touched by such consideration. Sometimes the remarks seemed too venomous but she always remembered that Hortense's life had been bitter with disappointments. She couldn't remember the time when Hortense wasn't full of little liver complaints or wailing against the awful weather, not fit for an Indian, or groaning under the hard work she and Milton put into their little business, working like convicts. Only in the last few years the tables had been turned on them again, the baking powder trust squeezing them to the wall with their nice little product, Ripley's Wonder Baking Power. They had forced the Ripleys to sell just at the moment when the product was beginning a return on their investment. But the deep trouble of Hortense's life was something that could only be hinted at. Years before when they were first married, she had spoken outright; now she was silent, scared of the prying eyes of Anne's girls. It was a curious thing that Milton was sick at last, crumpling up of some deep-seated trouble that had begun a long while back. It had begun so far back that it had sapped all the married life of the Ripley couple. It was really just a streak of luck that they had any children at all.

When Anne Wendel thought of all the good she could do with the eight hundred dollars and the extra money she might make on bits of property bought at tax sales, all her trouble seemed worth it. The girls would get some proper clothes, they could get the house fixed and maybe turn it into a duplex and rent half. It was a comfort to her to know that her two youngest were in Oxtail and she wrote them to air the winter clothes and put them in moth balls.

The day she fell from the spring wagon, coming in from the country on a visit to one of the lots up for tax sale, she argued and instructed the frightened young doctor. "Now this is nothing but a sprained ligament, it will be all right if I give it a little rest." She nearly fainted as she said it, groaning and turning gray as ashes. But she wouldn't let anyone wire her folks and it was days before she had the strength to scrawl off so much as a postcard.

The hotel took care of her in a slipshod way. "It's a judgment on me for taking those lots," she thought but the next moment she scorned such idiocy. She had a perfect right to the lots. If the wagon wheel hadn't been slippery nothing would have happened. She tried to sit up in bed but the hot applications burned, her back got sore, at night rats crept out from their holes back of the old furniture and stood rustling and squeaking. She kept her shoes handy to throw at them, and when they scurried away, bugs oozed out from the old walls to bite into her skin.

"Don't worry about me," she finally wrote. "I had a little

accident, sprained the ligaments of my leg but will be all right soon." Of course she'd be all right soon. She lay in the old hotel and listened for the trains that used to make her so restless as a young girl when Joe had run off to the Black Hills. She cheered herself thinking of how nice she would fix things up with her little inheritance. She bore her pains like a proper martyr for what she thought a due and sufficient cause.

If Anne Wendel's card had come on any other day, it would have caused more agitation among her family. As it was, the Wendels were stirred up about the trouble that might come to Gus's brother. Mayor Handy had been allowed to make his speech in spite of the sarcastic comments of big business in the town. Since that hour leaflets had appeared on the street:

NOTICE: THIS is a call to returned soldiers and sailors and all other patriotic citizens of Oxtail to meet at the courthouse square Monday night at 8 p.m. for the purpose of seeing that the name of Oxtail is unsullied and blackened by allowing a convention of anarchists, calling themselves Industrial Workers of the World, to continue in our midst.

The two evening papers had come out with nice little statements, one from Sheriff Jones who was sore because he had not had a free hand that morning. Said the Sheriff, "The I.W.W. stand for destruction of government and property and murder and sabotage and that is the sort of organization Handy stands for. But he can't run Oxtail. Even if a law and order committee to aid officials has to be formed. We must avoid what is going on in Russia." The other from a big creamery man, "Today is I.W.W. day in Oxtail. I am told that a tall weakling brainless spiritual mistake and business misfit who is at the head of our city government has welcomed the Wobblies. I am for the clean masses as against the highhanded masses."

In spite of these indignant statements the streetcars were

jammed with people going home from work who did not seem alarmed. Amos Wendel thought the boys were a little wild and hoped they would get away before trouble began. "Ed's a nice looking fellow," he told the girls. "I hope he doesn't get into trouble in this town."

Everyone in town seemed to want to be on hand in case of trouble and the downtown streets were jammed by the time the Wendel girls got there. Someone said there was a meeting of the new law and order committee at the courthouse and someone else said Sheriff Jones had better keep his own roost clean before he began on other people's. Everybody knew lower Fourth Street was a mess of fancy houses and gambling joints, and Jones got his divvy in spite of the Mayor's orders to clean up. A tense crowd jostled the streets. Jones and his cohorts appeared around nine o'clock, armed to the teeth and brandishing clubs. The American Legion boys in their nice khaki uniforms formed a wedge behind. Jones was unusually good natured.

"No, no," he assured Papa Blonheim who kept the saloon on the corner. "I'm not starting trouble. I'm for law and order, but," he swung his billy, "I'm here to see we get it." He stood near Papa Blonheim's saloon, a broad grin on his face. "I've got my orders. Hands off. I'm not touching that dirty nest. No sir. Just keeping order." When the American Legion boys charged up the stairs, he stood his grounds, smiling amiably, but it was hard to stick in that spot. By Jesus, it was downright unfair for the Chamber of Commerce to force him to play such a part, a fighting sheriff should fight.

The big cars of big business were out to keep an eye on the trouble they were sure would brew that evening. Cadillacs and Packards grunted through the slow moving crowds. "The big sows, you'd think we were nothin' but a crib of corn," said an old farmer, nearly shoved off his feet.

"Hey watch out, you bullocks, keep clear here," yelled a little group from South Dakota. Workers from the packing house district glowered at the big cars with the back seats filled with pretty elegant women, smiling like movie pictures. "Let them keep their bitches out. Get off the street." The big cars grunted their horns,

nosing through. The crowd had to give. At the same time a yell
went up, as the khaki boys came down the stairs of the I.W.W. hall
bawling, "We got the rats, boys, three cheers." Nobody cheered.
The crowd tightened and drew close together. The big cars began
to honk as if they were at a carnival. Behind the legion, pouring
redfaced down the stairs, tumbled the delegates to the convention.
"They don't look very fierce, do they?" said Amos Wendel.

"Haywood. Bill Haywood," began someone from the packing
house group. "Haywood, Bill—where's Bill Haywood?" Now the
crowd opened up for the delegates, leaving by some miracle the
sweating legion on the outside near the store windows.

"That's Bill, that big guy." "Where, get off my foot, I can't see."
"What's he saying? Quiet please."

"I can't hear a thing," complained Vicky. The big cars began a
loud honk on the outskirts of the mob. Some of the boys near the
edge went over to the cars and threatened the drivers. Sheriff Jones
began to look scared and to swing his billy. He was jammed close
to the saloon with Papa Blonheim's belly as a protection. And now
some of the words came hoarsely between honks of horns.

" . . . the very people who are abusing the I.W.W. today if they
had lived in the days of our forefathers would have been licking the
boots of King George. They would have said of the boys fighting
barefoot in the snow of Valley Forge, 'Look at them, they haven't a
shoe to their feet and they are talking of liberty.' Yes, we are
dissatisfied, completely dissatisfied with the existing order of
things. And this is the first reason and the main reason for the
existence of the I.W.W. We are absolutely and irrevocably dissatisfied with the present system of society. We consider it a useless
system and we mean . . . "

"What? What is he saying?"

"He says," said a man next to Vicky, "we mean to destroy it.
The system, he says. If you ask me, they're cutting their own
throats." He ducked into the crowd and Vicky and Rosamond
looked at one another. They had never expected to hear anything
like that in their home town. Perhaps it wasn't such a dead place
after all. Perhaps in this very spot something would happen.

The car driven by Meller, the newspaper owner, now bucked

again and the crowd slowly began to yield. A stone from somewhere smashed the windshield squarely. The car came to a full
stop. Whistles blew. Sheriff Jones bustled into action, hitting right
and left with his club. His cohorts followed, swinging at women
and children, young and old men, anyone who blocked the path.

Bill Haywood, taller than those around him, had vanished. The
delegates had vanished. No one knew where. The crowd milled and
churned and ran over into bystreets and the delegates tangled
among them, disappeared.

The crowd yielded and the Meller car wriggled through the mass
with police on the running board. "Too late, Meller," yelled a
voice. Meller turned his head and Amos Wendel said, "Look, he's
hit."

"Meller's hit," went through the crowd. "Serve him right, but-
ting in." Other cars began slowly to wedge in behind Meller and to
cash in on the opportunity, the Salvation Army charged down a
side street and getting as near the center of things as possible
began grimly Onward Christian Soldiers. A woman's nasal voice
shrilled above the honking of cars. A few stragglers stopped beside
them and lights in the Iowa Clothing Store went on in hopes of a
little business. No one could see a sign of the Industrial Workers of
the World.

"Maybe we hadn't better go to Gus's," said Amos Wendel.

"Why not? Only we won't find him there. Do you suppose they
will drive them out of town? Look at the innocent people they've
been hitting."

"Hard to say what these chumps will do," said Wendel. The
three had walked slowly down Fourth Street and, looking backward, saw the crowd still sticking like bees to the corner where Bill
Haywood had appeared and vanished. The sheriff was still bawling
to keep the streets open.

Gus was slouching near the backdoor of his house that stood on
stilts like a sick chicken with the pip. A long thin dog came
waggling toward the visitors.

"Say that's nice you could come," said Gus, coming toward
them. "She's been raising hell all day, say, this is fine, but I don't

know if we'll see anything of Ed. Did they walk off that pretty tonight! See them?"

"We were there but couldn't see much or hear much."

"Bill made a wonderful speech, what a talker." Gus shut his eyes and shook his head. "I'm afraid the bloody legion will make more trouble for him. He's getting out tonight," he said in a low voice as they neared the kitchen door.

Mrs. Gus came to the door and seeing the girls, flushed and pushed her hair back self-consciously. "It's a wonder he couldn't take you in the front, bringing you back here, I hope you'll excuse it."

"Why, this is fine," said Vicky. Everybody shook hands with Mrs. Gus.

"I'm just giving this fella his supper, if you'll excuse me," said Mrs. Gus, shoveling a hasty spoonful of bread and milk into the mouth of her youngest, who strapped to his high chair, opened his mouth and stared at the newcomers letting the milk dribble softly down his chin. "We have to eat around here in spite of all the big doings going on. To hear them talk, you'd think they had the power of the lord. I says this morning, look at you with holes in your socks, bragging around what you're going to do. Get your socks fixed, then talk."

"Guess you know what Ed said, don't forget," said Gus. "Don't put the cart before the horse, he says."

"I hear nothing but argument from morning to night," said Mrs. Gus, "and first one guy, then another. Who're you? I says this morning when a new face bobs up."

Mr. Wendel smiled dipomatically and said, "It's always hard on the women."

"You said it, Mr. Wendel," said Mrs. Gus, straightening her back and nodding vigorously. "Gus thinks no one is like his brother but I wonder how much bread Ed ever buttered."

"Say, you talk as if Ed didn't work. Why woman, he works harder than I ever dreamed of."

"Oh everything Ed does is perfect," said Mrs. Gus, whirling from the baby who kept his mouth open waiting for the spoon, and appealing to Mr. Wendel and the two girls. "Sure, if Ed spills something on the floor, it only polishes it. I've eyes in my head. Why this man is the better of the two, if you ask me, if he knew it. I say a man who shirks a family and hasn't taken on his share of the rearing and raising ain't one to go reforming." She set the cup of bread and milk down hard and the cat got up, yawned and began mincing over the dishes toward it. The baby, denied his food, set up a howl.

"Look at that, never mind, mamma's lamb, poor soul, no wonder he cries, what a time he's had today." She snatched the infant up, glared at her husband and the next moment, said in a company voice, "Excuse me, please, I'll put this fella to bed, then we can be more sociable."

Gus brightened when she left the room and, winking, said he was going to give them something good. "She can make good wine," he said, pouring out the glasses from the big glass jug kept under the table. "Ed's been hitting this," he went on, slanting his head to one side and measuring it with one eye. "How do you like it?"

"First rate," said Mr. Wendel smacking his lips. The girls smiled and smacked and Vic asked for the recipe.

"She'll tell you," said Gus. "I'm afraid we won't see Ed. And I tell you," lowering his voice and moving toward Amos, "he's a sick man. They got him at Tulsa and beat him up, shameful, poured hot tar on him. He's got a ton of sorrows in him too but he won't say much." Gus stopped anxious and suddenly worried that he had been talking too much. But Amos was like one of the family, and Amos's girls were too young in his opinion to take such questions seriously. Victoria sensed that Gus was a little sorry for saying so much and picked up the paper. She wanted to say something to show him they were all on Ed's side.

"Did you see where this smartaleck got into the convention today?" she said pointing.

"That? They got that stool pigeon spotted. He thinks he's so slick. Say, read that out loud. Read what he says they stand for, it's good."

"The purposes of the I.W.W. are to proclaim free love." Everybody burst out laughing and even Mrs. Gus who had come back into the room smiled.

"To disrupt the greatest American institution, the Home." Mrs. Gus looked grim but the rest laughed louder than before.

"To overthrow the United States government."

"To establish a local soviet."

"To free class war prisoners."

"Well, what's the matter with some of them aims, granting they are true and accurate," says Gus. "I don't see why men should be locked up in jail when they ain't criminals."

"I guess you'd like that free love one too," said Mrs. Gus, taunting him. "If the truth were known."

Mr. Wendel cleared his throat and said the wine was lovely. The atmosphere tamed down a little and everybody sipped their wine. It began to look as if Ed would not show up. When they finally heard steps outside, the girls set their glasses down and sat listening.

"There he is," said Gus, nervous and getting to his feet softly like a big cat he tiptoed to the screen and opened it. Ed and a squat dark fellow in a blue sweater came in together. They all shook hands. "Wet your whistle," said Gus, "here's some folks countin' on hearin' you sing."

"Not tonight," said Ed shortly.

"Oh come on, Ed," said Mrs. Gus, much more affable to her brother-in-law than the Wendels had expected her to be, "you know you want to show off that lovely voice of yours."

"Not tonight," said Ed.

"I guess you're pretty tired," said Vic. Ed turned and looked at the tall thin girl sitting loosely on the edge of her chair, he smiled slowly. "That's it," he said. "I'm all in."

"We better go home," said Rosamond, "and let you get some sleep."

"Aaw now," said Gus, disappointed. "Stick around a while, He ain't going to bed. You don't know him."

"Don't go," said Ed. "Can we have something to eat, Maud?"

"Eat, eat, eat, I never see such eaters in all my life. Sure you can have bread." She pulled the tin bread box toward her and raising out a big loaf began slicing it up. Ed and the blue-sweatered fellow edged toward the bread. They looked tired and like kids under the shaky gas light.

"One thing I want to ask you, is Bill all right?" said Gus leaning toward his brother foolishly eager.

"He's all right, sure, he's always all right," said Ed munching bread.

"I wouldn't call stewing in jail all right," said Mrs. Gus.

"What jail was that?" asked Amos politely.

"Oh he ain't perticular," joked Gus, "he's tried them all, ain't that right, Ed?"

"Just about," said Ed. He was provoked at his brother for getting people up here. How did he know who they were? Trouble with Gus was that he was just a showoff. Perhaps it would be better to sing something and get rid of them. The girls were pretty though. Too bad Big Bill hadn't come up, he liked a pretty girl, who didn't? God-almighty.

Swallowing his cup of wine he screwed up his face and began singing.

Scissor Bill, he is a little dippy,
Scissor Bill, he has a funny face,
Scissor Bill, should drown in Mississippi,
He is the missing link that Darwin tried to trace.

As his big voice, singing softly, began the words, Gus's face broke into smiles, he began clapping his hands to his knees and as Ed crinkled his cheeks to simulate the ugly Bill, he did the same, swallowing his cheeks, ogling his eyes. Even Mrs. Gus sat stiffly admiring.

Scissor Bill, the foreigners is cussin',
Scissor Bill, he says, "I hate a coon"
Scissor Bill, is down on everybody
The Hottentots, the bushmen and the man in the moon.

"Come on, now," said Ed warming up. "Everybody, what's the matter with you, Sam. Get in on this."

Gus, Sam, and Ed all edged together, their faces warmed and excited. "Ready now," said Ed. They sang through another verse, came to another chorus. "Come on, now," said Ed looking at the girls.

> Scissor Bill wouldn't join the union.
> Scissor Bill, he says, "Not me, by Heck,"
> Scissor Bill gets his reward in Heaven.
> Oh sure. He'll get it, but he'll get it in the neck.

As he said the last line, Ed doubled up and then threw his head back contemptuously. Gus spit out the words, Oh sure, with relish. Sam reached for another piece of bread and Mr. Wendel laughed softly. The Wendel girls were mortified not to know the words. "Let's sing it again," said Vicky. "Then we can learn it."

Ed had been feeling low but the words put life back into him. He was feeling good once more and ready for anything. Tomorrow there might be trouble, but tonight they could all sing. There were two ways to fight the jails, singing and silence. He'd seen both.

"Why don't we sing Casey Jones?" said Gus. "I like that one about the best. When I was a kid I always said I'd be a railroad man because we lived near the yards, but I never got any nearer than loading trucks to take to the depots."

"I'd rather sing, Come with me Now, My Girly for a change," said Sam.

"That's a wonderful song," said Gus. "But it ain't a real man's song."

"What song is that?" said Vic.

"It's a good song," said Ed, clearing his throat. As he began it, Rosamond said whispering to Vic, "It's got the tune of Meet me Tonight in Dreamland that we used to roller skate to."

Ed frowned and went on. Mrs. Gus put the bread knife down and leaned forward, breathing softly with open mouth.

> Come with me now, my girly,
> Don't sleep out in the cold,
> Your face and tresses curly,
> Will bring you fame and gold,
> Automobiles to ride in, diamonds and silk to wear,
> You'll be a star bright, down in the red light,
> You'll make your fortune there.

"See," said Gus. "That's an old hag trying to lure the girl."

"Sure," said Ed. "Do you want to hear it?"

Gus waved his hand to go on. Vicky thought of Papa's store on Pearl Street before he lost his business, with the red lights in the doorways of the houses opposite. Papa always thought she didn't know what went on there. Suppose he had known that she had really admired Mabel Moore in those days, that big handsome woman sidling down the stairs like a seal and standing on the pavement in the hot sun looking around her with big melting black eyes under a little black satin umbrella lined with shell pink? It took years to identify her with the Mabel Moore who got arrested regularly in the Oxtail papers as Resort Keeper, Gets Fine. She sat dreamily during the song and Ed feeling that he wasn't getting the attention, quit abruptly and poured some more wine.

"You ain't quitting," said Gus.

"Oh can't we sing more. Can't we hear Casey Jones?" said Rosamond.

"I'm afraid you're tired of me barking," said Ed. When the song stopped, he was tired himself. In his head all the plans for the work in the oil fields and for the coming harvest season jumped around. They'd try to suck them in for sixteen hours a day and rotten grub. Everything went too slow. Speed, that was what was needed. How were you going to get it? He looked around at Mr. Wendel and the girls who were looking at him. Nice friendly girls. Tomorrow they would be working in some dinky little job but tonight they could sing.

"No sir, you got to sing Casey Jones," said Gus.

"Then we'll really go," said Vicky Wendel.

Casey Jones went to Hell a-flying,
"Casey Jones," the devil said. "Oh, fine;
Casey Jones, get busy shoveling sulphur—
That's what you get for scabbing on the S.P. line."

As he sang, he tapped his knee and Mr. Wendel tapped his. Mrs. Gus with a kind of unfamiliar abandon, swayed her head, her cheeks flushed. All her bitterness toward her brother-in-law had vanished. The Wendel girls, and Ed, Sam, and Gus leaned toward one another, swaying as they sang. The girls uncertain followed as best they could. When they came to the verses, Ed took it up alone. His voice was strong and pumped fresh life into the stale little room. His back was turned toward the screen door and outside the earth slid away from the house on stilts to other shacks below where the packing house families lived on the muddy flats.

When the breeze shifted a nasty packing house odor of burning hoofs and hair drifted slowly over the helpless town and into the very room where the singer sat. But nobody noticed it much in that room. They were looking at Ed, beating time with his head, with his big hand. His eyes flashed from Vic to Gus, from Gus to Amos and back to Rosamond. Now and then he would take in Mrs. Gus with a long sweep of his hand.

"Where'd that song come from?" said Rosamond.

"It come from the whitest guy you'd ever have hoped to meet," said Ed. "The dirty finks got him and shot him." His mouth got ugly as he said it. Under his look they sat very still waiting for the next words that were certain to concern them all.

"They shot him at Salt Lake City," said Ed. "But you can't kill that bird. How do you want to die, they says, hanging or shooting? I'll die fighting, says Joe Hill, hitting out and they had to tie him to a chair before they could shoot him."

BEHIND THE SCENES

The night the Wendels went to Gus's house to hear Ed sing, the Troys gave an evening for Mr. Buckingham from New York. It was too bad poor Tim Meller came with a patch across his head.

"Poor little boy," said silky Mrs. Troy, passing behind his chair and drawing fingers that she fondly hoped were velvety across his forehead. "Did it hurt him?"

"You bet your life it did," said Tim, looking angrily at Mr. Troy.

"What was the big idea. I told those boys to throw something to start things but not at *me*."

"Well, Meller," Troy said, "I can't understand it. A little accident. Happens all the time. But I'd look into it."

"I said, plain as day, get something started, but I never said hit me."

"Of course not," said Troy. "Of course I think it was a mistake for you to go ramming your car in like that. Just antagonizes the crowd."

"Hell's fire, you didn't want to baby *that* crowd, did you?"

"No," said Troy, looking at Mrs. Denbar, the jeweler's wife, who was sipping a cocktail in an elegant manner. "But you got to handle this situation with gloves."

Mr. Buckingham spoke up. "If I might put in a word with you gentlemen," he said easily. "I've had a little experience with this kind of thing. The Chambers of Commerce recognize the danger. That's why I'm out making speeches. Not that I'm much of a speechmaker," he deprecated to Mrs. Troy who played up nobly with "I'm sure you are, Mr. Buckingham. You've got such a nice voice."

Mr. Buckingham chuckled but turning suddenly toward Mr. Meller said, "I'll tell you something, it's a stiff fight. What do you suppose we're turning loose so many speakers for, in a time like this? Not to help the boys through college, not by a long shot. This is an open shop drive and if we don't win, it'll be a setback. Of course," he straightened and smiled, "we'll win."

"Now you're talking," said Troy. "Well, the bankers did their bit today. We met and sent a stiff set of resolutions to the Department of Justice disapproving of the convention here. It puts us right and I think will square matters with the boys in the east."

"Credit men did the same," said Denbar. "Hey Flossie, don't forget your uncle." He held out a glass and Flossie Troy poured leaning toward him. A heavy perfume blurred the drink and Denbar sighed, like Valentino, sniffing up the rich odor.

"You boys don't know the half of it yet," said Meller. "They made a deal with Handy that lets Henderson hold the sack."

"What do you mean?"

"Well, the police lay off the legion and the gang lays off Handy. We got to go through the motions with Henderson and his outfit. He's pretty sure of himself, says he's got the people back of him whoever they are and now the boys think he was playing pretty smart and acting possum so he could draw them into this. Of course the I.W.W. were sacrificed. They're probably hoofing it out of town. But what are a few I.W.W. among friends."

"What do we go through with the recall for then?" said Troy. "I don't see it."

"Henderson has a lot of strong arms back of him, see. They won't listen to reason. If a guy won't listen to reason, I don't know what you're going to do about it. It looks bad. I feel sick."

"It's only your head," said Troy.

"Rot," said Meller. "I tell you we won't make much headway until we get rid of Handy."

"He's a kind of nut, isn't he?" said Buckingham.

"Oh yes, he's a nut. Believes in all sorts of isms. Now I believe in freedom, but not license. This I.W.W. business is just wanton license. And dangerous. It makes me see red."

"Well the point is, will he cooperate with us on the open shop programs? He's got to be made to realize the seriousness of the business. This country is going to be flooded with soldiers with no jobs for them. You got to bring down the scale somehow or the business man is going to be strapped. Then the country goes to the dogs."

"He's a union man," said Meller. "I tell you and tell you."

"Even so, Mr. Meller," said Buckingham, smiling, "we may be able to make him see the light. You can take the case of Mr. Gompers."

"Now that the excitement's over, we better have a look at Mamma's card again," said Amos Wendel. He read it aloud and shook his head. "It sounds bad to me," he said. "Bound to be worse than she says. Should we wire her?" The two girls read the card over several times. It did not make sense to them. Their heads were still buzzing with the songs Ed had sung. Every stick of furniture in the house looked unfamiliar as if they had only visited in this place, never belonged to it. They finally argued about the card and decided to wire the next day; she couldn't be worse or they would have heard and the card did not sound serious.

When their father continued to fuss a little, the girls could hardly hide their impatience. There he sat smoking his last pipe of the day and they felt as if they had just been to someone's funeral. Joe Hill was a young man that they could almost see.

Rosamond sat writing to Jerry, trying to hide her anxiety about him. Who cared about their life together? The war was over and there seemed no prospect of his coming home. The house, the town itself was as confining as a box. She cheered herself by writing a long encouraging letter to Jerry full of ideas about their future life. They would study and find things out and never get dull and never save to make payments on anything and they would keep alive. What if the war had ended in false and broken promises and everyone feeling let down? A new world would come. She felt self-conscious after some of her high-flown sentences and almost blushed to read them. Maybe the censors would make trouble, but, no, the war was supposed to be over. Surely she could tell her own husband a few things. He was feeling low enough, she could tell by the monotone of his letters. The songs kept repeating themselves and her pen almost swung to a kind of remembered rhythm. It was funny the lift singing gave a person. It would be fine to sing like that with hundreds, with thousands of people. She could remember the fun of singing with a crowd; not since she was a little kid had that happened. What a fuss the schools used to make on George Washington's birthday, herding them all together to march down the big hall in even rows to the roll of a drum. Then the flag salute and singing O Say Can You See. It almost seemed as if the song didn't matter, just the singing. But the songs Ed sang were important. The words were the kind that stirred you up; not like the songs on Mamma's piano that filled you with a pleasant sadness and eternal hopelessness.

As Rosamond wrote, she looked up and wondered what Vicky was thinking about. She was pretending to read. Every now and then in living something exciting happened to make life seem bright. Then dullness covered it up again. There ought to be a cue to keep that brightness. Vicky wished she knew where Caseman was so she could write to him as Rosamond was writing to Jerry. When she considered how little she knew that fellow, she couldn't understand why she always seemed to go back to him in her thoughts, except that he was alive and she wanted to live like that, without a settled kind of living. She really believed that she was very fitted for a kind of exciting existence that had its base in something besides the usual things people lived for. She told herself she was like Uncle Joe, like her mother's father even, both of whom had moved around, had been adventurous—and losers— you couldn't say that they had won. They had died, with thousands of other young men, trying to get success that she could very well see, in spite of Uncle David, came to the few. She even thought that she was making things easy for herself by not wanting that kind of future and not caring for property or silver tea sets. She really believed that she was pretty well stripped for action and would make a fine soldier in the struggle for a decent world.

The only trouble was that she had no idea how to go about it. Tomorrow, perhaps tonight, Ed would be gone. Caseman moved fast as lightning. She seemed always left in a house in the midst of chairs and mirrors and beds and plumbing that people gave up their lives for. At that minute she figured she was above wanting such things but the next she remembered that the Legion had that very night kicked the chairs in the I.W.W. hall to pieces. The kicked chairs made her blood boil as if they had been paid for by her own sweat. She wished she had been the one to throw a stone at Meller. The stone was thrown on purpose, Ed said, to start something. Their gang would not throw stones—not at a time like that. A complicated conspiratorial battle was going on all the time. The Mellers and the Troys and the Brackwoods were always at it, Ed said, always getting ready for it and spying and sitting tight. And the guys they were after were guys like him. Like us, Ed had said, looking at her. The guys they are laying for are you and me, Ed said, smiling his big smile. Papa had laughed as if Ed was joshing but Vicky took it very seriously. She was glad to find herself lined up against those small town snobs whose daughters had been the cause of one of her early hurts when she was almost too little to know what it meant. Nancy and Clara had been to a church party on the best side of town and Nancy had come home a little crestfallen. Telling about it, she said she and Clara had been walking along in the street in the dark and heard the "swells" coming, they could tell by the jingle of their bracelets. It was the style to wear bracelets loaded with gold and silver hearts, and the little girl could fancy the bigger girls coming with a jingle of finery that left her own two sisters in the cold. She had never forgotten that shriveling of the heart. It was not nice to hear Nancy's hurt voice. The swells had swept by the two girls from the wrong side of town and none of Mamma's stories of her family and their exploits could cover the discomfort. Only Ed and a street full of Wobblies singing and making things uncomfortable for these first families could wipe out that past.

Anne Wendel was pleased to have a wire from her little family. She had the maid at the hotel prop it up for her on the dresser and felt that her sacrifices were worth something when her family showed such concern. It was not easy to lie in bed but she comforted herself thinking how much worse off it might be. The doctor was hinting that it could not be a strained ligament or it would show improvement and he talked vaguely of muscle strain and maybe something fractured. Anne gritted her teeth as he touched the leg but she had more faith in nature than doctors and told him to run along and let time heal.

As soon as she could, she wrote a soothing letter to Nancy who was still upset about the highhanded way the girls had acted in Seattle. "You mustn't mind the girls, they're young yet and full of ideas. Vicky always was a little overbearing, it's her way. They mean well." She forgot her pain in her trouble about Nancy and her hurt. She took such things so to heart and had always been so helpful with the younger children, sending them little sums when they were in college. The year Papa's business had failed, Nancy and Clifford had moved in with the family just to help out. That's the kind she was. Yet she couldn't help but feel a kind of pride in those two stiff-necked younger girls. She told herself they were like her and she could see them reliving all her own aspirations. If only she could get her money out of the Grapeville property so she could help them. Rosamond was writing about wanting to go back to college, she and Jerry together, and there was nothing Anne Wendel would like more to see. Education was a fine thing, it lasted when money failed you. Even when health deserted you, you had it. She couldn't understand some of the slighting things Vicky said about it, but apparently they weren't serious as Rosamond still believed in college. Of course she didn't know as much about it as Vic. She wished she knew what Vicky was driving at. Sometimes the girl reminded her uneasily of poor Joe. She had that same kind of a drive but what she was heading for, Anne Wendel did not know. She used to think the girl wanted to be a teacher, she was so bent on education but now she wouldn't hear of teaching. Sometimes she talked almost wild in her letters. It gave the mother concern. She wished she had her Emerson here or Thoreau. It would be a comfort to read something steadying that took her mind off her leg.

Her sister Hortense wrote, but her letters were beginning to nag at Anne. She had used her Victory coupons to buy a Victrola and her daughter Eloise's baby boy was a joy, played pat-a-cake in the wash basin and then drank the water. Tossed sand in his hair. Was a great big Boy. No mistake about that. Milton was slowly wasting away and she could hardly bear to mention him to her sister. When she learned that Anne was flat on her back, she wrote the first cheerful letter in a long time. It was so full of good spirits that it almost seemed to Anne that her sister rejoiced at her ill fortune.

David Trexler showed real concern when he wrote. He said she ought to go back to Oxtail and he painted gloomy pictures of all the awful things that could happen if she didn't go. Anne Wendel had to fall back on her own resources and admit that even one's loved ones are a weak reed. But she hastily put that idea out of her mind, it made life seem very lonesome.

David Trexler was not in clover. Cushioned in a comfortable little town that had few labor troubles, his interests took him far enough afield to hear rumblings that disturbed him. His investments in spruce lumber that jumped from $33 a thousand to $115, government price, had been reinvested in good solid Roseland investments. Friends began to ask his advice on investments and he had managed to divert some Indiana Standard Oil to Wheatley's Tidbits, Roseland Linen Mills and Chumley's, Inc. He himself was pretty heavily involved in those transactions and new capital was needed at a time when the big trend in business affairs was toward centralization. He was backing a chain store scheme that would capture every important drug location in Oregon, Washington, and Idaho. From these states they could nibble inland. At noonday business luncheons he was beginning to be called upon more and more as a speaker.

His doctrine was simple; strict honesty, a fair profit to capital, and equitable wages for labor. It paid in his own instance and he was more and more inclined to give little bonuses to clerks in his store and to encourage them to buy homes, with himself as mortgage holder. "Give your employee a stake in your business, make him realize he is your partner, just as you are the co-partner of every business interest in this country, and you guarantee for yourself a safe and happy landing." He liked the way he ended such a speech, standing with his hand lightly resting on the table cloth, his eye glasses gleaming, his good clean skin radiating health. He could feel himself as a magnetic force in his community, it was a sweet triumph. His pockets were filling out but his heart was empty. His triumphs were not enough.

His son Dave, Jr., had returned from overseas with broken arches, falling hair, and rotten tonsils. He had had the temerity to stop at Arden, Pennsylvania, and look up his aunt Millie. He actually brought up that fatal name at the table, casually relating that the man she had married was a really nice fellow, lame in one leg from rheumatism.

"Rheumatism," snorted his father carving the roast viciously. "You believe that?"

"That's what Aunt Millie said," said Dave. He answered his

father squarely, without fight and without interest. What had happened to the boy? The spring had gone out of him; he was resigned to life, not excited about it. It goaded his father to fury to watch such passivity. "And they've got a fine little house, nothing fancy, but Aunt Millie and he run a little business, a grocery business, and she told me that one day they just shut up shop and took the Ford and rode around picking wild flowers." Dave said it lingeringly as if it was hard to believe.

"That will land them in the poorhouse fast enough," snorted David. His wife looked at him anxiously and at her son she looked with astonishment. What had got in the boy to bring up such a subject? But he was changed. His very indifference had finally been of good service to him in his love affair with Charlotte. When he came back she had actually gone to Portland to meet him, spurred on by the kind of quiet resignation to life that his late letters showed.

In the lobby of one of the best hotels she waited for him eagerly. When handsome officers passed in burnished boots and belts she half rose, expectant. That morning she had unfortunately cut her finger and the bandage bothered her. It had been difficult to force it into the glove finger but she would not think of waiting for him without gloves. She sat, fresh and sweet, flowers pinned to her jacket, her heart beating, anxious, some of her vanity about herself and life shaken. She was ready to be his now; it was time to make a home, to have a settled position in the town and who was better than David Trexler's son. Everybody said that Mr. Trexler owned the town really. Why, he had mortgages on half the business blocks and was putting up the new bank building himself.

She waited and the glistening boots passed by. She was staring across the floor at the desk when a hollow voice said, "Hello, Charlotte," and looking she saw first a pair of ugly shoes, unevenly taped legs, baggy pants, lumpy jacket, and then Dave's face, pale and not smiling.

"Why, Dave," she said, getting up and feeling suddenly lost and like crying. "Why, Dave."

Her "Why, Dave" told him there was a change but he knew that already. He had said that Charlotte was the one thing he would fight to keep but there was no need to fight. Girls were marrying fast and she was ready. He wished they had married before he went overseas. Everything that would ever happen to him would come too late.

David Trexler was almost as ashamed of this indifferent son as if he had been a criminal. It made the father more red-blooded than ever. He stayed late in his office every night, figuring, drafting letters, making notes for the next day. Sometimes very late he would shut his eyes and throw his head back and wonder what kind of a life he might have had if his sister Anne had not interfered when he tried to elope to St. Louis with that little actress so long ago. He still took an active interest in the stage and talked familiarly of the Barrymore family and their movements. But no one was like Modjeska and he had yet to see a performance such as Madame Jaunauschek gave in Marie Antoinette when he was a young man.

Sitting in his office he made up drafts of his life and saw himself like an actor moving in the scene he had created. Some of the scenes were not working out as he had planned. Millie had played a bad act. Dave, Jr., was not going to play the part he had hoped. His daughter Sue was giving him concern. It would be disgraceful to have an old maid in the family. His baby Pussy-dee was too young to worry about and his other son Daniel did not show signs of setting the world on fire. Still it was hard to tell; he was young and had just come home from cruising around with the navy. Both boys were back, a little the worse for wear. It was now time to consolidate his efforts, make sure that the foundations he had laid would be properly utilized.

Sometimes at night he made out little checks to people in distress. To the son of the washerwoman who had the broken arm. Of course, they had never bought the woman a machine and she had continually bothered them about it but when the wash was done so well without, why throw money away. Then his clerk's nephew was sick and had no money; a helping hand there.

Oh, it was a joy to reach out the helping hand and he craved more and more to be close to people, to have them look up to him, to fancy them pointing him out, "There goes Mr. Trexler, the

philanthropist, he does so many nice things, and all so quietly."
This rôle he liked better than any he had fancied himself in, better
than being the bank president although that ambition would soon
be realized.

No one could say he had made a penny dishonestly, it had been
aboveboard, according to law. Profits had been extraordinarily
high during the war but look at the munition makers, there was the
profit. Fortunately he had invested in Bethlehem Steel and liked to
think of his investment working for him back there in the little
town where as a boy he had visited his aunt and Uncle Blank and
the old mule had scared him bellowing that little boys should be
seen not heard. How aunt had liked the cigars he used to take her,
much better than cologne. Yes, if truth were told, it was that old
association that had led him to Bethlehem Steel. He explained
none of these intricate matters to his son who was a good clerk in
the store.

To his sister he wrote a long letter blaming Aaron for his neglect
and reminding her of their childhood together when they had gone
on Sundays to Chestnut Hill and jumped down the steps at
George's Hall. Did she think the trees were still in Geoffrey
Avenue where the cardinal bird sat and sang that time he escaped
from his cage, and where was the stuffed mockingbird? Mouldering in Hortense's trunk, or where? Did she remember the big cage
Joe had made for them and the morning that he walked in from the
South carrying the birds wrapped up in papers.

He would write like this and then sit back, his head aching.
Since Millie went away, it was not so easy to go to his wife for
consolation. He felt shut up in himself, and for business this was a
good way to feel. But at night all the rest of him boiled over and
kept him up late negotiating little matters for needy relatives and
hangers-on. It led him to write his coexecutor in his brother's
estate at Grapeville to please give Mrs. Wendel a helping hand and
see to it that her claim against the estate was settled up even if they
had to take it to court. Also if he could find a buyer for some lots
she had mentioned, Mr. Trexler would consider it a favor and
doubtless Mrs. Wendel would see he was compensated.

He loved the wording of these letters, sitting like a judge with the pen poised over his neat methodical writing with the even slanting letters. Walking along the quiet streets around two or three in the morning, he took pleasure in the sleeping town. He felt like a father who has been up at night with a sick child. The early graying light, perhaps a policeman pacing past the bank and his respectful "Morning, Mr. Trexler," soothed him and gave him confidence in his ambitious and benevolent projects. It made him pass over the letters from the farmer begging for a renewal and stiffened him when it came time to foreclose on Sam Blackwell. How much good could he do if he allowed shiftlessness to take a premium? Business was business and, if he was in the game, he must abide by the rules. Hard though it was to be businesslike at times, it would have been a criminal neglect of his duties if he allowed himself to slip through life as blithely as a boy. He hoped he had strength for his burden and it comforted him to remember the parable of the talents. Even the Lord recognized the benefits of fruitfulness. Increase. If you have a dime, make it a dollar. When a fine character who fought for the common people, like William Jennings Bryan, did not scorn to accumulate this world's goods out of purely saving qualities and smartness a little above par, he should accept his own destiny and bow to his responsibilities.

He hoped he had the strength to bear them, as with each step he neared his home after a long night session in his office, scorning to use his car, climbing toward his house that caught the first rays of the sun and sometimes the sun was beginning to fall into his bedroom as he wearily fell asleep.

When Amos Wendel heard from his wife that as soon as her leg was better she would come home, he strained himself to squeeze out every penny he could to make more payments on the house. He looked forward to her surprise and pleasure and could not understand the indifference of his two girls to his purpose. At night, as he smoked his last pipe of the day, he thought of them, soberly trying to understand why they wanted to bat around without possessions except what a small trunk would hold.

At the warehouse there had been some trouble. The Bryants had proposed another small cut in Gus's wages and his own. Gus got up on his high horse and said he wouldn't stand for it. The two of them had actually made a scene about it to Bryant.

"What's this," Andy Bryant had said, pulling his pipe from his mouth. "What's this," trying to make a joke out of it.

"We get low enough as it is," said Gus. "I can't feed my family decent, or buy them clothing as it is. What do you want to do, starve us off the face of the earth?" He stood there his legs apart like his brother Ed, his head up. He'd sure learned fight from that brother, not that it was, as yet, to do him much good.

"You don't like it, huh?" said Andy Bryant, shifting his pipe that he had stuck back in his mouth, then yanking it out like an all day sucker. He still thought he could kid the boys along.

"No, and neither would you. You think because there are a few soldier boys looking for jobs, you can give us a nickel and tell us to run along. Well, we can't live on air."

Andy Bryant colored up, particularly as a traveling man in the office, hearing the noise, edged to the door and stood looking on with a patronizing smirk on his mush.

"Let me tell you something," said Andy, taking a strong man pose, and tapping Gus on the chest. "If you hadn't worked here for years, I'd give you the can, as it is I'll give you another chance. Did you ever hear of supply and demand? You did, huh. Well, that works here as well as elsewhere. There's plenty of good husky boys who are going to be glad to step right in where you leave off. If you don't like it, try to suit yourself somewhere else. You know me," he whined, looking at Amos, "and you know that I wouldn't do this if the business didn't warrant it. Amos knows, he's had a business of his own."

"It's not the same thing," said Amos. "My business ran down, and this is standing up pretty good."

Andy got red and the traveling man made his grin wider. "You boys get to work and think this over after hours. Tell me what you want to do. That brother of yours ain't doing you no good Gus, I'll warn you." He whistled in a light and airy mood, went into the office, slammed the door and, sticking a pencil behind his ear, stood

up before the slanting high desk to run his finger down the column
of orders. The two men looked at each other. Gus swore. "God-
damn if he can treat us as if we were in didies." Amos didn't know
what to do. He hated to think that he would lose his job and the
house that was slowly getting paid for.

Gus swore all the rest of the afternoon. He was scared to quit
because he wasn't sure enough of getting another job. "Amos,
we're nothing, just you and me, but you take if we had one big
union, or organized like in Seattle Ed was telling us about, I bet
you he could whistle then. Say, wouldn't you like to see Oxtail on
its rump waiting for the dirty work to be done, the cars stopped, no
gas, no light, no deliveries, just a dead town with people walking
and everything tied up tight as a drum." The picture set him up
like a stiff drink and he shoved the freight onto the trucks with the
energy of two men. "Hey, take it slow," Amos warned.

The evening with Ed had left a warm spot in Amos, but that was
all. He got the idea of the strike though and wished he was
younger.

"Gus," he said, "we ought to belong to a union. But you take
some of the unions, I never liked what I heard about them, they
were not much good for the men, just fattened up some walking
delegate, seemed to me."

"Oh, we'd have a real union," said Gus. "But right now, I
dunno," he rubbed his head, squinting and thinking hard. He'd
never have the nerve to show himself again at home if he lost his
job, but he hated himself standing for it. How could he face his
brother Ed if he were to lie down and take it. Damn it, if a man's
mistake wasn't getting married. Marriage like all the other good
things was for the Andy Bryants. They could nuzzle at home and
have things nice and not worry about their kids getting a right
start. No sir, a fella should stay single and fight a two-fisted fight.
Amos was useless; he was old but he had had a fair life. Not a
house like a chicken coop, that's one sure thing.

The two men took their trouble home and Amos hated to admit
that his wages were to be cut. It made him out so worthless. Vicky
and Rosamond blew up at the mention of the cut.

"Why Papa, that's outrageous. You and Gus should quit. Just leave such a place."

"Where would we go?" said Amos quietly. "Oxtail isn't so big. There's a lot of young fellows looking around for jobs. But I tell you, Gus told Bryant a few things. He got kind of hot under the collar."

"He ought to have more of Ed in him," said Rosamond. "He ought to get into a union, and so should you." Both girls looked severely at their father who felt uncomfortably like a little boy.

"Just what we said," he said. "But where you going to find a union? We ought to have done it long ago. Bryant's got us in his power. Two fellows alone haven't got much punch."

The girls didn't know what to say to their father. "He's old," said Vicky as she and Rosamond washed the supper dishes. "We might as well admit it. But it's awful for Gus and those kids. Oh, why can't people *do* something." She squeezed the towel hard, standing there, helpless. The dishes bounced around in the suds, there was the plate with the gold rim that was a wedding present. The knives and forks with the pearl handles should never go in hot water. Uncle Joe had sent them to Aunt Catherine from the south. He had gotten out, as they were certainly going to do. They had heard that story and thought they knew it by heart. No one ever wanted to get out into the world more than Uncle Joe had.

Oxtail papers flippantly reported that as an outdoor sport revolution in Mexico had lost a lot of popularity in the last few weeks, Generals Zapata and Blanquet would both be missing when May first bills came in. They were jubilant too about the American troops making their spring advance in Siberia against heaven knows what enemy. It was confusing to Amos Wendel who read the papers from cover to cover and often thought of April as a cruel month. His girls chose April to go away and he felt the White Elephant like an octopus around him. He wished he and Mamma had a modern bungalow without so many feet of pipes and plumbing to make trouble. One thing was certain. His wages had been cut. The Wobblies were driven out. The papers crowed until Mayor Handy won out on his recall election. Then they settled down to business and sourly began reporting strikes that were popping from

one end of the country to the other. The Oxtail *News* that had so
cheerfully consigned to oblivion the "lost" Seattle general strike
was obliged to mention, one by one, strike by strike, five million
men swelling the "trouble" for the bosses,

    STEEL,

        MINES,

            PACKING HOUSES,

                RAILROAD CARMEN.

When they began singing the boy whose brother had been shot down in the march on Ford's sang too. His shoulder was painful and swelled in a big blue lump under the old sweater. He stood with his forehead resting against the bars, and Solidarity Forever rang through the hollow halls. Funny the way even the jailor had more or less fallen under the spell. When the fat old bird discovered the hammers and sickles they had drawn up on that wall on the way to the yard with VOTE COMMUNIST he had razzed them. "Say, what ya mean? Vote Communist. Didn't you guys ever see a ballot? Vote who for?" And Belton had yelled out, "Very good criticism, Comrade," and the next day by god if they didn't chalk up Vote for FOSTER and FORD. It was their jail. There wasn't a man who wasn't singing by this time. All the petty thieves clapped in for snatching at scissors, wrenches, auto parts, pieces of lead, brass knobs, for a few cents to buy grub for the kids, for themselves, to hold together until "something turned up." The boys from Ford's took turns on the soapbox, speaking out from their cells. If one was shut up another began.

Don't be afraid fellows. We are all workers. We were fired on by gunmen as if we were criminals. All we asked is work. You are here because society has no place for you. Fellow workers . . .

Silence.

A tread on the cold floor, rattle of god knows what, silence. But silence has many voices, the voices of the past, of our consciences. He is silent, the boy whose brother was shot down, leans his head against the wall, thinks that Lenin too lost a brother. At the hands of the Czar's hangmen. It is cold in his cell and he lets his mind trail back to the book he once read in a warm room, trying with his mind's little light to see the page, to chase the very elusive words that tell about that other brother. A brilliant student—like his own brother had wanted to be when he was in highschool before he had to quit to support them all—but the Russian, Alexander, had been interested in worms, and his brother was crazy about chemistry. Alexander had studied so much about worms that Lenin thought he couldn't be much of a revolutionist. They had been very young boys but the older had been considered enough of a dangerous man to kill.

The boy in the jail tried now to remember every living word on the page he had once read, he kept at it, steadily pursuing. "The fate of the brother influenced Lenin, all his life." There was comfort in those words. He tried to hold to them to keep out the look of his brother's young face, dead. But they were singing again and he got up and sang with them; his voice was unnecessarily loud and the prisoners hearing him made their voices louder to match his own.

III. AMERICAN DESERT

ROSAMOND set off for Detroit full of high hopes of getting an interesting job and meeting interesting people. In the summer she and Jerry could make trips on the lake, they could save money and take work at the university, they might manage to go to France and live a year. Anything might happen once she was out of Oxtail.

Corny Stebbins had run down considerably. He looked faded and shabby. They spent an evening in a dismal speakeasy and she had to listen to all his troubles; his kids had been sick that winter and his wife was afraid she was going to have another. He still had a lot of brag and insisted on taking her around town the next day and giving her a harangue right on the street corner about the lousy politicians and the betrayed boys who had gone to fight for a democracy that had never existed.

"If I told you all the dirt about this bloated town, you'd not believe it," he said. Someday he was going to write a novel about it. In spite of his boring attentions, he was helpful and got her in touch with some people who promised to introduce her to someone with pull. She took a little room pretty well out and spent a lot of time riding around on busses sizing up the town. After Seattle it wasn't much for sightseeing, but it had an air of being in the thick of things that was better. Scenery was all right, but boring, taken by itself.

On the weekend Stebbins insisted that she take a little outing with him and his oldest kid, a boy about ten. He made up an alluring story about the lake and for a terrible price she bought the cheapest bathing suit she could find. It turned out to be a sell and shrank in the water. They went down to Cedar Point in the pouring rain, but the minute she began to hear real breakers Rosamond was happy. "I never thought there'd be real breakers," she said, getting excited and leaning out the side of Corny's Ford.

"What'd you think there'd be," Corny's kid wanted to know.

"I didn't know the lake made breakers," said Rosemond, laughing at the kid. She felt friendly and happy toward Stebbins who relaxed and made a great to-do of ordering the best meal in the house. But when it came to rooms, there was nothing doing and Corny had to pull his press card out of his pocket with a big show and say he'd have to get rooms that night. There was scurrying around and rooms were found for them, Corny feeling very important.

"That's all those damned cards are for or the jobs either. I don't know how much longer I can stand it. I want to get out of this mess. Perhaps to Seattle where you don't spend all the time paying coal bills and wiping kids' noses, and besides look at the strike they pulled there. They're alive."

Rosamond thought it was a great joke for him to be aching to go to a place she had just come from. They both decided that everything was absolutely crazy. After a few glasses of wine Corny got a little loud and Rosamond hoped she wasn't going to have trouble managing him. A couple of fellows had come in and were sitting at the next table eyeing him in a suspicious manner. "I bet this country has made more millionaires during this war than widows. The interests own the country, they own the patriots, and if the returned soldiers weren't snagged by all the talk, they'd get on their toes." One of the fellows at the other table stiffened and came over.

"I don't like your talk," he began, swaying, resting a large hand flatfingered on the table.

"You don't. Say, who are you?"

"That's my business, but I'm something you never were, I'm a soldier that was in the defense of this country."

'Where," said Corny, "Camp Dix or Camp Lewis? It's you little halfassed stay-at-homes that make all the trouble. You ganged up on the finest bunch of workers in the northwest and committed murder."

"That kind of talk won't get you nothing but trouble, buddy," said the fellow getting red. The proprietor had come into the room and fussily answered Rosamond's warning look with a, "Here now, what's matter boys, take it easy, tame down now, no trouble." The boys, both a little groggy, sulkily retired to their drinks. Corny muttered to himself and Rosamond took the kid to his room and told him he had better go to bed.

Once upstairs, she felt suddenly too tired for another bout of talk below and locked herself in her room. Unsteady voices rose in quarrelsome tones from downstairs. She undressed and went to bed and, opening the windows, let the noise of the surf rising in the storm shut out the racket below. Several hours later she was still awake, in a happy doze, thinking of the time when Mamma had taken them all to Oregon. She lay in bed soothed and cared for by that remote past, forgetful of Corny and when she heard the handle of her door turned stealthily, she laughed a little to herself. The door was secure and in a few minutes his unsteady steps turned away and went along the hall.

Through Corny's efforts she landed a job in the clinic at Harper's Hospital and was elated to be interviewing patients and keeping records instead of hammering out business epistles all day long. The patients were mostly foreigners and the big room where she worked had long benches like those in the waiting rooms of the railroad station in Oxtail. She kept the records on nice little blue cards. It was hard to condense the human misery that boiled up from the huddled patients who sometimes whispered their complaints hurriedly and completely as if in a confessional: "I got body sickness, just body sickness. Baby died, his bones so little like chicken bones. Boils all over me after I got that dye on me. Baby cries all the time. Yes mam, four living and four dead."

At the end of the day she was glad to go to her room and sit looking out the window at a big tree with little green leaves. Sometimes a kid in rompers rolled over the grass and plunked down looking surprised. She wrote to Jerry pretty regularly but his letters were slow to reach her. A kind of leaden reserve in them frightened her. Once he wrote that they were handing out scholarships at the Sorbonne but he wouldn't be lucky enough for that. He had been detailed to a wood-chopping outfit instead. Perhaps they'd ship him back without once seeing Paris, but he had learned French and studied it all the time. Maybe they could both come back to France some day, he kind of liked the life. The little town of Limoges was not very large, but you never got to know it. A cathedral topped it off and the streets ran around and up to it as it squatted there like a big spider sucking up the flies. The idea of going to France suited Rosamond. She thought of Paris as a city almost enchanted. It had a kind of aura around it just as the name Sarah Bernhardt had. The future was certainly going to be a gamble but it didn't matter just so they didn't get stuck in stupid jobs and stupid towns. As the time came for Jerry to come home, waiting seemed an eternity and she was glad to distract herself with moonlight trips to Lake St. Clair or a dance at the Arcadia with a young fellow who had been introduced by Corny Stebbins.

Corny himself had taken his rôle of the somewhat elderly friend with good grace. Sometimes he thought sadly of their more romantic footing in Oxtail, and even Rosamond had a pang when she realized how little Corny meant, even as a friend. He was bent on getting out of his rut, and his own past with its continual intrigues with women made good copy when he was talking with the boys. He said that if he hadn't hamstrung himself with a wife and kids, nothing could stop him from jumping into the labor struggle. It was going to be, without question, the coming fracas.

Jerry had to go to Oxtail to be demobilized but he hardly stopped in that town long enough to say hello before he showed up in Detroit, all the nice country color drained from his face, thin, terribly shy and happy. Rosamond had got together a little belated trousseau of pretty nightgowns and underthings, but when she really had Jerry with her the things were forgotten. It seemed kind of theatrical to dress up in that way and she couldn't explain the kind of shyness she felt with her husband. Try as they might they couldn't quite get back to those first days in Manhattan, Kansas, with all the troubles of finding work for Jerry and the unsettled problems sitting like stones on their chests from the start.

The first thing was to get him some decent clothes. "You can't get a job looking like that. You need a suit," said Rosamond looking him over and shaking her head.

"All right," said Jerry, cheerful but not ambitious. "We haven't much money for suits but I have to get a job right away. The point is, what can I get?" He stood uncertainly feeling despair at the way all the initiative seemed to have deserted him.

"We have to decide," said Rosamond. "Not just fall into anything. This is our life we're deciding. I think we ought to work and save and maybe go back to college. We don't know enough and we're both pretty young." As she said it she thought of the campus at Wisconsin, the lake in winter, the sail on the iceboat and the way it cut straight across the black ice like a terrific bird.

Jerry wasn't certain what he wanted to do or could do. He still fancied he would have some kind of a choice. He had been jolted out of Oxtail and felt uncomfortable in Detroit. He refused to meet Stebbins.

"What do you want to be so old-fashioned for," said Rosamond. "He's just a friend and he's been very nice to me. You ought to know that."

Jerry shut his mouth stubbornly. "I don't intererefere with you," he said, "and I don't want to. You do whatever you like but I just don't like the man and I don't want to meet him." He had a terrible tight feeling in his chest even talking about it. He was bewildered by everything and didn't know where to begin to get a grip on things. More than a year, almost two years, obeying orders and getting up like a jack in the box every morning, didn't fit a man for much else. He tried hard to make himself like his own words. Maybe he didn't want Rosamond to do what she pleased but he thought he ought to want to. He thought of her as a wild bird who would hate him if he tried to clip her wings. He could stand anything except to live without her. It was an incomprehensible idea anyhow, his whole future revolved around her. He watched her now, how pretty she was, and how *alive,* as she sat figuring up their expenses, shaking her head, and he agreed to everything.

Even his suit. But he hated new clothes. His old suit that he had worn when war was declared looked seedy when they went into the clothing store. The neat clerk came forward. Jerry was stubborn and on the defensive.

"Wanta look at a suit," he said crossly. Rosamond tried to mollify him by holding tight to his arm and smiling at the clerk.

"What price suit?" said the clerk looking him up and down.

"Fifty dollars is top price and it's too much," said Jerry.

"A fifty-dollar suit is a cheap suit," said the clerk, shaking his head. "Its actual value is no more than a fifteen-dollar suit a few years ago."

"That's the kind I wore then and it's what I want now. I'm a cheap man." He looked the clerk, the little snob, straight in the eye. It was a real pleasure to say he was a cheap man. At least he knew where he stood. He had heard of a job in a real estate firm as a kind of errand boy running to the courthouse to verify deeds. It wouldn't pay much. He had hoped to buy Rosamond some little things, take little trips on the lake, but not on that salary.

"You oughtn't to talk that way, Jerry," said Rosamond when they were outside with the suit all wrapped up in a big box. "Or feel it either. You'll never get anywhere that way."

"I never will anyhow. I've not got the education. Thousands of kids are ahead of me. A living is all I hope for," he said with a kind of bravado, grinning. But at heart he wasn't cheerful and made a heavy burden for his young wife. She wrote her mother that she really had to think for both of them. Since he came home Jerry had no fight, it looked like. He seemed content to let the days slide.

Sometimes at night they lay side by side very far apart. Once he reached over and felt tears on her face. "What is it, darling?" he said snatching her to him and for the moment they felt close together again, both crying, like lost children.

She couldn't tell him. "I want it to come back," she said at last.

"Those days we had." He couldn't answer. His throat felt knotty. He hated the war, the long year, the anxiety now of trying to keep alive their young life together while all the time the long dull hours at tiresome work, the worry about the future, the monotony tried to rob them.

WHITE HEADED BOY

Jonathan Chance knew Detroit almost as well as his home town Benton. From the time he was a kid, he had gone on shopping expeditions there with his mother. When the Chance family bought the first big Oldsmobile in Benton, Jonathan became the chauffeur not only for his own immediate family but for all the connections who had a share in the car. In those days, taking a ride on Sunday was a ritual and the whole family equipped with veils and patience, went out the road toward Eaton Rapids with eleven-year-old Jonathan at the wheel. He was always big for his age and at eighteen was passing himself off for twenty-two.

It was because he could pose as older than he was that he wormed himself on the Detroit *News* as correspondent during his highschool days in Benton. It was all sport reporting then, but the job gave the kid a hunch and shifted him from the path that his father thought amply beaten to fame and fortune. The father never had an idea but that money-making was his son's aim, with naturally respectability as its chief ally. He was swept along by vanity at his son's enterprise to allow Jonathan to drift to Washington, D.C., with his old sidekick, Terry Blount, on the pretext of studying law at George Washington University. The two young bloods put in a good winter wedging themselves in as correspondents for Detroit papers and Jonathan had the distinction of being the youngest member of the press gallery.

He took a great deal of pride in this exploit and let it take care of itself. He was then trying to broaden himself and become a well-rounded man, making the rounds of tea-dansants with well-known

Washington débutantes. His handsome face, tall figure, and good dancing made him a valuable asset.

But in 1919 he had no idea of the way his life was to turn. He was taking it on the run and beyond having an aversion to his father's business and a liking for books that led to collecting first editions, he was content to let one day slide into the next. "I live in the present," he was proud of saying.

On his way to Benton on vacations he always stopped off in Detroit to hang around at different joints patronized by the newspaper crowd. He gradually concentrated on Vidisichis'. It wasn't so much different from the Krauses' house in Lansing, the same homely atmosphere and Mrs. Vidisichi was a wonderful cook. She knew how to spread herself when Jonathan and some of his cronies showed up. In about two mintues she had stoked the kitchen stove red hot, a pot of stuff smelling of herbs and meat was bubbling on the back, rice was boiling over, a couple of bottles of red were stacked on the table and the boys, arms crossed, sat waiting with wide grins, talking about literature and life in a way to make Jonathan particularly sensitive to the reception he was bound to get the next day in Benton. His father would have some puny job lined up for him.

"Say," he would begin, pretending he had just thought of it, "that wire clothesline is up in the yard, better get it down, Jonathan." Or maybe he'd even have the nerve to ask to have the car washed, even if it wasn't dirty. Whatever it was it was certain to take all the fine feeling out of the boy, and by the time Sunday came and he had accompanied his father to church rather than make trouble, he was thoroughly cowed. He sat during the sermon raging and sore and, during the heavy dinner that followed, only feebly resurrected himself enough to make a few sallies and eat his fill of the fine Sunday dinner. But his humiliation at being the perennial little boy sat heavy on him as he left his town for Washington and it was only by stopping again at the Vidisichis' that he washed it away with wine, good food, and the fond friendly Mrs. Vidisichi leaning in a flattering manner on the table fixing him with her mild blue eyes and beseeching, "Now Johnny, what you having, hey?"

He felt a man here, and if none of the other fellows showed up, the two Vidisichis sat down with him and they had a marvelous meal chewing up the fresh salad and lifting the crisp browned lamb to their mouths with fingers that often scorned a fork. He would relish every mouthful of food and all the time get the lowdown on the town, how Ford worked his men for every cent he gave them, and times were going to be bad again, and Mister Tolman looked frail, what was the matter with him?

He loved to pull out a cigar afterwards for Vidisichi and see Mrs. V bask in the pleasant after-dinner feeling that sat like a charm on them all. They would sit there dreamily and maybe Earl or Pete would come in. He had almost forgotten where he had found these guys; Pete had been in the *News* office one day when he came from Washington, as for Earl he worked a tool bench at Ford's and was a swell fellow.

By midnight the bunch were certain to show up. Room rent was high in Detroit and they hated to go to their narrow stalls after work. The V's kept a kind of open house for the little group that had discovered them. Later others were to find the V's and the intimate feeling went away as Mr. V's pockets filled. Not that he lost interest in the original claimants, but he no longer had the time.

When they all sat down to drink wine at the V's table, Jonathan, like as not, raised his glass proposing,

> I've seen my fondest hopes decay,
> Hooray, Hooray.

"Hooray, hooray," said Earl, tipping his glass. The good wine warmed him through and soon he could begin on his favorite subject, Rabelais. At night when he went to his room, it was Rabelais that he picked from the head of his hard little lumpy bed and read until he felt wafted enough from this life to go to sleep. During the day he sat at a tool bench at Ford's. He was an expert worker and he liked to think that someday he could use words with the same precision as tools. Rabelais was the one man who had done it. Rabelais had pressed all his hate and love of the lousy world into a book that reeked of the filth and fun of living. He liked to roll all the good fine four-letter words off his tongue and the other boys the same. Their language became a kind of Rabelaisian slang. Codpieces and codwallopers were dragged in familiarly with orders of wine and bologna.

"What about that fine bit of codpiece over there?" Earl said pointing to a salami reposing on the sideboard.

"Sure," said Mrs. V, beaming. One word was as good as another to her. "Sure, why not?"

But the curious thing, the fact that Jonathan in later years was puzzled to explain, was how the prime subjects of the day escaped them. None of them allowed the League of Nations to divert them from Rabelais or from a discussion of the importance of Mr. Cabell on which they were divided. The Sparticans in Berlin met defeat, Rosa Luxemburg was drowned in the Spree, and Karl Liebknecht shot in the back, and the young men at Vidisichis' continued to eat their salami and to discuss art and letters, to ponder over Joyce and Gertrude Stein, and to be set up more than any of them individually cared to admit, when a young man known as a book reviewer in New York and a New York critic in the sticks announced after an evening at V's that Detroit, not Chicago, was in his opinion the literary center of the future.

Each of the five young men who made up that little group at V's went away from the Hungarian kitchen that night a little groggy and wild, thinking of the rôle he might very well play in a new strong literature of a day to come. By 1929, the blasts from factories and the hammering of living were stronger than their individual voices. They were rallying to something besides wine and youthful hopes when the crash came, even though Tolman was out of the race, marooned perpetually in France, determined that if his life of Balzac were not published he would commit suicide.

But at the time, they were very young; sitting around the red table cloth, it was hard to say who led the talk. Perhaps Earl, the Ford worker, perhaps Tolman, or Guy who had fond hopes of writing a great American novel. Perhaps Jonathan, who kept his thoughts to himself and had a way of quoting Logan Pearsall Smith's *Trivia* that silenced some discussions.

"The trouble with you Johnny is too much trivia," said Earl, leaning back and looking at him, a little sore to be interrupted just as he was laying down the law about Cabell.

Jonathan wanted to spurt an answer that his trouble was too much Benton, too much mother, too much father, too much church, but he smiled instead and being tight quoted a line from Dowson,

"I have been faithful to thee, Cynara! in my fashion."

Guy finished it, waving his glass weakly, a subject who was to fall for one fair creature after another, but he did not know it then, thought instead that he was a pretty strong man with women.

They sat there then, five young men, not aware of their destinies or the destiny of their nation, talking about Mencken and his smart cracks and the booboisie that was important to them only as a class who bought the wrong pictures, ate mediocre food, read the worst books, sat on the most expensive and stupidest furniture, made love in the most boring way and were properly cuckolded for same, patronized the most banal shows, and appreciated meat rather than the joie de vivre in woman.

Sometimes out of a clear sky Mrs. V put a record on the squeaky Victrola and the most surprising refrains would suddenly be wafted over the little room:

In the land of the sky blue water

and the boys would stop involuntarily, all good midwestern boys with parents and homes and recollections, and they would listen, a little ashamed of their sentimentality that immediately afterwards launched itself into a Rabelaisian account of a tea in Washington at which a couple of pansies had tried to crash the gate on the strength of the butler's known predilections.

Jonathan would tell these stories of Washington life with his arms stretched loosely across the table, his dark eyes very blazing in his face that grew paler and leaner as the drinking proceeded, as if the flesh were being slowly consumed and soon nothing but the fine skeleton would look out at them. The boys had familiar cracks about most of the well-known figures and especially for the fat senator who had nothing to say to Jonathan and Terry Blount except, "Write me up, boys, I don't care what you say, so long as you mention my name." This craving was good for many a swell breakfast.

"Breakfast's his specialty," said Jonathan. "You should see me and Terry, stuffed and lolling back after all the waffles and sausages and eggs and grapefruit, and him handing us Corona Coronas or Laranguas. And help yourselves boys, he says, never knowing that Terry already helped himself and is sweating for fear his chest sticks out too much where he's hid them."

"To think those old farts run the nation," said Tolman.

"They don't run the nation," said Earl, "why deceive yourself, they are the camouflage. Wall Street runs the nation. Ford won't play ball and someday it will be dog eat dog. When the titans get through eating up the little fellows, they will begin on each other." He stretched his long fingers and the other boys looked at him with deep respect. He had the brains, and he looking at them envied them their college educations, which they had or were in process of getting, their nice clothes that they wore with an air, their appearance of being already somebodies.

Sometimes if the atmosphere were mellow enough he pulled a chapter or two of a novel he was writing out of his pocket to read to them. In it they saw themselves, howled down, blown up, tossed about as a Gargantuan Rabelaisian might have done. After the reading he would sit there, modestly, and wait for their enthusiasm. They gave it without stinting but something was lacking. These conversations repeated on paper, were all in a kind of vacuum that they themselves were in when they shut themselves up away from the harsh city, night after night, at the V's.

"Christalmighty, Earl's one of the best writers in this country," Guy said. The others agreed and believed, and when one of the college men from Ann Arbor was brought to Vidisichis' by Tolman one night, it was no surprise to any of them to have him go off his nut over the stuff and insist on printing it in the college paper.

Jonathan couldn't understand how a guy like Earl, who had the brains if anyone had, could be set up by any attention a college could give. He was taking his work at George Washington U. with his tongue in his cheek. He made fun of his fraternity, one of the best, and mimicked for the delight of the crowd at V's the way the men insisted he go out for something and worried for fear he read too much. They had even had a secret meeting to discuss what was to be done with Chance to get him into college activities more and keep him less "booky."

He let them worry and fuss around him, taking his law course lightly. The tedious briefs all about property and property quarrels got on his nerves, reminding him of his father's perpetual preoccupation with little belongings. He never went home that some new gadget had not put in its appearance to be solemnly and sacredly cared for. He let the law course roll off him, wondering a little what was to become of him, taking pleasure in feeling cynical and above it all. Technically, he still stuck at his law course and even read criminal cases with pleasure. He would sit in the window in the library devouring law magazines and their discussions of type cases. The case of a Salvation Army lassie and her captain was read several times. It wasn't that he cared about the technical question of rape about which the case pivoted. Sitting on the velvet cushions in the window seat of his room, the story had an ugly but realistic flavor. He began to think that maybe the law was a good handle toward prying into the world. A registry of lawyers convinced him that most men of law spent their lives in legal tangles about property rights, and he gave up reading the law magazines and dropped his courses in law, once and for all, as something he didn't want to bother about.

The boys at Vidisichis' had an almost other-world attitude toward the question of money. Earl was the only one actually at grips with making a living. The rest were pattering with newspaper jobs or notions about writing and they pushed aside such practical questions as where the money was to come from. Their parents still helped out, and they fondly thought of themselves as above wealth and one of a select company of aristocrats of the mind. Food for thought was the food of life, and poverty in an attic was romantic in a city devoted to a brand new bustling industry that turned cars out like strings of sausage.

"Let the lice keep their filthy lucre," Guy said in his funny cracked voice that always sounded as if about to break into tears.

"I don't want any of their damned geegaws. I don't want their lousy houses or their stinking motor boats or their yachts."

"Say, I wouldn't mind a yacht," said Jonathan. "You never sailed a boat or you wouldn't talk like that. Boy, there's nothing like it, you cut through the water and don't know if you're a bird or a fish."

"I'd rather have a speedy car myself," said Pete. "A long low racer."

"You've been reading those confession stories," said Guy. "Then they got into the long low car and swung out into the boulevard. The lights dazzled her eyes and she snuggled into his arms."

"You're getting good," said Earl. "First thing you know you'll be writing that stuff." Guy looked hurt. He was working in the secrecy of his room on a long story he hoped to sell to *Smart Set*. He wanted to get a letter from his idol Mencken even if he was turned down. Everybody said Mencken often wrote letters even when rejecting a story.

Jonathan would cackle his funny silent laugh, leaning his long body across the table to get nearer the others who always seemed a little apart from him as if the consciousness of his father's wealth was between them, unacknowledged but present. He made a clown of himself to break the barrier down and as a last resort would do a solo dance, contorting his long legs, doubling and turning, snapping his fingers, his face like a white intent mask. He'd have the whole place howling and clapping and Mrs. V beaming as if she were running a vaudeville number. Afterwards he felt tired out, the triumph went dead, he drank hard and fast and, out on the street hurrying to catch the Washington express, he looked back through the checked curtains at the boys thumbing their noses at jobs and life and he too felt keyed up for the second. But on the train, he could not sleep for the racket, thought pensively of some strange exotic girl who would love him with all her being, thought of never being loved but of living a brilliant isolated life, something like Henry Adams.

Henry Adams's *Autobiography* and Schopenhauer were bedside reading and he varied from the bitterness of the German to the pose of being a detached observer. When his father's check was late, he hated the position he was put in, necessitating a wire or meechy letter. He consoled himself with reading Henry George and was pleased to be convinced that if his father did not have landed property he would not be able to make his son feel like a little boy. Nothing could persuade him that his father did not delay his check on purpose to subordinate him, and it rankled in him and made it necessary to go to some tea and be the life of the party for a whole afternoon in order to get his feeling of self-respect back again.

BORN AGAIN

Victoria Wendel was slow in leaving Oxtail. She pretended that the curtains needed laundering, the house should be cleaned, everything made spick and span before her mother came home. It was not certain when Anne Wendel would come home. She still clung to Grapeville hoping for a few more crumbs. She wanted to sell one of the lots she had filched. Her lame leg was very stiff and it was a miracle that she could use it at all. Nothing except Trexler grit had pulled her through, she was convinced. It kept her on her legs while she negotiated with an Italian on the road to Millville. Before she owned the lots she used to carry on long chats with the Italians and sympathize with their troubles. It was plain to her that they got cheated. Now she had to keep her eyes open that they did not cheat her. Her brother David was always implying that she and Amos were easy marks.

"It's a dear price, missus," said the Italian. "That piece ain't good for much. I can raise berries on it if I manure it good. I don't see how I'm to get my money out of it then. But I got to have more ground, it's my one chance. I'm raisin' all the earth will bear on the bit I've got, I can't push her any more, I got to have your piece. It's right next to mine and it's the natural way for things to be."

"What would you consider fair?" said Anne Wendel standing as she had seen David stand, her head back, her mouth open a little, her eyes very steady on the man's face.

"Fifty is more than I ought to pay," said he, shuffling with his foot in the dirt. David would laugh at her. His scorn would blister her but she let the piece go. She would make real money when it came to cutting up the homestead and reselling it. But she didn't intend to tell David of her poor bargain.

When Anne Wendel came home, the entire family turned out to the train and pretended not to notice the cane and the limp. Her face was thin and strained, but once in her own house, her eyes brightened. She began snooping around, poking things with her stick. "Just think, Vicky," she said, "we can really have a decent bathroom and I'm going to make a breakfast nook out of that old porch and get electricity."

"I kind of like the gas," said Vicky. "It's such a nice soft light."

"Oh, electricity is so much cleaner and safer," said Mrs. Wendel, and she could hardly wait until a contractor had begun his estimates. The figures sobered Vicky. She couldn't help but think how much she could do with that money. When Rosamond heard of the improvements, the same thought came to her. Neither of the girls said a word. They thought their mother had a perfect right to improvements, but it made them more determined than ever never to own a little home if you had to sacrifice so much for it.

There was no more excuse for Vicky to stay in Oxtail. Bills from a swanky department store in Seattle began chasing her. She still had the coat and dress that she had charged in the early spring. Her father and mother spent evenings going over their debts that they meant to pay bit by bit even if the improvements had to be postponed. Some of the debts went back for years when Amos Wendel had his own business. She did not let her mother see the bills from Seattle and finally wrote boldly on the outside, *Deceased*, and dropped the envelopes in the mailbox with an arrow to return to sender.

She stood looking at the green mailbox where the letters were lying. It was as simple as that. She felt as if she had definitely decided on a new way of life; she couldn't say what or how it was to work out. It had to be, that was all. As she walked away, the big car of one of the Meyer Brothers passed. T. B. Meyer's daughter had lately married one of the small European counts and T. B. was wearing a white carnation in his buttonhole. They were enlarging the big store and making cuts in the girls' wages. Miss Button at the ribbon counter had told her about it. The store in Seattle had no connection with Mr. Meyer except that it was in the same business but the sight of Mr. Meyer obliterated any doubts she had about her action. As for *Deceased,* she was deceased. All that painful little way of living was dead and buried. It was a good feeling and she could understand for the first time what old lady Hoskins and young Nelly Turner had felt, when, in the revival meetings Nancy and Clara used to take the two younger ones to, they regularly and to the edification of all were "born again."

BLIND ALLEY

It was lucky for Jerry Stauffer that he had a job already cinched, because he had hardly worn his fifty-dollar suit two weeks before it began going to pieces and in the most embarrassing places. Rosamond was indignant. "What do they think fifty dollars is, it's two weeks' pay," she said, holding up the pants angrily and making the weak place worse by actually spreading the goods with her vehemence. "Hey, look out, don't ruin it," said Jerry, reaching for the pants. In his BVD's he looked awfully like the little boy picture on her dresser taken with his little sister years ago. The same bright eyes and rather round face. "What's happened to you?" Rosamond would say, pinching at his arm and dragging him along when they were out walking. They had been talking about the future and she had again asked him what he wanted to do.

"Nothing," he said, with that appalling cheerfulness.

"I don't know what I want to do. That's a fact. I know you want me to be full of ideas and ambition. I can't help it, I'm not."

"Well, we can't go on like this forever, we have to decide on something, this is bad enough, just going to work and feeding our faces and running into debt and worrying for fear we won't have money for proper clothing this winter, that's bad enough but I can stand it. I can stand anything if I see any future."

They had come to rest before a florist window and both gazed at the blues of iris and yellow of spring flowers in delicate vases. "Look at those orchids," said Rosamond, "not the gawdy ones they are tiresome but the little bits of wild brown ones."

"Say, it would be fun to raise those, wouldn't it," said Jerry, "we could raise orchids and make pottery. You know that's a wonderful thing, I used to watch them in Limoges."

"You see, you really have interest, you just choke it out all the time. Why do you do that?" She pinched his arm again and he laughed pleased to be pinched.

"Sure, I've got lots of interest but what good will it do us? We haven't any money. I can't go to school and learn anything, I just don't see the future, I hate this job."

"That job," said Rosamond, "why, of course you hate it. Nothing but office boy, really, for those real estate men. Hunting up deeds is no work for a grown man." All the same he was glad to have it. The initiative was all gone from him and one job looked like another. But the future haunted them both. They talked about it all the time. If Jerry has no plans, Rosamond had dozens. She thought they should save and go back to college the next year. They could both go and Jerry might begin a medical course. He was proud of the fact that his family had had a doctor in it for seven generations.

"You'd make a fine doctor," she said eagerly, "you've got such steady nerves and an interest in people. I can just see you, with a knife in your hand performing an operation. With a mask on. If I were you," she went on thinking soberly, "I'd make some one thing my speciality. Now what would you be interested in? Heart disease or lungs or what?"

"I haven't an idea," said Jerry. "It's crazy to think about it. But I used to pretend I was a doctor when I was a kid and get grandpa's spectacles and put them on and go around taking the family's pulse. Mother would stick out her tongue. You've got diphtheria, I'd say, and no one ever had any but terrible diseases."

They would talk a great deal in this manner because, when it came down to it, talk and being together was about all they had. Everything was terribly dear. Shoes were $10.50 unless you wanted the paper ones that wore out as fast as Jerry's fifty-dollar suits. Silk stocking with lisle tops were $3. Rosamond walked her shoes thin hunting for some that were cheaper but it looked as if prices meant to stay at the peak with wages dropping. Jerry got $100 a month and Rosamond $75 yet they could only pay for a room and eat half-way decently. Never a cent to lay by. Yet she kept right on talking of saving their money and going back to college.

It got to be a disease. They'd pinch on this and do without that and then get so bottled up, cooped together in one little room and going nowhere and seeing no one, because it was as hard to meet new people in this town as if they were all on different planets with a million miles between, that finally they would blow out the savings of weeks on a show. They had to see Mary Garden and came away in a kind of trance but the cheapest seats had cost $3.80. Walking swiftly up Woodward Avenue waiting for a bus afterward, Rosamond kept ahead of Jerry. She almost felt as if he were deliberately hanging behind, like a stone. Her feet went forward lightly and in her turquoise blue dress, made over from the dress she had worn at the dances at the University of Wisconsin, she felt gay and lighthearted as if anything might happen.

"Only think, Jerry," she said, stopping suddenly and tugging at his arm, "we can save and maybe go to France for a year. You said it would only take a thousand dollars." She said it as if it were ten dollars, a mere nothing. "We could make walking trips, sit around in the sun, study the language, *live*." She didn't know what she meant by living, but she was always saying it, pressing a great deal of meaning into it, feeling it very much, as if it were something in her body, tugging at her side, lunging against her ribs to get out. When she looked back at her own brief life, it was so mixed up with the worry of getting money, there didn't seem to be much living. When they were little, they played in the big yard and had ice cream every Sunday and whipped cream cake from their own cow and believed in Santa Claus, and then after that, highschool was fun and the two years she had taught in the country weren't lost but they had been pretty hard and lonely years. Then came the one year at Wisconsin, and sometimes lately it seemed wrong to have gone there at all. It was like holding out a piece of cake and then grabbing it away. "This isn't for you, get along with you." And she had had to get along, back to jobs again. The taste of the cake made everything else seem stale. She sometimes remembered the praise she had got in college, and how she had come down the hill after talking to the professor as if she were floating. The yards of the frat houses had been full of lilac bushes; as she came along she could breathe their scent. The whole world had been opening like a morning glory. Now it all seemed a dream. She'd never be satisfied, she'd never rest.

"Don't you see we can't just be content to drift along?' she said. But as long as she was beside him, Jerry didn't feel he was drifting. He was living. He could stand the dull work so long as in the evening he had her, with her quick way of talking and her look that seemed to touch everything it saw. What stories she could tell about the clinic. He felt as if he knew those folks. Of course, the nurses must be awful crabs and probably jealous of Rosamond. How could they help but be? The old man with the beard who stood in the door not understanding the nurse's angry, Too late, too late, and the fellow who had fits since he was shell-shocked in France, and the woman with five kids and two newborn wormy twins that the five loved as if they were angels, and the sunburned man in the fancy blue carpet slippers, where would you find such people except out of Rosamond's head?

Because, though they were living and real and had an existence of their own, leaving the clinic with their sores and backaches and nausea and fears of pregnancy and cancer to go to ugly rooms where there was never enough food or fire or clothes or bedding, still to Jerry, who saw the world through Rosamond, they were her people.

Sometimes at night lying in bed, she'd go over the whole day, and try to make him see how awful it was for the kid who had been in France to get his Wassermann test back plus 4. "He just couldn't understand it," she kept saying.

"Probably went with a French chippie and thought he was getting a nice innocent girl, lots of them did that and one kid I knew went crazy from shock when he found he'd syph instead." He said it evenly in his kind of hard young voice, and they both felt they had to face things with hard young voices, not mince around sentimentally anymore. Just the same, the feeling that they too could not understand their own predicament any better than the boy with the Wassermann, kept haunting Rosamond as she lay on her back looking out their window and feeling a thousand miles away from everyone. Like as not, Jerry, tired out with pounding around to the courthouse and different parts of the city, fell asleep and she sometimes raised herself to look at him, his face was so childlike and peaceful. It was hard to believe that he could be anyway content when in herself there was disturbance and urge to get out, to do something, to live.

Sometimes when they had had a particularly nice supper downtown together or had gone to dance at the Arcadia, she would slyly slide open the dresser drawer upon coming home and hesitate about putting on one of the fancy nightgowns she had made before his homecoming, but it always looked too fragile, it always seemed as if she ought to save it for a really big occasion, for the day when they started back to college or went off to France, or began living.

When letters came from Victoria, she had a pang of jealousy thinking that Victoria might get ahead of her. The two had always been close and now they had the feeling of rivals. She wanted and yet hated to think that Vicky would be meeting interesting people, getting into work she liked, while all the time she sat in Detroit, mouldering away.

Vicky's letters from the first made the most of everything. She had found a room in an artist's studio on Twenty-third street with another girl. They had the room at night, the artist taught art during the day to pupils. She worked at Jensen's selling children's books. There was only $16 a week in it and she got more than some because she had worked in San Francisco and because she went to college. Some of the girls told her she couldn't live on that and would have to make conditions for herself. One of them had made good conditions with a floor walker. Victoria had a lot of fun writing to Rosamond, coloring everything to sound fascinating and romantic. She didn't say how her back ached or that the room smelled of kerosene because the landlady soaked the bed with it to keep off bugs. Yet they paid $8 a week for their share. The artist also paid $8. It was a crime. She said nothing of such humdrum things but wrote airily of the skyline and the crowds and Broadway and the east side with the torches on street bazaars, and Rosamond began to talk to Jerry about both of them going to New York. It wouldn't be any worse there and might be better.

Jerry wouldn't hear of such a move. Sometimes on his errands through the city he would take advantage of the extra time he might have and sit in the park, let the pigeons wheel and strut around him, brood on Limoges, that town that rose up so strangely to the peak of a cathedral and all the life around had once strained to that one thing. He got Henry Adams's study of Mont Saint Michel and read it at night, in bed, with Rosamond beside him making lists of books or reading.

"My," he said proudly, "you've got quite a list. Are we going to read all those?"

"I am," she said stiffly, "and you ought to." But she didn't have to urge him. He waded through them. "Where Iron Is, There Is The Fatherland," kept them in a discussion half the night. "I'll never go to war again," sid Jerry, pacing up and down in his pajamas. "I'll go to jail first. I tell you it's demoralizing. Look at me. The fellows who were killed are better off. I don't know what's happened, but I feel shot. Perhaps it will wear off, but meanwhile here I am, too poor to go to college. Untrained for anything, trade or profession. Why a whole new batch of kids is struggling for a toehold. They haven't time for me. It all goes too quick. No one has time for us. Here we are, without a future and they don't even want to give a bonus."

When he talked, Rosamond felt happier than since the days they were first married. He seemed to wake up but the bitterness soon tamed down, he swallowed hard, said, "Well, what's the use?"

"There's lots of use," said Rosamond. "You can fight about it. No one should just submit to it."

"How? With a lot dumb guys who don't know what it's all

about? Who let themselves get sold like a lot of chickens for a war while Morgan cashes in and all the big munition kings ride around with gold-plate fixings in their cars? Hell, it's hopeless."

"I can't stand to have anyone say a thing is hopeless," said Rosamond. "Now I see how mad mother was when Papa failed in business and just gave up without a whimper. She said she could stand anything but that. What's the matter with you anyhow?"

They felt suddenly poles apart, standing there facing one another, he with a horrible sinking in his stomach that she was really discovering how inferior he felt himself to be and she that he would always be like this, that nothing she could do would change him.

"As long as I have you, I don't care," he said, like a little boy, sitting down beside her. But she didn't respond, sat stiff and unyielding when he put his head against her breast, her eyes looking far off, feeling suddenly trapped and as if she would not, could not bear it. Others fight, she wanted to tell him but hated to mortify him at that moment. She hated his giving in so much that she just sat there, her mind off a thousand miles. She kept remembering that I.W.W., talking in Gus's kitchen.

How do you want to die, they had said. 'I'll die fighting' said Joe Hill, hitting out, and they had to tie him to a chair before they could shoot him.

BUDGETS NEVER BALANCE

Anne Wendel wouldn't admit that her leg pained her most of the time and that getting around with a cane was almost as bad as not walking at all. She kept right on saying, "Oh, this pesky thing will get right in time, nature is slow, it's only human beings that must be always catching trains." As she got older she found herself using some of her mother's expressions, falling into her little habits of soliloquizing. But she'd never have the poetry Mem had, or perhaps English always made everything sound hard and bare while Mem's upcountry German made expressions like, "Here I sit on a naked twig, piping notes of sorrow," sound natural and poetical. "I need a new thatch to my roof," Mem used to say, when her hat finally gave out and she got around to buying a new one.

Nobody worried much about Anne Wendel's bad leg. Time alone could heal. But she slowed up on her activities and sat behind the grapevine on the front porch oftener than she used. When Nancy and Clifford announced that things were closing down in Seattle, the shipyard job was over and Cliff had not found anything else, she wrote them eagerly to come back to Oxtail. She was certain there were as many opportunities there as anywhere. They could stay right in the old home, it was empty enough with only Amos and herself rattling around alone.

Nancy hated to leave the marvelous scenery on the coast, but if you are homesick mountains are no better than an Iowa dust storm. Cliff had not been able to pick up a job in Seattle and they had veered to Chehalis, a small town, with no friends. Cliff had undertaken to sell Chevvies on commission, and at the end of two months saw plainly that he not only could not get rich but could not make a living. The owner of the garage told him if he had a little capital he could come on in his business, but he might as well have asked for the moon. Clifford was really relieved that his wife's homesickness and continual crying spells gave him an excuse to write to his old boss in Oxtail. Yes, there would be an opening for him, not quite on the old standing but the future was bound to be worth any temporary sacrifice.

When Nancy came back the three women, Anne Wendel and her two daughters Clara and Nancy had good times together and all three envied Rosamond in Detroit and Vicky in New York. It was really a kind of triumph to be able to say that the girls were in big eastern cities. "How're your girls doing, Mrs. Wendel?" "Oh, they're doing fine!" said Anne, smiling and happy. And in fact so far as Vicky's letters were concerned she seemed to be making friends, and only Donald grumbled that if they didn't watch out she'd get herself into trouble back there.

"What do you mean trouble?" said Amos Wendel with a grating note in his voice. "She's well, she's getting along all right. She's had too many different jobs to suit me. I don't like that but she's all right."

"All girls in cities get into trouble sooner or later, mark my words," said Donald heatedly. "New York's the loosest place on earth. I was there myself. We went all around, the aquarium, the nightclubs, saw the Follies. I could tell you things about that town would keep you awake nights."

But no one paid much attention to Donald. He was a wet blanket. The mother pumped away on her sewing machine with her one good leg to make pretty blouses for her two girls. They were always writing, one or the other, could she make them this or that. She was ready for anything to help them out. That's what she was for. Heavens, what would life be worth if she couldn't be doing things for her children.

All during that winter she planned on beginning improvements on the house in early spring. Toward 1920, people talked of property dropping but the house across the street sold for a terrible price, went way up to nine thousand and it had been only a little four-thousand-dollar house a few years back. Mrs. Wendel was certain her house could sell for more. She wrote romancingly to her two girls of making lots of money off the White Elephant and of everyone spending the summer camping on her share of the old homestead back in New Jersey, with a little car and Jerry to drive it and the rest of them, Clara and her kids and all, sitting in it in solemn state driving around. After a few months in the White Elephant, Nancy felt cramped as always when two women both try to keep house in the same kitchen and neither will admit the other is boss, and wrote her sisters that she and Cliff hoped to have a home of their own some day.

When both girls came down with the flu in strange cities, you could hardly keep Anne Wendel and Nancy at home. They were for flying to Detroit and New York to care for the waifs. But Amos put his foot down and said enough had been spent on railroads and they should wait until it was certain the girls weren't able to get proper care otherwise. Rosamond and Vicky dragged through, and wrote each other feebly that at least spring was coming, and

Rosamond reminded Vicky that in Seattle those enormous maple buds must be pink and swollen to bursting.

Sometimes Rosamond and Jerry would sit over their accounts, trying painfully to budget their needs. "We ought to be able to live on this, why whole families live on less," said Rosamond. "All the clinic people, with all their children, live on less, but of course that's why they come to the clinic, that's why they're sick and the babies look so ratty. I wake at night and think of them, they haunt me." With her hair pushed back and a wild look in her eyes, she had a haunted look that troubled Jerry. It made him feel awful not to be able to earn more. And then it wasn't as if they had his earnings every month. He got fired from the real estate job and was weeks getting a collecting job. That job didn't last when he refused to come to work at seven-thirty.

"If there was any use in it, I wouldn't care," he said. "But there's not. And they want me to keep at it until six. What kind of a life would we have that way? We're tired enough as it is." They both still clung to the idea that their life was important. They agreed to let the collecting job go. "You'll get something else," said Rosamond, "but your clothes are all wearing out, you'll look like a tramp soon." She looked him up and down, wondering what could be done with a suit that threatened to give out all over.

"I get furious remembering how we paid fifty dollars for that suit and you might as well put faith in paper."

"I can't get another now, but I'll sell my Liberty Bond, only they're only bringing $85 now. We can buy a lot on that."

"I wanted to save that for next year," said Rosamond. She still believed they should make an effort to go to college. Yet sometimes when she thought of college it made her angry. Her one year had equipped her with nothing to fight with, it made her long to read books she couldn't afford, many of them the libraries didn't have. College was not for them, it looked like, but she was so set on it that at night in bed she could only think of the time when they could be there, when at last it would seem as if they had begun to be started in life, not just beating time.

When Emma Goldman and Berkman got out of jail they went straight from work to the meeting but there was a line a block long.

"Look at that," said Jerry excited, "you can't tell me there aren't thousands of people interested in keeping out of war if they'll come to hear those two old draft resisters." They fought with the crowd to get in the door, but no success. When it looked hopeless, they went with the left-overs to a funny old hall belonging to the Wobblies and listened to a little man with a sandy beard. On the wall was a newspaper clipping telling about the I.W.W. meeting in Oxtail. Rosamond pointed it out to Jerry and several men hearing her, crowded nearer. The clipping was all about Meller's windshield getting broken in the mob.

"Served him right," said Rosamond. "I wish they'd broken more than the windshield." She felt all stirred up inside of her. When a young kid began telling her how they had painted his uncle's barn yellow out in Dakota because he was a Socialist, she listened with her eyes getting wider. "My folks shut themselves up in the house and laid low," he said. "But the dog give them away. He come sneaking around and when they thought the coast was clear, they opened the door a crack and my uncle said, 'Come on, Debs,' his name was Debs, see, and they heard him, one of the guys was hanging right around the corner and they drove our whole bunch out, tried to tar and feather them."

Afterwards on the street, she kept saying over and over, "Can't something be done, can't something be done," and she was angry at Jerry's taking it so calmly. He wasn't calm inside, he felt a dead weight in him. Lately he wondered if they had not kept fellows like him chopping wood, picking up iron, doing useless mechanical things until they got like wood, like iron themselves, with a purpose in view. "Hell," he said one night, when he felt that a chasm was between Rosamond and himself, "they did it on purpose. They wanted us to come home and be nice clods."

"That's the way I like to hear you talk," she said, starting up and looking at him as she used to when he began coming around in Oxtail begging her to go riding on the milk truck in the moonlight.

But it wasn't every day that there were meetings. Most of the time they seemed to be flung back into their own little nest and it got more cramped every day. Toward spring when Jerry decided to take a flier selling real estate, they moved to another house where

Rosamond was allowed to cook supper in the family kitchen every night. But it was embarrassing, eating their little meal with the real family of the house within earshot. A constraint seemed on the young couple, they seemed never at home.

"Let's go to the woods in northern Michigan this summer," she would plan, "think what fun, just live wild, away from everybody. I want to get away from cities," She even wrote Victoria who was beginning to let on that the city had gotten under her skin, too. But though they planned on a summer in the woods, they went right on trying to keep what jobs they had.

The babies at the clinic multiplied as spring came on. They were scrawny and cried too much; now and then a plump fair baby popped into the world to show up the rest for the miserable infants they were. The too many children, the too little to do with, the sitting there, day after day, taking down histories began to seem futile and heartless.

"Can't anybody *do* something," she kept saying, but on Saturday nights when the got their money and went dancing at the Arcadia she forgot everything. The music was wonderful and Jerry was proud at the number of good-looking boys who came up and wanted to dance with her. Sometimes he was perfectly willing for her to go ahead but he rarely asked a strange girl. When he did, it was only for Rosamond's sake, so she wouldn't think he was not a good sport.

When the real estate job went slower and slower, they put their heads together desperately. "What about a job at Ford's?" Jerry said. Well, he would have to start at fifty cents an hour, wouldn't he? And while she would just as soon he was making Ford cars as selling real estate, better, still you could see with half an eye that those Ford men had it taken out of them. Once they went out to the factory around five and the bunch of men who were loading flat cars looked ready to drop.

"That's the way it would be," said Rosamond, "you'd have it taken out of your hide. I'm not ready to give up yet, I'm not going to live just to keep alive." But when they talked lately they both had a trapped feeling as if something was closing in on them. Rosamond began to think with pleasure of the comfortable house in Oxtail. It was a big airy house. Home faces were good to see. The town wasn't so bad. Since her attack of flu, she had been rundown, the doctor told her she needed a rest. Why, he might as well tell her to go to the high Alps.

But no, that was where the special kind of chamois came from that the lady, who ordered a $16,000 motor car, wanted for upholstering. Her eye had fallen on the little account in one of the magazines. The company assured the reader that really one had no idea of how much pleasure the clients took in personally supervising their orders. It was quite a kick for them. They often spent several weeks at the plant supervising some special design. Of course each car was custom built. One crowned head was having his personally designed bar installed. Sixteen thousand dollars. Why, they once thought Uncle David callous enough, when he had gone off to Death Valley in his new Cadillac the time Mamma asked him for money to help pay the interest on the house. That was nothing to sixteen thousand. As she thought of sixteen thousand, it swelled in her mind to millions. It grew and grew and seemed to burst like a bomb through the long room where the patients waited in drooping rows. She couldn't see how in the world Mamma could be so pleased when Uncle David condescended to send her a little money. Something so shameful was in the world that at that moment she felt sick and as if there was nothing for it but to go home for the day.

When she wrote home, she began to throw out hints. Anne Wendel was only too happy to spy them out. "I think the child wants to come home," she said to Amos. Amos felt proud of himself. He still had his job, and look at his sons-in-law, out of work half the time. He was all for the young couple coming home.

But Rosamond held off yet. Jerry was determined to give the real estate venture a try-out. "If I'd only gone in it a year ago, when we first came here. Then there was money in it but then I had only sense enough to be an errand boy for them. Now nothing is selling. There are too many strikes. The place is full of them. People who would fall for a little home are out on strike or going out. And of course you don't get a word of this in the papers; but talk to anybody and they'll tell you how unsettled things are."

When everything had seemed very dark they had both fallen back on the bonus. "They'll have to give it to appease popular demand," Jerry said, but in May, he groaned one night as he read in the paper that the worthless old Congress had shelved it and the issue wouldn't be brought up until next session.

"What are they there for?" said Rosamond. "Riding around, enjoying themselves, talking their heads off. What about us?" It was baffling. She hated to give up but she felt tired all the time. Perhaps if she went back to Oxtail and rested up, things would straighten out. Jerry could try to stick it out a little longer, there might be an upturn, if not, things couldn't be any worse in Oxtail. The White Elephant was big, they could at least rest, and maybe get their forces pulled together. There was no use living as if life wasn't going on for years and years. Trouble was they were too greedy. They wanted everything to happen at once.

Jerry hated to show up at home without a job. His own father was sick, no one seemed to know what was wrong, and his mother was writing him uneasily that they should rent the farm and move to town. He hated to go back and be in the midst of family troubles again. But Rosamond seemed set on it. "If we haven't any money here, it'll be hotter than blazes, we can't even go on the lake. We might as well be in Oxtail." Truth was, she was lonesome. They had not been able to make any friends for the reason that they never met any people. At the meetings they went to, they were shy and kept to themselves. All the enthusiasm that was in them kind of burned out when they had to go back to their room alone. Sometimes when they rode along in the bus, Rosamond looked out at all the windows of houses where people lived. But most of them also knew few people probably; they just trimmed their lawns and tried to get nicer bathrooms and nicer cars and lived and died.

"The tower room is waiting for you any time," Anne Wendel wrote and, when Rosamond remembered that little white room at the top of the house that looked so far off over the Missouri, she longed to go home. "It's just for a little while," she told Jerry. "We are going to Chicago next January, you wait and see; or if you get the bonus we'll go to France. We'll live a year and maybe find out a few things. You can stand anything if you know there's something different in the future." She packed up her few things, and riding in the train across Iowa was cheered that the early June made it look so fresh and green. "It's a good sign," she wrote hopefully to Jerry, who was hanging on for dear life, trying to make a go at a business that had been suddenly and to all intents, inexplicably, shot to hell.

She hid her disappointment when the tower room turned out to have been painted a blue that Anne Wendel fondly thought cheerful. "It's awful," she wrote Vicky. "I can't tell mother but I was fearfully disappointed. A blue something like this ink. Oppressive blue pressing down on one—swallowed in blue." But she set out her little pieces of Limoges pottery that Jerry had brought her from France, the pin tray with the butterfly on it, and rummaged the family garden for a flower or two. Nothing much grew around the White Elephant except marigolds but she picked some to brighten the place. Everything was the same, she had to admit, only she did not belong anymore. She was lost, so dreadfully lost, and sitting on the porch in the evenings as she used to when a little girl, she felt she had never in her life been so alone, belonging nowhere and to no one.

Anne Wendel complained that no one was interested in the new improvements but herself. "It's all for you and not a one of you care a thing about it," she said at supper, her red hair bundled into a white cloth, and on her cheek a smudge of paint that wouldn't come off.

"I never said I didn't like it as it was," said Amos, winking at Rosamond.

"Well, you shouldn't," said Anne. "If you had had to keep house with all the inconvenience I have for thirty years, you wouldn't talk like that." Rosamond said, "It's going to look wonderful mother, never mind, Papa's only joking." But she had no enthusiasm for the new hardwood floors, the up-to-date bathtub and the electric lights. The broad boards on the old floor had been restful, the gas light gave a softer glow. When she looked at the improvements she couldn't help but think what she and Jerry might have done with the money. It would about solve their problems. Everything seemed simple if one only had enough funds for a little while, just a breathing space. But still she couldn't blame her mother. She'd had little enough all her life.

It was the same when she went out to Stauffers' farm. They were surrounded by tools, equipment, windmills, and all that goes with a dairy farm. Mr Stauffer looked seriously ill but Mrs. Stauffer was a dynamo and practically ran the farm. They would rent, she said, and live in town. But there was no way to ask for help for herself and Jerry. It didn't seem right to take away anything from such parents.

Nancy grumbled a good deal that summer because Clifford was not getting a square deal from his boss, and at night Rosamond and Cliff and Nancy rode around in the little Ford, buzzing out the Correctionville Road. The very movement soothed them all, they quit feeling peevish, eased back, and sometimes Rosamond would sing. The two girls talked of driving to Omaha to see the styles but Cliff wouldn't hear of anyone but himself driving the car. It was his choicest possession.

"I'd like to be a chauffeur," Rosamond wrote Vicky, who was writing that she'd like to get out of office work forever. She talked of raising bees, of learning to fly an airplane, of going to France. Rosamond wrote that her latest plan was to go to France and live there for a year. Jerry wanted to learn ceramics at Limoges and she wanted to take some courses at the Sorbonne. "I don't know whatever is the matter with those girls," Anne was forced to complain, partly with pride. "They just don't seem able to settle down. I never saw anyone turn and twist so, you'd think they were tied up with ropes. Sometimes I think it's the farm blood in them warring with the city. I don't know what it is but I wish they would reconcile themselves more."

Rosamond didn't find it hard to be happy in a day-by-day way in Oxtail. The sun was so nice and the bees flocked around the grapevine when it flowered. She took long walks with Clara's children, the lot of the, coming back torn with brambles, red faced and shouting. In July Jerry began to weaken, it was clear he could not make a go of it in Detroit. No one knew how he hated to give up and come back to Oxtail. He brooded about it and felt that he was an utter failure. If there was only time to turn around but without money there was no time. There was nothing to do but take it as a kind of joke, and he and Rosamond actually laughed the morning he stepped off the train at Oxtail. It was early and the stores on Fourth Street weren't open yet. They walked into an all night café for a cup of coffee. There was something crazy about being back in Oxtail, after the way they had razzed the town.

"Anything doing here?" said Jerry, looking at Rosamond, fresh and sunburned in a new blue dress and big black hat. "Say, you're looking wonderful, that's one good thing."

"It's the only good thing," said Rosamond. "We might as well store up strength, it's all we can store up. And I'm making myself a few clothes to get ahead of the game."

In the afternoon they took Cliff's car and drove out to the big bluffs along the Big Sioux. They got out and lay down in the grass and they could see the river crawling along placid and coiled in the bends like a snake waiting to strike. "There's an awful threat in that river," said Jerry. "Can't you see it, just waiting to rear up and strike and rip out more corn land? How's crops this year, does your father say?"

"They're fair," said Rosamond. She was thinking that this was the first time she had ever looked at that river with her husband. They had both been born in the same town and now they were lying on the bluff where Anne Wendel and the children used to go on picnics years before. She was married and yet everything seemed just the same. She was still worried about how to live just as they were as children when the crops failed.

Anne Wendel was almost smug to have the White Elephant filling up with her offspring. She had illusions of the New Jersey homestead selling for some miraculous price, the White Elephant itself she pretended would be put on the market in the fall and all of them could go to Florida, could go east, could do whatever they pleased, to hear her, on the proceeds.

"She'll never sell this house," said Rosamond. "She's in love with it and you can't blame her. It's the first time in her life she ever had a chance to fix a place up. It's gone to her head. She dreams of cupboards and breakfast nooks and is always making little drawings. She's used up her eight hundred, I'm sure, but no one dares ask. She didn't even pay the mortgage, Papa keeps the interest up but that's about all."

The work of remodeling, of shoving furniture into corners, of polishing floors, of selecting light fixtures went on in the bustle of the old house, and Rosamond escaped often enough to the blue tower. Sometimes, tired out, she would lie on the bed. There on the wall in a neat frame with a painted wreath around the words was a motto Mamma had given Vicky when she was ten years old.

> And so I find it well to come
> For deeper rest to this still room,
> For here the habit of the soul
> Feels less the outer world's control,
>
> And by this silence, multiplied
> By these still forms on every side,
> The world that Time and Sense has known
> Falls off and leaves us God alone.

She could remember when she was in highschool being quieted by that motto, of lying on the bed feeling peaceful and imagining she was face to face with God. Now it made her feel only empty and angry. Was that all they could tell you? How could that help? What she and Jerry needed was work that used what brains and energies they had, if such things mattered. Were they just fodder, waiting to be chewed up by their own mechanical processes of keeping alive?

What good did it do to have brains? What good did it do to fall in love? The world had no use for those things, they only pretended they had use, to kid you along. When Jerry couldn't find a thing but a night job at the express company they talked it over and accepted it with stoicism. "It can't last," Rosamond said. "After all, we are awfully young. Things will get better. They simply have to."

On Jerry's night off, they went to public dance halls and took pride in the way people watched and admired their good dancing. "Anyway we can dance, I was beginning to think I wasn't good for anything," said Jerry in his cheerfully bitter voice. On Sundays the Stauffer and Wendel families sometimes herded together for big dinners and the men congregated for political discussions. Donald like to hint at the gossip he had heard about Wilson's private life but the two older men, Mr. Wendel and Mr. Stauffer, discouraged him with their blank looks. They preferred to discuss crops and the tariff.

No one could say Sundays were exactly hilarious. Rosamond often used the excuse to write Vicky to go to the tower room and Jerry would tag along and lie on the bed in his stocking feet reading while she wrote her sister. Sometimes she would look up and watch the Missouri that from a distance had such a deceptively lazy look. Almost anywhere in Oxtail on high ground, there was a sight of rivers and, sitting in the tower, she had the feeling sometimes as if treacherous rivers were weaving around Oxtail, waiting to strangle it. Once years before, she and Vicky had almost got sucked into the Missouri at the mouth of the Big Sioux when paddling in a canoe. They were just little girls and they had worked several hours, silently straining with the paddle, dragging themselves back, inch by inch.

"What's Vicky up to?" Jerry wanted to know. Rosamond said, "She's in love with someone, he's married."

"Gee, that's too bad," said Jerry. "Oh I don't know," said Rosamond. She didn't want to talk about it. Vicky had left New York to sell stamps and cigars at a hotel counter in the mountains to get away from this man. Rosamond envied her a little; from Oxtail it seemed romantic. Sometimes Anne Wendel hung around waiting for everyone to go to bed so she could rummage for the little secret notes Victoria enclosed in her letters to Rosamond. These were intended for Rosamond's eyes only, and heaven knows how the mother knew they were there. At midnight, many a time, sitting on the rim of the chair, she read these scraps with a pang at her heart and yet not altogether with pain. Her girl was experiencing life, she was living. She didn't know what it was in her own past made her feel this way. She ought to be up in arms, but after all, you might as well look life in the face. Her own brothers had lived free as birds, and no one could have called Aaron's Mrs. Ferrol anything but a wonderful woman. All her opinions were shifting in late years. Papa's failure made you look at things differently. Just

so no harm came to her girl. She almost prayed that no harm
would come to her. But it was like a book, you could not get around
that. She carried the secret around with her, with a kind of sly
protective way about her. She wouldn't let Rosamond know she
had snooped, no, she would keep it hid until she died.

Rosamond could hardly sit around all summer. She had to find a
job. The *News* had nothing at present, would let her know. Not
that there was much difference between writing up society ads for
Oxtail matrons and taking dictation from some business man who
sold tires or shoes. Stebbins who had gone to Seattle wrote discontentedly of his job on the biggest paper there. He didn't like its
political tone, hoped to get on the Seattle *Union Record* as soon as
they made a Sunday edition. Perhaps she'd like to come out?

That would be crazy, not that everything wasn't crazy enough.
But crazier than anything was the discovery that along in August
the untoward had happened. She was up to her neck now, caught
midstream without a paddle. It looked, it certainly looked as
though, if something drastic didn't happen, she was going to have a
baby. Not that she didn't want one, she wanted several, but at this
time how could they support it?

At night she had horrible dreams and the skinny babies in the
clinic at Detroit grinned and shook rattles at her like human skulls.
Now she hunted jobs with a kind of frenzy. Anything would do.
Work would be a pleasure, any kind of work was better than sitting
at home, wondering, feeling caught in a trap.

"Hope you land a job," she wrote Vicky who was back in New
York looking for work. "It's more than I can do in this blasted
town. Why is it that I am reduced always to hunting for a
stenographic job? Went up Saturday to interview the Meyer
Brothers about an advertising job. All the brothers still wear
carnations and strut the floor like kings. Bill Brackwood has
bought an airplane for his wife, the ex-vaudeville queen, and she
threatens to drop Christmas presents on the houses of her friends
from the sky when that day comes. Nothing doing at Meyer's.
Feeling just the same, no matter what happens I should be good for
five months work anyhow and prefer it to rotting away here at
home. Send me the *Liberator*, will you? They don't sell it in this

town anymore. The fair is in full swing, autos carousing past at all hours. The droshky ride you had up Fifth Avenue must have been fun. I haven't had any sport for so long I'm disintegrating. We loathe this town, Jerry can't find anything that pays more than $25 a week. Imagine rearing an infant on that?"

If only Cliff weren't so tight with his car. She longed to drive with it at night, to take it alone and go out along the road and keep driving. Drive to the Black Hills where Uncle Joe had lived and had gone mad without finding gold. It would be great to hit straight across Nebraska out to the knobby country of the Hills. Perhaps get lost winding around in the hills the way she and Vicky were once lost in the cornfield. "Where are we, Vicky?" she had said, in all that green, green reaching to left and right, in front and back, nothing but the rustle of green and overhead a blue staring eye of sky. They had kept on marching through the rows, talking of perhaps starving like the boy in the story. They too might fall down between the rows, until they starved to death in the ripening corn and crows came to pick their white bones or the farmer cut the corn and the shocks would topple around their skeletons, bleached and clean.

The awful thing was waiting to find out if something couldn't be made to happen, but in spite of the nasty medicine, her body was as relentless as death. It was awful to think how one small factor changed a life, how people died because bones got in their throats, miners perished because it cost too much to buy new timbers, thousands drowned because dams were expensive. She got a kind of crazy feeling. "Jerry Jerry," but he wasn't even in bed beside her.

No, he was working at night and only at three in the morning would come up the stairs to the tower room, carrying his shoes so as not to wake her. The moonlight was often in the room; in its light he looked big and clumsy, like a bear, moving softly as if on paws.

In the morning at breakfast all the family looked as if they had not had enough sleep. Rosamond's trouble wore on them all but everyone pretended to be interested in the weather, and Papa said he would have to tie up that woodbine, it was shutting out the light at the kitchen. Rosamond would sit, feeling completely alone, trying to puzzle out some way to manage. Her whole being was focused on one idea. Sometimes in the midst of her desperate thoughts the idea of a baby would seem terribly sweet. She remembered Clara's babies and the way they splashed and squeezed up their legs in the bath, but then she would look around her at the old familiar house and realize that they had not even been able to stay in Detroit. They had no right to a baby now. No one could give any advice. What to do. Do Do Do. It was in her head every minute. Old wives tales that scared her. Anne Wendel could hardly speak of the trouble. She had taken her children as they came but she didn't want to be bigoted. It was against nature but the world was upside down with the war. Jerry had no job, he was indecisive and puzzled. He should have time to turn around. But when Rosamond began to be sick from that vile medicine she put her foot down. "It's the health I care about, that's all. It's not right, it's against nature," and her heart seemed to mourn over the baby that wanted to come into the world with all the familiar little traits of her own children.

Rosamond and Jerry tried to talk about it calmly. It was no time to be sentimental. The whole progress of the race had been a fight against nature, hadn't it, against letting nature run like a great lush beast through the land. Well, it showed you, you had to fight, you couldn't turn your back and hide your head like an ostrich. You had to act.

Jerry stood by the window. He wanted the kid. More than that, he wanted Rosamond to want it. Perhaps she didn't really love him enough. He felt so small with all his failures, how did he have the right to urge her to have the kid. He couldn't risk making her rebellious and what right had he, who could not manage his own life, to dare to want to manage another's.

"What should I do?" said Rosamond looking up from the bed where she was lying stretched out, very pale.

"You have to decide, it seems to me," said Jerry, biting his fingers. "It's your life. I haven't the right."

"I don't know who has, if you haven't."

"It's your life. I don't think anyone can decide but yourself."

"It would be your child." She looked at him desperately but he stood there frozen in his helplessness. He started toward her, making a small outward movement with his hand. "Gee," he said. "Do you think . . ." Then he stopped, frozen again by the sudden fright he thought he saw in her face.

What should I do? she asked this one and that. Even Stebbins in Seattle. "If you think you'd have responsibility only when it is a baby, you're mistaken. It lasts forever," he said with the bitterness of feeling hamstrung with five. Vicky wrote to beware of the doctors. But Clara hinted that people like Mrs. Troy went through it again and again. In the end, she made the rounds of doctors but no one wanted to touch it. Only the poor get the cold shoulder, she told Jerry, feeling as if she were in a fever, had begun to skip rope as the little girls used to do and would never be able to stop. One, two, three, how many carriages will I have, four five six.

When a doctor of rather shady reputation finally agreed to do the job, she got cold feet, remembered with terrible clearness the poor women brought into the clinic, their insides poisoned forever, their wombs spoiled for all time, never to bear again. It would be awful to be injured so she could not have children. Life wasn't always going to be like this. Better times would come. As soon as this was over, they would get out of Oxtail. To be free, that was all that she wanted. To be well again. To have her body to herself. She got up in the mornings while Jerry was having his much needed sleep. He looked more childlike than ever as he lay there. Poor boy, he slept hard after the night work. Sometimes she wanted to shake him. Wake up, wake up, help me. Help me.

In a few days it would be over. It was nerveracking to have to sit around in the evening and listen to Clara and Donald and Nancy and Cliff and some of their friends talking about Brown Lake and going swimming in that mud hole. She tried to get in the talk, but the babble went on. Anne Wendel looked at her daughter anxiously. Her whole being yearned over her girl. She longed to take her woe into her own body but life was so limited. You could sit and stare at the most serious things. It was only given to help in little useless ways.

Papa had nothing to say. No one told him what it was all about but he had guessed and suffered to be kept out of the secret. When the company came, he stepped in from the porch to join cheerfully now and then in the conversation. Rosamond slipped out the back door. Air, she had to get air. Cliff's car was parked near the curb. It was a marvelous night. How big the stars were, like you read about. When they were little their mother used to escape from the house on nights like this, just for a run around the block, she'd say. A breath of air. They'd look up from their books, feeling lost and uncomfortable in the house without her. The clock ticked too loud. "Wonder why Mamma doesn't come back," Vicky would say. The two little girls would feel suddenly strange in the big house. They would go to the door, walk out on the porch, smell the wild fresh air. Mamma would come running along the walk and laugh when she saw them. "Did you think I'd run away?" she'd say.

The car started up all right. Cliff would never know she took it, she'd bring it back after a little runaround. She headed north toward the road that she and Jerry had liked best in the milk truck days. The car ran smoothly with a curious click now and then but it was swell to move, to feel the fresh country air blow in at the windows and that dry warm smell that hung over fields in autumn even after dark. Only that day hanging up the clothes the sky had been full of wild white clouds. The sun had baked the back of her neck. Let's see, should she follow this road or go straight ahead. What fun it would be to start across country, driving fast, choosing roads, passing through the rich country with the different colored fields, the green ones with winter wheat and the red earth, like Mother said was back in Grapeville, with dark deep red clover not pale pink like Iowa clover, and then the rich purple black earth of the gumbo country in the Dakotas where Papa used to get stuck up to the hub when he went to fix farm machinery. Nothing was any lovelier than a field of corn, plain Iowa corn, and where would Oxtail be without that corn. Take a field full of shocks, nothing was lovelier and the golden ear and the stars coming out so cold, like the night they went on the party at McCook in the haywagon and had dinner on long tables loaded down with dozens of pies and cider and whole chickens and jars of watermelon pickle. Oh, there was good rich living in the land and why should it get pinched off, why should people feel squeezed and beaten, it wasn't the fault of the land. Heavens no, ask Papa or ask Jerry's father. Mr. Stauffer could tell you. There was enough to support all the children anybody wanted. Why Mr. Stauffer's cows gave wonderful milk, the very best, if it wasn't for the middlemen in town hogging it, so he got nothing for it but what skim milk should be worth, when it was really pure gold, his milk, the finest Guernsey milk.

She had run along without noticing the road and found herself at the end facing a big white house. It was a little trouble backing out but the trouble distracted her and made her forget that tomorrow she would have to face the music. Out in the country she thought almost with surprise of her plot. The ground was so rich and the insects were all humming when she stopped the car, very loud, as they do in the fall of year just before the frost nips them for good and all. She sat with her head on the wheel a few minutes, it was not too late, she could back out of it, just not show up at the doctor's. They'd find a way to manage. She started driving slowly and at the bend saw the lights of Oxtail reflected in the sky.

The ugly streets were waiting to suck her in, they'd never let her go again. Her foot pressed nervously on the gas and the car shot forward. Speed, that was fine. She was crazy to get cold feet. She'd have to go through with it, or get caught like a stuck pig. If only the foolish false optimism of people always expecting things to get better could be harnessed together. That would be some power, but no, people were slow, they'd drag you down give them a chance. Faster, and her foot went on the gas. The town lay there, like a little trap, but Ed and his friends had slipped out of its clutches. The liveliest night she'd ever known in Oxtail was the night Ed sang. Where were they now, in jail or where? Jerry was at work, piling up boxes, loading trucks. He would come home toward morning, and fall asleep like a log. Something had happened to them both, they weren't needed, weren't wanted but by God they'd live, just to spite the world. She pressed her foot sharply on the gas and the car shot ahead. Speed was fine and clean, it was a pure feeling and she'd have one fine taste of it before tomorrow. The long hill was clear and the headlights brushed the blackness of the road. The light to the left was dim. It was just like Cliff to have something out of gear. Easy now, easy, and she let it out, the car shot ahead, clean ahead, ripping out suddenly like a broken spring tearing down the hill and when it hit the big dark truck stalled without a tail light near the bottom, Rosamond did not even know it.

Summer in Many States 1934

The government expert was trying to explain. "Now you farmers are just nervous. There's no use in looking so far ahead. A step at a time. We're getting relief in here fast as we can."

"You're not paying us relief," said a farmer. "You're paying the banks relief."

"I don't understand you," said the expert, smiling nervously and looking at his assistant, a young man who was hoping to get through with these people so he could get on to see his girl. "You're getting two dollars for your sheep and goat skins."

"I get you," said the farmer rising and presenting one of those bull necked fronts so antagonizing to a well meaning expert. "The government pays us two dollars for a skin. We got to sell because the drought kills the sheep and goats. They got no feed. First you told us we had too much. Now we ain't got any. So we have to kill. Who gets the two dollars? Is it us that took care of the flocks? Right off the bat the banker gets a dollar that we never even see. Then on that other dollar, we don't get more than thirty cents because by the time we skin them and take them to a point of shipment, it costs plenty. So when this feller Richberg tells how he puts two billion up for us farmers, he's talking through his hat. He's handing over one billion to his buddies, the bankers, first of all. Then we get about thirty cents, see."

"Well we can't go into that," said the expert uncomfortably, looking frantically for a friendly face. "But if you have any suggestions of any better plan, I'll be glad to hear them. As for debts, I'd be glad to get rid of mine that easily." He tried to chuckle, gave a half hearted imitation and stuffed his watch in and out of his pocket, his eyes shifty beyond the door to the hot land. He'd got hold of a tough set of farmers this time and no mistake. He began to see why the small town storekeepers were afraid of them.

When he was whirling off in his car to the next point, he continued to feel the cold arrows of that farmer's speech. He felt as if they were at his heels, with their cold determined eyes. The worst of it was, they were right. He groaned within himself, wishing he had never taken any courses in sociology and had stuck at something simple, easy to understand, if there was such a thing nowadays. The bleak horrified countryside turned up its stiff bones of dead grass, crucified corn and wheat beaten savagely to earth by heat. His very flesh crawled and he longed for fresh green country to the east. This landscape was swept bare as a stage and maybe the small town storekeepers were right. The farmers would refuse to starve, they would come in droves, they would pick the cans from the shelves, they would fill their old cars with flour and tins. They would be at each other's throats, storekeeper and poor farmer and now another cog had been found to throw into the machinery, the poor farm hand, his threat to the farmer with his strikes won on big farms for higher wages. The trick was to keep them apart, to keep them fighting, let dog eat dog.

The poor fellow, still human, groaned but he could see an implication when it stuck out like a sign post. My God, if they ever realized they were in the same boat, if they ever quit tearing at each other's throats, if the little storekeeper ever got it into his head that his friend, his only friend was the poor farmer, not the rich banker, where in hell would the system be then? I ask you, where would it be then, and where in hell would his job be too? So let the feuds brew and the nightriders ride, let them go to it.

WHITE HEADED BOY

Abel Chance did not worry about his soul. As a deacon of the church his soul was taken care of. He loved the Sunday ritual of waffles for breakfast with the Sunday paper crisp and unopened waiting for him in the living room. He did not believe in reading the paper at the table on Sunday. And in fact, not until his wife died, did he ever make much of a practice of table reading. He was always shaved and bathed before Sunday breakfast and sat in his lounging jacket with the consciousness of clean underwear, the finest woolen socks and pure linen helping him to savor the special Sunday quality of the day. His wife poured from a silver pot that was always burnished. Sunlight flooded the breakfast room and on winter mornings he could look straight through the back windows where the bird box on a tall pole sheltered birds that he fed regularly. He would as soon think of going to church or office unshaved as to leave the house without giving the birds their morning meal.

He would as soon think of not winding his watch as of not going to church and when Jonathan was home, he accompanied his father. He never had the necessary hardness to defy his father and stay away from church. His sister as a child had locked herself in her room, kicked and bawled, but he had been choir boy. It was easier to go his own way, do what he liked, and say nothing about it.

On Sunday afternoon his father's idea of a good day was to have Jonathan drive them to Eaton Rapids to see Aunt Sadie or to take the Kempers, who had no car, for a drive. It was a satisfaction to sit back, to feel the car on the best hard tires run along smoothly and evenly, to know it had the right amount of oil, air, and gas, and was washed and polished as well as any car in Benton. To come back to Sunday night supper that his wife had prepared because that was the girl's evening out, the meal spread out temptingly on a fine lace cloth, the lights burning richly in the crystal chandelier. He did not even read the descriptions in the Sunday paper of trips to the south or west or abroad although his wife did and would sometimes broach the subject.

"Wouldn't you like to go to Florida, Abel, the Wilsons are going and want us to go, too."

"Well, yes," he would answer slowly, keeping his eyes glued to the paper so as to avoid his wife's, "that would be nice all right, but who would do the work at the store? I'd like to ride around, nothing better, but with taxes and school expenses, I don't feel like Mr. Rhingold, not yet."

You'd think to hear him he was head over ears in debt. Every time he sent his sons money at school, he dinned into them that money was scarce, and he had "borrowed" this from the bank. The older he got, the more he held to this fiction. Certain expenditures were good investments but he had too much homespun in his nature to take to travel or the arts. He pooh-poohed his wife's interest in milk-ware, hobnailed pitchers, and antiques but as the articles won respect from callers, he gave her more or less of a free hand. She concentrated more and more on these objects and saved all Jonathan's letters.

If Jonathan could slip out of it, he liked nothing better on those Sundays he was home than to go to Krauses'. Krause was still at the Chance store and he still had his bitch hunter. Mrs. Krause got out cookies and homemade beer and the two men smoked and chewed the fat. Business was fair. There were more unemployed than Krause liked to see. His nephew had come home and couldn't find a job. He was sitting around looking lost as a needle in the haystack. It would be better for him if he had a girl.

"Sure he needs a girl," Jonathan said, spitting carefully in the woodbox.

"That's what I told him," said Krause. "You need a girl, I said, to take you out of yourself. He won't even answer. Just glum, but he's got ambition or used to, I don't know what ails the kid. Do you think he's sick?"

"Might be," said Jonathan. "Shell shock maybe."

"No," said Krause, "not shell shock."

"He's lazy, if you ask me," said Mrs. Krause. "Still he's looking for work. He makes a pretense. My sister, she's sick about him. Says you'd never know he was her boy." From talk like that the two men would meander off into politics, and Krause was a greater hand at it than any of the boys who hung around at Vidisichis' in Detroit. From their talk you'd think Rabelais was ruler of the world.

If he didn't go to Krauses', he went out to the Beckers'. Their boy had joined the navy to see the world but had been stuck for months in some little pit of a town near Baltimore. "It ain't even Baltimore," Becker said, "and the kid bought the postcard he sent us of China from a fellow in a boat that rowed out to meet them. That's all the world he's managed to spot so far."

Old man Becker made his own wine and treated his vintages with respect. When he poured out a glass, that had first to be carefully rubbed with one of Mrs. Becker's best tea towels, he liked to stand, legs apart, face flushed, staring at Jonathan who stood with legs also slightly apart, head back, the glass raised and looked through, the color of wine admired and then slowly tasted, smacked, rolled on the tongue, all the time Mr. Becker suspended and waiting. "This is first rate, Mr. Becker, first rate. A real bouquet and flavor. One of the smoothest wines I ever tasted."

"I thought you'd like it," said Mr. Becker modestly, at this point taking up his own glass and going through the same ritual, as if he were still a stranger to his own brew.

"You certainly know the trick," said Jonathan.

"None of your damned essences for me," said Mr. Becker, "this is the pure juice of the fruit. Nature has worked her miracle in this little glass, not a jumble of chemicals out of a bottle." They would then sit down, at the kitchen table, the wine bottle between them.

"The boy says that Pershing began as a private. Do you think that's right?"

"Wouldn't be surprised, but come to think of it, he went to West Point, didn't he? Those fellows get the breaks. Not that privates haven't worked up, but how many do you ever hear of?"

"You're right there," said Becker. "And for every fellow who gets to be president of a bank there are hundreds of thousands who don't. Yet we run the country for the bank presidents, that's the way I look at it." Mrs. Becker had come out to look on and she gave a little grunt.

"There he goes—off on his favorite hobby—but what he never stops to reflect, Jonathan, is that this is a free country and you can get what you want with the vote. If people haven't sense enough to see to it that they get a different government, why let them suffer, is what I say." She nodded her head virtuously, sniffing and glaring a little at her husband who glared back.

"Do we have to have that old argument?" he said, in his excitement actually gulping his wine without reverence.

"Oh, you and your bankers. He's just got a grudge because he lost a thousand dollars in the 1907 panic. Can't get over it," she said nodding her head as if to make the shot tell.

"All right, that's a grievance, granted. But when did it come? Just when I needed that thousand. Why, that was the first necessary thousand they are always talking about. Save a thousand, they tell you, then invest. Then your fortune is made. But before I got to use it, by gum, if they didn't swipe it."

"You should begin again," said Mrs. Becker. "Instead you've been content to work for others all your life instead of working for yourself. That's what I can't get over. I just wish I was a man, I'd show you." She steamed out of the room and out to the front porch. They could hear her rocking back and forth, the noise was grim and emphatic. Becker grinned at Jonathan. "Well, here's to the women," said Becker, making a wry mouth that reminded Jonathan of Bert in the bicycle shop days.

> Rat nip catnip pennyroyal tea
> I saw a bedbug buggering a flea

Bert used to recite, smearing gum on a patch and then suddenly galvanized in a squatting position staring out the open door where a woman in a thin dress had just passed. "Never trust a woman who will smoke a cigarette or take a drink," he used to say irrelevantly. "She'll do anything." In those days Jonathan had not taken such remarks to heart. He thought Bert old-fashioned and didn't agree with Becker now, but he grinned and swallowed his wine, women had a terrific way about them of wanting to swallow a man alive. His own experiences had shown up girls as always wanting to show off and to get what they could out of you. At least the girls of his own class. He liked to think back on the West Virginia days, the summer he was selling garden seed. He remembered a little cigar clerk in a dinky hotel and another girl, who rode a horse like a boy and could whistle and had beautiful breasts under an old Sears, Roebuck sweat shirt. They knew how to love, he liked to tell himself, and sometimes at Vidisichis' he would refer to them, darkly, and say that a fellow didn't know anything who hadn't got himself a woman who knew what it was to work.

Earl would look up, one eyebrow raised pretty high. He was courting a girl in a Detroit factory, a young fresh thing and he was going to marry her. His book had slowed up, he was not taking so much interest in it any more. His girl was putting ideas into his head about being somebody, about getting up in the world and not just squatting at Ford's all his life. The other fellows were all uneasy about their futures. Tolman was beginning to think he could never do anything in such a commercial country. Pete was saying that if you really faced reality, the answer was suicide. Guy was trying to duplicate his one success and sell another story to *Smart Set*. He kept retelling the same piece in a little different way, each version a little thinner than the last.

But the one young man that the Chances liked to have Jonathan bring home with him was his friend Terry Blount, who was all on fire to make a fortune.

"I'm going to own a big house, have a beautiful wife and a dozen kids," he boasted, sitting in the Chance parlor and making Abel Chance burst out into little deprecatory yet appreciate chuckles. He was sensitive that Jonathan did not talk this way, was in fact curiously reticent about his future. "You have to begin planning. Look at Terry. That's the way to go at it."

Jonathan found it very hard to open up with his family. Sometimes they would work him into a confidential mood and he would confess that he occasionally drank too much. His mother would pretend to take it lightly, to laugh at it, his father shook his head but not severely. Jonathan had the momentary feeling that his people were pretty darned nice and broad-minded. But in a few days, a week, some occasion would come up to make him regret his confidence. His father would doubt him because he had admitted he drank too much. His mother accused him of taking the old whiskey that had been laid by for sickness. When he denied these accusations, they laughed good humoredly and reminded him that he used to deny he drank a drop and had finally admitted it. "How can we trust you, you lie so," his mother said. Or she would look at him if he were telling the smallest thing. "Now Jonathan, are you sure that's the truth."

At last he made up his mind he wouldn't tell them a damned thing but it took a long time before he could break himself. He kept forgetting that he must be suspicious of them. Often he would have liked to confide.

When he lost his job on the Washington paper he tried to make up his mind if the truth or fiction were better to tell his folks. He felt bad at losing the job but, it was true, he didn't care much about running his ass off chasing senators. The press gallery was funny but you couldn't write about it that way. You had to write up everything as if it were in dead earnest. Then he guessed he had too many irons in the fire. He was going to too many Washington teas, he slacked his studies for the press job and the press job for his studies and the whole mess for a good book. He had a hankering to write, not newspaper stuff, but the real thing. Not Guy's pap, that was no better than newspaper jargon and as for the *Smart Set*, in his opinion it was a snobbish shallow paper. He finally evolved a pretty good excuse for losing the Washington job and said that he had known all along it was coming. He said he wanted to go to a real school, perhaps Columbia, and study hard.

"That's too far away," said his mother, "and I don't like a boy of your age in New York. If you want to go to another college, go to Ann Arbor. It's your own state and you can come home on Sundays."

"Why yes," said his father. "You told us that Washington was just the place, you said you could study law and politics at the same time, now look what happens. Now you're telling us New York is the only place and in about six months you'll be telling us you were wrong. No sir, I just wish I could have jumped around like that. At your age, I was paying life insurance, yes sir, and had bought a lot. I was making payments on that property out on Chisholm Street, I thought then I'd build on it but never did. Sold it without using it but at a good profit. It just shows you."

Jonathan tried to answer them with arguments but it was no use. They wouldn't hear of it. They finally laid down an ultimatum and said he could go to Ann Arbor or forget college entirely. They looked so solid and unshakeable it was no use bombarding them with words. Words were nothing to them. His father could shake out his paper and hide behind it, his mother could go on counting the pieces in the linen closet. He might as well try to describe a trip to the moon as to make them see what he wanted. He didn't know what he wanted, just so it wasn't what they had.

David Trexler knew of the Industrial Workers of the World only through the newspapers. They were in his opinion the misfits of society, men who had marital trouble and were made drifters, they were the bellyachers whose lack of industrious application kept them castoffs and unsuccessful. As Roseland was a Pacific Coast town and a good deal of the money in the town was by this time Trexler money, it took on the Trexler complexion in its attitude toward these migratory birds, as Trexler called them in his quaint way at the meeting of the bank directors. Not that anyone at the meeting was giving them more than cursory attention. The strong arm of the law was putting them safely behind the bars and Trexler knew for certain that only the firm action taken by the lumber men had prevented real red trouble throughout the lumber belt on the Pacific. Trexler was still congratulating himself on his entrance into the lumber interests. They had been as profitable as steel.

His rising position in the town gave him the feeling of wanting to do good with his wealth. He was still Dave to the town and there was nothing he wanted so much as to assure his townspeople of his abiding interest in their welfare. He figured about a fountain, an endowment to education, and finally a park. The land in question was costing him too much in taxes and it would be ideal for the kiddies to play on. He was, however, not without a rival, and on the city council the problem of the gift park became a ball that got tossed back and forth and finally out. His rival's park was taken and for a while David Trexler sulked at the ingratitude of the world.

Dave, Jr., had married and the wedding, an outdoor one, under blossoming trees with little children scattering rose petals in the path of the happy pair, was the talk of the town. Trexler felt he was

beginning to reap a reward and he got the young couple established
in a brand new house on one of his own pieces of land. The couple
were to pay for this property, with interest, in regular payments.
Dave, Jr., was also to repay his father for his education, just to
teach him the value of money, and in fact the young pair suddenly
found themselves in their little bower, completely hamstrung so far
as the enjoyments of life went. The relentless payments had to be
kept up and besides Dave was working in his father's store. To be
sure, it would someday be his store, when he had made the
arrangements to pay for it bit by bit, but in the meantime, it was
Trexler senior's property. The old man had too many strings to his
bow to give it his attention, Dave ran the place and at the salary,
arbitrarily fixed by his father.

"Why, we can't even belong to the country club at this rate,"
said Dave's young wife, looking at him doubtfully and feeling
horribly let down. They would be old before they had money and of
course Mr. Trexler was the kind who would live forever.

Dave said they were going to belong and he'd find a way. But he
felt mean. The meanness seemed to spread like oil. It made his wife
cross and irritable even in bed together. It spread over their life, it
made it hard for him to be nice to his mother. She was in high
spirits and hoped her son would have offspring soon. Then she
could make lovely baby things all handmade with real lace.

One Sunday night after Dave and his young wife had had a spat
because there was hardly a cent left over to have any pleasures on,
he walked up the hill to the big house moodily. He hoped he would
find his father and he meant to tell him a few things and have it
out. For one thing he meant to tackle him on the subject of his
salary. If his father didn't pay him more, he'd quit and get a job
working for someone else. The grass had been freshly watered by a
big elaborate system of automatic sprinklers. As he turned the
corner he came upon his father without a coat, in his Sunday white
shirt, playing with the sprinklers, turning them off and on.

"Did you ever see such contraptions?" said Trexler to his
gloomy son. "Look at this, there are three different streams, fine,
spray, and strong. Why, it's magic and this one little lever operates
the whole lawn." His face was red with enthusiasm and looking up

he caught the unresponsive look on Dave's face. It soured him at once. He hated to see his son's unenthusiastic way of meeting life. Why, at his age, he had had the world before him, he had his own way to make, to carve it out by hand, out of stone, you might say, and yet he had never pulled a jaw like that. He snapped himself upright and said crossly, "Well, Mamma and I are going for a little drive, but you'll find Sue in the house."

His way of saying this, of dismissing his son, reduced Dave to nothing. He followed his father, rebellious but dumb and sank down on the porch chair. His mother sailed out in a lilac silk dress and began telling him about the lovely flowers in church that morning. He nodded but could not conceal his grouch. There was no place for him to go. He couldn't go home where Charlotte was crying her eyes out and making him feel a spineless fool, he couldn't sit here and let his father ride him. He got up and mooched up stairs. The big empty hall was filled with heirlooms, the old hand loom that they had used back in Pennsylvania, the big chest that had come from his great-grandfather's farm. There were even the guns that had belonged to Uncle Joe on the walls. All the things in this hall had belonged to people now dead. Standing there and looking out at his father's big Cadillac sliding slowly down the drive, he thought that the lucky people were the dead people.

At the end of the hall Sue's door was open. He walked down the hall and stood looking in at her. She looked up from her desk, saw him, blushed, and covered a sheet of note paper with her hand.

"What you doing?" he said, coming over toward her.

"Nothing, I'm writing a letter," she said self-consciously. "Go away," she went on still laughing a little. He hated his sister suddenly for having a big room, no worries, and being able to write letters. Their father had not made her pay for her education. She had gone to college too, but whoever heard anyone tell her to get busy and pay it back so she could learn the value of money. He sauntered nearer and picked up a magazine.

"What are you reading this stuff for?" he said.

"It's not stuff, it's just not the *Saturday Evening Post*, that's your speed."

He leaned over her, his face suddenly beetling and looking very much like his old man's.

"And who are you writing to?"

"Quit bullying me and go away, Dave, please," said Sue, keeping her hand over her letter.

"Let me see," he said, pushing at her hand. She fought and they both laughed a little. He read. "Sounds like a love letter. Um. Well, who is he? I'm sure glad to see you're writing a letter like that. I thought you never saw anyone but that girl at the library. You had me worried."

"What do you mean worried, isn't that all right?"

"Oh get wise to yourself, you know what I mean."

"I certainly don't," said Sue, getting pale.

"You don't?" said Dave, feeling ugly. "Well, there's a name for that kind of thing but I won't tell you." He felt as if he wanted to wipe that smug look off her face. So she could get away with murder, could she? She said, "Quit your insinuations, and tell me what you are talking about. I don't like the way you look."

"Well, you can't have everything the way you like it in this world, haven't you found that out yet? Here give me another look at that letter." He tugged at it and she held to it, they struggled for the letter. Tears came into her eyes. "Please Dave, you frighten me, what's wrong with you?"

"I just want to see that my sister isn't making an ass of herself, that's all," said Dave, tearing off a corner of the letter. But he couldn't read it. Then he looked at her. "I'd like to know who that letter is to, I've a notion to tell Father."

"It's to no one," said Sue, "I tell you it's none of your business." He stood staring at her desk as if to wrench her secret from her.

"I think you're lying to me," said Dave. "But whether you are or not, it's time you got some sense. You and that girl are too mooney to suit me."

"Go away," Sue said. "I'm sick of hearing such talk. What do you want to do now? Leave me nothing at all? Papa never had a day's rest until he broke up my engagement with Ralph. When the poor fellow was drowned, Papa was really glad. He said it was providence. Now you come along. This is all I've got, a friendship is all I've got and you want to spoil that. You want to degrade everything and what is it all about? Go away." She was screeching at him now, tears running down her face. "I'm sick of all of you, of everything, I wish I was dead." She burst into sobs, put her head down on the desk, on the torn letter, and sobbed. Dave, suddenly sobered, stood watching her. He cleared his throat. "I'm sorry Sue, I didn't mean anything, but Charlotte is all upset today too and Dad never gave me a chance to talk, just drove off. Forgive me, can't you."

"Go away," Sue sobbed, moving her hand, pushing him with it. "Just go away, that's all I ask." He tiptoed from the room. Outside he stood drearily in the midst of the loom, the chest, the guns, the handwoven quilts on the wall. These solid things out of the past surrounded him in his misery, but Sue's sobs could still be heard as he silently tiptoed down the stairs.

IV. CLOUD OF FIRE

JERRY STAUFFER moved his things from the blue tower room to a room on the second floor but he did not leave the Wendel house. He went to work every day and found a new job in the shipping office of the packing house. At night he came home and tried hard, as he walked up the path, not to look up at the tower room and not to think. His room was on the other side of the house now, away from the river and away from the cottonwood tree where he and Rosamond had watched the robins making a nest that summer. He lay in a white bed that was once golden oak and that Rosamond and Victoria had enamelled years before to keep up with the times. He lay there with his eyes wide open and he could often hear the big clock downstairs ticking away. If he went to bed early he could listen to Mr. Wendel come upstairs in his stocking feet, then Nancy and her husband go to their room. Last of all Anne Wendel went to bed.

She made the rounds of her house with its fine new floors and its electricity and its little breakfast nook that she had waited so many years to have. As winter came on they put up a new storm door, the kind she had always wanted with glassed windows so you could see

210

out. Never had there been so many little comforts, they had not had things so good all their lives and never had it meant so little.

She would sit a few minutes before going to bed, trying to read with no heart in it. Many was the time when the children were little when she was on the go until late at night, setting the bread for the next day, darning stockings, perhaps the room would be strewn with their flannels that had been washed that day and hung near the register to dry. She would sit, trying to read the paper so she wouldn't get stale but could keep alert and be interesting to her family, and her head would droop. Then was the time, that she used to think, Oh for a little leisure for self-improvement. She expected to look forward to that day when she could read and do some of the idle things many women did. Now the time had come, forced upon her, and she did not know what to do with it. She had not been able to save her girl. At night alone she had a dread of her house. She would sit very still and look intently into the darkness of the next room. Where had her girl gone? People who were able to call accidents the hand of God were fortunate. She was not that kind. Sometimes sitting at the table in the dining room in the silent house she had the feeling that she could unravel the mystery. Then her life as a girl with its joys and sorrows rose before her. Her dead sister Catherine who had been no older than Rosamond seemed now the freshest in her memory. If she could think that there was a heaven where those two young girls were wandering now, hand in hand, it would be a happy way perhaps, but she knew better. She hadn't kept up with her girls for nothing. She knew better than to believe myths. All the same, it was hard, sometimes late at night to suddenly remember how small the box was that had contained the ashes of her girl when cremated. Victoria and Jerry had insisted on that way, and she was willing, even though Amos Wendel cried to himself with horror. She wanted what the young folks wanted, she wanted to be abreast with changes, and yet at night, she suddenly caved in, inside, her very vitals seemed to crumble at the thought of that sweet flesh burned and charred and lost forever.

Sometimes step by step she would go over the last months of her girl's life. Suppose things had turned out better in Detroit; if Jerry had been able to get a job, the accident would not have happened.

Rosamond wouldn't have felt so desperate at her plight, wouldn't have felt like rushing off with the car. It would have been then, what it should always be, a happy time for a woman. Anne Wendel still believed that children were worth all the sacrifice, but it seemed harder and harder to have children. With all the inventions and all the improvements in ways of living, life itself seemed never so difficult, jobs seemed scarcer, food dearer, living more complicated and bitterly hard. Looking into the darkness brought no answer. Better to get up, to set the bread. Jerry liked homemade bread, the poor boy, there was oatmeal to start for the morning, a letter to write to Victoria, poor child.

"I was down town today at Meyer's store. They are making big improvements but as Rosamond always said, when weren't they ripping out and adding something. The store has grown over a whole city block, just sprawls there and looks very nice toward the front but in back where cheap stuff sells, it is kind of a jumble with narrow aisles. That is where the farmers do their trading and I guess the Meyers think it good enough for them, but I'd like to know where this town would be without the farmers. A girl your size waited on me at Meyer's. She slipped into the waist I liked, only it was not the color. It cost $17.50, but I can make one like it for $5 and use the same material. You are all we have now and if I couldn't do anything for anyone I'd die."

She would sit there, looking at her letter. She longed to ask her girl to write to her as she used to write to Rosamond and to tell her the secrets she had confided in her sister. What was Victoria doing? She could not tell. The little notes would not come to the house any more for Anne Wendel to pry into late at night. It was as if a door had slammed shut in her face. She felt very alone and timid and lost and just held the pen there, trying to think of a way to say what was in her heart. There was no way. She would make the blouse, after that some pretty underwear, there were all those old clothes in the attic she could tear up into rags for rugs. She thought of her own mother's life and its busy end. Once she had been consoled to think how occupied Mem had been in her old age, with painting china, with making rag rugs, with her thousand and one tasks to the day of her death. Now when she thought of Mem's last years, she wanted to cry. A tight hand seemed to clutch her very heart.

In the morning there was breakfast and she started her family out with nourishing food. Jerry never would wear rubbers, he wouldn't take care of his colds. Nancy helped with the housework. If one or the other woman was left alone in the big house, she would make some wild excuse to hurry off, to go to town, to mail a letter, anything so she did not have to sit and think.

The White Elephant was really not a shelter for anyone any more.

Jerry Stauffer had no idea of working up in the packing house industry. There were men in his own department who had been faithful and industrious for years and who still held very minor jobs. He had always believed that if he had more education he would have stood a better chance at life, but he was surprised to find that a number of men pulling down only $25 a week at Cumley's were college grads. At least six or seven of them. One fellow had graduated from Princeton and before the war got $300 a month. He had been a civil engineer in Detroit and had lived only six blocks from where Jerry and Rosamond had lived. He was gassed in the war and had a pale skin and often a dry cough. For a while he had been civil engineer for road work but that had been stopped and he was laid off with the rest. When Jerry came home at night he liked to relate these stories. Sometimes the whole Wendel family sat around the fireplace in which a few logs were burning, not for heat as the furnace was enough for that, but for cheerfulness, and the unfortunate histories of others gave them the feeling they weren't alone in unhappiness.

But still you couldn't sit around the fire every night. Amos Wendel was getting to be a first rate story teller, pulling out old recollections and swapping yarns with Jerry. For years his wife and the girls had monopolized things, all unknowing, but now they liked to listen to him. "Why, I never realized Papa could talk so interestingly," said Nancy. "Oh you should have heard him when I first knew him," said Anne Wendel proudly tossing her head, "Why, he's a wonderful talker but in late years saves it I guess for men at the store."

Sometimes Jerry would pull himself away from the family group and go see his own mother. The hungry eyes of the two mothers made him feel cornered. He wished he had the guts to pull out, to go away. When one of his old friends talked of driving a car to California, he was all on fire to go. "What do you think of that for an idea?" he asked the Wendels. Nancy was all for it. She thought Jerry was in a terrible rut and after all he could earn $100 a month anywhere. He should get out, meet other people, start living again. She yearned over her brother-in-law and tried to spur him on in his plan. She and Anne Wendel actually quarreled a little about it.

"It's no time to strike out," Anne Wendel said. "He should save his money first, look around and try to locate something first."

"He'll never save enough, he'll just get cautious. I think you shouldn't try to hold him back Mother, he's so wretched."

"I wouldn't hold him back, the idea," said Anne. "I'm only thinking of his welfare. It's no time for changes like that, let him wait a little. I hear jobs are scarce on the coast."

It didn't take much discouragement to drive the idea out of Jerry's head. All the same when his friend started off on the train, after giving up the idea of driving, Jerry kept tab of his trip. "Tom's at Kansas City now," he would say, looking up with his bright alert eyes, his voice falsely cheerful. And the next day, "I guess he gets into Denver today. He'll be at Salt Lake tomorrow."

When good music came to town you couldn't keep Jerry away. His only purchases for himself were victrola records of Beethoven and Bach. One night after a fine concert he was walking out of the auditorium alone and at the door hesitated looking at the sky, hating to go home. One of the young musicians came out carrying his instrument in its case. He asked Jerry where the Hotel Martin was. His English was bad and Jerry, proud of his accomplishment, answered him in the German spoken in his home for years. The two young men delighted at their talk walked along the street talking of the old country.

"Were you in the war?" said Jerry.

"Yes," said the other. "And you?"

"I didn't see any fighting but I was in France. Stationed at Limoges."

"I was in Paris once, what a jewel of a city," said the German.

"I didn't see much of it but I'd sure like to see it again, don't suppose I ever will." He thought he would never see it again, he had the feeling nothing would ever happen to him. Everything important that he wanted was done for. He could have little pleasures, like music and books. The cloud of fire that led some people was not for him. He had not been able to manage his life, had not been able to keep Rosamond. He thought of his life as a long dreary road and yet as he listened to the young musician talking of the Rhine country and his home at Köln, he longed for a sight of the slow moving Loire again gliding through the vineyard covered hills of Burgundy at Nevers or down past the lush gentle country at Tours. He longed for a sight again of the river that his angry repressed rebellion at that time had not let him enjoy. In memory he enjoyed it and longed for it as he longed for the anticipation of a future that had come only to vanish.

At the hotel door he said goodnight, they shook hands cordially. He envied the musician pushing his way into the brightly lighted lobby. Tonight here, tomorrow in Omaha, the next day Kansas City, Denver, Salt Lake, San Francisco. He lit a cigarette and a woman in a white coat and furs smiled straight at the young face under the hat pulled down. A newsboy sang out, "Big Strike at Cumley's, night crew walk out, big strike threatened, mayor urges arbitration."

He bought the paper, read it as the street car jogged toward home. Talk of strike had been going around for weeks. He hadn't taken much stock of it. He was too sunk in his own trouble. Everything that happened lately seemed to be going on behind glass. It was as if nothing could possibly concern him any more. He remembered now talk that went right on under his nose. The higher-ups treated the office men as if they were dummies. They were certainly darned sure of them. The strikers didn't even bother with office help. He could tell them a thing or two like the talk he'd overheard about wage cuts scheduled for next summer. If they took it now, they'd get it in the neck again when summer came. Perhaps they did know and that was what blew the lid off.

For the first time he was interested to get to work the next day. It was bitter cold and he kept thinking of one of Rosamond's letters describing the Seattle general strike. He had been on the woodcutting job at Limoges and he had quit work, dog tired. When he read the letter he had tingled all over with a kind of reflected excitement, and a guy from a Washington State outfit had gassed for hours. That fellow had boasted that he had bummed all over the Northwest but you couldn't ride the rods if you didn't have a Wobbly card.

It was a little disappointing when he got out to the yards to find only a few men bunched near the gates. No one challenged him as he went in. But once inside, he could see the place was practically empty. Klingan the office boss was nervously fretting from one room to another. About a dozen office men stood around trying to look helpful.

"Now I'm going to need all you boys today and we'll eat here, I've arranged for stuff to come in. They're quiet out there now, but no telling what will happen. This will all blow over but we've got some important shipments that can't wait." The men were assigned jobs and went off down the hall. Jerry went to the scales room with Klingan. The room was down to 29 degrees. There were no windows. An electric bulb burned in a mean hard way. The two began weighing the meat. In a half hour Jerry's hands felt numb, his feet heavy as frozen clods.

"Get yourself a pair of wooden-soled shoes," said Klingan. Jerry went to the storeroom, stuck his feet in the heavy wooden-soled shoes, like peasants's sabots. Putting on the wooden shoes, pretty good. He came back clumping along the hall, wearing a pair of clumsy mittens he had found on a chest.

Klingan was raging at the office crew who were trying to cut up the meat. "Look at those hams, they're so thin you could eat them with a paring knife. Call that a cut? Why, my god, you've left the tenderloin on the cheap cut and there's not more than a cube of highpriced stuff on that hunk." He couldn't get very sore at the men though or they might quit. "Listen men, we've got to do this job, so hammer along on it but try to make those hams lifesized, not as if they were dying of t.b."

By the end of the day Jerry was all in. When he got home Anne Wendel was very indignant. "Look at you, frozen, why you'll get pneumonia at that rate. You're not used to it." In bed he couldn't sleep for several hours. He wondered how in hell the regular men stood it. The next day he chose the lard-rendering department. The temperature was 92 degrees and he got out of his suit into a pair of overalls in double quick time. That night he came home with a band of blue from the overalls sweated to his skin across his shirt and back.

Amos Wendel told him the papers said work was practically normal.

"They lie," said Jerry. He was all in, but reached for the paper. PACKERS ASSERT CONDITIONS PRACTICALLY NORMAL.

"Why there's no killing to speak of, every department is at a standstill except for the office men."

"Then if it wasn't for you fellows, things would be shut up tight," said Amos Wendel. He sucked his pipe with an audible sound and Jerry turned his head to look at him. "Oh we don't amount to anything," he said. "No one pays any attention to us. The strikers don't. Say they're holding out though, they haven't let a strike breaker in. We can't hear inside but I went outside this morning and it was noisy by the gates. I'm just afraid the packers will stir up something to break it, because the way it's fixed now those boys aren't going to weaken."

In spite of being so dead on his feet, Jerry got to work on time each day. Each day he lined up with something different. He helped load meat for Portland, Maine, destined for Europe. Then he chose to inject salt solution into the hams with a hypodermic. A dose squirted in his eye and half closed it. The best job was copped by Klingan himself. It was the box-making department in the basement where the temperature was normal. There was no end to the strike after two weeks, and one day when he got off the streetcar in the morning the packers had a truck for the office boys. They weren't going to take any chances.

Going to a movie late one night, he was surprised at how bored he was. He felt nervous and impatient, anxious to get out on the street, to be home, to be asleep, to be up and at the packing plant. The strike stirred up the whole Wendel family and for the first time since Rosamond's death they did not sit around the fire talking. Anne Wendel cooked extra muffins for breakfast because Jerry needed more nourishment now, she said.

It began to get under Jerry's skin that he knew so little of what was going on. He was a dummy going and coming, owned by the packers. When it was his turn again at the scales room; he put on the wooden shoes and tried to feel good humored and above it all. Clumping down the hall he heard a skirmish outside and yells and somewhere a whistle was blowing frantically. Klingan came in and said if they made trouble it would be reason enough to call out the militia. Rolling out in the truck with guards bristling with guns on the running board, the gang at the gate yelled "Scab." Someone threw a stone. Jerry was quiet all evening and about eight-thirty decided to take in a late movie. Coming out the newsboys were shouting extras. He bought one. A nightwatchman, an old fellow with a tobacco stained moustache, had been stabbed.

Anne Wendel was the only one up when he got home. "They've stabbed a man at the yards," said Jerry. "An old fellow who doesn't know what it's all about." He couldn't sit still, kept walking up and down, smoking, and finally went out to the kitchen to find something to eat.

"Who did it?" said Anne. "Who could do a thing like that? That's what comes of those packers giving such little wages and look what we pay for meat? Why, I paid nearly ninety cents for that tough piece we had tonight." "I bet my hat no striker stabbed that fellow," said Jerry. "I've got a hunch, don't know why. But if I'm right, I'm getting out myself."

"What'll you do?" said Anne. "Times are bad now." She didn't want him to quit and maybe get discouraged, drift around, and then leave home. The home was empty enough without that.

"I don't know what I'll do and it doesn't matter," said Jerry. The idea of being out of work excited him. If he was fired or quit, he'd have to go away. He would be forced to live again, not stay here forever brooding about the past. Rosamond would hate him if she could see him now, spineless as a jelly fish.

Bluecoats stood near the entrance gate next morning as the truck rumbled in under a yell of "Scab" and a few stones. Jerry wondered why Klingan was not more upset at the stabbing. He shrugged instead and said what could you expect. A strike was like war, someone was certain to get it in the neck. That night, at dusk, a shipment of guns came in packing cases out of a high-powered car.

"Hope we won't have to use these," said Klingan busily, ordering the placement of the guns in a cupboard, "but if the scratch comes, guess it's up to the office crew, hey Jerry."

"No me," said Jerry firmly.

"What, you'd turn yellow?"

"It's not a question of color," said Jerry, "but you don't get me to use a gun on strikers." Klingan turned around. His face turned ugly. "Jesus, don't begin any baby talk, I've got my hands full with worry as it is. The guns aren't to play with, that's certain, but who says they are going to be used. They were brought in in case of trouble. After that stabbing—"

"Who did the stabbing—"

"God, how should I know? Some striker, naturally."

Naturally nothing, thought Jerry beginning to feel too wise for the office. He started down the hall toward the cold room, even put the wooden shoes on his feet. There was a lot of shouting going on outdoors. A big truck was bucking and grunting at the gates. They were trying to highpower through with scabs. "Scabs," "sons of bitches," "hey, cut that out," "look out for the brick," "watch it," then a shrill whistle, another, a shot. Jerry straightened and kicked his feet out of the shoes. Put on his coat. Found his hat. At the door he was stopped by Klingan. "Where you going, for god's sake, we got that weighing to do."

"I'm quitting," said Jerry. He felt lighthearted. A chorus of shouts and jeers came from beyond the gate. Klingan looked at the door nervously. "I haven't time to argue if you want to be a fool."

"No one asked you to," said Jerry, "so long." He walked almost jauntily down the corridor. Not since they had grabbed him into the army away from Rosamond had he felt so lighthearted. The war hadn't been his war, but then he hadn't known how to get out of it. He could get out of this. He was getting out. He got out into the clear cold air. "Scab" yelled a voice seeing him. A big hunkie picked up a piece of brick.

"Not on your life," yelled Jerry ducking. He didn't know what he intended to do with himself now. A policeman jabbed him from the rear. "Clear the gate," he was saying. He tried to walk with dignity away from the gate but a new truckload of cowering men came rumbling up. "Scab" yelled the crowd massing and getting ready. Someone had ripped out a fence with barbed wires, the poles stuck up like stiff legs. The contraption was flung across the road, Jerry found himself pushing and shoving with the rest. He felt a little awkward but no one noticed him. He couldn't stand watching and he wasn't going back inside. He pressed with the men and when they yelled, he yelled too. His hat got crushed and he fumbled for a cigarette. There was no time to light. The cigarette was knocked from his mouth and the truck bucked a little, stood head toward the plant, like a bull pawing ready to charge. Police began whacking through the crowd.

"Hold ranks, stand together, push," and locking arms the men held, gave like rubber where a vicious blow from a cop knocked the line. "Hold now, for Christ's sake." The fellow next to Jerry had his overseas cap knocked off. He let his arms go to pick it up automatically, smiled, and said, "Don't want to lose that, it's all I got out of the damned war."

"They got a shipment of guns in there, did you know?" said Jerry.

"We guessed. What do you s'pose the old fellow got stabbled for except a good excuse to turn them loose?"

"You mean . . . "

"Sure, watch out, here she comes," and the truck bucked again. Stones chipped its nice red sides. The windshield bent and cracked in grinning zigzags. The police patrol clanged up and cops poured out. A blow hit Jerry from the rear. He tripped, fell, was lifted, flung, hit, kicked, raised himself painfully on all fours, and found himself on the floor of the patrol bumping over the narrow streets leading from the packing house district. As he looked up a cop hit him over the head. Someone near him was bleeding, drops of blood were plumping down on the floor near Jerry's hand.

"Hey," the cop by the door yelled to one on the seat, "did you see we got that big bastard?" Jerry did not lift his head; he looked at the feet, all old shoes. Another guy was crouched on the floor and looking at Jerry from a bloody face. He grinned faintly as Jerry looked at him. "You got it pretty bad," he said leaning toward Jerry. "Hey, shut up, you bastards," yelled the cop, leaning over and whacking the guy. The guy crumpled and lay still. Someone on the seat began to sing. Jerry wished he knew the words. If he wasn't kicked to death, he'd learn them. The other guys were joining in, even the fellow in the corner. It nearly drove the cops crazy. They couldn't hit everybody at once but they began clanging the foot bell on the patrol and busting through the streets like a house on fire.

"You'll have to get someone over here quick Mr. Purdy," said old Miss Peck into the mouthpiece, her hands trembling so that her words came over the wire in gasps and splutters. "Hoodlums are at the very door. By the million." She listened to the strong male voice over the wire and dropped the receiver as a brick crashed through the window. Oh they would kill her. She'd die and never get a chance to scrub Papa's tombstone as she did every Decoration Day for years on end. Something was tied to the brick. She crawled from behind the filing cabinet and reached out a hand. Mercy, suppose she couldn't get away. Whatever would they do to her? Stories of Huns and barbarian hordes swept terrifyingly, refreshingly through her parched mind.

Lord help me, she prayed as she tried to read. The words shivered. Demand. They were demanding again. Always demanding. Never a pretty please. No manners. Demand. Demand. Poor people should take what they can get and be grateful. Why should they have cash? They no doubt spent it on drink. All poor people drank or wanted to. They guzzled it away. Well they could shout and howl all they wanted so long as that door at the foot of the stairs held. Maybe Mr. Purdy would get here. Or she might try getting out the back way. Shouts came from that entrance also. What if those beans were mouldy? What did they want for nothing. Don't tell her. She'd suffered. She'd walked the streets more than a year looking for work until she was in tatters. But she guessed she knew what side her bread was buttered on and had sense enough to be grateful when a job was made for her.

The whole town was suffering. Nice people, educated people with sensitive feelings were suffering. Why poor Mr. Brackwood had lost his business. He had shut up his fine big home. Folks said his creamery was run from New York now and he was only manager. Think what a comedown and how painful. She sighed at the pain of poor Mr. Brackwood and tried to keep calm. A boy stood on the burning deck eating peanuts by the peck. Oh why couldn't she think of some fine strong quotation. Not even the Bible. The verses all slipped from her like water tumbling down hill. They were coming up the stairs. Oh oh. They were big noisy louts and dear knows where they would stop. The phone rang and she edged toward it. "Yes, Mr. Purdy. Yes." She heard the command of her master's voice and it was do or die. The books out of the safe, the money; now for the firescape. How thoughtful of dear Mr. Purdy to have a car waiting at the foot of the firescape. Maybe the police were handling the crowds from below. It had become quiet for a minute. The buzz of voices, feet, shouts, kicks, seemed to have been suspended. But only for a second. *One— two—three. Ready* someone was ordering and *All together now—* and yes the very door was quaking and bulging and Miss Peck ran, scuttling down the firescape oh shocking, terrible if a Man should be below and look up when her arms were full and she couldn't hold her skirts. No, she was down, safely, so nice of Mr. Purdy, she smiled, as from above a great crash like the side of a house falling made the man at the wheel step on the gas and nearly shoot through the brick wall. So nice, murmured Miss Peck but she could hardly wait to get inside her own little house, to lock the door, to stand panting, gazing with tears at the dear goldfish that she had thought for a minute, yes really, never to see again. She wiped her eyes and called up dear Mabel. "Oh you'll never guess. Yes, just hoodlums. They're mad because the food wasn't A 1. Why should it be? But Mabel the real thing they're sore about is that last night you-know-who took that fellow out of jail and beat him up and dumped him across the river in Dakota. He was the ringleader and we think came from Minneapolis. Our town wouldn't grow his kind, Mabel. Yes sir, and if the farmers would keep their noses out of what isn't their business, things would be all right, but they brought that fellow back to town, I say they brought him back and dear knows who all is outside my office. Mabel, it was just like the war. I tell you I never heard such a racket. I never seen the like. I thought I'd die, Mabel, I thought I'd die.

JAILBIRDS, GO FREE

Victoria Wendel lived in a basement apartment with three other girls. The front windows looking out on the street and school grounds opposite had bars like a jail. People came and went at all hours and sometimes at night one of the girls, sitting on a couch near the window with a man, would look up and see the curious brazen stare of a street child peering down into the room. Often bad words were chalked up on the stone front of the house near the mailbox by the wild street boys. The Hudson Dusters and other street gangs of big boys hung out nearby, but the little children were wild as hawks and screeched and tore by the house late into the night.

Until the time her sister died, Victoria thought she liked this life. In the afternoon the girls would hurry home from their different jobs and have tea in fine china cups. The tea was a gift and was a high grade tea from China in an imported package a foot high. They cut oranges very fine and floated a slice in each cup. A good many young men came to the house and in the evening some or all of the girls went out with different young men. When they came back it was very late and they always knocked on the door before opening it from the hall. Some man might just be leaving. They would talk a little, joking, making light of things because during the day they all had tiresome jobs.

Now and then one of the girls, Bernice, overcome with her domestic impulses, insisted on cooking dinner for them all and to oblige her they ate the delicious food, the rice, the chicken, the fine salad. But in the bathroom they grumbled about it, were up in arms against a régime that was too much like the old living at home with parents. One night no one came home to the fine meal and Bernice cried into her chicken and rice and ate gloomily and omnivorously alone.

Whatever they had done as children in their homes they thought

224

they hated to do now, but Victoria carried little keepsakes around with her in her trunk and each of the girls had some little vase or knickknack that had once seemed desirable. If they came from different parts of the country, they had one thing in common, they came from homes where the parents had had the same struggle to hold up their heads, to educate their children, to see them started in life. Sometimes the girls would start talking about their home backgrounds and Victoria would tell how her two older sisters got married on a white fur rug taken out on approval at Meyer's Department Store.

"And the next day mother always sent it back. She felt bad that my younger sister didn't get married at home so she could stand on the white fur rug, too." Everybody laughed and Victoria had a twinge at the exaggeration. She knew her mother had no such thought in connection with Rosamond's marriage but it sounded funny.

After Rosamond died Victoria did not feel like sitting around in the evenings and she dreaded to meet new people who might drop in for the slice of orange tea. She usually ate by herself uptown and came back to the apartment around seven for a few minutes before going out again. One night when she came in and went straight to the bathroom, Esther Whittaker hurried in after her. When they were both shut in the room, Esther said, "Don't go in the back room just now. George Gates is in there."

"All right, I won't," said Victoria, powdering her face.

"I have to tell you about it," said Esther and her excited voice made Victoria turn and look at her. "He's hiding here. No one must know he's here. As bad luck would have it, he was in the front room when Bill came, and hurried back while I answered the bell. He'd been lying down and had taken off his shoes. The shoes were standing right there. I passed it off though. I saw Bill looking at them and said, Oh, that's someone seeing Vic."

"For heaven's sake," said Vicky. "I guess I can stand it." They both laughed quietly. "What's he here for?"

"He's hiding. He just got here from Chicago. Don't say a word to a soul. They're fixing up a passport and he'll go to Russia. It's that or twenty years in Leavenworth. Some wealthy Chicago woman put up bail."

"Should I go in there now?" said Vic. "I'd like to change my dress."

"Sure, go on, only he's awfully nervous." Vic went to the door, softly opened it. "It's only me," she said in a whisper. The thin dark young fellow shot up from the corner of the couch but, when he saw Vicky, smiled and pretended he was looking for a book. He tiptoed around in his stocking feet keeping out of line of the two long windows that looked out on a little weedy backyard. Then he picked up a book and sat down determinedly. He tried to read to show how much at ease he was and Vicky had to smile as he turned pages too rapidly. From the closet she looked out at him as he sat with his back turned. He turned more pages, lit a cigarette. When she came out of the closet, he said in a low voice, "Did you notice anybody outside?"

"Watching, you mean?" said Vicky. They did not turn lights on for fear someone outside might see in and the dusk in the room added to the kind of heavy silence. It was as if George Gates had brought his year at Leavenworth on his shoulders into this room. "I didn't see anyone. I'll look when I go out. And I'll see you later." George smiled again at the tall girl who was looking so delighted to see him.

This was a good place. No one would think of looking for him in an apartment full of girls. He could even slip out without suspicion. Men came to see the girls. It was ideal. If dicks should surprise him from the front, he could get out the back. He had looked out the windows with a good deal of scrutiny. It was fine to see other buildings, firescapes. It was fine to think of himself in an apartment of nice girls, fully protected, at least as much as it was possible to be. Lights were beginning to go on in houses across the backyard fence and a man came to a window and looked out steadily. It gave George the creeps. Not that he could be seen. He was safe. He was only obeying orders, that came only twenty-four hours before it was time to report. Too bad to lose that big bail, twenty thousand dollars. They had certainly stirred up the dust. A lot of hysteria and fear and frothing at the mouth. He wanted to double up with laughter. When he was clear of the whole thing, he'd laugh. He'd roll and laugh like a big dog out in the grass for the first time after a hard winter. Serious as it was, it was comic to think of the chattering and quaking. Why, they were doing such a favor to the cause as no one could estimate. Cramming the I.W.W.'s into jail was a favor. Thanks mister, for the favor. He'd never forget the surprise some of those women showed at the Chicago trial. "We thought you must be a gang of cut-throats." Let them cram the jails. But even a dam won't stop a cloudburst. You could pile stones higher and higher and the water would leak through.

He got to his feet nervously hearing footsteps. Only one of the girls from the front room going into the bathroom. He waited tense until she went back again; voices laughed and talked and then a clatter of footsteps moved out through the hall. The front door slammed. It slammed twice, the signal to him that everything was o.k. Smart girls. He chuckled. A kind of nervous laughter seemed tearing at his insides. He sat down, picked up the *Saturday Evening Post*. Why, if the bulls tore through the place, he'd be sitting here. "I'm a brother of Miss Wendel," he'd say, indignant at being interrupted. But no, they wouldn't tear through without more of a tip. He'd tear out the back. Too bad there were bars on the windows. He'd have to get out the back door leading into the hall. But there was no use thinking of such things all the time, it was all taken care of. Dozens of people were smoothing the way. For all the thousands beaten up and jailed there were thousands more, sprung up from the wreck. They were making reds so fast, you wouldn't be able to count them some day. He laughed silently, looking at the *Saturday Evening Post*, the ads were certainly fascinating, big cars, swell women. Fisher Bodies. Beautiful bodies made in Detroit F.O.B. by men too tired to know the difference between one body and another.

The apartment house opposite was lighting up fast. The long windows downstairs had gauzy curtains and it looked as if a party were to begin. Dinner probably. Women in pretty dresses and bare arms. The gauze curtains made it seem miles away. Later on, one of the girls would bring in some sandwiches. That was a good

dinner he was eating when the order came. A quiet tap on the
shoulder, "Want to speak to you, George," and all the women
having the time of their lives looking up as he left the room. He
hadn't gone back, just slipped out the door and gone forever. He
would never see Chicago again, the windy city, the hogbutcher
town. If they weren't passing cocktails in that room. He walked
close to the window watching. The man was passing cocktails on a
tray and they were standing up, sipping; someone came near the
window and pushed aside the gauze and looked out. Suppose they
had someone planted there to watch? They couldn't see him; he
stepped backward into the room, way back and over by the far wall
sat down, looking. It was like being in a theater. Way down in the
theater looking a little up, at the stage. There was a lot of money in
that apartment, those women were dressed up like plush horses. A
high board fence, two little weedy plots of grass and that was all
that separated them. Let them swank around. Drink, be merry, for
tomorrow you die. That was a good line, but not so good as that
other about take the beautiful princesses to wife. That held the
meat. He was thankful for a good memory, it had saved him more
than once. At first when he was locked up he hadn't wanted to
think of anything. The best way was just to be as much like a
fungus as possible, don't expect anything, don't hope, just sleep.
But then he couldn't keep it up, he had to fill the vacuum in his
skull; many a night he tried to remember things he had learned by
heart as a kid. Then work up gradually to his young manhood. And
swing at them with a right upper cut with *Continue to struggle
bravely forward, most worshipful matters of capital. We need you
for the present*. He began to laugh. He got up and walked back and
forth in his stocking feet, still silently laughing. *We need you for
the present*. He pulled out another cigarette and pulled himself
together. Lit it and puffed solemnly for a second, his eyes on the
big windows where the party was commencing. They had put their
cocktail glasses down now and all the men were standing up for a
latecomer. A woman who was apparently the prima donna of the
evening. That was the one really swank apartment in the midst of a
lot of little mouldy ones. It set the pace and the rest kept trying to
break their necks. *We need you for the present . . . You have to*

convert the more or less owning classes into genuine proletarians, into recruits for our ranks. It gave him a sinking feeling to remember the many times he had said that over, just to keep his head straight. And then bits from Shelley. He'd talk out loud but not for long. Silence. Light out. Silence. Sometimes he'd pretend to talk in his sleep. He'd shout out the words. The guard would rattle angrily. Quiet. Shut up. He'd snore and turn over, groaning. But lots of wakeful guys heard him. *You must create the material means which the proletariat needs for the attainment of freedom. In recompense whereof, we shall allow you to govern for a while. Dictate your laws, bask in the rays of the majesty created by yourselves.* The men were now singling out the women in the lighted room, getting ready for a sally to the dining room. The prima donna woman was, of course, still the center. *Spread your banquets in the halls of kings.* He snickered and wondered if it would be safe to tiptoe into the kitchenette to look for even a crust of bread. He should have asked them to bring the sandwiches earlier, it was his own fault. *And take the beautiful princesses to wife—but do not forget, that: The Executioner waits at the door.*

Although he had spoken not a word aloud, he felt that the room was ringing with sound and he quickly tiptoed toward the hall door and listened. No sound. He would have to sit down and wait with patience. He'd better read the *Post*, not keep thinking of what had gone on in jail. Some of it sounded cuckoo.

He was waiting patiently when Victoria came home. She had the sandwiches and they sat on the floor near the windows so that the reflected light from the big apartment across the way could shine on what they were doing. "How do they taste?" said Victoria.

"Fine," said George Gates. "I'm making some coffee, too," said Vicky. "That's fine," said George. He laughed. The coffee was steaming and it tasted wonderful. "It's like a picnic, isn't it?" said Vicky. "I mean the eating, you know. You're not nervous?"

"Not now," said George. "Say," he said getting up, carrying his sandwich. "Let me show you. What do you think of this?" He went to the closet, pulled out a checked cap. He put it on, cocking it over one ear. "A sport," he explained. Then he took a copy of the *Saturday Evening Post* and pretended to read it. "Pretty good, what?" he said naïvely, smiling. "They'll never know me with this outfit." Vicky laughed so loud, they both suddenly stopped and listened.

"It's only one of the girls coming in," said Vicky. They went on eating their sandwiches.

Hortense Ripley was often envious of his sister Anne Wendel's more agitated life. But when he saw her brother David she always deplored the upside down existence that Anne's girls lived. When Rosamond died, she shook her head as if it were only to be expected. The girl's death melted Hortense for the time being and she wrote more often to her sister. They exchanged Christmas presents for the first time in years and, when Anne sent silk stockings, Hortense wrote a long homesick letter about the old days in Grapeville when they had never seen a silk stocking. They were so nice on the feet but not for them as children. Nowadays everyone had them even if they didn't pay the grocer.

Milton Ripley was sinking and his end was taken for granted in the little family. Things went on as before only in a softer key. When he actually died, it took them months to raise their voices to normal. Milton had had his heart's desire before he died, he saw his daughter married. And Eloise had her heart's desire, she was married and had a white dress and her father was alive to see the wedding. She did not leave her father's house after the wedding and, as Sue wrote her cousins, there was certainly no honeymoon nor anything approaching it. But in her solid quiet way, she was happier in staying to see her father decently dead than she would have been gadding off.

Death or no death, the business went on and with retail prices suddenly taking a sharp decline it meant a terrible loss to little grocery people like the Ripleys. Their stock had all been laid in at the old prices and it meant something like a three-thousand-dollar loss. There was no backing out of it, it was an old man of the sea. All their lifetime they had gone into debt only to shovel themselves out again and the process kept repeating itself.

It was getting on Hortense Ripley's nerves but she wouldn't admit it only wrote an angry letter to Anne saying that if Sally persisted in saying her age was 47, when everybody knew it was 55, it was a crime. She was only doing it to make trouble and they should beat her at her own game and expose her to everyone. She deplored all the trouble and worry Anne Wendel would have with the Grapeville property and its final settlement but she didn't discourage her and in fact no one could have made Anne Wendel swerve from that path now.

She had nothing to hold her in Oxtail. She dreaded the day by day life in that town. Jerry was packing up his things, getting ready to leave. He was talking about going east. If she was back in Grapeville, who knows, he might come to see her. She clung to him and told herself he was all of her lost daughter that she had. She tried very hard to be independent and the property in Grapeville was a steadying positive thing. After all, Vicky still needed help. When she got her money out, they could do things together. They might spend a summer by the seashore, something must be made out of their lives.

Hortense often spent Sunday afternoons writing to her sister after her husband died. The modest rooms back of the store always seemed a little mean if by chance her rich brother condescended to drive up in his Cadillac and get out for a little talk. She resented his presence and when he didn't come she resented it. Who in her life had she had for a friend? Why had she lived? Her children, of course; but they could not keep her peaceful or content. When Milton was finally in his grave, Eloise went to her husband but the mother had doubts of the outcome. Her only son was beginning to get bald with no signs of wanting marriage. She made fun of him and held on to him firmly. When they went out walking people looked at them as if they were a married couple. Her handsome figure and face looked years younger than her age, and as for Milton, Junior, he had the heavy set of a much older man.

In the evenings, she rummaged in her yard, planting every square inch. "I don't know where to stop," she told Anne, "I'm like the woman back in Grapeville who made her own house, built a chimney and planted a garden, all with her own hands, and then began making artificial waxed leaves under glass." The yard boiled with fuchsia and heliotrope. The house was buried in trumpet vine.

"Oh, Anne," she wrote, "I truly think that this life is just a preparation class—in the better world Milton will get what he so longed for here. I must go to bed and sleep now. That creek has been rising and rising until a half hour ago when it began to go down. Now I can feel safe."

When David Trexler became a grandfather nothing could contain him. He phoned the news to Hortense at three in the morning, sent telegrams all over the country, then sat down to write the details to his sister Anne. He had to get in a dig at Millie back in Arden. "If you should happen to correspond with the madame in Arden," he wrote, "don't mention Dave's baby daughter, it would only embarrass her." This sentence penned viciously made Anne Wendel shake her head. She was astonished that bitter feeling could last so long between relatives. As for Millie, Vicky saw her now and then on weekends when loaded down with presents of fresh strawberries or out of season asparagus she took a train to the New Jersey resort where Millie and her husband had gone from Arden.

No one even told David of the change in Millie's location. He continued to speak of her contemptuously as the madame from Arden. As for David, Junior, he got no real joy from his little daughter after seeing his wife's face, pinched and bitter, looking out at him from the hospital bed. "I hope you're satisfied," she said, but in a few days she was reconciled to the child, would hardly let the nurses take it from her and picked its name, Cynthia, from her side of the house. Trexler Senior was hoping they would name the baby Mary after his mother, but Charlotte said there wasn't a chance. It was enough that her husband's father took practically all the credit for the child, carrying it around in its long dress with its little wobbly head, insisting to everyone, "Look at her, a regular old Trexler."

WHITE HEADED BOY

During the year that Jonathan Chance went to the university at Ann Arbor he felt that great changes were going on in himself while at home his folks were standing still. Every month his father sent him a niggardly check with a long precise letter telling him the news. Uncle Jake had run a nail in his foot while superintending some reconstruction work in the old barn. Aunt Hettie had a cold and the church was giving a bazaar. The Rhingolds had gone to Florida; too bad he couldn't take a vacation but with such a big family it looked as if he were saddled for life. Seemed to him expenses were higher than they should be at the university; when he was Jonathan's age he thought he was lucky if he had money for church. He was borrowing the enclosed from the bank and expected a careful accounting of same with love from all, your father.

The communication always depressed Jonathan for an entire day and he wished he did not know that from one store building alone his father was raking in five hundred a month rent. He wondered what it was all about as long as it gave so little pleasure and, since he got very little out of his classes, turned over in his mind different plans of escape. He could earn money all right, he knew that. Go out on the road and sell. He was the type they wanted, tall, well dressed, Anglo-Saxon. The boys in his fraternity said he would make an ideal bond salesman. Everybody was talking bonds and prosperity, even when the gloom of 1921 slump was still upon them.

Only old Mr. Snyder, an alumnus from '83, sighed at the tragic fate of Wilson. He thought the Hardings poor makeshifts and groaned at the collapse of Wilson's plans for a League of Nations. "What this country needs is far sighted unselfish men like Wilson," he said in an orating tone of voice while the boys listened politely because of his donations to the house. "We need men with

233

vision but when we get them what do we do? We crucify them." As
he said this he ground the fist of his right hand softly into the palm
of his left. But a few minutes later he was spurring them on with
their singing. They were lucky if they escaped without having to
repeat his old standby back in '83 about General Grant and a
cannon ball that come a-flyin' through the air. The boys were
ashamed of this bucolic nonsense but Mr. Snyder revived with its
singing. He lost his martyred look and plunged into a discussion of
politics. Jonathan was practically the only one in the house who
cared to listen to him. The old fellow was troubled about Harding's
high tariff promise. He couldn't get his mind off it. "It'll sink the
ship, you see," he nodded prophetically. It pleased him to see
Jonathan pay attention to his remarks. He had never been chosen
as a Minute Man during the war and he resented it. In the bosom
of his old fraternity, he had the audience denied him. Jonathan got
his first touch of curiosity about politics from this man and he
found out how few up-to-date books on the subject the university
had. Nobody could tell him much about what was going on in
Russia. They were tickled though at Germany and said that it was
a triumph to see those people realize that a democracy such as the
United States had was the only proper system. The Russians would
come to their senses too someday. They would have to, it was the
only way to develop a country and everyone knew that Russia had
the resources.

All the talk seemed going in circles, and the resentment
Jonathan felt at being forced to stick around Ann Arbor when he
might be east, kept him always lagging in everything he did. He
put off going home as much as possible and when he showed up was
continually disappointed that his mother never showed any swift
demonstrative affection. Once he went to the home of one of the
boys at the house and his mother had been so tender to her son that
the tears had come to Jonathan's eyes. He grieved that he did not
have something of that kind in his life. Girls made a big fuss over
him but he was on the lookout. They wanted to get married and he
didn't want any of that yet. He wasn't going to be tied up until he
was ready. His mother was always warning him against girls.
"Now Jonathan, you be careful, don't get them all worked up, it's

not nice. It hurts girls and is very wrong. I don't like all this petting that goes on. You have no business to get ideas about girls until you are able to earn your living. Your father never got married until he was thirty and that's the proper age for a man who wants to make something of himself."

If it hadn't been for Vidisichis' and the Krause family, he would have taken to drink more than he did. But he was tight pretty often and gradually his father began to get in little digs at him. He had a good answer. "Why father, Charles Graham drinks more than I and look at his father, he practically owns the Rhingold plant. And Charles is going to be a big shot there himself some day." But all that year his father kept insisting on accountings for his allowance and, when he was home, made life a misery with petty jobs about the house.

Sometimes Mrs. Chance in her room upstairs felt sorry for her boy. But she had only to go into his room and see the big pictures of girls on his dresser to harden and feel that her husband was quite right to insist on discipline. There was no turning Mr. Chance. Under his quiet manner he could be a regular mule. Look what a to-do he made about every bit of antique china she bought. And the pewter. It practically took the joy out of it to have him pick it up, look it over, lay it down with his everlasting, "Hum, almost as good as new. Now if I were investing, I'd buy something that wasn't secondhand." As the boys got older and her one daughter drew near to the marrying stage, the mother felt curiously alone. She went often to her room to sit quietly rocking, wondering why her heart was so heavy. When she saw the little photograph of her small daughter dead for many years, tears came to her eyes at the lovely childish face. She would nod at the little one, her throat choked up. But for the most part there was always shopping to be done and she had the big linen closet to keep filled and in shape, the maid to supervise and all the new kitchen equipment that had to be struggled for because, for some contrary reason, Mr. Chance always acted as if his own mother's ways were good enough for anyone. Once the new stove or new kitchen cabinet was in, he got all the pleasure out of it anyone could expect, but before it was installed, you would think he had no intentions of ever buying anything.

He kept his whole household pared down to modest ways of living and if they had not known his income, they would have thought themselves lucky. As it was, Jonathan fumed that he was not sent to an eastern college and that his request for a typewriter met with suspicion. He actually had to make out that he wanted it to write orders on when he went on the road next summer.

One night when he had left Ann Arbor in disgust he walked into Vidisichis' pretty late. It was raining and inside the fire and the smell of wine and garlic made him feel as if he had stepped into another country.

Earl and Guy were sitting at a table toward the back with a stranger. Mrs. V had to slap Jonathan on the back and V himself stuck his head between the curtains and said in a minute he would have something fine fixed for them all.

"All dressed up, aren't you?" said Jonathan, kidding Earl who looked self-conscious in a new suit and semi-stiff shirt collar.

"Earl's on the up and up," said Guy. "Haven't you heard? He's on a trade magazine now. He used to make tools, now he writes about them. Pretty good, hah."

Earl said the pay was no better but it was a lot easier. The strange guy grinned and said, "You're trying to work up, I'm trying to work down. At least that's the obvious way to put it. Maybe it's the other way about, all depends."

When they began to eat, Jonathan went to the front for a package of cigarettes and to give Guy a chance to come along for a little private conversation. "Who's the new fellow?" said Jonathan out of the corner of his mouth.

"Awfully nice guy," said Guy. "Kind of a nut. Talking against what he calls intellectuals. Says we all talk too much. He's seen a strike—see—thinks he knows all about everything now. Out in Iowa. An Iowa man. Used to live here he says. Seems awfully nice, reads good stuff. Nice guy."

"Seems like a swell guy," said Jonathan, feeling free and happy. He went back to the table. "I hear you've been in a strike," he said.

"Well, just on the edge, I didn't have guts to get in soon

enough," said Jerry Stauffer. "But it pushed me out of Oxtail, that's something. I lost my job, see, and thought I'd come back here. I came back to the snake that bit me."

"What do you mean by that?" said Earl.

"Oh nothing," said Jerry, embarrassed, "I just mean I got it in the neck in this town when my wife and I were here before, couldn't make good, see, no job and had to go back to Oxtail. I thought I'd come back and try again, meet my enemy right on the home grounds if you see what I mean."

"Sure," said Guy not seeing in the least. "That's the stuff. You in the war?"

"Yes—if you call out of fire in the war. But I was in France."

"I sure envy you," said Guy.

"You're a fool to do that," said Jerry sharply, then catching himself added, "Excuse me, but I feel kinda strong about it."

"Sure," said Guy, "I know what you mean, and with me it's only that I feel that I'd like to be in France. The little cafés, the leisure to enjoy life."

"There aren't many do that even there," said Jerry, "but at that I guess they get more out of it than we do here."

"They haven't prohibition, that's one thing," said Earl. "It takes a snide country to put that over on you."

"Nothing's the matter with the country," said Jerry. "In fact I'd rather live here than anywhere. It's got wonderful scenery, plenty to eat, excitement by the carload."

"Don't call that civilization, do you," said Guy. "What I mean, say Earl, get out Tolman's letter. We've got a friend over there—see—he writes it's wonderful. He's wandering all around Germany on next to nothing. Took a train to Dresden from Berlin, cost him a dime. Went to the Rhine from Berlin. A quarter. Lives in the best hotels, buys Rhine wine at each meal. One dollar. What a lucky break. Jonathan, why don't you get your old man to stake you? Believe me, if I could get across, I'd cross."

"My father's only interested in getting me in business," said Jonathan. "Punching the old time clock." He reached out his hand for Tolman's letter and read it enviously. What a chance. Jerry looked on, feeling a little out of place. He supposed it was because they were all college boys. They were probably as old or older than himself but they seemed like kids. He wondered if any of them had German blood like himself. The way they talked, Germany was just a big ball park. He might think the same if his mother's folks were not all the time writing about the schrecklichkeit and how every day the Egg was leaping to the sky in price, something way beyond them. Earl wasn't a college fellow but he couldn't make him out. An awfully bright fellow but he was on the wrong tack. That single tax bug didn't get you any place. Earl told him not to try to buck the game at Ford's. Said he'd get his fingers taken off, wouldn't be able to stand the speed. He wanted to take a shot at it the way some fellows did at college. There was a lot for him to learn. In fact, pretty nearly everything. He wondered what kind of a guy Jonathan was. He looked smart. He was certainly tucking away the liquor.

Another party came in and occupied a table near by. With ladies present everyone got noisier and wittier. Jonathan turned on the victrola and did a solo dance, contorting himself until Guy yelled out and called him a human pretzel. The girls at the next table begged for more. He repeated, his face very white and his dark eyes blazing. Everyone stopped drinking to watch him. Papa V dashed around in a greasy apron and Mamma V smiled from one table to another. "I just love to see people enjoy themselves," she said. "Just love it."

She put her hand on Jonathan's coat lapel and he smiled like a little boy. "It's nice to be here, better than home," said Jonathan. Earl was beginning a long Rabelaisian account of what went on at Ford's. He was describing operations as if it were all part of a huge alimentary system. Jerry listened fascinated. He was flushed and looked happy. Why was it he and Rosamond had never known about this place? If it hadn't been for that engineer at the packing-house he wouldn't have known of it now.

Much later in a daze with ears ringing he found his way to the basement can. Jonathan was sitting on the bottom step, his head on his hands. "What's the matter?" said Jerry.

"Look at me," said Jonathan, "I hate to go into business, I hate Benton. Here I am dead drunk, look at me, I was the white headed boy and now look at me," he shook his head, very tight, his face white, taking a pleasure in his downfall. If he could feel he were in the gutter, utterly fallen, it would serve his father right. To hell with that kind of ambition.

Jerry was impressed. "My father's got money, I've got education, and here I am, good for nothing." He cried. Jerry took hold of his arm. "Come on now, it can't be so bad." He felt suddenly very strong and cheerful. Why, this fellow had everything he had thought necessary to life, and it was practically useless. "Come on, now," said Jerry. He had the feeling they were going to be good friends. Jonathan got up and went into the toilet. When he came out, he was almost sober. An evil light was in his dark eyes, he looked around wildly.

"I'm all right now," he said in a perfectly sober voice.

"Sure," said Jerry. They went back up the stairs together. The girls beckoned to Jonathan but he waved them away. "Can't dance now," he said, "busy," and turning to Jerry he said, "Say, did you ever read Schopenhauer?"

"Ask him, did he ever read Henry George," said Earl.

"What about Anatole France?" said Guy.

"Nuts," said Jonathan. "Did you?"

"Yes," said Jerry. "He said some good things."

"Very good," said Jonathan. "About women."

"Oh, I don't know. You have to remember his mother was a bitch."

"Where did you get that?" said Jonathan.

"Why, it's history. She was always screwing around. She was a bitch."

"That's women for you," said Jonathan.

"What you got against them," said Jerry, "you sound soured."

"No," said Jonathan. "Why doesn't my mother make my father loosen up? All they want out of me is to make a respectable organ grinder of me." Everybody laughed. Mrs. V came over and rubbed Jerry's head. Mr. V said he loved to see people enjoy themselves. Jonathan drank more than any other two people and yet when he got up his long legs were pretty steady. When they all filed out, he and Jerry had arranged to meet again.

"Haven't heard about that strike yet," said Jonathan.

"Oh, the strike," said Jerry, laughing a little. The next minute he was ashamed. He had forgotten the strike.

"I don't feel like going to bed," said Jonathan. "How about you?"

"Me either," said Jerry. They walked along the cold deserted streets.

"And I don't want any more to drink either," said Jonathan. "Let's get a cup of coffee."

They turned in at an all night coffeepot and slumped down on high stools. A couple of taxi drivers were arguing and the boy in the dirty white apron was leaning against the counter, half asleep, listening. He stirred himself when he saw the two customers. Jerry and Jonathan gulped their coffee, their heads half turned listening to the drivers. They were wrangling about some prize fight.

"What kind of a strike was it?" said Jonathan.

"Packing house," said Jerry. "But they were sold out. I guess the cards were pretty well stacked against them and they got folks out there so scared of reds that the first sign of a strike the whole town is on its ear. Funny thing though, I learned a lot. I was just a clerk but before I came to my senses I was working every day, strike or no strike. One of the above-the-battle boys. But you have to be one thing or the other in a strike. We were getting out shipments every day and helping out the packers. They finally got the militia out, and the chamber of commerce was in cahoots with the packers and put the screws on the mayor who had let the convention of I.W.W. meet there a year or so back. Tried to make him feel he was to blame. I don't understand all the workings of it yet but I know whose side I'm on, from now on."

Jonathan said he'd seen his father's workmen go out on strike but there wasn't any doubt as to whose side he'd been on. "I was out with the men, down in Krauses' basement all the time," he boasted. "They won too."

The drivers on stools nearby gradually shut up and began listening. Jerry and Jonathan felt very good about having an audience and raised their voices a little. The drivers leaned nearer. One of them piped up and said if they wanted to see a strike they should have been in the 1919 steel strike. That was a strike. His brother-in-law had been killed in that strike and, goddamit, he was supporting his sister ever since. "She's got six kids, too."

"Is Rockyfeller supporting six kids?" said the other driver. "Is he sitting up all night looking around for a fare? Oh no."

"Shut up," said the first driver. "Rockefeller didn't have nothing to do with this strike."

"Gary," said Jonathan. "Isn't he the steel king?"

"I don't know who the king is but all I got to say is that my brother-in-law got shot in the back and she's got six kids. No insurance either. The strikers did their best, buried him swell, took up a purse, but it's a life job if you get what I mean." "Jesus, yes," said the waiter. He was leaning over with his sad young face. "It's hell."

"You said it," said the driver.

"Jesus, yes," said the coffeepot man unable to get beyond that phrase. Jonathan and Jerry finished their coffee, passed around cigarettes to the crowd. "What about some more coffee on me," said Jonathan. "And pie," he added as he caught a look on a driver's face.

They all ate their pie without speaking. Jonathan was ready to buy cigarettes for the bunch but he found his pockets practically empty. It made him sore suddenly. He had visions of his family at home all snoring away under the finest sheets. Dammit. He said to Jerry, "Let's get going." Outside they walked along briskly. "My folks have the dough," said Jonathan, "and I got the feeling I could have a million on my own if I want. But what for? I wish I could knock around the world for a while. Give a fellow a chance to think."

"I have to get a job pretty damned quick," said Jerry. "No time to think." He kept thinking of Earl's advice to come around to the trade paper. He wished he could talk to someone like the fellow at strike headquarters in Oxtail. There was a fellow with a clear cut path. Since he got away, his own path had not seemed so clear cut. He would not be able to stand the speed-up, Earl said. He'd lose some fingers. He'd get licked. He hardly listened to Jonathan until he caught the words, "And what I'm going to do is just light out, go to New York. I'm sick of these halfassed towns."

"Oh," said Jerry. "If you do, wish you'd look up someone for me. My wife's sister."

"Sure," said Jonathan. "Is she good-looking."

"Kind of," said Jerry. "She's a swell girl. I wish you'd meet her."

"I will," said Jonathan. "Just write her name down here." He got out a book. It was thick and full of names.

"Jesus, you must have your hands full keeping track of all those dames," said Jerry. Jonathan laughed and slapped the book.

"Love 'em and leave 'em," he said, but after he said it, walking away, he wondered why fellows always talked like that, he didn't love 'em and leave 'em. The trouble was no girl had got under his skin so far. He was beginning to want one to come along and break his heart. The world was empty and cold. He wanted to suffer.

V. DWELLERS IN THE SWAMP

JUST when things seemed most stagnating in Oxtail, Billy Sunday arrived for a big revival and Uncle David Trexler came back east. David Trexler came east on a business trip and the need for the trip arose only after news that Millie's husband was dead had reached the coast.

Victoria was the only near relative to Millie in the east and she wrote her a brief little note describing her husband's end. The strange romance of the big luscious woman and the tiny thin man with a limp and great blazing brown eyes was over. They had spent an idyllic year doing absolutely nothing in a Jersey coast resort and then, spurred on by dwindling finances, had gone to Philadelphia to buy a little clothing business and general store. The enterprise had put too great a strain on Mr. Shane's already weak heart.

"He got up, same as usual," wrote Millie simply, "and shaved as he always did. There was never a day when he didn't shave. He went into the bathroom and shaved and I lay in bed. Then he came back and sat down on the edge and said to me, I feel kind of tired, guess I'll rest a minute. He lay down and that was the last. His last words were to me, guess I'll rest a minute. He was always my lover,

Vicky, and we had the best time, one day I just left my washing and we rode around picking flowers. He had a weak heart but as he said we couldn't vacation forever."

When David Trexler heard the news, he turned red and said brusquely, "Well, poor woman, she's paid for her folly." He was very quiet for days and announced abruptly that he meant to go east to attend to business. No one stopped him. His wife had a sudden chilled feeling. Much as she loved her sister, she had enjoyed the peace of being the one woman in the house. Without saying a word, she knew Millie would come back again. To make it easy for David, she said timidly, "Life's short enough, better bring Millie back, she's no one else." But David had not answered her except to say, "Don't know as I'll be able to get in touch with her, I'm going to be pretty busy."

All the same when he came from the east stopping in Oxtail, Millie was in tow, a big thoughtful woman with dreamy eyes, who sat in the room with the air of being somewhere else. No one spoke of Mr. Shane when David Trexler was present and when he was not present, Millie did not feel inclined to discuss her husband. She said that Victoria could tell them what a wonderful time they had had in Jersey, that was all.

Billy Sunday was kicking up a rumpus in Oxtail and he had brought along his Don Juan male singer whose love troubles in the papers had so entertained the Oxtail ladies. They fluttered to meetings and the big grown women took delight in the reunions of the Sunshine chorus of former days. While the meeting was assembling, Mayor Handy came in to shake hands with the leaders and the women near Nancy began hissing and cackling that he certainly had his nerve.

"Why?" said Nancy, disturbed and on the defensive. After all Handy had defended the I.W.W.'s and she remembered only too well poor little Rosamond's stand on that questions.

"Don't you know? Why, he is an I.W.W., and look at the stand he took on saloons. Wants prohibition repealed."

When the mayor in the midst of the talk asked for a wave of human kindness to sweep over Oxtail, the bristling backs of the women stiffened virtuously. Nancy felt cut off from the others, wondered why it was that so much rancor filled a town like Oxtail. But when the music began, tears filled her eyes. A warm wave of feeling swept audience.

> "Shall we gather at the river,
> The beautiful, the beautiful river,
> Gather with the saints at the river
> That flows by the throne of god,"

with their heads up, voices pouring forth, their faces changed and softened, their warm feelings drained off in useless song. Nancy felt mellow and loving, swept along by the great waves of song. The only trouble was, the feeling disappeared so soon. It did not really last until she got home. Once there, she had to admit she felt sad and more let down than ever. Her feet hurt. She wondered if she would have had such moods if her sister had lived.

But Uncle David put pep in them all. He was in a capital mood, red-faced and blustering. When his eyes met Millie's he looked sheepish and turned away with a joke. Millie looked at him calmly, often as if he were made of glass. The two sons-in-law were anxious to get advice from their prosperous uncle. Donald tackled his wife's uncle after a good solid dinner at their house. The older man had his coat off and was standing on the porch, thumbs in his vest. Donald broached the subject of opportunities in the far west.

"If you know of any good money-making business on the coast, wish you'd give me a tip, this town's pretty stale," he said, handling one of his cigars in an expert way and lighting one for his uncle with pleasure.

"Well," said Trexler slowly, "the only way I ever found to make money was to save a little out of every dollar I made. The only way to accumulate money for the late years of your life, is to save while you are young." He said it solemnly, looking sharply at Donald and figuring that there was a shaft that hit home. A young man with such a big family smoking cigars of that quality was likely as not near the rocks. "Save," repeated Trexler firmly, "that's the ticket."

To Nancy's husband he had something of the same advice. "Do good work, it is bound to be recognized, you'll be promoted." He was very cheerful and urged both men to begin buying little homes.

"This country is founded on home building," he said. "It's the rock on which we stand. Without homes we'd be a wasted migratory lot, without roots. Save, that's number one, number two is buy a home." He was very well satisfied with this advice and Anne Wendel was so comforted to see an old home face after losing her daughter that she too lapped up his words and spun around him with little attentions as if he were the center of the universe.

Only Amos Wendel sat with a cynical expression on his tired old face with the drooping moustaches. He had heard that story all his life, had lived by it, and he was still working at Bryant's for a little wage, had lost his business, and had all he could do to keep the interest paid on the home that was his wife's heart's desire. He had seen his young daughter die. His sons-in-law never seemed to get ahead, yet none of them were wasters. He was frankly jealous of David and kind of sore at his wife for always laying it on so thick about his success. He bet a nickel that something crooked had gone on sometime or other. Never knew a rich man yet who could show a clean slate. Thinking such thoughts pleased him, and he was the only one who did not think Uncle David wonderfully thoughtful when he departed leaving a twenty-dollar bill.

"If I was president of a bank, I wouldn't be a piker," he thought bitterly, but said nothing to Anne who kept repeating how much good an old home face had done her.

After he left, it was the natural thing for Nancy and her husband to find themselves one day the owners of a lot. Yes, they would pay for the lot bit by bit and then someday they would build. To tell the truth they had bought the lot without realizing how it came about. A new addition was being auctioned off and they went with the crowd hearing that dollar bills were to be handed out to bidders. Every fifth bidder got five dollars. Clifford, his eyes bunging out, piped up in time for a five-dollar bill, had just clutched it in his hands when the gavel came down. The agents, check books in hand, surrounded him. He turned red, fumbled, hoped he wouldn't get fired from his job if he should back out. But Nancy stood by him.

"It's a good lot," she said. "Let's go through with it." But neither of them got much sleep that night. They owned a lot. Of course it was to cost $1370, a terrible price, but still not so high considering the select neighborhood.

Nancy quoted Uncle David to her husband and the young couple finally decided they had done something pretty bright after all. They went to a Billy Sunday meeting to celebrate and, as times were none too good, it was surprising how many came from towns around for a little free entertainment. When Sunday left town taking $13,500 with him, Clifford remarked that revivals were a pretty good paying proposition, but then Sunday had figured the converts at around 15,000 head, most of whom never showed themselves in church again.

BITTER SISTERS

At about the time that Jonathan Chance came to New York and began to know Victoria Wendel, Anne Wendel began making plans for her Grapeville campaign. She pushed along with her idea to make money out of the homestead as she had always pushed her whole life with her projects. The White Elephant was still unsold and it clamored for paint and a new roof. She kept telling herself it would make a fine duplex house. It would make a nice little paying property. She could rent half of it and she and Amos could live in the other half on the rent. She would make money on the Grapeville property to pay for the repairs and she did not forget to add that when she got her money out she would certainly help Victoria.

Her first job would be to expose Sally and show her true age as 55 not 47. Then if Sally wouldn't sell her share for a decent figure, they would put the property up at auction, she would buy it in herself, pay Sally her share, and resell it after cutting it up into lots. This plan give her a new lease on life and she lay awake many a night, cutting up the land and naming the streets. She had decided to name the main street in the addition for Rosamond. If she could see her daughter's name on a little sign on the street and feel that it would go on being called that name, even after she was dead, it would give her comfort.

On her way to Grapeville she stopped off to see Victoria and was a little shy staying in the shabby basement apartment. She felt like a little girl visiting grownups and sat timidly back during the evening when callers came. But no one enjoyed the talk more or looked more sharply at visitors' faces to try to see which were important to her girl. The memory of some of the notes Vicky had written Rosamond made her uneasy, but alive in all her bones. She could see that Vicky knew what to drive for in life, it wasn't surface things, and she hoped that she would come to her senses and have children before it was too late. She couldn't imagine a woman's life without children. She had by this time even persuaded herself that Rosamond had died making plans to have her baby.

There were only two girls in the apartment now, Victoria and Esther, and during the days she was there, Anne Wendel made nice little home breakfasts for them and deplored the tiny slovenly kitchen. She couldn't see how you could call it living to be cooped up in these dingy holes. The garbage lying around on the streets near her daughter's place led to the one quarrel between the two.

"There's no sense in being so dirty," said Mrs. Wendel severely.

"People are too poor to be different, don't you understand, too tired, too poor. There's no space. All the garbage gets picked up uptown, not down here. They don't care if people live like pigs down here."

"That's no excuse," said Anne Wendel firmly. "If I had to live in a tin can, I'd keep it clean. I'd be clean if it was the last thing I'd do."

"You don't know what you'd do, you always lived in a whole house, you'd don't know anything about it," said Vicky crossly. She actually felt like snapping at her mother who looked scared and little at the harsh words. But she couldn't bring herself to take back what she said, only when the two of them went for a long bus ride uptown she put her arm around her mother as they sat on top looking at the scenery. Anne Wendel beamed happily. "I was cold," she confessed, "in this evening air. But I'm not now, not when you put your arm around me." Vicky squeezed her and could say nothing. What was the sense of all the deprivation in the world? Anne Wendel longed to live with her daughter but she did not even dare propose it, instead, got on her train to Grapeville pretending that there was nothing she wanted so much as to get out of the beastly city, New York. "I'll be glad for a breath of real air again," she said fiercely so as to keep from crying. "I don't see how you stand it here. Well, as soon as I get my money out, we'll go some place together, won't we?" she said, yearning, her eyes eating up her daughter's face.

"Yes, we will Mother," said Vicky. "You have a good time down there." But she knew it wouldn't be a good time. She walked away from the train with a heavy heart.

George Gates had left the apartment and, so far as the girls knew, had safely made his exit from the country. A kind of conspiratorial excitement hung around the place and particularly after it came out in the papers that more I.W.W.'s, including Bill Haywood, had skipped out. No one in Victoria's circle doubted their right to jump bail with red raids still going on and with feeling high against them. They wouldn't stand a chance of a fair trial, and being hung up for twenty years couldn't help. There were fellows in Walla Walla and Kansas and California, rotting in jail, helpless. Enough was enough. If they had been bankers, they might hope to win, but no, they were only people who wanted to change the world.

Anne Wendel never looked more like her brother David Trexler than on that day when she bid in the Grapeville property against her sister-in-law Sally's bidder. The two women fought it out, in the open, on the property that had been the Trexler homestead for years, where Anne as a girl had let the white pigs into the clover and fed the cardinal and mockingbird in their great cage. From that house poor Joe had burst to run away from the sheriff, never to return until he was mad and done for. She stood very upright, supporting her bad leg on a stick, a short wiry little woman with greying red hair sprouting under a smashed black hat, her chin the regular Trexler chin and the blue eye fixed now as intent as death on the auctioneer. The crowd stood expectantly. Mrs. Aaron Trexler did not appear. Her son stood by the official bidder, his sullen mouth resentful as Mrs. Wendel's $7225 won.

"Good for you," said Roundtree, wiping his hat band. "You'll make something. Expect to resell, of course."

"Of course," said Anne, trembling a little now it was all over, tiny beads of sweat on her creamy skin. Already she was at work in her mind's eye, clearing away brush, getting a survey, naming streets. "Don't let them frighten you, you'll get your money out," said Roundtree.

"I expect to do more than that," said Anne Wendel facing him squarely, feeling for the first time an equal, a property owner, one who could buy and sell, could even name streets.

Her sister Hortense was a little dubious. She would have been content to let Sally gobble it up and get out a sure few thousand dollars without the bother of reselling. Why, trouble was nothing to Anne Trexler. If she could improve a thing when had trouble ever been a consideration? How many times she had scrubbed old paint, peeled off old wall paper, ripped up old clothes and dyed and resewed them for the pleasure of making something a little better than it was.

If Hortense couldn't see the results she could. She could resell at two thousand profit, to say the least. Amos could stop that drudgery and have a few easy years before he died.

Not that he seemed to want them. He had complained when Bryant Bros. told him not to come to work so early during the winter. It only took fuel to start the stove so soon and business didn't justify it. Actually Amos had grumbled and fumed that things were deadly slow. He hadn't a lazy bone in his body but all the same he caught colds too easily, got limp as a dish rag in the terrible summer heat, needed a well-earned rest. Not to speak of Victoria, who had lately lost her job and needed a boost if anyone did.

No wonder that when she got a letter from Victoria, all about a young man she had met, Jonathan Chance, and a picture somebody had snapped of him one day when they went on a trip to the country, she stopped everything, sat down in the field where old Pony used to go to grass, and looked at the picture of the boy a long time. The man she had hired and took such pleasure in bossing went on cutting down weeds. Several piles of brush were already in flames. She forgot the whole business for a little. Sometimes there really seemed a kind of unseen destiny that linked life together in a way too mysterious to divine.

Why, that boy looked for all the world like John Gason. It was in that very house across the meadow that as a girl she had waited for seven long years for John Gason to return. It almost seemed as if he were coming back, to her own daughter. She loved to think such thoughts, felt suddenly happy for the first time in years. If only the girl kept her head and didn't do something wilful and foolish. He was a fine boy, she knew it from the minute she set eyes on him. He and Jerry were fine boys.

Her hands trembled a little, she tucked away the letter, got up with a groan, her bad leg tugging and aching her. She would clear the land, cut it up, sell it. It was a pleasure to hold and to walk over and to belong to but she couldn't expect that. She needed the money too badly. Victoria ought to have some pretty clothes, she was too indifferent about such things. Oh, but she would name a street for her poor girl, for Rosamond, who seemed sometimes to be a little child again following around beside her, tugging at her hand. Look at me, here I am. It was terrible to have only a street to name for her child.

She stumbled as she walked away very fast, almost forgetting her cane. Even in her uneasy joy for what she stubbornly envisioned as Vicky's future, bitterness at the inequality of life filled her eyes with tears. She plucked clover heads roughly, stuffed some into her trembling mouth. As children they used to suck out the honey, looking up at this same sky. Larks had wheeled overhead and they had wheeled there too on that long ago day when she had run out of the house terrified to fling herself down in the tall grass and clover, raising her head now and then to look back, at the blank windows of Catherine's room, where her young sister lay alien and dead.

In the evenings she would often leave the modest boarding

house, where she was friends with the landlady and where she took
an interest in the daughter's little problems, for a stroll past the
hotel. She would stop in at the post office and take pleasure in the
respect people showed her. Somehow it consoled her for the
obscure years she had spent here as a girl when they had all lived
under a cloud, so to speak, on account of poor Joe. Not that he had
been guilty, quite the contrary, it was a sin and a shame to think of
guilt in connection with him. Perhaps he had been indiscreet; yes,
even after all these years that was all the guilt she would attach to
him, shutting her mind stubbornly from staining in any way the
memory of Joe, the most generous brother.

But when she remembered how quiet a life they had had,
grubbing away like moles on that place, it was a consolation to see
herself now, walking along, and to know that from behind the
porch vines where families sat taking the cool of the evening only
the most respectful comment was made about her. It was a real joy
in its way, not of course like the joy of seeing her little flock of girls
all dressed in their best sailing down the street together for a
Sunday walk. Or like sitting at the foot of the table to a real good
dinner with the children on either side and Papa at the head
carving their own bird that she had fattened and fed.

It was a different satisfaction and not so sweet, still at her time
of life, she was pleased at herself and when the day came when the
whole plot was laid out in black and white on paper with Rosamond Avenue running down the center as straight as a die, she
could almost see the trees and the houses where people would
actually live and breathe and children would be born and life
would go on, forever.

After George Gates left, there was no more excitement until
Vicky got fired from her job. She was fired for a reason that Mr.
Ravenwood considered good and sufficient. He wanted to oblige a
young friend, a handsome boy from Princeton. The boy's mother
had a nice apartment and was threatened with eviction if she didn't
pay her rent. He had come to Mr. Ravenwood and put up a long

sad tale. Mr. Ravenwood had promised a better job to Victoria when she came into the publishing firm. She would be promoted to an editorship if she was willing to read detective stories for a few months. It would give her experience. It seemed to Vicky that she would always be taking cheap jobs to get experience and, as soon as she got it, she would be fired or would quit and then it would begin all over again. Considering how many times she had found new jobs for herself there was no reason to be worked up at the loss of this one.

She made up her mind to rest for a few days, mend her clothes, and try to think of a plan for the future. Everyone she knew was making some kind of a new plan. Those who could were getting abroad as fast as possible. No one seemed to want to hang around in the States anymore if they could help it. Tales of cheap living abroad and of music and art galleries and disturbances threatening every country made sitting at home, where troubles appeared to have been settled with a good strong arm and an incipient dose of prosperity, very tame. Maybe if mother got her money out of the Grapeville property she could go abroad herself.

Such an idea made a job look very sour. Day after day went by and she read the want ads and took in movies and at night went out to dinner with some man or sometimes went alone and tried to feel that she had really been living and had experienced life. She thought she knew a good deal about love by this time and liked to throw out hints about her experience to other young women who had not been so adventurous. It gave her a satisfaction to put herself in the role of the beautiful Mrs. Ferrol who had been betrayed. But away from the girls, her good common sense made her ashamed of her stories, she sometimes laughed to herself in bed thinking of them. Whatever she had experienced of love, it seemed all pain, and romanticizing about it was like sprinkling sugar over bitter berries. For all that happened, she was still in the basement apartment looking each morning at the daylight through the window bars. The grime that settled on the woodwork began to look like plain dirt. She spent a whole afternoon scrubbing the paint, dusting and sweeping and in the evening sat in the midst of the spick and span place with a real pleasure. Maybe she was just an old-fashioned girl, as her mother used to say when she caught her sweeping and dusting as if her life depended on it. "Heavens," Anne Wendel would say, "you've gone to work and raised a dust again. The minute my back's turned, you begin. Sometimes I think you are going to be just like that old Aunty back in Pennsylvania who spent her life cleaning and scrubbing. You're half funny old Pennsylvania Dutch and I don't know what the other half is. It beats me."

Sometimes walking in the afternoon the feel of the air was like that in the cornfields at home. She'd imagine she was lying with some young man who looked like Caseman. "You're lovely," he was saying. "You're a sheaf of wheat, an ear of corn." But often as not she and Esther merely kept very late hours, making tea with a little something in it for young men who poured out the stories of their life. She would see the young man to the door and in the dark hallway he would urge her to go off with him, for a weekend or to a hotel. Sometimes very late, she would find herself in a room she did not know, whispering and laughing, hearing the rumble of trucks as far off and unreal as the remembered Iowa storms. She could forget her troubles for a little and shut out of her mind her unhappy adventures into what she termed real love. She had to tell herself that her experiences had taught her lessons and that her life would grow up out of those experiences as from rich ground. It was not an easy consolation. She was lonely and cried suddenly at night thinking of her sister plunging helpless down the long black hill into the fatal truck. She began to fear to read certain radical magazines with their vivid descriptions of the terrible beatings in Centralia. A kind of thickness came into her very eyeballs, her eyes felt all cried up, she would crumple up inside of her, even in a public library, and choking, feel as if she must leave the room. Her sister's death, all the deaths of the broken and bleeding, of the young who had wanted to live in a fine world, seemed part of herself and she dramatized their suffering and linked it with her own. When she got hold of some man who "knew something" as she termed it, she felt better, all the hopelessness took a cheerful form. He could explain to her that nothing was final, that even the deaths had been far from in vain. If she had any pang it was that

her sister seemed to have died so futilely. It would be a consolation
to die for a cause that would go on, forever.

One Saturday afternoon, when she was furbishing up her ward-
robe and mending, rubbing too hard and tearing the needle
through the stockings with too fierce a hand, one of the girls who
used to live in the apartment came back for a visit. The apartment
was a magnet for all those girls who once lived there; when they
left, they came back as long as Esther and Victoria still had it.
When they finally departed, they still clung to the idea it represented of their first early days in New York when some of the
things that they had expected began to happen a little. When Cora
came in, she opened her pocketbook mechanically, jerked out her
scrubby mirror and powdered her nose. Yes, she had come back.
She had been to Boston, cooped up in a boarding house with
antimacassars and birds under glass. A woman with steel beads
and a rat under a pompadour ran the house and read out loud in
her bible every day, with the door to her room open so the odor of
holiness could percolate through the halls like a bad egg. In New
Bedford she had dug up some wonderful material about the old
trading vessels and the seamen who ran them. But. She stopped
suddenly in her rapid narrative, her voice in its swift confidential
flight turning suddenly very grave. But.

"Was everything all right when you came back?" said Vicky,
looking up quickly at Cora's face that was contemplating not only
the floor but the bathroom of the apartment she had just left.

"Oh, I wasn't going to tell you," she lied. "But it's like this.
After all, I have to tell someone because I can't go back there."

"What's wrong?" said Vicky, thinking of the little dark thought-
less man who traded on his ability to paint and had this really
talented girl running around wiping his brushes, arranging his
shows, meeting his friends until she had walked out one day quietly
about her business but not to leave him, just to earn money so they
could have the good food he liked and she could buy a new mattress
as the old one hurt in the middle of the back. What had he done

now? Cora said, "I've nothing against him. After all, what's done, is done. But I had no idea in letters. None. When I pushed open the door of that apartment I had a funny feeling. Beware of surprising anyone, my dear. It seemed totally strange. The things stood in the same position, the chairs, there was my picture on the wall and my shawl over the bed, but in the bathroom there was some outlandish powder and one of those terribly bright lipsticks. So I just walked out again and here I am now."

"Not to stay?" said Vicky putting down her work and looking straight at her.

"Yes," said Cora. "Why not? I don't like things like that. I'm not made that way. Never liked muddy rivers. No, he is gone, so far as I am concerned, forever." Her mouth did not shake but her fingers quivered a little as she lighted another cigarette.

Vicky looked at her. "I'm not made that way. Why, it might be nothing. Nothing important. You should fight for what you want, not walk out." Cora agreed. Trouble was that she wasn't that way, she admired it, but she wasn't like that, when a thing is finished, it's done. She didn't want it anymore so how could she fight for it.

But, began Vicky. No, she couldn't remind Cora that she had often said fervently and trustfully that this time she really believed, she actually thought it would go on and on, perhaps forever. What was it about that word that was so haunting and desirable. It was the word engraved inside of Anne Wendel's wedding ring that came off her hand so seldom, only sometimes when she had been kneading dough and took it off. The children had picked up the ring, caked with the white dried dough, to read the initials and the date and word *forever* that was so much more amazing than their father and mother could ever be. What ideas had been given to them that secretly they longed for love that would go on and on like a great stream. She couldn't say anything at all, looked sideways at her friend and finally tried to laugh a little.

"Here we sit like two solemn magpies at a funeral, let's do something to cheer ourselves up," and it ended with them going to the little Spanish place where they had flaming punchinos and the young daughter looked like a Spanish dancer as she served the food.

They sat huddled over a little table avoiding reference to the lipstick and the powder and indulging in their childhood pasts. Say what you pleased, there was a time in childhood when a ghost could be real. Cora remembered as clear as day, not that you could explain that kind of thing, when they had taken her as a young child back to the house where her little brother had died before she was born and she had started up the stairs alone, had seen as clear as daylight another child in blue pants and a little collar and a fall of light hair and had stared a long time while he stared back. Then she had come back and told and the hushed grownup awe, the fear; and someone said that was a sign on her, she would be snatched from them but, no, it was only her aunt who had been snatched from them, falling from a spirited horse as she jumped a fence in her wild free fashion. And, of course, who can tell what caused such a memory, in what it rooted, what superstitions, what mirages, but there it was, as firm as the iron hitching post of the little colored boy holding a hoop in his hand.

The two young women had hushed their voices and the ghost from the distant past had succeeded in making even that very afternoon seem a little misty to Cora. Almost at the same time they both launched into a new kind of reminiscence as if to recall life with a bang. Vicky told about Mrs. Bolton who baked fourteen and twenty pies just like nothing during threshing season and had six tall sons who thought her the salt of the earth and Cora said that Mrs. Schultz of Texas could not be beat. An ox of a woman who carried a little calf as if it were a baby, having her being in the midst of cheeses and piles of golden butter and crocks of home made jams.

"And Mrs. Coney," began Victoria, trying to get her word into a conversation that for some reason suddenly seemed exciting and real. From the other side of the room a party that had been getting increasingly noisy now burst into loud tones and a voice in the silence said, "I tell you his life work is to accumulate two things, wealth and respectability. Well, let's have another little drink. Here's to crime and fornication." Turning, the two in the opposite corner of the room saw dark backs of coats, a woman's hat with a bright green band and a tall thin young man facing them. As he looked at them, he stiffened a little, then stared back. One of the young men turned, said, "Oh, hello Vicky, come over here." Both girls carrying their flaming punchinos, now flaming no longer, went across the room a little reluctantly.

The noisy group made way for them, the two newcomers sat down. Victoria sat opposite Jonathan Chance. Cora's pale face brooded under her thick dark hair. The noisy talk clamored and rang, she could no longer focus on that little bright point of her childhood. Someday this moment would be like that point to her. She would be old, with luck surrounded by her grandchildren. In the rush of years, what would a mere lipstick in the bathroom matter then? Her back stiffened but even as she sipped her punchino, now rather tasteless, she thought that at this very hour she had planned to surprise him, to have a good dinner laid out, a bottle of real wine, and herself, like a feast.

Jonathan Chance stopped his speech after the new arrivals joined the party. He got out his little address book and looking through it pointed out to Vicky her own name. They talked about Jerry and after a little he went on being the life of the party. What was this girl thinking about? The discussion the two girls had been having put a spell on Victoria. She almost missed her future.

It was a short quick step from the time when Victoria Wendel and Jonathan Chance met in the flaming punchino place to when they picked up and disappeared from New York. It was only a good while afterwards that they began to be romantic about those days. When they were happening they took them for granted, even the second evening of their acquaintance when at a Saturday night party Vicky had suddenly and surprisingly made a scene. A plump little bantam of a woman had been making shameless advances to Jonathan, dangling herself and her income and trying to tantalize the boy with visions of trips and cars and leisure. Without any intention of falling, Jonathan had listened, flattered and smiling, all the time conscious of Vicky's eyes upon them. When they got up to dance, the little bantam's arms were wound firmly and openly around his waist and Jonathan docilely danced with his head in the air. They had only made a few turns in their corner when Vicky was across the room like a flash, had wrenched the little bantam from Jonathan's embrace and had quietly but firmly placed herself in his arms. They danced very close and even up to the corner where the poor woman was spitting out her venom against that little bitch.

Hearing the words, Vicky smiled straight at Jonathan and they caught their breaths a little. "Aren't you ashamed of yourself?" he said.

"No," said Vicky. "That lollypop. You're not for her. You're much too good."

"Who am I for?" said Jonathan grinning triumphantly.

"For me," said Vicky. "For me and me only."

"You're not the jealous kind, are you?" said Jonathan.

"Maybe," said Vicky, "that's not important." What was important was that from that night they began being together and almost at once decided to get out of New York to go to the country, where they might really begin to live. Without a cent between them, Jonathan sailed into a fine salesman's job for a publishing house. He would be on the road six weeks, net around four hundred dollars. They could live for ages on that.

"It's spring," Vicky said, "we could have a garden, but no, by the time you come back it will be too late. Anyhow it won't cost much in the country. We don't need much. Everybody has too many things, all we really need is a table and a couple of chairs, a stove and a bed."

"A bed is awfully important," said Jonathan. "I think we should have a good bed if we don't have anything else."

There were really only a few weeks in New York before the road trip and Jonathan liked nothing better than to get a little wine and go up to their room where he could read the *Waste Land* or Gertrude Stein or a long poem by a man called Kurt Schwitters that repeated over and over, "Mamma, the man is standing there," until it was like drop of water endlessly falling. When Jonathan came to the last lines, where the spell was broken by elephants bumping together, he was relieved himself, though he would never admit it, and charmed, would read the piece to anyone who would listen. It was almost as if the life his father was holding out to him and he was refusing, had its last gasps in his determination to feel a part of dying things. To hear him read,

> April is the cruellest month, breeding
> Lilacs out of the dead land, mixing
> Memory and desire, stirring
> Dull roots with spring rain

was enough to raise the roots of your hair. A kind of prickling went up and down the spine. His voice and long body, the strong hands holding the little book; Vicky liked nothing better than to lie on the floor on her back, her arms stretched out, her eyes on his face.

When he was gone, when she was really alone, she felt terribly alone and was frightened at the future about which she had no idea only a deep need and conviction. They were going away, they would be together, they would be happy. They would have a house and a garden, he would do what he wanted and not what his father wanted. It was a miracle to her and a horrible example of the way people were warped all out of shape to find out that a father could have it in his power to help his son and not help him. Jonathan actually got a little tired at hearing how different Victoria's parents were, how they shared what they had and how her mother at that moment was planning on helping her as soon as she got her money out of the lots.

"People get different when they begin to get money. You were lucky to have parents who didn't have much," said Jonathan. But he was already wondering what kind of a plan he could make to convince his father he was working when in the country.

"What do you have to think of him for?" said Vicky. "He's not giving you any money. You should put him out of your mind and forget him." It was easier said than done and Vicky was the last person in the world who could do such a thing herself. You were brought up with your parents, it took time to shed them and their influence, didn't it? It was very slow and yet when Jonathan's reports came of the good trip he was making and she could figure on just what they would need, dishes so much, window curtains, a stock of staples for the pantry, then the future seemed really coming true. His letters, all homesick, all wanting to be back, restored everything to her that she thought she had lost when she had loved that man who had not needed her enough to matter. She remembered the agonized notes she used to write Rosamond about him with wonder. Once in Chicago Jonathan wired her to get him on the phone at his hotel at a certain hour and she had done so, issuing from the telephone station with bright eyes and blazing cheeks, repeating to herself the commonplace conversation with its halts and repetitions as if she would memorize it forever.

Sometimes on the train hurrying from city to city Jonathan would stretch his long legs in their expensive trousers, that his father continued to provide out of pride that his son might appear as the best, and feel surprised at himself that he was actually back on the road and no longer working only for himself. In Benton where he stopped to see his parents his high spirits aroused suspicion only in his mother. His father was tickled at what he diagnosed as a return of early ambition. He took his son around the house, pointing out the wonderful set of china with the onion pattern from Dresden that his grandmother intended the boy to have one day.

"You want to get a fine home for that china," said Abel Chance. "It would only look well in a nice house on nice linen. Never buy cheap stuff, it doesn't pay. The best is cheapest in the long run." All this settled convinced life only amused Jonathan now that he saw prospects of going his own way. He listened attentively, sat during the Sunday dinner while his sister's husband expounded on what he expected to have in ten years, detailing with a terrible patience the sum set aside for education for potential children and foreseeing the day when, sufficiently successful, he could retire on his income. Mr. Chance nodded his head approvingly.

Mrs. Chance kept a sharp eye on her son. Unknown to anyone she had quietly steamed open a letter from Victoria, had read amazing matter. Her son was living with a woman. Her skin from neck to feet seemed flooded with blood at the idea. Some bold person had imposed on her boy, had worked her way into his life. He was foolish enough to be taken in, had forgotten the good bringing up, had forgotten everything for some woman's arms. The visions that came to her thick and fast tormented her. She took soda for heartburn, sat for hours in the chair by the window gripping the arms, looking out at a blank street. She had fought to keep him from marrying, now he had fallen into something blacker, deeper, more deadly. Sin. Lust. She had sense not to say a word, kept her secret, kissed her boy with a kind of repugnance and let him go. It was no time to tell his father. Better to wait.

But when her boy was gone, and she was alone in the house the maid's day out, she went around gathering up his things, his letters, his notes to her in school, his baby pictures, weeping terrible tears and tying up bundles with shaking hands, locking the letters finally in a drawer of her desk together with the bottle of old whiskey that she had so often venomously and mysteriously accused Jonathan of having pilfered. When she came to a picture of herself as a young woman, with round sweet face and happy eyes, staring out eagerly at the future, she hid her face in her hands, sat a long time seeing as well as if she faced a mirror, the discontent, the lines around the eyes, the proud and bitter mouth. And as if to restore her youth to her, she slipped the picture in with Jonathan's things, among those snapshots taken up north of the boy in the sand with his fair hair and dark eyes.

She went on an orgy of buying to forget and so long as she bought only the best and often useless things, Abel Chance paid the bills, grumbling a little, but prepared to accept his situation as a responsible man in the community. And of course, buying was a good thing for everyone, it gave jobs to the needy, it was, in fact, something like a contribution to church.

If Jonathan had kept his secrets to himself at home, he couldn't restrain himself with the boys at Vidisichis'. He had a mistress. They were going to live in the country, he was going to do as he pleased. He was going to write. As he told of his plans he rather pitied the boys, either contenting themselves with girls they couldn't take seriously or tying themselves up with marriage.

Jerry was the only one he had trouble seeing. He boarded with a worker at Ford's and was working there himself. When the two finally met, Jonathan was embarrassed at Jerry's seedy appearance. Jerry listened to his story, staring into space. "Well," he said almost rudely, "I hope everything works out fine for you." He looked fiercely past Jonathan as they stood outside a cigar store, up at the cold outlines of the buildings against a pale evening sky. "When you going?"

"Right away," said Jonathan. "As soon as I get back. I'm out now getting the dough together. It costs next to nothing in the country, of course."

"Guess you'll find you have to eat there, same as anywhere else," said Jerry. He still could not look at Jonathan. He felt a little contempt for the plan that would take the two out to the country where they would live as if on an island. He could fancy them together in a little kitchen with an oil lamp and he felt bitter that he would never have that life. He had come to feel that his own earlier failure in Detroit had been responsible for losing Rosamond. Once he had turned his anger against Detroit but he was learning; it wasn't a city to blame, it was a system. His country had taken him when it needed him; when he had needed it, it had no use for him. The little bonus that the state legislature had finally shelled out to the soldiers had come too late.

Jonathan was beginning to get uneasy and to wonder if he should have told Jerry about Vic. Perhaps the fellow was conventional. He began to fumble for something to say when Jerry pulled himself together and laughed. "Let's go out to the V's and get some food. I'm starved. I guess that's why I'm so absent-minded."

But all the way there and during the evening Jerry could not quite pull himself together. He was glad to get away from the cheerful Jonathan. Let him imagine he was on top of the world if it did him any good. He felt cut off from all the crowd at V's; working at Ford's made him want to cut loose from all his old ties. He had only one consolation in the world and that was finding out more clearly every day where he stood. He turned as he left Jonathan and looked back at the tall well-dressed fellow walk off. He wondered what kind of life he would have with Vicky. Whatever it was, sooner or later they too would have to face the music and decide what side of the fence they were on. He'd chosen his own people, they would have to choose theirs. With a father like

Jonathan had, it looked as if they would be on different sides of the fence, still you could never tell.

He walked home, entered the Schultz kitchen quietly and passed through to the cubby-hole where he shared the iron bed with ten-year-old Rex, the oldest son. Rex's dog Sam lay on the floor and began wagging his tail in a heavy thump. He shushed the dog, pushed the boy's thin legs over on their own side, climbed on the squeaky springs. It was late. A street light shone through the broken cracks of the shade drawn down. He couldn't sleep but he slowly began to doze. Let Jonathan be happy. Christ, was he getting such a dog in the manger he couldn't bear people to be happy. All the same it was easier here, with the Schultzes who had so little. Among them, the hard tight ball inside him seemed always to unroll and his insides eased and felt peaceful as they used to when he waited in the farm kitchen for the cake dish to lick. Even his fingers had tasted good as the spicy flavor had penetrated to his stomach and his heart. He shut his eyes but as he dropped off to sleep and long line of cars at the works began coming at him in the dark. He stirred, woke up with a start, rubbed his numb arm. The night was no good for sleeping. Rex had kicked off the covers and Sam had crawled to the foot of the bed and was scratching his fleas. He carefully covered up the little boy. Yes, this was the right place for him. He would stay down, he wouldn't be foolish and try to rise on someone else's neck, he'd stay down, right here with his own people until someday they could all rise together. And let Jonathan go to the country and think he was living if he wanted to.

When Pete Schultz came home and told his wife he was out at Ford's she said, "Thank God for it."

"You're crazy woman for thanking God. What'll the kids eat now. Shoe leather? Only there ain't any of that to spare either."

"I'd rather have you home alive than dead. You'd be dead if you kept it up. We'll get along. I'll take in washing."

"Who for? Nobody can pay for washing. You got to wash for your kids enough as it is."

"Never mind," said Mrs. Schultz. "Never mind." She looked around her as if she could pick bread off the floor and patches for kids' clothes off the wall. "Just as I thought you were going to take it a little easy again," she said sorrowfully. Why for the first time in a long while things had slowed down. That was when they thought there would be a strike. Pete had come home like a human being. He had enjoyed his supper. But they had just used that strike to make things worse. They had double crossed the boys, called it off and they were all pleased as Punch. It was a good excuse to fire a lot of men. To stay slowed down. What was the use making cars no one could buy? She knew they had never owned a car except once for a few weeks. There were too many mouths to feed and she wasn't going to turn Jerry Stauffer out, even if he had no job. He'd stuck by them, paying board and helping with doctor bills, she'd see they stuck by him. But merciful mother of God shoes, food, gas, to say nothing of the very clothes on their backs.

Pay a dime and buy a diamond, why she could remember when they had jokingly begun doing that and she had kept it for awhile too. She and Pete used to study things like that and wonder if it paid in the end. There was one about *it doesn't pay not to mortgage your home* that Pete used to marvel over. Seems you could get more money for what you borrowed by puting it in stocks

than what it cost in interest on the mortgage. There was no end to
the get-rich-quick schemes but now they were over.

Schultz was out of work. The parks were full of bums. If you sat
down and looked a bit tired someone told you to move on. But
thank god they had health, they had the gas stove paid for and it
was a blessing they had never owned their own home to get them
into trouble and to be a worry and fret.

They certainly was getting to be a great big army of people who
just had their noses out of water. A great big army of them and
sink or swim they used to say. People couldn't starve in America,
they said. There was always something around the corner. They
just couldn't couldn't starve. All the same they were pretty hungry
and she wished someone would explain to her why they were
hoeing under them crops out west. And killing them hogs. Her
family could use some of that stuff. Could use plenty. And she
whisked around to look at Schultz who sat there, staring, you'd
think he'd seen his own ghost.

IN JOSHUA'S COUNTRY

When Jonathan Chance got back to New York, he was pretty
chagrined to find out that his savings from the trip were nearer two
hundred and fifty dollars instead of four hundred.

"That can't be right," he said as he and Victoria huddled over
the paper scrawled with figures.

"It's right," said Vicky. "I've gone over it three times. No, the
trouble is, you spent more than you thought. You can't eat dollar
steaks and stay at the best hotels and save much. You see they
allowed your expenses but only up to a certain point."

"The cheap skates," said Jonathan, "they expect a man to sell
big and then live like a chewing gum salesman. You don't understand Vicky, you can't do that high-powered stuff without good
food and good rest. It just can't be done and they know it."

"Oh they don't care, but you see how it is. You're used to doing that way and I can see that's the only way to do on those trips."

"It's a dirty trick on me," said Jonathan. He felt sold out, after he had expected to save all he made. This way he had paid for the trip, taken at high speed, and the firm had got the benefit.

"Two fifty's not bad," said Vicky. "We can do a lot on that and we'll just go ahead. And I have sixty saved. I've been doing odd jobs all the time, that's a big sum. Three hundred."

"Three hundred ten," said Jonathan. He looked sharply at Vic. Was she criticizing him for not bringing back the whole four hundred? He was one of the best high-powered salesmen in the country but you couldn't sell and live like a chewing gum salesman. You had to have elbow room. She was studying the figures and did not look at him. She brooded over the possibilities of their life in a kind of trance. "Nobody could have done any better," said Jonathan. "It just can't be done."

"Oh, of course not," said Vicky looking up surprised. "No one could." He fancied her voice sounded a little hollow. He felt grieved but forgot it in the hurry of getting away before the precious money melted. They went straight to the little Pennsylvania town where Jonathan had heard houses could be had cheap in nearby country.

It was the goldenrod season and asters and goldenrod covered the little hill. The house was on the hill and had six handsome rooms with dozens of windows. There was nothing to put in the house but the new bed they had bought in the city and a couple of second-hand chairs. As for a table, Jonathan hadn't been a boy-scout for nothing. He made a table. He made a bench. After one trip to the village he came home with friends on both sides of the road. They heaped the back porch with tomatoes and peppers, onions and squash.

"Look at that, why they are giving us all that truck, think of it."

"It's the same as if your father gave you a check," said Vicky, hands on her hips calculating. Nothing for it but to buy a big kettle and glass jars. They canned, they pickled. They had an orgy of chili sauce, grinding frantically in the light of the kerosene lamp.

"A little more red," Jonathan called, grinding fast. "Now some yellow. Aren't there any more beets?" The lovely colors fell into the boiler, the mass bubbled in the kettle, was poured into jars and stood in rows on the pantry shelves, with the canned goods from town and the sack of flour, the sack of sugar and the dried beans.

They stood gazing at their larder. "Nothing can touch us now," said Jonathan. "We got enough to eat all winter. We'll lay in coal and wood. What more could we want?" Well, they wanted blankets and a few dishes and a second-hand coal stove and, as winter came on, they shut up the different rooms and narrowed themselves down to the kitchen and the sitting room with a room above for Jonathan to work in and a hole in the floor for the heat to rise to warm him. They settled down in that house and began to look at the stars again the way they had as children. When the snow came down they slept late in the gray light of the morning and stayed up late at night in the yellow light of the good oil lamp with the practical shade.

The snow plopping on the windows sounded like water drops and they were cut off as if on an island. The snow swirled around them and piled in waves against the door. Little animals nibbled around the house for food, a possum stole the leavings of the cat's dish and rattled the plate for more. In the long evenings they sat close to the fire in their sweaters, sipping cider, reading aloud. They went back to Shakespeare and Marlowe, they took turns reading, and when the book changed hands sometimes an owl hooted his three mournful toots. Once a coon screamed. The book dropped, they looked at each other, smiled and went on again. In the morning the windows were heavy with frost. The room was a cave, the blankets were a cave around and over them and inside they felt warm and living. They relished their victuals, scraping the food from the plate, scrunching the thin buttery toast, pouring more coffee and, after breakfast, like as not, they'd read awhile again. There would be wood to chop, washing to do, because every penny needed to be saved, the freezing clothes hung stiff as dead men on the sagging line. A rat haunted the kitchen, clawed around, chewing a big hole for himself next the sink. He came in boldly and took the meatloaf from the open oven, dragged it to his hole, was surprised with his gray head rearing angrily, his claws on the prize. Nothing to do but hunt him with a trap, a good strong one, baited with cheese. But he was too smart, wittily nibbled the cheese, left the contraption unsprung. They couldn't get him. The rat was the center of their life for days. Get him, and they admired his cunning, but Jonathan fixed him with silk string craftily imbedded in the cheese.

"This will fix him," he said, laying the trap carefully and, when it finally sprung, they felt sorry for their victim and actually missed his sneering snout. Time was measured for awhile from the day the rat was caught, then it faded, it became just winter. The wagon with butter and bread came around once a week. They bought a quarter of a cow and hung it frozen in an empty upper room. Together they studied the cook book, concocted a dozen different ways to eat beef. "There might be a war and we wouldn't know about it," Victoria said.

They thought they didn't want to know. The island was enough. Their first suspicions about each other were wearing off. Others began slowly to take their place. When Victoria began hinting that now was a good time for Jonathan to work, he had an involuntary angry flash as if it were his mother talking. Sometimes he began to wonder if he had really understood Vicky. The little hollows in her neck were filling out. He was a little afraid of the blissful look she sometimes had but he loved it too; it made him feel good to be walking around in his own house making someone happy. When she got on her high horse and stormed around because he had spent too much at the store, he had a terrible uneasiness. She was then so much like the temperamental woman he had always dreamed of having who would break his heart. He now thought of his old boyish ideas as past and done for and he was sometimes, in spite of his reasonable attitude toward those things, a little jealous when Vicky told him about her past experiences. He raked up his own but they had all been easy conquests and no girl except Vicky had ever touched his heart.

When the effects of the selling job began to wear off, Jonathan mounted the crooked stairs every day and sat pounding away on his typewriter. Victoria liked the sound. Seated below she loved the industrious sound coming from above. But Jonathan was not happy about his work. When he sat in the little empty room bitter ideas and words from his past came to his mind and poured over the paper. He wasn't satisfied with his hatred of his old life. He began to look out the window and sometimes as he sat there a spring wagon drawn by an old skinny nag went past. It was Jake Colburn's and his three tin cans of milk covered with the old blanket went by regular as a clock. Once Jonathan was up early enough to see him on his way to the milk station. It was half-past six. After that, he often heard the hoofs ring out on the cold hard road. Around eleven, Jake came back again and Jonathan might be hauling in an armful of wood. He would stand still, raise one arm, shout "Hyyuh Jake," grinning all over and Jake never failed to raise his arm brightly, grinning too.

By the time Tolman's letter came they were already beginning to feel a little out of things. Tolman wrote from Germany about going to the opera in Dresden, of finding himself wedged in a big square with thousands of red flags, of shops smashed and girls selling themselves for a slice of bread or a postage stamp. In Munich he was in the center of artistic life, had tea at the American church and talked twaddle with old ladies and leftovers of the German upper-crust, spent evenings in the homes of American painters, who, suddenly valuta wealthy, hired whole orchestras for all night parties where orgies went on behind palms and a German with a Harvard accent talked seriously about an incredible little pansy who was trying to push over affairs in the south.

The long letter, written closely in bad diluted German ink, tantalized them both. Tolman was living. They suddenly felt left out of it, quit reading, sat silently in the evening, each with a book and suddenly proposed that they take walks to the village every day for the paper.

Yes, affairs were stirring in the world. Germany could not pay her debts except with goods and if she did that it would not be long before she quit being underdog. New wars seemed popping all over. A university professor was preaching a millennium where poverty would eliminate itself by the natural process of increased production carried to the nth power.

Icicles snapped and broke from the roof, the little creek muffled in snow purred and burst in soft spots through the ice, melted the snow in large oozing pools, broke out one morning in a mild roar. It was nearly spring. Figuring one night, they decided to plan on summer. They had stuck it out through the winter, summer should be easy. Even though they had only thirty dollars left.

Anne Wendel had put in a bad winter at Oxtail. The Grapeville property was cut up and ready to sell as soon as it was spring. She had borrowed money from her sister Hortense to go back to Oxtail and Amos Wendel had come down with the grippe that took weeks of careful nursing. Sometimes in the big hollow house, running up and down stairs, waiting on him, Anne had the awful feeling that she would get her money out of those lots too late. Amos looked so waxlike, pulled through so slowly, there were nights when the house seemed screaming at her. What good would the house do if he died?

But as soon as he began to mend, she was right back at her eternal figuring. No matter what happened, she and Hortense would be several thousand to the good, that is if the lots sold for what she had bid them in for. The property had been theirs as a gift to begin with, you couldn't take away that. Hortense was drumming at her as spring came on. She could certainly use some money. She had advanced expenses to Anne, she was beginning to feel cramped. Business was slow and they had lost money in 1921 that had not yet been gained back. It was a dog's life, so hard to get up in the mornings. She was up at quarter to six before it was light in the hopes of catching a little early trade.

The two women thought of their little inheritance as the long dreamed of capital. One thousand banks had failed in Iowa and the Dakotas, but, thank fortune, Anne Wendel had lost only fifty dollars. She was determined that Vicky get some help. When she thought of her daughter, she was anxious and tried hard to believe that everything was all right with her. She wished she would marry that boy. Did Vicky think she had pulled the wool over her eyes when she talked of spending the winter with friends in the country and helping with the housework for her board? That didn't sound

like Vicky. No, there was something back of it and she knew very
well what. In this day and age unprecedented things happened. But
now and then in letters she wrote little homilies about life and
marriage and having children and that life was not worth much
without children.

As soon as Amos was better she went back to Grapeville. With
two daughters in Oxtail they could surely keep an eye on their
father. It was lonely in the Grapeville cemetery where she went the
first thing to look at the graves and see if the rose on Catherine's
grave had not been winter-killed. It was putting out little leaves
and the ivy on Joe's grave was thick and green. Mem's stone had
sunk considerable and poor Aaron had not yet a sign of a stone due
to the miserliness of Sally and her son.

When handbills were finally printed of the coming sale, and the
day arrived, Anne Trexler was on the ground almost at sunrise.
Suppose things did not go well. Roundtree had warned her that she
might even suffer a loss and until time for the sale she stumped up
and down with her cane, her hat pushed off her forehead, picking
up sticks, examining all the little stakes that marked the new lots,
gazing with admiration at the street signs with their bright new
paint and anxiously tidying up as if the earth were a parlor and a
little neatness might save the day.

When people began coming with lunches and little stools, she
buzzed around happily. "I always like to see people have a good
time," she confided to the auctioneer who stood waiting with a
cynical expression on his face. "You what?" he bellowed. Anne
repeated but he shook his head carelessly. What he was after was a
good commission and this crowd didn't look any too tempting.
They were out for a nice day, that's about what it looked like.

Anne Trexler sat on an overturned barrel with a pencil and
notebook and when the bidding began, started to scratch down the
bids. Each time the hammer fell, she could feel it in her body as if
it were her heart. Dear God, surely she would make something.
What had she had all her life? Surely it wasn't presumptuous to
hope for a few crumbs so she could take her husband, who had
slaved all his life for her, out of that hard work and give him a little
comfort. It wouldn't take much to fix up the duplex and if Vicky

had a little nest egg, who knows, that boy and she might get married. The means for a steady way of life makes people do steady things, she thought hopefully.

When the day was finally over and Roundtree and the auctioneer figured things up, it had turned out fair after all. "That is, if these folks really pay up their mortgages when due. Part cash, part mortgage." She took the cash and made careful records of everything. She sent jubilant wires to Hortense and Amos. Actually it almost seemed as if money had dropped from the skies.

If David Trexler had presented his two sisters with cash out of hand, he couldn't have been more pleased at the news that Anne Wendel had made a good deal on that Grapeville proposition. Of course his giving up the share left by Aaron's will did not come to much, still in David's mind the principle of magnanimity represented considerable.

"I don't know why she doesn't send me *my* money," said Hortense discontentedly when a few days went by without a check from her sister.

"Now Hortense, don't be grasping like Aaron. Mem used to say she hoped he would see the light one day, but he never did. Affection outlasts dollars, give your sister time. It's a nice little nest egg for you girls." It would certainly relieve him of a feeling of responsibility toward his sister Anne. Hortense had a nice little business but Anne was always on the rocks and, if he had not helped her oftener, it was only out of respect for her and because he didn't believe in pauperizing people. Independence and the exercise of individual initiative were the foundations on which this country had risen to first rank, and he had risen also and hoped he used his means wisely and with due regard to the laws of nature. Lately he often found himself soliloquizing in a way that surprised him and when it came to speechmaking he was one of the best.

The night before he had presided at a Chamber of Commerce dinner and had had occasion to remark that never before had the country seemed so prosperous, so headed for prosperity for all. Businesses were wisely sharing profits and taking their employees as stockholders—co-partners.

Several melons had been cut in the last year; he had got a bonus as director of the new lumber enterprise in southern Washington. Tel. and Tel. and United States Steel were high. He had begun to buy for friends, make investments that invariably turned out profitable. Lately he was seriously considering breaking in his daughter Sue to take over this phase as a paying business. She could make ten thousand a year easily, to say nothing of fliers she could take on her own by a study of the market. He congratulated himself, and at that very moment, any number of other gentlemen were congratulating themselves on what they considered their own individual acumen. They thought of the sky as the only limit to legitimate profit.

Sue did not become overly enthusiastic about the stock transactions. "I don't know what is the matter with my children," David stromed one evening as he sat on his veranda with Ella on one side and Millie on the other. "No enthusiasm. Dave acts like a dead man half the time. Sue gets a proposition that would set any other young woman on her toes. Why one of Anne's girls would jump at the chance. But no, my children act as if they were martyrs when a little money-making propo comes their way. It's your blood, Ella," he said looking at his wife venomously. "I tell you you haven't warmed your bottom porchsitting all these years for nothing. It's coming out in the children. I never saw the beat."

He groaned and rolled his eyes but he really was enjoying himself. Privately he thought that it was quite true that a really first class man rarely has children that come up to snuff. The law of compensation. Still he had hoped his children would show more ambition. Half the time they acted scared. And what glum faces. His son Daniel was actually acting as if he were doing his father a favor by going to the agricultural college. The boy had shown no other talents, so he might as well farm. "My God," said David, "see if you can't talk to Sue, mamma."

"Sue's busy sewing," said Ella morosely. She knew that at that moment Sue was in her room putting her eyes out making a fine handsewn nightgown for her friend in the library who was going to be married. She didn't like such intensity, it made her uncomfortable. She was glad the girl was going to be married and out of the way but what would Sue do then? Why, the stock business, of course. She could become independent and make contacts, even marry. The mother suddenly felt more cheerful but she did not know why her heart was so often heavy. It was nice of course for Millie to be with them, the poor creature had to have a home; still sometimes when it came to an evening drive she did wish she and Dave could go alone without him singing out, "Hey Millie, where are you? Going driving, hustle now." The two women and the man sat stiffly on the porch chairs like stuffed pigeons. People in cars driving by looked enviously at the handsome house and grounds, even at the three stout persons with bilious faces seated solemnly in a row, staring down the valley.

When Victoria got a check for fifty dollars from her mother she couldn't help but crow a little. "That's the kind of people I've got, when they've got anything themselves, they just naturally share it. Fifty dollars, why we can buy tools for the garden and seeds and a nice steak to celebrate."

They went to the village and came home loaded with bundles. But she couldn't let up on the kind of people she had. It made Jonathan a little sore. If he had any hopes of getting something out of his father, he would, but there was no use trying unless it was for a business. "If it was business, he'd come across quick enough but he doesn't see any sense in writing."

All the same the proximity of the money his father had was a kind of poison to them. Jonathan felt that secretly Vicky had a grudge against him for not trying to get a loan from him. He put it off, and wrote home seldom. His father answered briefly, demanding to know what he was up to and when he was going to get to work at some respectable occupation. Someone had written an account for the Benton paper saying that Jonathan had had a piece in a magazine that had been published in France and the United States customs had stopped it as obscene. He was mortified to death to think that his son would write filthy trash and wanted to know when he meant to get down to business and make a decent living.

When Vicky read this letter she almost hit the ceiling. "Filthy—
he doesn't even ask you, just swallows an ignorant custom official's
word. Oh what a father." Jonathan felt white hot himself but he
wasn't going to begin trying to educate his father. "He doesn't
know, what's the use of getting worked up." All the same neither of
them enjoyed their supper, it took several days to tame down again.
As if the piece the father had referred to wasn't something to be
proud of. Why, it had been Tolman's idea. He had finally got to
Paris, was in with a group who were the vanguard, so he said. They
had printed a piece Jonathan had sent, together with selections
from Gertrude Stein, Joyce, any number of people to be proud of.
Jonathan had been proud himself, the book in its paper cover was
in the room where he wrote. He liked to see it, it made him feel as
if he had already published many volumes.

Not that it made it any easier to write. Something was plugging
up his mind and when he began writing the dollar world of his
father dragged its way across the page and put hatred into every
word. You have to believe in something to write, he concluded,
feeling shut-in in his little room, tied down, sick of his own efforts.
Hatred didn't feed you. He loved Vicky, their house, the long
evenings and the farmers leaning over the fence admiring his new
garden and examining the fresh turned soil. All these good things
found no place when he sat down to write. He couldn't seem to tap
them. His fear of being sentimental, of writing dishonest stuff kept
him dipping into the past where there was no danger of being
anything but bitter. But it was certainly not enough. Aldous
Huxley was cheap compared to a first rate writer who really
embraced the world. He longed to embrace the world, to take it as
he took Vicky and as he took the little valley sloping away from the
house. Coming out late at night, he loved to stand, to see the hills
spread like the naked thighs of a woman, a great warm and loving
woman. As he stood there the land rose to embrace him, sudden
and sharp as if a naked woman had risen from the earth.

By the time June came, they had quite a sizeable garden and
way ahead of some of the neighbors. "Chance has got the best peas
in the region," they said at the store. His corn was ahead of them
all. He worked hard and fast, the garden would have to keep them

all summer. But their shoes wore out, it took kerosene for light and the oil stove, a dozen needs drained the good money away.

One night a neighbor strolled by and said that it looked as if city folks were going to buy the Weaver place. And more city folks had looked at the Barton house. After supper Vicky and Jonathan both had the same idea. "Why can't I ask father for a loan to buy a place, just as a business proposition? That fellow said these places went for five hundred cash, the rest a mortgage. We could ask for a thousand, use five hundred to get the house, the rest to live on this summer and fix it up. We could fix it up ourselves and sell in the fall. We might make five hundred dollars, even a thousand." Vicky was already figuring. "Do you think he will do it?"

Jonathan was certain he would. "When it comes to making money," he explained, "father isn't tight. He's quick to see." They went the next day to the owners of their house; yes, it could be bought, five hundred would cinch it. They could hardly wait to get home, to write the long patient letter, to draw the plan of the house, to point out its many advantages, to urge that now was the time and this countryside was certain to be exploited as Connecticut had been. It was late when they finished but they walked the two miles to the village and dropped the letter for the early mail. On the way home the stars never seemed so big, they were like the stars in southern skies you read about. They stared up at them, stood a long time listening to the sound of their brook.

"That's all this country is good for any more," said Jonathan, "city folks. Weaver says he falls behind a little every year. Can't make any money. All these people just raise garden stuff for themselves and send out as many members of the family as they can to the porcelain factory. Now if we could raise some crop to help us out, sell something, say onions or peppers." When they reached home, late as it was, they wrote another letter to the department of agriculture for a bulletin about onions.

In the mornings the sun came early and waked them. It was no longer like a sleepy cave. They were up with the sun and out at the garden. It was a joy for Vicky to look out the kitchen window that was as clean as any farm wife's, shining in the sun, and see Jonathan working with the hoe, turning the soil, keeping the new green shoots spotless of weeds. To wash the lamp chimneys in the suds and see them shine. To put herbs in the pot of meat and smell it in every corner. But all the good could turn black and spotted, with fear that the money would run out, that Jonathan would have to go back to hateful selling on the road, and a kind of peril was in their days. When she thought of the future, she feared New York as if it were a blister; anything but that. She'd work her fingers to the bone and probably would, she thought bitterly, but anything was all right so that they got somewhere, so that they kept a decent purpose in living.

When the fifty dollars came she wanted to pretend to her mother that she was married to Jonathan, and often in bed composed letters telling her the news that she knew would make Anne Wendel so happy. But she was afraid to speak of it to Jonathan for fear he would think she was asking him really to do it. She felt timid and uncertain and in her heart doubted that he loved her.

When Mr. Chance got the letter from his son asking for a thousand dollars he was very pleased at its energy and tone. He thought it was about time for his son to cut out his foolishness and get down to business. He had wasted precious time staying with friends and trying to write but he was pretty young, he could make it up. And a young man has to sow wild oats.

It was a smart idea to try to make money on a real estate proposition and as outlined, his father was solidly behind it. He put it aside to sleep on and decided to act at once, as Jonathan had intimated the deal might be snatched from under his nose if he didn't seize this opportunity. Usually Mr. Chance consulted his wife on these matters but she had gone north to open up their summer cottage. The cottage was called that only out of tradition; actually it was a huge house with several bathrooms and big airy rooms. They had put around twelve thousand dollars into the house and only that spring were considering further repairs; but these things were inevitable and incidental upon owning property. Mr. Chance would not hesitate to spend money on a house. It was only when it came to giving money to people that he hemmed and hawed.

He slept on it and took a walk around the garden, peered into the wren house where a new nest was going on. The roses needed fertilizer; he must see to that and only the best paid. The maid came out to hang up the washing and he stood in his fine pressed gray suit that so perfectly matched his graying hair and took pleasure in the handsome linen that was gradually being hoisted to the line. Then he walked to work, and at his office, quietly wrote out a check for his son.

> Dear Jonathan;
>   Mother is up north and I am alone. I am sending you check for one thousand dollars to use in purchasing *real estate*. You may send me a note of even date with this check at six percent for one year. I have had to borrow a very considerable sum from the bank this year and will have to add this and it will be some time before I shall be able to pay any of it back since we had to borrow $12,000 to swing a deal. Rev. Burgess died suddenly a few days ago. We are all well and send love to you. I hope you will write more often.
>   Your Father

He got off the letter and the check and felt good about it. He often thought of the future and the pride he would take when his son would really make a mark in the world and be looked up to by everyone as a successful man. He couldn't understand how he had gotten bit by the writing bug. That kind of thing didn't run in his family. By this time he had forgotten everything about his father except the strict discipline the older man had given his sons. He forgot his diaries and the letters to the newspapers and the burning interest the old man had taken in politics.

No, he remembered only one Chance virtue, the ability to get and hold money and to use his position for purely respectable and selfish purposes. Abel Chance himself lived for these things and so far as the rest of the world and its happenings were concerned, they might as well have occurred to a blind man.

He was still pleased with himself five days later when his wife came back with a long list of articles to be bought for the cottage. She came in just before dinner, drawing off her immaculate gauntlet gloves, looking as if she had stepped from a bandbox even after the long drive. Abel put his paper down, went over and kissed her. "How's everything?" said Mrs. Chance.

"Oh pretty good," said Abel. "Mrs. Grace is sick and they've sent for her son. Uncle Megs was in the store this morning, he says he and Aunty want us to take a little trip with them this summer." He paused, waiting to spring the big news. "Had a letter from Jonathan. I guess the boy is through sowing his wild oats. He wants to go into real estate."

"He what?" said Mrs. Chance, galvanizing as if for action, her mouth tightening.

"I say he wants to go into real estate. He wrote a very sensible letter, all that country is beginning to boom like Connecticut. He wants to buy a place and fix it up himself and sell it this fall. Sounds all right to me. I told you he'd get over that foolishness."

Mrs. Chance snorted. Her face turned suddenly white. "I hope you don't believe any such cock and bull story, Abel."

"What do you mean," said Abel.

"Why, that's nothing but one of his lies. He lies all the time. Just the way he lied about drinking for so long until he confessed. You *are* easy, Abel."

"I wouldn't say that," said Abel, disturbed and a little on the defensive. "It sounded all right to me. He's to pay me interest."

"You mean you actually put up the money."

"Yes, I sent him a thousand. He'll be able to get the place on that, and you can't lose on real estate."

"Well, Abel Chance," said Mrs. Chance. She was speechless. Her skin looked livid, around her nose purple patches began to show. "Abel Chance." She couldn't find words. Her husband looked at her in alarm and resentment. She opened her mouth, shut it, said, "I'll tell you after you've had your dinner. I think it's about time you knew what's going on. As for me, I don't want anything to eat. I couldn't swallow a bite." She sailed up the stairs carried by the fierce hot pumping of her blood. So Jonathan could fool his father, wangle money out of him to spend on some hussy. Oh, it was terrible. It would surely leak out through the town. To think that Abel was such an easy mark. Like taking candy from a baby. She pulled off her gloves, propped herself on the bed, rolled uneasily. Where could she lay her head in peace. At that moment her boy was disgracing them. It wasn't enough he should write filthy literature; no, he must flaunt his immorality in their very faces and brazenly expect his father to finance his little amusements.

When Abel Chance finally came upstairs he was very grave. "Now Millicent, what's the trouble?" he said. She sat up in bed, sniffed angrily. "Well, I didn't want to worry you before, Abel. I have known of Jonathan's goings-on for some time, and to make sure I wasn't just fancying things, I spoke to our lawyer and he's been doing a little investigating for me. You can ask him."

"I'm asking you," said Abel.

"Jonathan doesn't want to buy real estate. Why, he's living with a woman, openly *living* with her, do you understand that? It's been going on for months. I suspected it when he was here and read a letter he got and I put Mr. Buckle on the job then. No Abel, I didn't tell you, I thought perhaps Jonathan would see the light, but when it comes to a question of getting money out of you . . ."

She spread her hands angrily. Yes, when the pocketbook was touched it was high time for action. Abel Chance got up stiffly. "I'll go around and see Buckle and have a talk with him," he said. Mrs. Chance shrugged her shoulders. She felt suddenly relieved and as if she could eat a morsel. She wasn't going to finance her boy in sin. Let him settle down and live steady and get a decent job like other people. She went to the kitchen and, getting out a cold piece of chicken breast, ate it morosely.

Several hours later Mr. Chance came back, walked firmly upstairs to his wife's desk, sat down and wrote to Jonathan.

Dear Jonathan:

Since mother arrived home I have learned of things which have shocked your mother and me very much. Your mother has had suspicions of your actions but has had no definite evidence until she found some letters which lead her to believe you have been living unmarried with a woman. This has been going on for some time. We learned through our attorney how you are living and other things concerning you and have evidence to substantiate our information. I have immediately stopped payment on the check and will absolutely not back you while you are living as you have been. It would be aiding and condoning a moral and civic crime to do so, and you know very well that you are liable to the law for your conduct. You will have to either marry the woman or quit her immediately. While the woman in this affair is no better nor worse than the man, yet no one would want to harbor such a person or have anything to do with her. Get a job at honest work and quit or marry and if you write any smutty stories, please have enough consideration for me not to sign your name to them. Any time you can show me that you have gotten to honest work and decent living I shall be willing to back you to the best of my ability but to think that your mother and I have worked hard these many years and denied ourselves many things with the view of bringing up our children to be decent, honorable and useful citizens and then have developments of this kind brought to our knowledge is extremely distressing. I hope you will let me hear from you soon and that you have enough character to turn away from the path of vice and vagabondism upon which you appear to have considerable start.

Your father.

P.S. I mailed you a thin summer suit recently.

When he finished the letter, his face was quite gray and Mrs. Chance looking at him, subdued her growing cheerfulness to remark, "Abel, just go to bed and try to forget this. You look done in."

"I am," said Abel. He felt as if someone had given him a body blow. All the expectations he had for his son seemed to have crumbled. He couldn't understand it. His own terrible austerity concerning payment of debts and rigid conduct as to money and to regular living, made his son seem the blackest of sheep. He could not sleep but felt relief the next day when the check had been finally stopped.

For three days Jonathan and Victoria had been possessors of the thousand dollars. They had at once walked to the town, put it in the bank and now had the bank book on the mantelpiece. The negotiations for the house were not yet completed but would be shortly. A great deal had happened in the three days. The neighbors up and down the road knew of the proposed sale and were dropping in to find out if Chance meant to farm. Jonathan looked at the check book often and couldn't resist telling Victoria that his father was "a nice person and not actually stingy."

"Why, of course," she said, but all the same she privately considered the interest on the note a curious thing for a parent to demand. Catch her people doing a thing like that. Now that they were to be property owners, even if only for a summer before they could sell, perhaps she might pretend to her mother that they were married. Not that it was important, to anyone but her mother. Still, she knew her mother worried and she couldn't think up any more good reasons for lingering in the country.

"Why sure," Jonathan agreed. He had a brief uncomfortable moment but after all one should consider one's parents a little. And it wouldn't change anything between Vic and himself. Besides he felt a lightheartedness now he saw a chance to get some independent way of living. If he could be sure of a little money for a while, who knows what he might not do. He was still stuck with his work as if he were in a swamp. He couldn't seem to write anything but sneers at the world. When he was in the little room uncomfortable doubts made him fumble. His mother standing big and dominating seemed ever behind him. "Now Jonathan, just stop that and get me those brass nails I spoke to you about."

The uncomfortable and doubtful nature of the kind of writer he wished to be, didn't bother him. What stopped him were the recollections that sucked like parasites at all he proposed doing. If he could someway throw them off, be free. He thought he didn't care a damn about the people he had been brought up with. Why did he keep on putting their dead souls down on paper? Let the dead shovel under the dead. He wanted to get ahead with his life, tap the ground not the top soil. If he could get back to essentials, to the very barnyard, the manure pile that, once spread over the fields, made stuff grow.

All the same, it was fine of his father to help him out. And he got Joe Riegel up to look over the place. "I thought of knocking out a few partitions," he said. "What do you think, Joe?"

Joe stood with his old sweater bulging, his eyes gimleting the plaster and stones. "That's easy," he said, "You just take a hammer and knock away. These old houses were never strong on partitions, they put all their strength in the outer walls." He went around knocking with his thumb against the inner walls, wrinkling his forehead. They had a tiny drink of dandelion wine just to celebrate and Joe sat sipping his as he gave advice about paint and sound beams. As he talked he rambled on about jobs he had done, parts of the world he had seen.

"Yes mam," he said, "I'm not one of your native barnacles, I've been around, all over. Them hands don't look like much," he spread them out with all their nicks and calluses and bruises. "They ain't much for beauty, but they got me around a good bit. I've covered some ground. I've worked about everywhere in this country where there was work to do." He leaned back against the pillar of the porch, sipping his wine with pleasure, clearing his throat and smiling in a deprecatory way at his hands, that he kept stretching and spreading out proudly. "No, they ain't much for beauty but let me tell you," he said looking at them, "they saved my life." Jonathan and Victoria nodded in appreciation. They were in a state where nothing that was said mattered much. For the first time in months, they weren't worried about the future. The future was going to provide.

"I was working on that railroad down on the Keys, a couple hundred of us on a raft and one of them tornadoes blew up before we could get off, we were blown out to sea as if we'd been a chip. You never saw such water, it came down on us like a wall of ice and washed off dozens at a time. The old raft stood it and bobbed up again. I looked around, seen all them men gone, and held on for dear life, I don't know how I did it. I held on and the water come down again, lifted us up, threw us about, there was no end to it. Each time men washed off. When the sea finally let up, there was only three left of all that outfit. I was one." He looked at his hands again. "Never went near the water after that," he finished. "And who was we making that road for? A bunch of crooks, that's who. A bunch of crooks." His mildness had disappeared and he shook his finger threateningly as if about to make a speech, thought better of it, reached in his pocket for a chaw of tobacco. Jonathan walked toward the road where the mailman had just stopped. Vicky was still feeling the heavy rise and fall of the sea, the men swept off like seaweed, the hands struggling to hold on. She looked up as Jonathan came back and, as she saw his agitated face, again felt a sinking and terror. "What's wrong?" she said going toward him.

"It's from father," he said. "He's stopped our check."

"Stopped our check?" said Vicky. "Why he can't do that."

"I guess he can all right," said Jonathan. Joe Riegel got to his feet embarrassed and looked around for a hat he did not have. "Guess I'll be going, Jonathan," he said. "Anything I can do for you, let me know."

"I guess I won't need that advice about the house, Joe," said Jonathan. He had stuffed the letter in his pocket. They had already cashed several small checks on the new account. He wondered which way to turn. "I got some bad news, Joe," he said. Joe nodded. He had overheard a little.

He said, "And say listen, Jonathan, if you want any money, let me know. I ain't got much, but what I got is yours. I'll be glad to loan you anything I got."

"That's swell of you, Joe," said Vicky.

"That's all right," said Joe. "Absolutely all right." He walked off down the road muttering. Jonathan and Victoria went inside and shut the door. "I bet my mother put him up to it," said Jonathan, flattening out the letter. He was very pale. The two looked at each other, speechless, in anger. "I can't believe it," Victoria said. "Whatever for? As if we were insects. What for?"

When Anne Wendel got the news saying Victoria was married, she called up both her married daughters. Clara began crying into the phone but Nancy came right over for the details. The whole household was in a flutter and Amos Wendel picked up the snapshot of Jonathan and looked at it a dozen times. "He's got a nice face," he said.

"He's the very one for Vicky," said Mrs. Wendel. "I can tell a good face everytime." When Papa was out of the room she told her daughters that he looked like John Gason. They both looked at the snapshot again and agreed. The news took the sting out of a very painful exchange of letters that had begun between Anne Wendel and her sister Hortense. Both women were getting to the time of life when they dreaded old age and dependence on their children. Anne had finally sent her sister a check for part of the proceeds of the sale but she had reasoned that she should have something extra for her trouble and had subtracted a matter of eighty dollars.

This eighty dollars was pounced upon by Hortense who used up all the repressed rage of a lifetime in worrying and wrangling about it. She had begun a whole series of abusive letters and had mortified Anne by actually wiring her threats to get that money to her by a certain date or she would have one big trouble. It was an entirely different woman than Anne had ever known that she now had to contend with. A kind of frenzy was in her sister, all the injustices heaped upon her during a lifetime of petty storekeeping raged now at Anne whose own situation she completely overlooked.

The happiness that Anne believed was Vicky's made up for this battle with her sister and for several days she distracted herself planning a present for her child. Nothing is more useful than a quilt and she washed the lamb's wool out of the old blanket, picked it and spread it, covered it with a nice blue and pink cover tied with pink and it looked and felt like new. Light as down. But what a pity that there wasn't a cent for a new present. Not until the payments on the lots began coming in. If only she hadn't been so anxious to pay up the mortgage on the house. But it did seem good for once in her life to have a house that was really their own. Mr. Mortell the cashier had acted disappointed, as if he had expected all along to finally put his cat's paw on the property. Well, he was cheated of that but it was a pity not to have cash around the house and with Hortense carrying on like a wild cat, she hardly knew where to turn. It almost seemed as if they were really about where they always had been. They owned the house but for spending money, you couldn't see it.

Now that her daughter was married, she began to wonder what kind of place the girl lived in. During the winter she had never examined the conditions of Vicky's life too closely. She had not even inquired where the town was. It was better to let it remain in a kind of mystery. Now she dragged out a map and hunted with a pin over the surface. It hardly seemed true, but yes, that town was not far from Locust Valley. It was in the very county where her father had surveyed the roads and she herself had been born. "Vicky is back in that part of the country where I came from," she said to Amos that night. "Think of that." They both marveled. It was as if some unseen hand was directing their daughter. Bad luck they had often had but surely now and then good signs appeared. Perhaps in her daughter's life all the wrongs that the Trexlers had suffered would be made right. Amos Wendel and his wife discussed all the circumstances of the past until late that night and Anne finally decided to send her daughter some of the old Trexler papers for a wedding present.

"There's nothing like knowing what soil you've sprung from and that's one thing the girl can be proud of. A good honest line." She didn't have any new present but her girl could hold up her head when it came to folks. She packed up some of the old silver spoons that Joe had sent them from Atlanta back in the days when fortune seemed dangling before his eyes, some of the old letters and diaries, and went to bed with a quieted heart. Even if Hortense raged, she had a good conscience. She knew she deserved that eighty dollars and as for her sister being in dire want, it was all bosh.

The old letters and papers did not have the cheering effect on Victoria that her mother had hoped. She did not have her mother's glorified ideas of the past. She suspected that her Uncle Joe had really got into trouble down South, had probably taken funds along with the rest of them. She didn't blame him, she pitied him and she was tired of pity. The world was still full of young hopeful men, who like Uncle Joe, turned and twisted hoping for fortunes. All their good generous qualities were in danger of trapping them, not helping them, in a world where the plums went to the biggest thieves. Money, money, money makes the mare go, was one of her father's sayings that came from dear knows where. It was a kind of crime not to want money and only money, witness the way Jonathan's father was behaving. His hardness of heart froze the blood.

In the night she woke and lay very still longing to burst into tears. Jonathan had been blighted enough by his parents whose notions of success had become part of their boy. She was certain that his battle with his work was due to the parents and it gave her consolation to blame them. Her letters had been opened wilfully, an attorney had been put on their trail like a bloodhound. And what had they done? They had slept together. Why, it was enough to make anyone laugh and they should laugh, not let it gangrene their very vitals with hatred and bitterness. The parents weren't good enough; such energy should go somewhere. It should hit straight at the real enemy that had made the parents in the popular image. Even lying in bed, so angry and confused, a kind of tranquility came over her as she tried to piece out all she knew about the world and what was happening in it. Let the parents have their day, it would not last forever. George Gates had said it would not go on forever.

In the morning the two would look at one another. They would even laugh about it and there was always the garden and Jonathan could make another trip on the road in the fall. Now the season for a job was past. The young couple put their heads together and defied The Father. From that date on, Mr. Chance was The Father and Mrs. Chance The Mother, and the two together represented The Parents. They told The Parents that they were married and they wrote a long serious foolish youthful letter indignantly denying the charges and reiterating their belief in literature, life and love.

When The Parents received this letter, Mrs. Chance snorted. "I suppose you believe that," she said. Mr. Chance did not reply. He felt bitterly toward his wife and wished she had never told him what she knew. Jonathan had been his favorite, it was all spoiled.

"It don't know what to believe," he said in a tired voice.

"Just take him up on that," said Mrs. Chance. "Take him up and ask him if he's married to send on his license. I guess that will keep him guessing." She charged up and down the room as she spoke, everything in her seemed turning to water when she thought of her boy. And to such a shameless woman. A woman who wrote about past relations with other men. Yes, actually in black and white she had referred to these affairs and had had the effrontery to pretend that they had been nothing in comparison. Why, in a short time she would be telling that to a new man. That kind always tired. Unless she was after Jonathan for his money, or the money she fancied he would get. That was possible.

And then as if drawn by a magnet, she went upstairs and opened the drawer of her desk where she kept a copy of the letter she had secretly read. She drew it out, the copy was in her own firm familiar hand, but the words could never become quite familiar to her. Her eyes ran down the page, riveted on one passage, stopped and reread: "And it's as if I saw the world all new again. Like once when I was a child, very young, perhaps not yet five, and I got up early in the morning. I had never been up so early before. Mother and father were eating breakfast. The long shadows were on the house and road. There was dew over the grass and roses and I had never seen it before. In those days a boy used to drive the cows to pasture and a drove of cows came along, splashing in the soft dusty road, booing and pushing and the sun began slowly to rise higher. I can remember clear as day, the delight. Why, this is what early morning is like. That's it, my darling, the delight." When Mrs. Chance read this her very teeth scrunched together, she pushed the letter aside, muttering and troubled. Now and then doubt entered her mind about That Woman. But time would no doubt prove that she was right.

As for the young couple when they got Mr. Chance's insulting demand for the license, they scrunched the letter in rage and then laughed and finally got good and tight on cider brandy. Jonathan's work was almost a thing of the past. He hated to go upstairs and when he did, sat sullenly before his typewriter wanting to damage it. Who bought the damned books anyhow? What was the use of turning out any more fodder for people like his parents. The two young people were in a continual state of bile, wasted the whole day rambling over the country, talking to the farmers and when one began a hard luck story, they felt happy as if now they had company in misery. With the good milk bringing around three cents and selling in the city for eleven cents, who got the money? "You don't have to be a fortune teller to find out who gets it," said Mr. Blum. "I know I don't. I can't never break even, my place is running down, it's only the big fellows can be sure they got test-proof cattle. Where do I stand? Hey, I ask you, where?"

Well, where did *they* stand? They went back to the house but there was a comfort in not being surrounded by the rich and prosperous. When night came and lights began to show in kitchens, day closed on the same anxieties over all. Jonathan pulled his father's demand for a marriage license from the wastebasket where he had scrunched and thrown it angrily, sat down to his typewriter, wrote on the bottom of it,

"My wife and myself do not want to be further insulted. Your conduct has made my wife suffer a nervous shock that has forced me to put her under the doctor's care. Jonathan."

When Victoria read it she laughed uncertainly but it pleased her to have Jonathan defy his parents. "Oh Jonathan, that's not true," she said.

"It could be true. You don't eat, you've got circles under your eyes. If you were my mother it would be true. She'd be having doctors in to hold her hand. I don't care if it isn't. I'm tired of the whole business." All the same he did not feel heroic. They both felt humiliated and all their plans seemed shaken by being treated like bad children. Being a writer was not a noble game. To get the respect of his father he would have to make loads of money, write junk that he despised. When he went into his little room, he could not seem to make his mind work. If he had a Rolls-Royce and drew up in it before his father's house, what a kowtowing he would get. But when he needed help, he was treated like a criminal.

He finally shut the door to his little workroom, locked it and hid the key. He didn't think he wanted to open it for a long while. He was through with his father's world and he made up his mind that that world was dying. Joyce and Proust had said all that could be said for such a world. His mind's eye knew that the cue was buried in the very farms around him. He could realize the pattern, the system that was creating topheavy wealth for the few and misery for the many. It was just a mental conviction in him during the last of that summer and he began hunting around for books to substantiate himself. He got into arguments with Vicky. She was vague in her ideas but strong in her feelings. It was the other way around with him. The I.W.W. had been licked. Why? Where was the stream now? It must be there, under the surface. Through what channels was it working? He felt cut off, out in the country he began to realize that he really was on an island. The farmers were too patient, they trusted too much. He felt discouraged at his very first researches and went off on a sidetrack, just gassing and drinking with the farmers and the old characters who had given up the struggle and had holed in on some small patch of land with a gallon jug as consolation.

Sometimes when Jonathan turned up very late, wild eyed, Vicky had a terrible fear and premonition that he would end like Uncle Joe. One night when he did not come home until late she heard him stumbling up the steps of the back porch. He was trying to bring in a load of wood for the kitchen stove. It was a bright moonlight night and she was so glad to see him that all the reproaches she had been storing up for letting her worry, fell off and were nothing. As he saw her, he stumbled, his hat fell off, the wood spilled. He sat down with the wood, his face deathly pale, his eyes black. He couldn't speak. "You're tight," she began reproachfully.

"What of it?" he said. "Why not? As for the aristocracy of the mind, it's plain crap. The great minds are the great bunk. They made a miserable botch of the world, look at it, a lousy place." He began to cry, and she felt a kind of terror. What could she do to comfort him? He couldn't love her or he wouldn't feel so terrible.

There was something crazy about his sobs, she had a cold chilly reminder of Uncle Joe. "Don't Jonathan, please, please."

They leaned together on the steps, crying and holding to one another. "Everything will work out all right," she said cheerfully. Of course it would. They were young, strong, nothing could stop them.

That is, she thought, suddenly remembering Rosamond, nothing but death.

SHOT GUN WEDDING

When The Parents got Jonathan's brief retort, they hardly knew what move to make next. Mr. Chance's conscience began to prick. After all, the boy might be married; he was right when he accused his mother of never wanting him to marry, of being afraid to take her into his confidence. "Jonathan's got a few facts on his side," Mr. Chance pointed out. "You never did want him to marry."

"I was only thinking of his future," she said. "And of course when the right girl came along, it would be a different story." She bit her lip thinking hard. For the moment her son eluded them. Heavens, he might just ignore them, not try to get money again. "Abel," she said, "I think we ought to go right after this until we find out what is wrong. If he is married, all right. If not, he should marry or leave her. That kind of woman thinks nothing of stirring up scandal, she'd think herself justified in having a child and making a scene. You don't know what hot water is yet."

This new idea of a probable and terrible future dug into Mr. Chance's very marrow when he tried to sleep. What kind of a spectacle would that boy make of them all yet? And also, he might be wronging the boy. He was after all his flesh and blood, he would inherit property someday. Mrs. Chance kept at her husband and succeeded in starting him in their car toward the east. Stopping at the nicest tea rooms did not lessen the heavy outrage that turned Mr. Chance a bilious color and contorted Mrs. Chance's once amiable face into a hauteur. With an eyeglass swinging on a long chain she mentally focused That Woman with a scorching eye and the image she had conjured up of a dissolute creature with disordered hair, smoking of course, like as not continually in a red kimono, taunted her and at the same time gave her satisfaction. It would be a genuine pleasure to floor such a person, to show her up by her own gracious manners and she rehearsed her gracious manners and hoped she knew enough to keep tight hold of them no matter what the provocation.

When Jonathan Chance raised himself from the onion bed to see what car had stopped, he saw his mother stepping out and his father peering around the wheel at him. He dusted his hands on his overalls and came toward them, calling toward the house, "Oh Vicky, here's father and mother."

When his voice reached her upstairs, Vicky slid out of her large rather dirty apron and smoothing her hair, went down the stairs. The large handsome woman coming toward the house like a battleship did not relax as she shook hands, but Mr. Chance smiled uncertainly and with obvious relief. The girl looked thoroughly respectable and even quite nice. He had a moment of envy of his son, able to bamboozle such a girl. He was amazed and affronted at the unexpectedness of the situation.

"Your father would like to see the house," said Mrs. Chance, as if she expected to catch her son in another lie and unable to produce a house. Vicky opened the kitchen door with the nice new netting Jonathan had fastened in place himself. But the house smelled of flytox and, after a little sniff, Mrs. Chance elected to sit on the porch. They sat there, Mr. Chance rambling on about Uncle Megs and Aunt Hattie and everybody wondering when the demand for the marriage license would be made. When they were finally tired out, Mrs. Chance suggested they go to the village for a steak and stop on the way at the owner's house. She was really disappointed when the owner actually materialized and hardly knew where to begin the next attack. They ate the steak, on the porch, the house being out of the question and after the meal Mr. Chance quietly took himself off to the garden. Vicky gave Jonathan a poke and he disappeared upstairs. In the room above he could hear the two women having it out below. Vicky was crying. His mother was crying. Strange and horrifying, the two women were crying in a kind of mutual sympathy he could not understand. He sat with his head in his hands and could hear Vicky tell his mother that he had always loved his parents but they had wanted to dictate his life to him.

"Oh, we never cared what he did, so long as he was respectable," his mother was saying and the way she said the word, wringing it out of her heart, was as if it held all the virtues and all the good in life. Vicky was silent and it was very quiet. Suddenly he heard her coming upstairs. He raised his face and sat waiting. "Shall I just kick them out?" he said. "Tell them to go and let us alone?"

"No," Vicky said. "I've told her we are married and the license is in New York with my things. I guess that will end it." They kissed each other and went downstairs together. Mrs. Chance was attempting to act natural and sociable and had called Mr. Chance in from the garden. He was standing amiably hoping he would not be called on to say anything. No one said anything and they talked about houses. The Parents implied that a House was a fine proposition and everyone should own a home. Jonathan no longer was interested and looked tired and anxious. It was late afternoon before they got rid of the parents. They were going to drive to New York.

The young couple were exhausted. In the midst of it, the Blum boy had come over and asked if Jonathan could please come help pa with the cow. When he got to the barn, Blum was sweating and anxious. "I owe the vet and he won't come till I pay him. Besides we can do this. Just let's get this down her throat." He had the medicine ball ready and thrust his arm down. The cow's bloated sides heaved and panted. The two men sat with the animal, warming blankets, rubbing her legs. When it was dark they lit the lantern. Mrs. Blum peered in the door with her drawn anxious face. "Is she going?"

"We'll save her, mamma, don't worry," said Blum. The entire family came out one by one, the old grandma, the kids, they stood in the door looking and hoping. The cow was about all they had, where could they get another? When she finally seemed better, it was near midnight. They went into Blum's kitchen for a drink of wine and now that the cow was saved the man and wife were smiling and happy. "I'll give you some cheese next week," said Mrs. Blum. "That cow gives rich good milk. She makes fine cheese." They all nodded and smiled and the business of the afternoon was like a bad dream.

When he reached home Vicky pounced on him. Only think those dreadful parents had phoned to the store and Joe Riegel brought the message. She had gone to the store, had talked to The Father, The Parents had got no further than Allentown, had decided that they wanted to see the license and requested the two meet them in New York the next day.

"Now what will we do?" said Jonathan. He hated being further humiliated, having his mother say triumphantly, "I told you so. Another of Jonathan's lies." A horrible disgust of the whole business made them long to run away. "If they had a few sick cows to worry over they wouldn't stew around about us," said Jonathan in a sour voice. "And anyhow they don't care a damn about us, they never left a penny and they know we are broke, all they think of is their precious respectability. Let's just pay no attention to them."

He looked at Vicky hopefully. He knew before she spoke that she wouldn't agree. "That would settle nothing," she said. "We can't do that. It's not a question of deceiving your parents. We aren't really deceiving them. We told them we were married and to all intents and purposes we are." She looked at him solemnly and he waited. He lit a cigarette and felt unaccountably nervous. His mother had left one of her handkerchiefs on the table and its whiteness, its lace edging and the precise folds, so different from Vicky's little handkerchiefs of cheap stuff, washed out by hand and almost never ironed, angered him. He picked it up and holding it toward Vicky said, "A handkerchief. That's all they care for me."

"We told them we were married," said Vicky, "and we should stick to it. We could have a paper. We could have signed it ourselves. We could even have witnesses. Cora would witness it. We could date it back, at least to the time when we first came to the country. I remember I knew a girl who got married that way, I don't know why." The whole idea as they talked about it seemed silly but they had got themselves into a tangle, they felt all around them obligations that they had never wanted, that were somehow obscuring their real struggle, but the idea that he might really be able to face his parents with a paper pleased Jonathan. It pleased them both.

"They want a paper. All right, we'll give them one." They took the early train to the city, made out the paper. Cora and Esther signed and with the brief statement the two called upon The Parents at their hotel. The Father was in a gay mood and when the paper was handed him smiled a little.

"I have to explain," said Jonathan. "This is not a regular license, but it's as legal as one. It's what is called a contract marriage." As he said it, in the presence of his well dressed parents in their handsome suite of rooms, he felt suddenly ashamed and hated them and wished Vicky wore a more elegant dress. But she stood proudly enough looking straight at The Parents and wearing the old locket and ring that had been in her family. Even The Mother noticed the beautiful locket. She was glad to see that the girl probably came of good family.

The Father was calm about the document and looked at it carefully. Jonathan, who had consulted a friend in the law, now added, "To make it fully legal we should have had a signature of a Judge of the Superior Court but we couldn't get to town before, we didn't have the money." With this he hoped they would be satisfied. That something had been left undone was enough for The Parents. They had their hats on, a taxicab called, and before the miserable young people could extricate themselves they were whirled to the down-town building and found themselves in a queue outside the door behind which some judge sat who would undoubtedly refuse and humiliate them.

As they waited, The Mother walked Vicky up and down, making little sympathetic remarks in an effort to draw her out and later betray her. Jonathan, pale and bored, wondered why he had ever let himself get into such a mess. When two hours passed, the young people deliberately withdrew and left The Parents to face it out alone. They took a cab with money given by The Father.

"He's going to pay our expenses, so let's have a good time for once," said Jonathan. They drove up to The Brevoort and took a room, suddenly enchanted at being in the city and having a chance to have breakfast in bed. They kept away from the hotel all evening, went out with friends, drank, laughed, talked loudly and excitedly about the future, analyzed the Russian revolution and the future of art and civilization, listened to a long account of the Passaic strike from a young man who had been arrested for picketing. Jonathan looked at this young man with envy. The story of the strike made the battle with his parents seem puny. He thought of them somewhere in the city, probably worrying and fretting about the marriage license. They would be discussing solemnly changes in their Will. When the young man described the battle with the police, Jonathan saw it all and wished he had been there instead of in the country carrying on a foolish feud with The Parents.

But when they left their friends and went back to the hotel feeling pleasure at the good bed awaiting them, they found numerous memoranda to call The Parents. The Parents were called. Vicky sat yawning on the bed. What was the matter now? The matter was that the judge had refused to sign, that the Corporation Counsel had been called in, that all the heads available had got together, that they couldn't figure out what was the matter with The Young People, that it must be that Vicky was already married and trying to commit bigamy, that in short, The Young People would have to cut out the foolishness and go to the regular bureau tomorrow and be married decently with no more monkey business or else The Will would be changed. Their so-called marriage was nothing better than commonlaw. Did Vicky want to be a commonlaw wife?

They shouted with laughter, then got sober as judges.

All the brightness of the evening vanished. "My God," said Jonathan, "is this never going to end? They make us feel such fools, how will we ever do anything again?"

They had been wrong to put themselves in The Parents' power. But what a temptation it had been to get a little help. The whole senseless accumulation that was now embodied in The Will taunted The Young Couple. Jonathan was for telling The Parents to go about their business. "You've always had money, you don't know what it is to be poor," said Vicky. "Even when you were earning money, it wasn't the same. If you got sick, you knew your father would take care of you. If you chuck The Parents over, all that security will be gone. We shouldn't just be romantic. We should try to be smart. After all, we don't care about the license, really. And if they cut you from the Will, you'd begin to resent me."

"No, I wouldn't," said Jonathan, resentfully. He felt tied and crushed by the events. The easy calm reasoning that had been his during the evening was gone. He felt it was absolutely wrong to let The Parents get the upper hand but if he refused, Vicky would think he didn't want to marry her. That wasn't it at all. He wanted to be free, there was no freedom if his folks thought they could run his life. If they won now, they would always win. He felt it in his bones.

But Vicky's advice sounded so practical that when morning came they found themselves escorted by The Parents to the Marriage License Bureau. Standing before the city clerk, pale and sullen, the two answered the ritual indifferently. The smiling Father and the grim Mother stood behind the two, like batteries of guns.

When the Young Couple got back to the hotel they took their marriage license and tore it into little pieces, flushed it down the toilet, watching the particles sucked out of sight without relief. No, that wouldn't end it. They felt defeated and humiliated and Jonathan got tighter than he had ever been before in his life.

Every Christian ought to observe Rogation Days, since such observance helps to increase the sense of dependence on God. I wish everybody could be in Spain on a Rogation Day and be fascinated by the charm and the beauty and the poetry of the processions that go out from the little villages. Writers with a good deal of truth call attention to the monotony and drudgery of American farm life. I am sure the festivities of what in England they call "gang days"—the processions into the fields—would do a great deal to relieve some of this and would add the picturesque, certainly the needed element in the farmer's life.

"Turn that damned thing off, turn it off," and the little boy scraping his bare toes along the floor turned off the radio, the only thing that was any fun any more. "Turn it off, I say," and he looked up frightened at his father, rubbing his hand in his eye. "I turned it off," he said. "What's the matter here?" The mother frowned at the father. He was trembling all over, putting his trembling hands into his overall pockets. "I told him to turn it off, if I hear another crack out of that thing," he raised his hand as if to strike.

"Now shush, it ain't so bad. Why there's been a big black cloud back of the barn all morning. It's apt to rain any minute. I was out sniffing the air, and it doesn't smell so dusty. Seems kind of clear and fresh."

"I tell you if rains don't come tomorrow, I'll shoot them cows," said the husband, glaring at his wife.

"Oh come now, it'll rain maybe. Don't let's talk of it. I got a nice pie I'm making."

"I don't know whatever of," he said.

"Well I ain't decided yet. But I remember my mother telling about pies she made on the Dakota prairies. Out of any old thing. A molasses pie is the tastiest pie I every saw but I ain't got no more. A brown sugar pie is nice. If I had dried apples even I could make a wonderful pie."

"Once we had strawberry pie," said the boy.

"You remember that pie? I'll make you another, don't you cry, I'll make another someday." They had moved out to the back door, slowly inevitably as if pulled by magnets. The great copperish fields were pulling them, they were lying bald and angry with tufts of sour dust whirling in spikes of revengeful horns. A long painful moo weak and blasted made an echo that sounded like a horn blown a long way off. The three listened to it, looking around a little wildly but there was nowhere they could go to escape that cry. The wind would carry it straight to them on any part of the farm. The wind was blowing off the fine top soil, it had blown away the seeds, blighted with wrath all the turnips and garden greens. When it got through with the soil, it would begin with them, and no one would prevent it. It was helping the powers that be. It was destroying crops, animals, life.

"You put that radio on again and by god," but the father did not mean to strike his boy. His hand just fell to his side. The kid looked up sniffling a little. The bare foot of the boy touched the bare foot of the father. The father turned and started to smile. He'd worked that land and plowed it and tended it like a baby. Now it was being scorched in an oven. The crops were frying like eggs. All over the west the pebbles were hot as baking stones. You could cook in the naked grass. The birds were deserting. They were deserting in clouds to make room for the grasshoppers.

"Don't you worry," says the misses, "I'm going to make you a pie, I don't know out of what but out of something."

"You're damned right I ain't worrying. This land will raise us a crop or we'll know the reason why. We ain't going to starve. I'll guarantee you that. There's money in this country, we been sending it east out of the west for a long time. Let them bring out the food, if they got so damned much of it. They got so much they didn't want what we could make. Don't bother, they says, we got enough. Plow it up. Kill them pigs. We got too much food in the world. All right bring on your too much, is what I say. Let them fill our bread basket, as they seem to have so much in their own."

"I'll make you a pie with tomatoes in it," she said. "They ain't all gone yet."

"Let them bring it on," he says, savagely. The sky was brightening. Over all those states it brightened. Then clouds came. There was no rain. There was wind and it smelled sometimes like the desert.

BITTER END

Anne Wendel had no idea of the turmoil that was going on in Pennsylvania. She was in hot water with her sister Hortense and a stubborn fight was going on between them. Even if Anne had been able to lay hands on the money, she would not have felt justified in meeting her sister's demands. Her sister's demands were unjust and they were so far from sisterly that every organ in her body seemed to bleed when she read the letters from that woman's pen. They might have been written with vitriolic acid. Where did such enmity come from?

Anne Wendel could think of nothing else. Grief took the heart out of her. She sat for hours in a chair looking out the bay window, seeing her life, herself as a mere child kept from school to pedal the sewing machine so that the boys of the family would have a chance in the world. The long years at Grapeville when all their energies and all their cash had dribbled out to help the boys out of trouble, to give them a start. Then her married life, one long struggle with the natural joys of a mother and wife always scarred by worry and anxiety. Now she was to be cheated at the end of her days by injustice and bitterness.

It was right she should have more of the proceeds than Hortense. She had done all the work, spent weeks with her lame leg scratching away at the lots, getting red and exhausted helping the men burn brush, rake, tidy up. She had had the responsibility of the whole project, Hortense had stayed in Roseland with folded hands, so to speak, waiting for the golden egg to drop into her lap. It was bitterly unfair and worse, so unsisterly, to begrudge her the money.

In vain she tried to imagine how nice it would be when the future payments on the lots would be made, when she might have a little car and drive around. Hortense owned a car. Everyone was owning cars. They bought them on installments. The whole country was installment crazy. Other people had victrolas and radios. She had never had one. She had been content to live along, surely it was not right to begrudge her a few years of ease. She wanted to go back to the country where Vicky now lived, to visit the old landmarks, to take joy in her daughter and her husband.

Sometimes she had a pain in the pit of her stomach as if she had swallowed a knife. It began when the astonishing letters from Hortense first began to arrive. She had to keep quiet, gently sipping hot water; and her father's old diaries of the trip he had made to the rich luscious country of early Wisconsin distracted her and helped her to an old pride. She made up her mind she would go to New Glarus and see the town that had started on the site he had helped select. But the letters from her sister came like blows. Before she could help herself, she was really sick.

"It's time to stop that foolishness," said Amos. "You girls write your Uncle David he's got to put an end to Hortense and her mad dog ways. Why, they want to kill mamma." He stood looking in the door at his wife, suddenly frightened that she might die. He had never thought of the possibility of Anne's dying first. He was the older, he had kept up insurance all his life to protect her, what good would that do her if she died?

When news reached Roseland, Oregon, even Hortense relented; she had a sudden fright and wrote her sister a long letter about the water cure and keeping the bowels open. David wrote a letter about symptoms of his own and gave her an invitation to come to God's country and get well again. "It won't cost you a cent," he said. "Just say the word."

Anne Wendel did not feel the gratitude that she should at the invitation. Why had it come now, when she could not move hand or foot? Still David had been a warm and loving brother. She had to believe it, she could not bear to lie there and feel the old family ties all disrupted and sour. Mem would writhe in her grave if she knew that petty quarrels about money were tearing them apart.

She kept her mind fixed on the past, on the wonderful trip David had paid for back in 1904 when the children were so small and they had all gone to the coast in a carryall with horses and slept in tents. She made Nancy bring her the big sea shell and lay in bed with her ear to the shell, the way she used to as a child, pretending the roar was the sound of waves. It distracted her and helped her to remember her children as little ones, running in and out of the waves with their tiny feet, shouting, happy and strong. She sat up and tried to write her brother but her writing was wavering and feeble, the hand of a woman shockingly old.

David Trexler took to his bed with his symptoms and he was anything but a good patient. His food bolted up on him, he began to pour with blood. When he saw the blood in the basin, his blue eyes popped. He felt doomed. He was already convinced that Anne would not get well. The blood sent him into a frenzy. He was furious that he could not tame life as he had wealth and his children. He sat up in bed, angry, his back stiff. When the door opened, he had a nervous tremor. His hand jerked up like a traffic cop's. Stop, death. When Ella tried to come into his room with little timid ways and attentions he roared at her, "Keep away from me. Let me alone. All I ask is time to make my will. Just get out of here and give me the same privilege that an animal has of dying in peace." Nobody could get near him except Sue.

With her father's illness a secret understanding seemed between the raging parent and his child. He let her sit by the bed, hold his hand. His yellow eyeballs rolled at her, he moaned, made a baby of himself. She didn't wince, just sat there, quietly, talking to him. "Now father, you'll be better."

"Won't," he said stubbornly. "Just do me a favor. Keep those females out. Let me alone, tell them to give me air. That's my last wish. Bring me an attorney, get him here, I have to make a will." In his will he determined to do right by everybody. He had the feeling that if he could make a will and do right by everyone, by his sons and Sue and his sister Anne, then he might be allowed to get well.

The doctors could not seem to diagnose his complaint. He refused to be X-rayed, bellowed and howled when he could not eat. He kept the house in an uproar. But he got well. He actually pulled out of it. The will was made. Everything was in order. He went to sleep and came out of the sleep smiling like a child, asking for a little weak tea and toast. When he had gobbled the food, he waited for the nausea and the blood. But nothing happened. It was all a dream that he would die. He would live. In a few days he was dressed, bustling around. Why, with the market on the up and up there was time to do even better. He could leave even a more astounding piece of property. He would be the talk of the town.

Even the telegram announcing that Anne Wendel had suddenly died did not quench his new thirst for life and power. He drooped for days, appeared red-eyed at meals, bullied Ella and Millie and had long confidential chats with Sue about his boyhood and how good Anne had been to him, but inwardly his spirit did not flinch at this death. He himself was miraculously alive. And he had been cute enough to back Wall Street when the La Follette scare pushed stocks down.

When Jonathan and Victoria Chance returned to the country after the bout with The Parents, everything was changed. They could no longer feel content and in fact, there was no money in sight to give them a feeling of security about anything. The grocery bill was bigger than anything Jonathan could hope to make with his typewriter in the near future. He wasn't going to write pulp. If it came to making money there were hundreds of ways. He could go on the road again. When Vicky tried to keep him from drinking he had the sharp feeling she wanted to dominate him as his mother had done. But when they were in bed together, the feeling washed away, he was ashamed of his suspicion. Sometimes she was in tears at his reproaches and wildness, a frightened look came into her eyes but she quickly tried to hide it.

They locked up the house, stored their bits of furniture, trailed to town. Time had been lost, the good jobs were gone for that season. they scurried around, piled themselves and their suitcases in a rented room, took jobs clerking in stores, waiting on the Christmas trade.

Vicky in the toy department and Jonathan in books, could do no more than pay their rent, buy their food, hope for something to turn up. When nothing turned up but word of Anne Wendel's serious illness, Vicky was frantic. "I've got to have money, Jonathan, I must go to mother. She's really ill, she keeps asking for me."

Driven by the urge, Jonathan tried his best to raise money. Nobody had any. A measly twenty dollars wouldn't get Vicky far. He was ashamed of her reproachful face. In her despair she called him names for not being smarter about his parents. "Why did you let them go without getting help? We did what they wanted. Then they clear out. They don't care if we live or die. You should have struck up a bargain. It's shameful."

It was shameful to have Vicky so bitter. He spent an evening composing a letter, taunted by a premonition of certain failure. Many a time he had said that, regardless of anything, his father would come to the rescue in case of illness. Perhaps it would be simpler now to say Vicky was ill, needed a doctor's care. He wrote a vivid letter, feeling horrible to have to come around his father begging. But when the reply came, enclosing ten dollars and asking for the name of Vicky's doctor and advising him to get a responsible job where he could support his wife and pay his debts, the dam burst.

Vicky flung out of the house and came back at midnight, very pale. "Here it is," she said. "I took up a collection from everyone I know. Tell your father to eat his money. Tell him to choke." When she looked at Jonathan's white face she burst into tears. She wrapped her arms around him and rocked him as if he were the injured one.

"We'll get better jobs," she said. "We'll save every cent. We'll begin again. I was wrong to believe in your people. You were right. We should have thumbed our noses. I see it now." But all the way out to Iowa on the train she could not get over The Father and his hardness of heart. She felt hard and as if she had swallowed something that would never digest. She still felt hard when she reached Oxtail, took a cab to the house, and surprised them all as they sat in a hushed terrible calm, downstairs, waiting for Anne Wendel to die.

Anne Wendel had been struggling all that night to keep from sinking into unconsciousness so she could look her girl in the eyes with a clear mind. She was troubled about her swollen face and insisted on hot cloths that might reduce the swelling. She lay there fainting and dizzy, stubbornly holding the cloths to her face so that her poor child would not be terror stricken when she saw the change in her mother. When Vicky looked at her mother she tried to see nothing but her blue eyes that steady and loving looked out of their swellings. The mother gripped her daughter's hand, in her warm rich voice she asked about the farm, about the jobs in the city.

She tried to talk, "When I get my money out of the lots," she said, "I can help you." Suddenly tears came into her eyes, she let the girl's wrist fall. She could see in Vicky's face that swift tragic look that meant she was going to die. She had felt all along she would die but time and again strength surged back, it was all a fancy, she would get well. They would have a few nice years. They could get rid of the White Elephant, go to Florida, buy a little place and live in the sunshine. But how childish all such ideas were. She felt ashamed of her sudden tears and blinking said with her thick tongue, "It's my eyes, they seem to bother me. I ate something the other day that brought on all this, I was getting better and this had to come along." She looked searchingly at her daughter and felt as she lay there that it was no use trying to fool her.

"You'll be better soon," said Vicky in a timid voice. She couldn't bring herself to tell the lie easily. Her mother's sharp eyes seemed to make fun of such pretenses. Yet the whole household was busy keeping up the illusion that she would get well. Day and night they tried to wrench her back from unconsciousness so she would suffer. Mrs. Stauffer came from her farm and her big strong frame put fresh life in the place. But she resented Mrs. Wendel. Deep in her heart she resented the mother of her son Jerry's wife. She thought Mrs. Wendel should resign herself, should let herself go. To hear her, you would think life was attached to a cord, you had only to pull it, it would loosen from the human frame and float free as a bird.

During the hours of waiting, she and Vicky stood on the front porch. The streets were paved now, not like the days when they used to watch the buggies go by to the fair and their mother had thought nothing of ironing the dresses and brushing the hair of her four little girls, packing the big lunch basket and then staggering out to the fair grounds for a brief attempt at a day's pleasure. All the trouble had been nothing to her. She had not spared herself and Mrs. Stauffer did not know why she begrudged the poor woman a few last painful breaths. Her own sister had not died like that, she had fought a good fight. When it was useless, she had folded her hands. "Sing a song to me, mother," she had said, and their tiny old mother had lain down on the bed beside her, had taken her in her arms and had sung the old lullaby. That was the proper way to die. And she had trouble too concealing her impatience at the way Anne Wendel's daughters seemed to hang on to her old bones, to her disappearing flesh.

"It's the young I'm sorry for," she said, her eyes burning. "It's not her, but Rosamond I'm thinking of." She thought if Rosamond had lived she might still have her son. Now he was far away, he was strange, never wrote and, when he did, had impatience for her trials with the renters on the farm. They could not pay rent, she accused them of being lazy, of wasting things. If her struggles had not got her the right to ease at the end of life, what were they for?

Amos Wendel, who had taken pride in everything his wife did, took pride in her dying. Her demands for food widened his eyes, made him chuckle, like the pranks of an overly bright child. From her bed Mrs. Wendel could see the doorway and room filling and emptying with useless people. A nurse in a white apron made her appearance and gave her pleasure. So, they were watching out for her, they were doing it right. But what about Hortense, what would she suffer when she heard the news?

In her pain she could not forget her sister who had betrayed her, who had forgotten all their long life of blood sisterhood. No, she should be punished, coals of fire should be heaped on her head. "Do

Hortense justice," she said faintly and Amos stooping to listen, repeated, looking around at the others with a proud nod. See, she thinks of everything. She should hate her sister and she talks of justice. He could not get over it and talked with Vicky who, of the three girls, was holding up remarkably well.

Vicky wanted to put her arms around her father but the hard cold undigested lump of feeling would not let her. She felt impatient at his pathetic face with the pouches under the eyes and the tiny tears. The roots of his life were being torn up and she could stand there, unable to do more than repeat like a parrot, "Yes, Papa, I know, Papa, yes I know."

When the electric fan whirred upstairs with a loud buzz of some trapped bottle fly, she wanted to rush up, to turn it off, to shake an indignant fist in the nurse's smug wailing face, "Can't you let her alone, why do you want to revive her, can't you let her die in peace?" But she had to grit her teeth, hand out coffee; to keep herself busy she washed and ironed, she cooked and scrubbed.

Mrs. Stauffer came every day, and now and then stomped down the stairs carrying sheets that were unquestionably burned in the furnace. The filthy business of dying contaminated them all. A puppy was bumped by a passing car, his yelps brought them all to the door, their faces contorted. "Can't they put the poor creature out of his misery?" Nancy moaned and no one could believe that the dog had not been mortally struck, that it was at that moment scrambling to its feet, licking itself, hobbling away.

"Listen," Mrs. Stauffer said taking Vicky into the pantry. Her voice trembled. "This is a hard thing to ask but someone has got to speak to your mother, to tell her to let go, she's holding on for dear life and soon she'll suffer. She's not now but the morphine won't take soon, the nurse says." She bolstered herself, her strong face looked dragged down, the skin empty of flesh. "You speak to her, Vic, you'll know what to say."

Yes, speak to her, tell her to die. Easy. It should be easy. Take a good stiff drink of the brandy that that nurse sucks up like water. Now then. She charged up the stairs and at the door the nurse met her with rubber gloves. She put the big gloves on automatically, went toward the bed.

"Here's your daughter Vicky," yelled the nurse as if Anne Wendel were deaf. "Here's your dear girl." Vicky looked straight at her mother who was struggling in her welter of swollen inflamed flesh. She looked at her mother softly and the hard lump inside melted. "Don't struggle so," she said gently, as if to a child. "Go to sleep." She waited a minute, took a deep breath, looked again at the eyes that looked back at her like far-off points of intense pinpoint blue light. "Go to sleep, it's easy. It happens to the birds, the grass, to us all. Just sleep."

"Go to Jesus," babbled the nurse, "Jesus is calling."

At the vulgar words Mrs. Wendel shook her head slowly, heavily, denying, the heavy tears squeezed from her eyes and soaked into her cheeks. "Never mind, mother," said Vicky, "never mind. *We* know." She gazed at her intently, feverishly as if the two could communicate in that moment all they ever knew. "We know." The mother sighed, shut her eyes obediently like a child, as if she had been waiting for some command. Then she looked at her daughter, gazing at her, yes, she was looking for the last time. She tried to talk, words came. "What does she say?" said Vicky. "What was it?" She strained nearer, her hands in the rubber gloves huge and grotesque on the white cover.

"She says, you're my sunshine," said the nurse bawling out the words cheerfully. Thank God, her patient was shutting her eyes, she hoped she'd make no more trouble; why, she never saw such an old volcano.

"Poor mamma," they were all crying but pity could not help her. Now when it was too late Hortense sent boxes of flowers, Uncle David a blanket of roses; friends who had no more than a speaking acquaintance stood around the grave.

VI. THE FUTURE BELONGS
TO THEM

VICTORIA WENDEL returned to her husband with the silver teapot that had been a gift from Uncle Joe, her mother's favorite brother. Her traveling bag bulged with its weight and bumped against her legs as she climbed the five flights to their apartment. Jonathan was about to sit down to a little meal he had fixed for himself. "Why didn't you let me know you were coming?" he said.

"I wanted to surprise you," said Victoria. She felt shy of him; even the kisses didn't take the shyness away. "I thought maybe you weren't coming back," said Jonathan, "you were so mad at me when you left."

"I know," said Vicky settling down and taking half of the omelet. There was a bottle of red wine and cheese. The room looked very bare with its simple bed, table, and few chairs, not to count the bookshelves that Jonathan had built himself. "It's nice to be home," she went on. "I'm sorry I was so mean," she said.

"You weren't mean, I was just helpless, that's all," said Jonathan with a new kind of bitterness. "I might as well realize I

310

can never expect any help from my father. Not for what we want to do. Those kind of people only help you to their kind of world. They want to perpetuate it and they hate anyone who won't play their game." He broke off a bit of cheese and put it on bread, poured some wine into his glass. "I began eating here to save money," he said modestly. "And I'm not going to get so tight any more. We've got to get out of this."

All that winter he said, "We've got to get out of this." He said it on Sunday mornings when after a Saturday night of drinking he had forgot his promise not to get tight any more. He would wake in the big dim room where sunlight never came except for a few minutes every day, lie still watching sun on the wall of the apartment opposite. Vicky with her arm thrown back was still asleep. Her childish face looked pale and had a hurt look that he resented. She would open her eyes, look at him reproachfully. He couldn't bear the reproach. He wanted her to be as she was when they first met. Laughing and crazy about him, not scared. Lately she had a timid scared look when he wanted to celebrate. He shouldn't want to celebrate. There was nothing to celebrate except that they weren't starving. They had enough in their bellies, it was only their spirits that seemed to be battered to death.

He wasn't the only one. Tolman came back from Europe with a hunted look. He stayed only long enough to get money from his father and to make arrangements about his future. The evening he spent at the Chance apartment was not so much of a success. Tolman was inclined to patronize his old friend. He had been sitting in cafés for several years, knew Ezra Pound and had sat behind James Joyce at a recital of George Antheil's music. He told with great effect about Joyce coming in very quietly and sitting just ahead of him. "Another guy I know was next me," said Tolman. "He didn't like the music, kept saying to me, it's lousy. But when Joyce raised both hands, see like this," illustrating, "and began clapping, this guy began pounding too, and yelling bravo, bravo." He paused significantly as Jonathan began laughing his long silent laugh, slapping his knee. "I could tell you who that was, but I don't think I should, he's a very well known person."

"Oh, come on," said Jonathan. "No," said Tolman, "I better

not." He sipped his wine. His thin intelligent face tilted to the wine glass and he half shut his eyes. "Not bad," he said, "but you should taste the real thing, a real Burgundy for instance is good, but of course there are much better wines than that, at least to my taste." Jonathan was sitting with drooped head. He felt completely out of it.

"Aw come on, Tolman, you ought to tell us who that guy was," he said. Vicky looked sharply at Tolman. She disliked him for making them feel out of the picture. What had he written? Nothing, he just talked about it. Jonathan had written. He had even gotten into trouble about it. His folks blamed him and called it smutty stories. She was wondering if Tolman was not something of a fake.

"Well, Jonathan, if I told you I'd feel like a skunk, gossip would get started, and soon it would get back to me." He was turning over in his mind whom he should name. He would be glad to name someone but the truth was, that the young man was himself. He had heard the story since that time a dozen times and he himself was the hero. He knew it for a good story and thought it showed what a broad minded fellow he was to appreciate it. But he didn't want to tell Jonathan, who might not see it in its proper perspective. He turned the talk to Antheil's music. But he continued to treat his friend with a certain aloofness. He was jealous of Jonathan's appearance in a magazine with such illustrious names. It meant much more to him than it had ever meant to Jonathan. He thought of himself as Jonathan's benefactor and he resented the kind of independence Jonathan showed.

Jonathan couldn't resist showing off his friend. He invited all their own friends who were stuck in advertising and publishing jobs. They came loaded with expensive hooch and sat around envying Tolman.

Tolman said the old realism was dead. The old language was dead. The old literature was dead. It was all dead. People like Joyce were creating a new world of language.

One of the advertising men said he couldn't understand a word of it. "I don't know what he's talking about," said the fellow miserably, at the same time trying to give the impression that if he didn't understand there was probably nothing there to understand.

"I could read you some of it, you shut your eyes, listen, it's all sound, when you listen long enough, a real meaning comes out of it." He shut his own eyes and with the air of a priest turned his head listening. Even Jonathan was embarrassed at the pose of his friend. He coughed and said that he had read Ulysses so many times he almost knew it by heart.

"But the last part, that nighttime monologue of Mrs. Bloom's, that's the most marvelous thing," said one of the girls rolling her eyes. She just wants the men to think she's pretty hot herself, thought Vicky. Nine chances out of ten, the girl did not know what it was all about. A kind of bitter doubt seemed to have settled over the room. But it immediately got gay again when Jonathan began reciting "The man is standing there."

> Mamma the man is standing there,
> Mamma the man is standing there,
> Mamma the man is standing there
> A man *is* standing there.
> Mamma, the man is standing there.

And when he came to the end where the elephants went bumping together his voice became positively inspired. The beautiful words filled them all with the ecstasy of the jungle. The elephants go walking . . . bumping together . . . bumping . . . bumping. The hollow bumps shaking the forest shook them all.

"Drink up," said Jonathan, pouring drinks wildly. "Here, what's the matter with you guys, drink up." They drank up and someone brought in a borrowed victrola and played some Argentina tangos. They tangoed, they danced, they improvised, and Jonathan danced and spun alone, clearing the room by his agile steps, until they sat down, on the bed, on the floor, and his feet twisted and turned on a dime and his white face was as intent as a chalk mark on a blackboard. His fingers clicked clicking a challenge to his friend Tolman who remarked that Jonathan reminded him of a character out of a sur-realist play. Jonathan stopped. Everybody uncurled and looked for glasses. "What does this remind you of?" said

Vicky maliciously pouring drink into Tolman's glass. She was getting tired of his Paris allusions. Could nothing remind him of what it was in itself! Always something had to be like something else.

Now the party was breaking up into knots. She felt on the outside, a domestic woman, pouring drinks. Listening. Tolman was holding forth again. He was now contradicting himself. He said words must be rediscovered for their own uses, they must be refound in their native significance. He struggled to make himself clear. Words should be used with the precision of tools, delicately and surely.

"And for what purpose," said Jonathan. "Include that, Herr Professor."

"Why to reveal the inner reality, of course, to unfold the inner consciousness of the mind, that works in the dark and does not know itself."

"Balls," said a voice, but everyone turned to look with disapproval at the speaker who retired to the toilet in chagrin.

Six glasses were broken, wine was spilled on the cover of the bed. Everyone except Tolman left feeling thoroughly inferior and stupid. Tolman bid his friend an affectionate farewell. "I couldn't live in this country any more," he said. "Life's too short. It's a bloody battle here, too raw." Jonathan envied Tolman his experience but he stuck by his guns. "Oh I don't know," he said. "We have to have roots, even for writing and it'll be bloody enough anywhere before long from all I hear. All that you say is right but it's all wrong, too."

Tolman did not even bother to ask an explanation. He yearned for civilization and went down the steps feeling a lucky fellow. Poor Jonathan had brains but they would corrupt in such a life, they would be eaten by worms. He thought of his own brains in a precious chalice and while a few years back he had contemplated using those brains for creative uses, he was now beginning to ask himself if, after all, the most useful function in the present civilization was not tending the altar, as it were. It was not only the Holy Ghost, it was the altar cloth, the incense, the waving censer that was responsible for the perpetuation of the great religions. The great literatures also must have their attendants who could wisely pass the wafer of the communicant. He was, however, dissatisfied with the communicants of that evening's gathering. He was, in fact, sick of America.

Jonathan and Victoria swept up the glasses and by that time were completely indifferent about the wine spotted bedcover. They crawled into bed, overslept, and were late to work. Coming home that night Jonathan bought a copy of a yachting magazine and while waiting for Vicky to come home looked at the beautiful pictures of lovely boats cutting through the water. They were all owned and earmarked by persons of wealth but as he sat there he couldn't see why he and Vicky couldn't have just a very little one, say a twenty footer, a double-ender because they were surefire sailors and took any sea, and they could make a trip. He could almost smell the sea breeze and, when Saturday came, he went to the shipchandler shops near the Battery and came home with charts of the coast of New England. "We've got to get away," he said that night. "We simply have to get away."

Well, they could go away when summer came but where would they be then. They couldn't live in a boat, they couldn't fish for a living. The sea was choked with too many fishermen who couldn't make a living.

"Listen," said Jonathan, "maybe we won't settle anything by going away but if I don't get away—" He got up, paced the room. He looked hunted. "What do we live for? You had to pay dentist bills, gas bills, rent last week. It nearly cleaned us out. I tell you we have to beat this game. Got to." He looked so wild eyed that Vicky again had that curious stirring of fear. He was like her Uncle Joe, he made her think not of Uncle Joe, whom she had never seen, but of the mental image she had made of an Uncle Joe who had finally lost his mind.

The next minute Jonathan was walking the floor again. "Let's look at it straight if we can. We can play the game everybody thinks they will play who doesn't like business. Lots of people like it. Those who don't or who like other things more, kid themselves, they say, oh I'll make some money and then quit. They never do.

Or if they do they do, they're only lucky. They live on islands in a sea of people struggling to keep heads out of water."

Sometimes at night when, very late, they would decide to take a long walk, they would feel all around them the push of the city, cars, subways yammering underfoot, skyscrapers yelling to the heavens. They would push along with their arms locked together, building a bulwark of their plans.

"We can get a boat or we can go to the country, which shall it be?" said Jonathan. "A boat would cost next to nothing." Victoria knew these next to nothings. All the same, she was game for a boat even if she couldn't swim. They made trips to the water fronts and stood watching the brutes of ferries, the big liners, the tiny craft plowing their straight and narrow paths. Up above the tall buildings they sometimes sought for the north star and imagined their tiny boat in a vast waste of water with no other guide than that star.

When they came back to the apartment, often very late, the silver teapot had an ugly way of standing out conspicuously from the top of bookshelves. It glittered in the simple room like an evil warning. Now and then Vicky had letters from her father who was trying to fill his wife's shoes. The White Elephant was taking more money than it brought in rent, it had been heavily mortgaged to pay debts incurred in Grapeville. The property there was also at a standstill, many of the buyers had proved poor pay. Amos Wendel had also put another little mortgage on the White Elephant to buy a good solid family stone.

But he wrote about the wonderful look of the land when it was turned fresh from the plow. "Times are getting bad again, not that they don't stay that way for most. But all the farmers are grumbling. Some say it's because there is no more free land in the whole country." He tried not to show that he was lonesome with his daughter Nancy in spite of her goodness to him. They had taken a bungalow and Nancy was enchanted with the breakfast nook that had a view toward the sunset and open country that made her feel as if she were riding in a train.

Amos Wendel did not want to travel. He was lost in the small house and wished he had a bit of land to work.

When letters came from her father, a deep sadness seemed to engulf the very room. It was so easy to mourn. To sit brooding over the dead and gone finding a meaning in all the lives. Vicky did not want to be a mourner, not even for her mother whose dead face, rigid and lonely as a face on an old coin, was so hard to forget, nor for Rosamond who was embalmed forever in a perpetual springtime. Memories had been all right for her mother, stranded in Oxtail. She and Jonathan were not stranded anywhere. They had plans for a future.

Many a night they got out their little records and figured up the total, just to reassure themselves that it was working out all right. The blackness outside pressed against the panes of glass. Only little by little talk of the boat died down. Then one night, "I don't think the boat would be the thing. I thought so once. But right now, it would take us away off from everything. Things are going to pop here. I think I'll get our money out of the bank," said Jonathan. They plotted about their money as if it were a precious only child. Their money would fool Jonathan's parents. They could start on their own account, they would know this time just exactly where they stood. No more playing into hands that had no use for them.

When Jonathan came back from his long spring roadtrip, dead tired, all the fire and enthusiasm burned out uselessly on a job he hated, Vicky would wonder if the wounds his family had so righteously struck, would ever heal. But Jonathan was not the only one in the world to be hurt. The world was full of the injured and lost. All the injured and defeated ones of her own family pressed at her back demanding new life. Though dead, she could feel the pressure of their hands, so misguided in life; she would look frantically at Jonathan whose likeness to Uncle Joe was like the stab of a knife. But he could rally in a few hours, be laughing and cracking jokes or sitting solemnly, his hands hanging, staring at something she could not see.

Young man, dollars do not grow on trees, ran an advertisement. No, but they are watered with human blood, thought Jonathan, and he was lonely for the men in his father's workshop who had always chuckled with pleasure to see him. He wondered what had happened to Bert, the bicycle repair man and hoped that when he got back into the country, Blum would not have forgotten him. Tolman was forgotten.

One night Jonathan's younger brother Tom sailed in wearing an elegant top coat and fine white silk muffler, a girl on his arm. Jonathan and Vicky were cordial, hauled out chairs, found a drink. The girl flicked cigarette ashes on the floor, as if she were slumming. Tom laughed at the ridiculous little apartment and kidded his big brother. "What you trying to do? Be an O. Henry?"

"Nothing so funny," said Jonathan, losing his sense of humor. He was out of patience with the kid and his air of riding the world. Jonathan had begged in vain to go to an eastern school. Now Tom was reaping the reward of a boy who had no idea of opposing his parents. He was already mulling over his future. He was sure of the future as if he expected to be on top forever. He talked of coffee plantations in the Philippines, of rubber in Central America. He was going to a college where he met only the best people and although he had nearly flunked out he was a star track man. He belonged to one of the best fraternities whose connections would last him a lifetime.

"Mine never did me any good," said Jonathan.

"You never tried to use them. You're a cynic, that's what you are," said Tom, feeling a little uneasy and embarrassed that his brother might not show off well. Jonathan found it hard to take the stiffness out of his manner. He and his brother were strangers, opposed to each other as much as if they had been fighting on different sides in a war. The kid would get help from their father, he would get what he wanted, what his father thought all people should want, a house, cars, things. Well, let him. He drank his drink hastily, couldn't keep back a sharp query, "What's it cost this year, Tom?"

"Oh, around three thousand. Dad sent me around three thousand. I've been careful but it takes the dough. You can't be a piker."

"Sure," said Jonathan. "It costs money to make an athlete."

Still you couldn't blame Tom who looked hurt and uneasy. But when they went to the little Italian restaurant, Jonathan quit rubbing it into his brother, laughed, called out his friend the proprietor and introduced his brother with affection and pride. The little Italian pumped hands delightedly and rushed around them in an excess of solicitude. The small room bubbled with warmth and good smells came from the kitchen. Vicky took off her hat and consulted Jonathan about the food and wine as if they were at home. Jonathan was determined not to be grouchy but to talk about upnorth and swimming and the time he tied Tom to a tree when they were little. The memories brought big bubbles of laughter out of Tom. He enjoyed himself. He was going to tell his father that old Jonathan was O.K. Yes, sir, he was all right. He'd come to his senses some day. He leaned over the table shaking his head. "All the same Jonathan, big boy, you make a mistake when you don't play up to the old man. Why cut your nose off to spite your face? Kid him along. He likes it. You can wangle anything out of him if you take some trouble."

"Suck around, you mean, no thanks," said Jonathan, "forget it. And don't give me advice please."

"Oh all right," said Tom uneasily. He looked around longing for a bright topic to restore the conviviality. "Who're those old birds?" he said pointing to two enlarged pictures on the wall that looked down at them from a wreath of green leaves and a red ribbon bow. Jonathan turned and said, "Sacco and Vanzetti."

He looked at the pictures himself and a warm strong feeling made him smile at his brother. His brother wouldn't understand. There was no use trying to tell him. Let him keep his topcoat and his white muffler and his fancy cigarette case. At the moment he forgot that he too was in excellent clothes, had a cigarette case that was also fine. He thought of himself as in the kitchen with the cook and the waiters. He was back there with them and they were talking about Italy and Mussolini who had crushed their unions. But not forever.

When they came back to the little apartment Jonathan read "The Man is Standing There" and Tom and his girl felt that they were now getting the real lowdown on advanced literature. They laughed themselves sick as Jonathan repeated the solemn phrases with emphasis. Jonathan also laughed and he had the feeling that he was laughing at himself. He picked up another book and turned the pages, looking at Vicky with a bright conspiratorial look. She shook her head but he began anyhow, with the same serious voice. "A spectre haunts Europe, the spectre of Communism."

"What's that?" said Tom a little uneasily. Vicky was frowning and Jonathan put the book down. "Oh just a book," he said but he continued to handle it, to turn it over, to run his finger along the beveled edge as if it were the blade of a knife.

"Sounds like hot stuff," said Tom weakly.

All the same he would like to see how a book like that would affect a fellow like Tom who made a point of knowing nothing about the world. He would like to hear his own voice rolling out the language that was so satisfying and he thought of himself in the years gone by as a callow youth. He was different now, he told himself, but he still had a long way to go. His learning still came from books and he doubted books, as if they had betrayed him.

When Tom and his girl left the Chance apartment, they took a taxi to an uptown roof. It was late but just the time for the crowd. Tom felt a little apologetic about his brother. "He's got the bug hard," he said laughing. "Oh well, lots of fellows get that way and they get over it. Give them a little money and they begin to see the light." He made up his mind to have a serious talk with his father. If his father quit being a mule and helped Jonathan, his brother would stop running around with wild-eyed people. Tom had not seen any wild-eyed people in Jonathan's place but he fancied that there must be such people, lurking in the offing. "And you take this dividing up business," he said. "Suppose all the wealth was divided up tomorrow, why, in a few days it would be right back in the hands of a few. It's human nature."

He was pleased with his argument and the two young people went out on the parapet that looked over uptown New York. The dazzling buildings cut into the sky, people on the streets below were tiny and Tom thought, futile. He felt philosophic and wise. He couldn't imagine mobs churning in those streets. That stuff was all right for Europe or for Latin America where they had revolutions for no reason except to work off the hot pepper they imbibed with their food. He communicated these thoughts to his girl who admired his wisdom.

Tom kept the promise he had made to himself about his brother and as soon as he was home went into a session with his father. "I told him I'd back him when he gets himself respectable work, settles down," said the father with a set jaw.

"He's living like anyone else," said Tom. "I think you ought to help him."

"Let him come to his senses," said Mrs. Chance. "And let Victoria come to her senses. It's her fault. I pity the poor thing. She'll get tired of wearing old clothes and doing her own work. Then she'll put Jonathan to regular work and he'll forget books and make the money he should be making. Just keep firm Abel and starve them out. It's the only way."

Even Tom was a little revolted and tried to melt the parents. But when she was alone, Mrs. Chance felt panic lest her son might not ask for help any more. Suppose that little creature proved really stubborn and did not demand finery? And if she did would it budge her boy? It looked black and she sometimes felt as if life were a kind of nightmare.

Her married life and the life of her girlhood had no connection. Thinking back to her youth often made her cry. Why should she cry? She was married to a good man, who had means. She had fine children. She did not know why she cried or why she now and then opened the drawer containing Jonathan's letters and the bottle of whiskey and had the feeling as if her son were interred within. She wished Victoria had turned out really bad, a smoker and drinker, running after men. Then the whole thing might very well be over.

In the midst of her thoughts she would run to the linen closet and count the sheets. To distract herself she made plans of alterations for the summer place. New bathrooms blossomed on paper. They put another bathroom in the summer cottage that spring just as Jonathan and Victoria were at last moving to the country with the oil lamps, the pump, the old-fashioned backhouse.

Back in the country Jonathan got into his overalls and ambled around to the neighbors. "How's everything? 'Bout the same?"

Blum had his hands full with the new chicks and Jonathan followed him around and helped him give the serum against disease.
"Abe Zimmerman's sold his cows," called Blum from one end of
the chicken house. The white hens whirred and skurried underfoot,
cackling and nervous. "He's been keeping books for ten years and
says that now it costs him three cents an hour to sell milk, so he got
rid of the cows."

'What's he plan to do?'

"Don't know," said Blum. "Blast these hens. I got trouble with
this bunch, they're regular cannibals, pick each other to pieces.
You can't blame them, it's this forcing. I got to force them to break
even and it makes them bleed. Then they pick. And the price for
eggs is terrible. They're too many doing it but milk's no good.
Nothing is any good, that's about it. Guess we'll have to take to
grass, hey Jonathan?"

"I was thinking of raising peppers," said Jonathan. The two shut
the door of the house carefully. "You pay two cents apiece, sometimes more for them."

"Say that don't mean a thing, the store price. Don't figure on it.
Look at milk," he groaned and waved his hands helplessly. "I bet
you a few folks are wishing they'd let Al Smith take a whack at
things."

"Do you think he'd done better?"

"No question of it," said Blum. "He's for the common people,
the Republicans have always sold out to big interests."

"They all work for the same boss," said Jonathan.

Blum peered at him. "Say, you talk like that fellow Tentman.
He's back again. Was here fifteen years then lit out for New York
but lost his job I guess. They say lots are losing jobs."

"I lost my job too," said Jonathan. "Lots of people are getting
out of work but the papers don't say much about it."

Once the garden was in, there was plenty of time for visiting
around. Zimmerman's place looked desolate, Waltman's had the
same broken down barn door, the Bleekman place looked good
because his wife worked in town and brought home her money.
Everywhere they heard a little of this fellow Tentman. Some said
he was a foreigner. Some said he was the best chicken farmer in

these parts. The garden took all their time and almost all their strength. They were laying in enough to feed them a year. When a storm hit the valley they would stop work, huddle together on the porch, their arms around each other, watching water pour in spouts from the roof of the porch, the corn flatten and a kind of wild sweet devastation lick the land. Great clouds boiled over the wild moon at night, rain clanged like iron on the slate roof. The electric air seemed to clear out all their troubles and doubts. But the farmers grumbled.

They stuck, each in his place, like hunks of sour dough. But in July, riding along in Zimmerman's old Ford, Jonathan saw straight ahead at a dangerous bend in the road where a big rock teetered, a new sign below the old dismal PREPARE TO MEET THY GOD. It was scratched in red paint, the kind he had noticed that fellow Tentman using on his barn. WORKERS OF THE WORLD UNITE.

Stocks continued high through the dog days of that summer but in Detroit Jerry Stauffer and many others were quietly let out. Cars were piling up in factories like so much useless tin and piles of unused men accumulated, one by one, in parks and railroad stations.

David Trexler sat behind his mahogany desk in Roseland, Oregon, buying stocks for a select circle of friends all that summer. Corn accumulated in the midwest and wheat filled to overflowing the grain elevators. Trexler bought all that summer and toward October an uneasiness held back the market. On October 24, buyers everywhere fell over one another, clamoring to sell.

Bucks County, Pennsylvania, 1934

I told them, I says May Day is a first rate American Day. It was made in America. "Tell that to your Aunt Fanny," says he, "it's a foreign institution, Labor Day is the American workingman's day." That's the day the bosses give them, I says, you don't need to argue, you can look it up, May Day is an American Day and moreover was made in Chicago. You can't find a more American city; May Day was born and raised, I says, right with the hog backs. Why that day is old enough to be your mother I says, it was sprung back in 1886 by a bunch of fighters who didn't intend to lie down and take it. And neither do we. "Oh as to that," says he, "I guess it's up to the board of commissioners. I'll have to consult the board, because right now," he smiled and pulled out his fat watch, "right now I've a little wedding to perform. One of my duties. But I'll warn you. I haven't anything against you boys, but you see, court meets here, why you'll disturb the court, he says, and the legion claims they won't let you march." He thinks that will fix me but I just laugh. When it comes to the legion, I guess we got some of our own, I say. We got about five tough roughnecks that have been through the war. One was even in the Spanish-American war. A real vet, I says. He wormed out of it but we got the permit, of course we got it, we got the courthouse lawn and we paraded with an American flag and we had a couple of speeches about our troubles here and fighting against mortgage foreclosures and how the next step was cancellation of our debts that could never be paid and if they could wink at big countries like Germany and France slipping out of it, they'd better wink at us if they wanted any bread or any butter either, and then by golly, the best part of it came. Why I tell you even I wasn't expecting it from that bunch of old Mennonites and Dutchies. I don't know who started it. But I could hardly believe my ears. They was about two hundred hard shelled farmers standing there around the American flag and by golly if they didn't pipe up and sing the International.

I guess that was the first time Doylestown, a good old town that belonged to William Penn, had ever heard that tune. And did I tell you? They raised their fists too. I don't know who told them about that, but they all did it and the Spanish vet was grinning all over. Court was going on inside, we could hear the clerk droning on like a man in his sleep.

WREATH, YOU'RE TOO LATE

David Trexler had always prided himself on having his ear to the ground. In the summer of 1929 he had warned the other directors of the local linen mill that if they did not watch out they would hold on to that little proposition just too long. The mill had begun, in the eyes of the town, as a nice little booster for local industry. The papers ran pictures of the model plant and long analyses of the flax that could be raised in Oregon of the same quality as in Ireland. The company had been formed by leading men and the intention, according to newspaper reports, was purely altruistic and solely to boost Roseland and a new state industry. The directors had a few meetings but they were busy men with fingers in many pies.

Trexler did not suspect that anything serious might happen that fall but he was expecting a little slump. He had noticed a weakness in the drug market and the foreign situation was not all it might be. The Republicans were, of course, bound to be bad. With the possible exception of Theodore Roosevelt the only sound administrations in his recollection were those of Cleveland and Wilson. The little linen mill began to look like an expensive toy. It had been running at a loss and it was time to unload.

A little earlier in the day, a sucker could have been found who would have netted the public-spirited gentlemen a neat profit but as it was, they barely cleared their skirts.

They cleared out with a bare margin and Trexler had no sooner absolved himself of that transaction when a dozen others clamored for attention. By Thanksgiving Day he was beginning to feel that old discomfort in the pit of his stomach. He stood a long time in the bathroom looking at his smooth-shaved face, the bald head, the sharp blue eyes. He pulled the skin of his cheek down and looked at the whites of his eyes that were faintly yellow. He stuck out his tongue. He felt sick.

When he was called to carve the turkey for the long table of family connections, he sliced off a final sliver of meat for himself and trifled with it. "Papa, you're not eating," said Sue from her place half way down the table. Ella from the far end looked up and Millie laid down her fork and stared at David, quietly and with an ominous long contemplation that made him hastily stuff cranberries into his mouth.

"Don't mind me," he bawled, shouting and irritated, his face flushing angrily. "I'm not stuffing like the rest of you but give me time." The words begun with his old bullying manner flagged off weakly. He felt tired and childish and looking at his hands thought how much they were getting to look like his mother's. He had the same blue veins, the same square capable thumb. He put small and trembling portions of food between his teeth and grimaced at Dave, Jr.'s baby in her highchair but the food would not force itself into his hollow body. He chewed it tiresomely and quietly spit it out into his napkin. Hortense with her head high and the old hoop earrings in her ears sat near Ella. There was nothing the matter with *her* appetite. Why, she even had her cheeks painted and rouge on her lips. At her age to fix up like a Jezebel was too much. He cut another slice of meat, called out sarcastically, "Hortense, some more bird?"

"No thank you David," said Hortense.

"Oh yes, Hortense, you'd better load up. A woman of your calibre running wild like a girl needs sustenance." The words added color to his sister's face and a sharp fear to Ella's but he was too indifferent to follow up his humor, sank back, sucking the corner of his lip. In the living room, he sat smiling among them all, for the moment forgetting the telephone calls, the upbraidings, the mortgages falling due, the houses unrented, Tel. and Tel.—bought at 198—down to 76, U.S. Steel preferred 45, that on the next day would begin a barrage that would last for how long? He should tighten his belt but his stomach was hollow. The trouble in the world made him surprisingly indifferent to his discomfort. In his bed that night he thought soberly of the pain and touched the skin of his stomach gratefully as if an electric bell were attached to his organism that might summon the old symptoms at will.

He trembled not for his own safety but for the safety of his Last Will and Testament. He had fought death a few years before in order to construct that Will and he had held on grimly to make substantial all its ramifications. He and Ella had spent hours during pleasant evenings calculating every possible contingency. They had worried over the big house with its objects so dear to them. David could not bear to think of this house torn apart after his death, the carpets ripped up, the pictures yanked off the walls, the rooms ravaged by strangers. They would rip out its bowels, tear loose its heart like savages. It was his house, it should stand there, just as it was, every picture in its place, the piano and the mementoes picked up by mamma and himself on their trip around the world in their rows on the what-not. There was the cigar band off the cigar that Al Smith had given him at the Democratic convention in Texas.

He thought with pleasure of the perspiring crowds and Millie and Ella in their pretty flowered chiffon dresses flanking his white flannels, the three of them making quite a swath as they marched through the hotel or entered the convention hall. The banners, the cheers, the happy warrior himself, beaming and simple. The great men of the world were those close to the common people. He thought of himself as such a person, able to crack jokes with the lowliest. He liked to think of the time he and Mamma were in Death Valley and he had strung along an oldtimer about the Elk convention to be held in Atlantic City. Why, he almost had the old curmudgeon packing his bag. Bryan had been such a soul, and yet substantial, he had found time to roll up something like a million.

All that winter he watched his diminishing accumulations with a jaundiced eye. When one of his oldest friends shot himself, he shut

himself up in his office, shivering as with a chill. He wanted to
propitiate the fates that were drumming away on his own board.
He got out his Will and looked it over carefully. If conditions
continued many of its phrases would be hollow. He didn't see how
he could leave so large a sum to the Salvation Army or to the
University for a scholarship a year to the brightest boy. He
couldn't bear not to leave such a bequest. Many a time, in a boring
meeting, with some old crony droning on he had let his thoughts
wander, a pleased smile had come over his face thinking of the
grateful bright boys who would keep his memory green, of the poor
that would be clothed and fed. It gave him stamina to put through
some pretty difficult deals and he did not see how he could go back
on those provisions now.

And if he was worried about his private affairs, he was even
more deeply concerned about the affairs of the bank. Only that
morning Mrs. Benton had come in for his confidential opinion,
hanging to his desk as it were a lifebuoy. He had found himself
fumbling when he tried to explain the transfer of her Standard Oil
stocks to some local investments that he had certainly considered
sound. And they were sound. It was only a paper loss, he told
himself, but he felt shaky.

At night in bed, the darkness gave him shivers and he tried to
warm himself against the mountainous form of his sleeping wife.
Her flesh could not warm him. No, he was cold to his very marrow,
his stomach turned in his sleep. But he was no longer the traffic
cop, holding up the white glove. Stop death. He only wanted a little
time, he told himself, but his banker's instincts were strong. He
made a little deal behind his back and told himself that if he could
only make a trip east, visit his father's grave, look up Anne's
children, maybe a trip to Grapeville to see Mem's grave and look in
on Aaron's son, then he would be willing to die, and perhaps then,
he need not die. Perhaps he would be healed miraculously as he
was that time several years before. The world also might turn for
the better. Each morning when he was certain to find somewhere in
the paper the prophecy that prosperity was bound to be around the
corner, he longed to believe it. If only the Republicans, shifty souls,

were not back of it. He had no faith in them. Their chicken in every pot, car in every garage was proving the joke of the ages.

He must go east again, make Anne's children some little present, lay a wreath upon the grave of Millie's husband. With a peculiar intensity he had fixed upon a wreath for the late Mr. Shane. Sometimes as he sat during dinner, pretending to eat his eyes would fall upon Millie, large and impassive with her morbidly pale skin and eyes that never seemed to see. He would try to placate her.

"How about a little more of this lamb, Millie?" And if she reached her plate, slowly, deliberately, he was grateful for it, heaped it with food, joked, laughed, rubbed his hands, did everything but eat. Millie, like a clay monument sat at his board and now that his last Will and Testament was in peril he remembered his youth. The sharp memories that are supposed to come to the dying came to the living.

When he looked at his wife, he saw her as a slim young thing with a wasp waist. Millie was a girl boarding a train for school in the east. He had managed her and broken her in to his business and his life. It was a satisfaction even now to feel that he had had the power to keep her for the best years of her life from that man's bed. Old as he was, he felt a snort of anger at the thought of that bed that had finally claimed her. But the next moment tears were in his eyes. He would think of his brother, poor Joe, who had been bedevilled to death. In the cupboard the handsome china that used to seem so out of place in Joe's cabin in the Black Hills, stood now, neglected show pieces.

He wanted to put his hands on something living, to go back to his boyhood, to listen to his father's voice. What had happened to those old papers, the diaries, the letters? Why, it was a sin and shame that they should pass out of the family name. He should round up such treasures, see to it that they came back to the proper Trexlers. Thinking of this transaction pumped fresh energy into him. For a week he almost forgot his pains, and when fresh gloom fell over the nation he was scared that his symptoms might disappear and leave him standing in the wreck.

Sue was frightened at his loss of weight. "Why, Papa, pull

yourself together. Depressions are nothing new, they're old as sin."
She said it easily, casually, picking up the cheerful thought from
the columns of the daily paper that retailed such ideas to the
people. The hand of God, forever passing the buck to another
generation. David Trexler's hand twitched as he signed checks. He
concentrated on his Will and became a pillar of determination,
joked at the luncheon club, and made a playful speech about the
time he was presented the pin by the brothers in old Shanghai.

But more ominous than the fall of stocks were the growing mobs
at the unemployment offices. It was no longer a pleasure to walk in
the park and he was astonished at such conditions in a nice little
town like Roseland. Of course cities always knew of unemployment
but Roseland was a town of little home owners. It gave him the
shakes and he was only too ready to believe when some of the boys
told him about agitators in their midst. The authorities had not
been able to spot them yet, but they would be certain to, nobody
else could be responsible for scenes such as were beginning to be
carried on.

He was glad to get on the train and away from it all. But even in
Oxtail his nieces and their families did not respond to his visit as
they used. Clifford was not so timid and even said brazenly,
laughing a little, his nose pinched in as he enunciated the disagreeable pleasantry, "Well, Uncle David, we never got to own that
home you advised us to invest in. We got as far as the lot and have
been paying light, water and paving assessments ever since. It's a
pretty valuable lot by this time only it won't bring any money."

"Give yourself time," said David Trexler, "why in my day I've
outlived many a blow. You can't always be on the up and up. Real
estate is something that no one can take away. It's earth itself."

If Nancy had not frowned upon him Cliff would have answered
that even the ground can slip from under your feet if you can't pay
taxes but the retort stuck in his throat instead. An unpleasant
strain fell over the company not improved by Amos Wendel's
sarcastic smile. It was a good thing that Nancy turned the conversation to the old days, to the old piano. "Remember the old piano,
Uncle David?"

They went into the living room where the old square piano

looked crowded and stuffy and overgrown among the smaller furniture. He went up to it, touched its keys, yellow and broken. In the old days how they had gloated over that piano. Joe had bought it for them when he came on a tide of fortune from the South. Many an evening David had bickered with his sister because they wanted him to practise his flute so they could all play on their different instruments for Joe when he came home. What wouldn't he give to play that flute now, to be that chunky boy again, with bulging front, standing beside his sisters and waiting for the chords of the piano to strike the opening note. Tears of self-pity came to his eyes. All the same that piano should belong to a Trexler. He would pay for it, yes, he would certainly buy it and this was the time, nothing was worth what it had been, certainly not antiques.

"Oh we couldn't sell the old piano, Uncle David," Nancy said as if it were sacrilege. In bed that night Cliff talked a little stern sense. "I guess if I lose my job, and I've got so many cuts already I might as well lose it, we'd be pretty glad for some money. We can't support a piano without a job, my dear." Nancy fell to sobbing and her husband lay there feeling mean and spiritless, resenting the role he was forced to play. Even Donald Monroe was not so generous with his cigars any more. But he still kowtowed to Uncle David and got up very early to see the old man to the train.

On his way east he told himself that Vicky had always been his favorite niece but he was disheartened by the reduced trains and the few passengers rattling around in the once well-filled Pullmans. When he finally arrived at Vicky's house, he pumped up all the enthusiasm he could muster. "Here we are, here we are," he shouted, eyeing the little country house with pleasure, kissing his niece, and proud that she had captured such a fine husband. But his shouts and jokes seemed to be yelled over a high fence. The young couple were polite, smiled, and did everything for him but he could not feel as if they were real kin. He fell to praising their home.

"Why, Vic, you've got a regular old Pennsylvania home. What's nicer than clean whitewash, these old twisting stairs and old beams. You can't beat walls a foot thick. Those old ancestors of ours all had faith, the faith that moves mountains, and you know," he said turning toward Jonathan, his mouth slightly open, his blue eyes wide, "that's what we lack today. Yes sir, faith." He ground his hands together softly and when Jonathan answered that maybe people still had plenty of faith only none in the old faiths, he looked puzzled, shook his head, sighed, took off his necktie and, opening his shirt collar, turned and twisted his neck as if it hurt. Jonathan made a mint julep with fresh mint from the garden and Uncle David sipped it gratefully. "My only quarrel with Billy Bryan was on the subject of prohibition," he said. "I never could see why man should limit his capacities for enjoyment."

"That's right," said Jonathan smiling. He was determined to be nice to Uncle David and not to get into any arguments. The poor fellow looked sick. "I guess you admired Bryan," he said.

"One of the great men," said Trexler. "But they had it in for him because he served grapejuice at a state dinner. That's about the size of it. I call that narrow-minded." He shook his head, sipping slowly because as he swallowed the julep tiny beads of pain broke out along the rim of his stomach. He kept on stubbornly, sipping, looking in a friendly almost beseeching way at Vicky and her husband. When he left, he'd leave a little surprise, yes sir, he'd pin a nice five-dollar bill to his pillowcase. Maybe even a ten.

Vicky tried hard to feel warm and friendly to her uncle. He was her mother's brother but she could not forget the many times her mother had asked in the old days, "Do you think I might ask Uncle David to help a little?" It had become the regular answer to say, "What's the use, he'd have an excuse." What's the use, what's the use? How many times, dear god, they had said that, almost wringing their hands, so anxious for a little help that seemed hung up above them like a drop of water that never falls to the thirsty man on the salty rocks. Uncle David belonged to another country; she and Jonathan belonged here surrounded by people who had no more than they did.

He and Jonathan played along pretty well as Vicky made dinner and set the table on the long trestle bench Jonathan had made out of boards from the old barn. But with all the nice food before him, David Trexler could not eat. His eyes kept wandering. Wasn't that an old daguerreotype of his father on the wall? It looked down on him, the youngest son, the fine passionate eyes in the long sensitive face, the bushy brows, the thin hands resting on a table, on a book. Yes, the book was the bible. David Trexler walked over to study his father's face. He had never set eyes on the man who had died just a month after his own birth.

"What a pity, what a pity," he murmured, sorry for himself, the fatherless child, for his mother whose life of toil had begun in grim earnest with that death. "What a pity." He longed to rescue his father from the ignoble forgetfulness of the grave but he could think of no way. Monuments crumble. The thought that he was his father's monument could no longer console him. He too would fall and that the weak sandstone characters of his own children must sustain the line, was bitter as dying. A kind of confused sense of fever rushed over his body under the nice fresh underwear with the embroidered monogram.

"What's it all about, can you make out?" he said appealing to Jonathan but he did not wait for an answer. Something in the young man's face made him afraid that an answer might really come. He preferred to look at his father's picture and to be saddened by the past. At least he forgot here the troubles of the bank, the threat to his fortune more disastrous than the threat to his life. He hinted until Vicky brought out the old diaries and letters and sat hunched and brooding, poring over them, a bright spot of color in each cheek.

Jonathan walked out toward the barn. He had heard an auto horn and grinned as he saw Tentman drive up. In a very short time he and Tentman had become good friends. When Jonathan realized that the short squat little man had almost escaped death a few months before, he was ready to listen to him. Here was a man who had been ready to die. "They meant to get me," he had said. "And they got Steve Katovis." He frowned modestly, angry that he had escaped so fine a death. "It was my good clothes, see, I was furniture carver and had good clothes, that was one day I had on my best and they thought I was a business man." He laughed delighted, the whole grim battle, the lines of pickets, the fire, the rush of feet and the blood, all fading for the moment and then coming back into his face, into his solemn eyes. "Steve was a good fighter," he said.

He was driving up to the barn now, slowing down the car as if it were a race horse. "What's on your mind?" said Jonathan.

"What did I tell you?" said Tentman. "That fellow over at the Bridgeman place is going to have the sheriff crack down on him. He began going around himself, getting his neighbors together. He come over to me this morning. They've got a mortgage of five hundred and they'll sell him up for that after he's sunk more than four thousand."

"We'll have to get going fast, in that case," said Jonathan. "My wife's uncle is here, they'll have to get along without me for a while. We'll round up a committee, see old man Snow. He's got the mortgage and we'll put the screws on him. We might as well begin now or never. It's bound to come. Then if he doesn't relent, we can call out the countryside."

"They'll come, by jesus," said Tentman. "I tell you the only way to learn is through the belly." He laughed, shaking all over. Jonathan ran to the house and tried not to feel guilty at Uncle David's dropped jaw. This was no time to pity that old trapper, but he reminded him of his own father who lately seemed a lonely man. The two men headed toward the back country, where bankrupt farming land still yielded crops on either side of old roads that Joshua Trexler had surveyed in the early days of plenty.

David Trexler was too tired to sit up late. He preferred to lie in bed in the low-ceilinged rooms that were so exactly like the rooms in the house where he was born. He tried to distract himself but the pleasantest thoughts revolved around his last Will. Some of his gifts would have to be modified. Only one gift he kept intact during the dark days that had fallen upon him. That was the house he had willed to Millie.

In bed that night he examined with his mind's eye the consoling paragraph of his Will dealing with this gift. He could hear Vicky moving around quietly downstairs, later he heard Jonathan come in and the two talking in low voices. Then they went to the kitchen and shut the door. The sound of the brook became louder, it reminded him of the ocean near the cottage that was to belong to

Millie. I do give, bequeath and devise to Mrs. Millie Shane the following real estate, to wit:

He licked his lips gently, the unpleasant taste of old iron reminded him of the shaky structure of the world, of his Will that was being threatened, of the prestige of his life that was trembling. He drank the glass of water by the bed, sought to calm himself. He saw the cottage half way up the little mountain, the pine tree behind it, the low roof and fireplace where they had burned the red wood log washed up by the tide, the wooden duck the boys found rocking on the waves, the old fishnet, and the wooden ship in the bottle. The sweetest freest times of his life had been spent in that house. If his Roseland house had been a wife to him this house was his mistress. He was old enough not to be disturbed by guilty thoughts, he let himself sink into an imaginative enactment of the reading of the Will, saw tears roll down Millie's face. Yes, it would be nice if he could be present and see Millie's face.

As he could not, he would lay a wreath on Mr. Shane's grave. He would tell Millie when he went home, say it casually, offhand, "Well, Millie, I went out to your husband's grave and placed a little wreath there. I thought it was what you would like." Then the light bursting into her eyes as he had not seen it for years, the quick rush of words, the soft grateful, "Oh Dave."

The need to lay the wreath was so urgent that all during breakfast he was distracted. The pain in the pit of his stomach knifed him and he finally felt driven to tell Vicky that he believed he would make a little trip upcountry first and then come back for the rest of his little visit with her. He sat fiddling with his father's old letters after he had eaten, his vest buttons open, his mind wandering among the old boyhood days, Joe the admired brother, Aaron who had been the steady one. He read and reread his father's last letter written to Aaron who had taken the little girls to Aunty Blank at Bethlehem while he, the baby, was being born.

Dear Aaron:

As the children are going to write you, I thought I would add a few lines. The Gap is on the same old footing—much talk and very little money—weather very changeable. Frank

Gerhard has not rented a place yet and James is very sick, much reduced. The scholars all cried when he came to school last week to get his books. It is consumption and there is little chance of his recovering, medicine can do little, air and water must cure him if he can be cured. If you wish to see him, come next Saturday or he might pass away before you came. Perhaps I may come up this week but I have a bad cold.

                                               Joshua Trexler

David Trexler read this letter with special emphasis several times. He followed his niece into the kitchen to read it again. The drama of his father writing about the boy who was doomed to die while he himself was soon to die, struck David as profoundly sorrowful. He could feel tears in his eyes and only gained composure by wondering how much to offer Vicky for some of the old papers. She guessed his desire and offered them to him. "You take what you like, Uncle David." she said. "I'd like to keep a few, but you take all you want." He flushed with pleasure but when he came to leave, hesitated about pinning a ten or a five to the pillow. He decided a five was best.

It was not much of a ride to the little Pennsylvania town where Mr. Shane was buried but he was surprised to see that the railroad was diving into the coal region. Piles of gray slag made the lovely hills unsightly, mill towns dogged one another's heels. The red plush of the day coach gradually flecked with dust and ashes. His collar rubbed and his hands began to itch. The itching reminded him of his symptoms, the bile that did not run properly, the organism gummed up with the accretions of disease.

He was relieved when the train stopped at the little station. As he began walking through the town he remembered now that Mr. Shane had worked for the railroad for years. He had been a timekeeper or a ticket seller or some such job, David Trexler could not remember. The town had the matchbox quality of a mill or railroad town and it depressed him. He thought that during the years that Mr. Shane had lived in this town with his mother, Millie was in Roseland writing to her lover secretly. Probably the man used to come to that old post-office building for his mail. He stood looking at it, fancying Shane, handsome even with his limp, coming with his secret, unlocking his mail box, putting the letter into his vestpocket over his heart.

His thumb fingered his vestpocket, he was all out of bi-carb pills. He had better get some and clear that taste from his mouth. In the drugstore he looked contemptuously at the thin anemic clerk behind the counter. Why, even the calibre of drug clerks was running down, not like the old days when a good man had all the status of a doctor. This was nothing but a salesman, an order filler, who sold rubber goods and rouge for silly girls.

All the same, he couldn't resist, "Business good?"

"Naw," said the clerk, "it's rotten. This town hasn't any money. The mills been shutting down, those left open just made cuts. That's what caused all the trouble."

"What trouble's that?" said Trexler putting a bi-carb on his tongue.

"Oh that shooting, cops tried to break up picketing and the mob got out of hand. The cops fired, some say they just fired in the air to scare the crowd but funny thing is, one of the local boys got hit. 'Course agitators caused the rumpus."

"Naturally," said David righteously. "If outsiders would only keep their hands off. We've had trouble in our town too, I'm from Roseland, Oregon. Trexler's my name." He reached his hand across the counter. Shook. "I'm in your business, too. Drugs. But that's only a sideline now. I'm in banking now." He pulled out his cards with his name and the line President Roseland National Bank in the lefthand corner, handed one pompously across the counter.

The clerk was impressed and a rush of old-time power put color in David's yellowed skin. He said authoritatively, "There's too much loose talk around, it's bad. Times are bad."

"This town's all right but outsiders got in and there's been trouble."

"That's it," said David in a deep damning voice. "You fellows have to keep a tight hand. Where's your cemetery here? I want to

take a look around, got a relative there, relative of my wife's
sister."

"You go out Palmer Street, turn left at Bayside, keep on till you
reach a big white house and turn right and it's straight ahead.
Expect you'll see quite a crowd out there. They're burying that
fellow. They've been going past here all morning. He's left a widow
and a little boy."

"Too bad," said David shaking his head. "Maybe they'll learn a
lesson." He decided to walk the distance and at the next corner he
went into the florist's and looked around for a suitable offering.
The shop was meagre and there were no rich wreaths such as he
had envisioned. There were artificial leaves of too green material
and there were potted plants. The potted plant was a compromise
but he at last picked out a blue hydrangea and decided to plant it
on the grave. To console himself he reasoned that the growing plant
was even better. Some day Millie might come here herself and she
would see the plant, still growing, the work of his hands. He bought
a little trowel and with his bundles trudged along the tedious
village street.

When he reached the cemetery he looked for someone to tell him
where to find Mr. Shane's grave but a small crowd of people with
hats off stood near a freshly dug grave and appeared to be waiting.
The raw yellow earth was ugly as a sore. How much nicer they did
things in Roseland, covering such a sight with an artificial blanket
of grass so that it might not torture the bereaved ones.

He remembered the photograph he had once seen of Mr.
Shane's grave with the monument Millie had erected for him. At
the time he had thought it generous but extravagant. It had taken
a lot of money. Mr. Shane had left a small insurance and Millie's
own savings, covering her eighteen years with him, were meager.
He reminded himself that he had always given Millie a beautiful
home with himself and wife. He had taken her on trips, like one of
the family, had given her a wonderful Oriental rug.

Suddenly he spied the stone. The grave itself looked ragged. This
was not a well kept-up cemetery. The stones looked poor. Some
graves had only crosses of wood or were outlined with little pebbles
and shells. The poverty stricken look of the place took the heart out

of him but he dug away and set his plant upon the grave. The rich blue bloom distinguished this part of the cemetery and David Trexler stood up to look at his achievement. As he got to his feet, a thick crowd oozed into the far paths. They were singing. He wondered if they were Catholics but saw no priest. Men at the head carried a long box and behind came a woman and a little boy.

He watched them as they moved toward the raw yellow wound and the little boy stared around in childish wonder. He felt a pang for the child, losing a father like himself. But the mother's pale face disturbed him and he turned away, embarrassed and walked toward Shane's grave. He had promised himself that he would go over in his mind the events of his life and enjoy the salutary effect of this act of retribution. But as he stood there, he could think of nothing but dreary thoughts. The hydrangea looked gaudy and out of place. Underneath the ground, Shane, the railroad worker, seemed to be looking up at him with a stern triumphant eye. Words from the side of the newmade grave echoed across the plots to where he stood. Someone was making a speech. The crowd had pushed in from all sides, it stood curiously quiet and well-ordered. At a distance the pale faces had the appearance of looking exactly alike. The people even stood alike, arms hanging loosely, and for all Trexler knew they no doubt lived alike in rows of montonous identical houses. Mill people.

He tried to turn back to Shane's grave again and to conjure up the bright look Millie would give him when he told her about the plant. But he could only remember her young face bathed in tears when he had denounced her as a traitor and cheat for writing to and conniving with a scoundrel behind his back after he had paid for her education and expected to get some use out of her in his store. He could see that face after all these years, suddenly contorted and making its false renunciatory promise. Oh, she had bitterly deceived him, writing to Shane all those years, but at least he had kept them apart. At that moment it was no triumph. He kneeled and began plucking weeds from Shane's grave uneasily but a sudden louder voice of a new speaker boomed across the graves.

They shouldn't allow such speeches. Phrases angered him, he got to his feet, dusting his trousers and started righteously back along the path. The idea of talking about rights at a time like this. When the foundations of business were cracking. He started along the cinder path toward the crowd, his feet scrunching importantly. He only wished this was Roseland. As he neared the speaker, he half expected that his important appearance would halt the speech. No one paid any attention to him. He stood on the outside in his nice gray suit with the purplish tie.

All the eyes of the crowd were focused on the speaker, a lean man in a stringy coat who talked straight at them, leaning across the coffin with his body as if he would reach them all, touch them, one by one with the contagion of his confidence and power.

"And now friends," he said. "Now friends. One thing to remember. They can shoot some of us down, they can't shoot all of us. Everytime they make us dig a grave for one of ours, they are digging the pit from under their own feet. Every time they fire us and cheat us and drive us from our homes, they only increase the forest of hands that will rise up against them. Comrades. One word to remember. The word of Joe Hill, himself shot down in cold blood." The voice choked with rage, waited a minute, went on. David Trexler, stirring uneasily, looked around frantically for a policeman, some friendly face. Police were on the far edge of the cemetery. There was no moving thing except a woman pushing her baby back and forth in its perambulator.

"Don't mourn. Organize," said the voice, the body leaning toward them, the hands out, then dropped quietly. A deep silence followed the words.

David Trexler shivered on the ignored edge of the crowd but when the yellow lumps of earth began to fall, he shuddered as if they were falling into his own grave, upon his own unprotected flesh.

The crowd stood tight, a hard nucleus like a fist that would never open, and he looked toward it appealingly for sympathy for David Trexler, the little orphan, but it was staring at the grave and did not see him.